Beyond the Badge: Nox

Blue Avengers MC
Book 6

Jeanne St. James

Jeanne
ST. JAMES

———

Credits:

Photographer/Cover Artist: Golden Czermak at FuriousFotog
Cover Model: Mike Crowson
Editor: Proofreading by the Page
Beta Readers: Alex Swab, Author BJ Alpha and Sharon Abrams
Logo: Jennifer Edwards

———

www.jeannestjames.com

Sign up for my newsletter for insider information, author news, and new releases:
www.jeannestjames.com/newslettersignup

about her upcoming releases: http://www.jeannestjames.com/newslettersignup

Blue Avengers MC Series

Beyond the Badge: Fletch (Book 1)
Beyond the Badge: Finn (Book 2)
Beyond the Badge: Decker (Book 3)
Beyond the Badge: Rez (Book 4)
Beyond the Badge Crew (Book 5)
Beyond the Badge: Nox (Book 6)

Author Note/Content Warning

Please note:

For the most part, the timing of this story runs parallel to Beyond the Badge: Crew (BAMC, book 5).

Content Warning:

Grief from death of a spouse
Past pregnancy loss

Glossary of Terms

PSP - Pennsylvania State Police

DEA - Drug Enforcement Agency

The Plant - A place away from stations/barracks/etc. for law enforcement/a task force to conduct clandestine criminal investigations.

Plant Manager - Person in charge of wiretapping/transcribing calls

MC Chapter - The national club with a national exec committee (President, VP, etc.); Ex: Deadly Demons MC

MC Charter - Each charter is run independently, does not answer to a mother charter or a national chapter; Example: Blue Avengers MC

Sled - slang for motorcycle

RICO - Racketeer Influenced and Corrupt Organizations Act

Eight-six - Get rid of something

Jag-off - Western Pennsylvania slang for someone who is a jerk, stupid or inept.

PennDOT – Pennsylvania Department of Transportation

Character List

BAMC (Southwest Regional Charter):

Axel Jamison - *President* - Sergeant, Shadow Valley PD
Shane Fletcher (Fletch) - *Vice President* - Trooper, PA State Police
Antonio Alvarez (Rez) - *Sergeant at Arms* - Officer, Southern Allegheny Regional PD
Aiden Cross - *Secretary* - Corporal, Southern Allegheny Regional PD, Nash's (DAMC) husband
Mike Miller - *Treasurer* - Officer, Pittsburgh PD
Daniel Finnegan (Finn) - *Road Captain* - Officer, Southern Allegheny Regional PD
Bradley Lennox (Nox) - Officer, Shadow Valley PD
Colin Crew - Senior Special Agent, DEA, Tri-State Task Force Leader
Owen Decker - Trooper, PA State Police
Danielle Montgomery (Monty) - Corrections Officer, SCI Greene

Timothy Frasier - Liquor Enforcement Officer, PA State Police
Roland North - Lieutenant, Pittsburgh PD

Other Tri-State Drug Task Force Members:

Luke Rodgers - DEA Special Agent
Luis Torres - DEA Special Agent, Plant Manager
Ken Proctor - Officer, Uniontown PD
Carl Powers - Trooper, PA State Police
Sam Kruger - Corporal, Greensburg PD
Warren Reynolds - Corporal, PA State Police
Don Mullins - Narcotic Detective, Pittsburgh PD
Nova Wilder – FBI Special Agent, Organized Crime Division
Camila Cabrera - DEA special agent

Others:

Aaliyah James - Magnum's oldest daughter
Sapphire Loukanis- Current dancer/former hostess at The Peach Pit
Sloane Parrish - Legal assistant, Decker's woman
Melina Jensen (Mel/MJ) - Finn's fiancée, former manager at The Peach Pit
Bella Jamison - DAMC, Axel's wife
Valerie Decker (Valee Girl) - Decker and Sloane's adopted daughter
Viper - Deadly Demons president
T-Bone - Deadly Demons former prospect
Sadie Parrish - Sloane's younger sister (deceased)
Saint - Deadly Demon in charge of The Peach Pit

Ringo, Popeye, Mutt and Chubs - Prospects working at The
Peach Pit

Clark - Monty's boyfriend

Magnum (Malcolm Moore, Sr.) - Dark Knights MC's
sergeant at arms; Aaliyah's father

Caitlyn Moore - Magnum's wife; daughter of Dawg, a
member of the Dirty Angels MC

Mercy (Ryan Mercer) - Army vet, works for In the Shadows
Security

Prologue

THE POUNDING on his apartment door had Nox cursing under his breath.

"Nox," he heard yelled through it.

It sounded like Cross.

What the hell did he want?

Pulling in a breath, Nox tamped down his annoyance. He loved his brothers and he'd do anything for them, so he wished he didn't get so fucking irritated when they tried to include him in shit.

Some days were worse than others. There was no rhyme or reason for it, but today was one of those days.

He'd even struggled with working up on the third floor with the task force and had headed down to his apartment earlier than he should have. If Crew had a problem with it, the task force leader knew where to find him.

Normally, Crew left him alone because Nox spent more than a normal amount of time upstairs working. Usually late at night when he couldn't sleep.

Or when he didn't want to sleep.

When he knew closing his eyes would be more difficult than trying to keep them open.

More pounding. "Nox! You in there?"

"For fuck's sake," he muttered, putting down the biography he was reading, then forced himself to his feet and over to the door.

With his hand on the knob, he took a few seconds to brace himself before flipping the deadbolt and yanking open the door.

Aiden Cross, the Blue Avengers MC secretary and a Southern Allegheny Regional PD officer, stood before him with concern not very well hidden on his face. But that wasn't all...

He was nervous about something.

"Need you downstairs."

Dread filled Nox's chest. "Who does?"

"Jamison asked me to come get you for a quick meeting."

It had to be Blue Avenger business since the prez wasn't on the task force. But their club's meetings took time and effort to schedule since it was difficult to get all of them together with their various work schedules. So, *yeah*, something was off with this whole thing. "About?"

Cross shifted from one foot to the other. "He didn't say. He only asked me to get you."

This was smelling like bullshit. "Everybody else here already?"

"Everybody who can be. We're only waiting on you."

"I must've missed the original memo," he said dryly, since they did not schedule BAMC meetings on the fly. "You could've just texted me."

"I needed the exercise." Cross's Adam's apple jumped.

Nox wasn't liking this.

Not at fucking all.

Cross tipped his head and turned. "C'mon. Let's go before we're late."

"Cross," Nox started with a warning in his voice, but the man was already jogging down the steps.

Setting his jaw, he stepped out and locked the door behind him.

He paused on the second-floor landing and stared down at Cross now waiting at the bottom. Sucking on his teeth, Nox slowly followed.

Every step he took down the stairs felt weighted. As if he wore cement blocks instead of boots.

When he got to the foot of the stairs, Cross opened the building's side door and waved him inside.

He met the man's eyes for a moment, took a breath and then walked through the BAMC's meeting room, the only way to get into their church besides the rear entrance.

Two ways in.

Two ways to escape.

With Cross close on his heels, Nox stepped out of the room where the executive committee met and into the clubhouse's common area.

There, he stopped short and took them all in.

Grim expressions. Nervous gestures. Perched stiffly on the three couches and some chairs set around that sitting area.

All eyes turned toward him.

This was not a goddamn BAMC meeting. "What the fuck is this?"

Cross was suddenly crowding him and pressing a firm hand to his back, urging in a strong voice, "Go have a seat."

Nox's nostrils flared and his jaw flexed. "No. We had no meeting scheduled, so I don't know what the fuck this is."

When he turned, Cross quickly blocked him from leaving the same way they came in.

He spun on his heels and was about to head toward the back door when, just as quickly, Decker was there, blocking his path.

"Get out of my way, brother," Nox warned just loud enough for Decker to hear. "Don't fucking do this."

Decker's lips pressed together so tight, they were nothing but a slash.

Nox's heartbeat thumped in his ears. "Deck..."

"Have a seat," Jamison called out.

With a glance over his shoulder, Nox saw the club president pointing to the only empty spot on the center couch. The middle cushion, of course, so he'd be flanked by two of his brothers.

"Is this task force business?" he asked Crew, not bothering to mask the betrayal in his voice. He already knew it wasn't because only BAMC members were in the room, but he was looking for any way to stall what was about to come next.

The task force leader answered, "No, but you still answer to me."

"Not off the clock," Nox reminded him.

Before Crew could respond, Jamison rose from his seat. "If you want to be that way, you do answer to me. I'm not only your sergeant at SVPD, I'm your prez." He jabbed a finger toward the couch. "Now sit the fuck down."

Nox's spine snapped straight, and his chin lifted in defiance. "You can't force me to do shit." He turned again, only to find himself toe-to-toe with Cross. "Get the fuck out of my way." His fingers curled into fists, an automatic reaction to the flight or fight instinct since no one was letting him leave.

Cross shook his head. "No, brother, I'm not going to do that."

"Nox," Jamison called out. "Do us a favor and give us a few minutes of your time. That's all we're asking."

"You're not asking. You're telling. I don't like being ambushed."

"And we don't like having to ambush you," Crew insisted.

"But you did it anyway."

Finn threw his hands up. "Because we had no choice! C'mon, man, just sit so we can get this over with."

"You're family and we all love you like a brother, and you have us all worried," North said next.

Nox pulled at his chin and let his gaze circle the group. "What's this about?"

He knew. He fucking *knew*.

"Sit and we'll explain," Jamison urged. "If you want to keep your job at SVPD and also stay on the task force," Nox did not miss him and Crew exchanging glances, "you need to sit."

"What are you going to do, fire me?"

"I'll put you on administrative leave," Jamison threatened, "and if you're on that, you'll be automatically removed from the task force."

Jesus fucking Christ. If he lost his job and was also removed from the task force, he'd have nothing left to keep his mind busy.

His own brothers were hobbling him. "For my own good, right?"

Did he sound bitter? *Yeah well*, he was fucking more than bitter.

"Yes, Nox, for your own good," Jamison answered. "Now, don't make me do shit I don't want to do."

"Then, don't."

Pinching his nose, Crew dropped his head. Without warning, the man surged to his feet and yelled, "You're off the task force!"

The room went dead silent at that outburst.

He glared at Nox as he spat out, "You made your choice, now you have to live with it. You can go back to SVPD and working patrol."

"No, he won't." Jamison shook his head. "Like I said, with the way he is right now, I'll be talking to the captain. He won't be on patrol, either."

Nox's gaze bounced from Crew to Jamison before it dropped to his boots. He pulled in a deep breath, held it and, after a few moments, released it.

He needed to go.

He needed to get the fuck out of that room.

He masked his expression when he lifted his head and considered them all.

Everyone in that room loved him like family. They cared about him. They were worried about him.

That was cemented when Rez said softly, "We love you, brother. If you love us, then you'll hear us out."

Fuck.

His heart knew they cared about him, but his brain was still screaming at him to escape. They warred with each other.

The bottom line was, he needed his job, he needed the task force, and he needed his brotherhood.

The last being the most important.

He'd be nowhere right now without them. Maybe not even breathing.

With a single nod, Nox went over and sat in the spot where Jamison had pointed.

Avoiding everyone's eyes, he stared straight ahead at the wall. "Let's get this over with."

"You've fallen down that deep, dark well again," Jamison started.

Nox's brow furrowed. "I'm fine."

"You were getting to that point," Rez agreed. "Until we found Sadie. Something triggered you when we did."

A switch flipped inside him when he saw Sloane's sister was nothing but a cold, defiled corpse on that bed. Even though he knew the woman had been dead long before her last breath.

She had given up. She had let her addiction rule her life.

No differently than Nox giving up and letting grief rule his. It smothered him like a weighted blanket he couldn't shake free.

"We can guess what," Decker added, "so we don't need to discuss those details, but we do need to discuss you."

He definitely didn't want to relive the moment when he stared into that motel room in Ohio.

"I'm fine," Nox repeated, trying to stay focused on the blank screen of the TV, instead.

"I wish that was true."

When he heard Crew's agonized whisper behind him, Nox yanked his baseball cap even lower to hide any reaction.

Cross spoke next. "We're here for you. No matter how bad it gets. But none of us have the skill or experience needed to truly help you."

"I'm fine."

"Christ almighty!" Crew barked, making Nox jolt in his seat. "You're not. Did you forget we knew you before..." The man blew out a breath and continued, "We knew you when you *were* fine. You are far from that now, brother. You can keep saying that, but it's all bullshit."

The view of the TV disappeared when someone stepped in front of him and a hand appeared before his face. In Jamison's hand were a business card and a pamphlet. "Take them."

Nox wouldn't take them because he wanted the info, he would take them simply to get this shit over with.

He quickly scanned them both.

One was a business card to a cognitive behavioral therapist, the other for a grief support group. Not the same group he had attended right after Jackie's death.

Thank fuck. He had hated that group, and he was never going back.

The group leader had constantly urged Nox to "get in touch with his feelings." That was impossible because, at the time, Nox didn't have any. He'd been nothing but a hollow shell.

This pamphlet was for a group specifically meant for spouses and loved ones of law enforcement and military, whether lost in the line of duty or not.

Nox asked, "I get to pick?"

"No," Jamison answered. "You're going to do both."

He squeezed his eyes shut, fighting the urge to argue. They weren't doing this to hurt him. They were doing this to help.

As he stared at the back of his closed eyelids, he relived something that had stuck with him.

A conversation that took place on the day of Sadie Parrish's funeral.

Right after the graveside service, Nox had picked up Val, Decker's four-year-old, and set her on his hip to carry her back to the line-up of parked vehicles.

Valee Girl had wrapped her arms tightly around his neck

and pressed her forehead against the side of his head. "Uncle Nox?"

Her soft, cautious whisper got him right in the chest. "Yeah, baby?"

"Why are you so sad?"

"Today's a sad day."

"But... you're always sad."

Jesus.

"Daddy says it's 'cause of Aunt Jackie."

Your daddy isn't wrong. "Do you remember her?"

"A little bit."

"What do you remember?"

"I remember her sneakin' me a lollipop after Daddy said I couldn't have one."

At the time, Nox had closed his eyes and swallowed down the uncomfortable lump wedged in his throat.

That lump had returned, and no amount of swallowing could get rid of it.

When he finally opened his eyes, he looked directly at Jamison.

He gave the man a single nod and an, "Okay."

Chapter One

"I SEE a couple of new faces tonight, so just a quick reminder that this bereavement support group is open to any members of law enforcement or military who lost a loved one or significant other. As well as family and partners of law enforcement or military, either killed in the line of duty or passed away in any other manner."

Just like it stated on the fucking pamphlet.

Nox had slipped in the door and found an empty seat in the back row at the last minute.

Like he had for the past three weeks, he'd sit on his bike out in the parking lot and watch the time. He'd wait until only two minutes were left before the weekly meeting started, then he'd head inside to avoid getting caught up in any conversation beforehand.

He also ducked out immediately afterward to steer clear of the same.

No coffee, no donuts, no chit chat.

He came, did his required time and split.

He wasn't there to make friends.

He wasn't there to socialize.

He wasn't there to compare scars to see whose ran the deepest.

He was only doing what was necessary to keep his job, stay on the task force and make his BAMC brothers happy.

And, more importantly, keep them off his ass.

"Since this is my last meeting here, I will miss you all and I truly appreciate the support you've given me as the host of this group these last three years." The older woman sniffled, and tears filled her eyes.

Nox ground his teeth. He had no tolerance for this emotional bullshit.

"Once I found my dream retirement home in a state without snow..." Bonnie chuckled at that and so did everyone else. Everyone except Nox. "I began to search for the perfect replacement. Someone who's experienced what we have and would understand what we've dealt with. It wasn't an easy search, but I finally found her. We can't be any luckier to have her step in to take my place since this will be my last night. She ran a similar group for years in Pittsburgh until life got too hectic for her to keep up. We all know what that's like, right? Now, she's ready to get back to it. Without further ado, I want to introduce Aaliyah James."

Clapping ensued as a woman rose from the front row and stepped up to the dais.

Nox blinked. The new host was nothing like the old one.

Bonnie's head was full of short gray hair. Glasses covered her light blue eyes. Her loose jowls shook when she spoke. Her skin was pale, and her hands were full of age spots. She wore clothes that had been tucked in her closet since the early 2000s and her feet were encased in tan orthopedic shoes.

This Aaliyah James did not check any of those same boxes.

Nox inspected her from head to high heels as she stood tall next to Bonnie. Her black hair, just shy of shoulder length, was full of curls and not neat like Bonnie's gray helmet after she got it freshly set at the hairdressers. It was sort of wild and loose, like the wind had styled it. It fit her face perfectly.

The style of her hair was as current as her clothes. A bright red button-down blouse emphasized her curves and the deep dark tone of her glowing, flawless skin.

Black dress pants fit her long legs well and red heels encased her feet. Gold hoops hung from both ears, a thin gold chain, with possibly a pendant, disappeared into her cleavage, and several gold bracelets circled one wrist.

As for rings, from what he could see, one circled her right thumb. He couldn't see her left hand to check out her ring finger.

Her makeup was perfectly done to highlight her cheekbones, her eyeshadow emphasized the deep brown of her eyes, and her full lips were bright red to match her blouse and painted fingernails.

She was a lot younger than Bonnie, too. But Nox had a hard time guessing her age. Even though he didn't see any wrinkles at the corners of her dark eyes, they reflected a lot of life experience and maturity.

She was definitely *not* in her twenties.

This woman had been through some things. Nox could guess an obvious one.

She had lost a loved one, whether it be spouse, partner or family member.

Either she was a member of law enforcement or her loved

one had been. Nox assumed he'd find out soon enough, once the woman introduced herself.

Did he even fucking care what the woman's story was?

No. She was just another talking head standing at the lectern once a week to guide the group. She was there to coax them to "share." To encourage them to empathize with the others. To coordinate who brought snacks and coffee the following week.

To strongly suggest they return week after week.

Like he had a damn choice.

"Thank you for the very warm welcome. As Bonnie stated, I used to head a group in Pittsburgh and..."

He was caught off-guard when her voice, with a tone reminding him of warm honey, wrapped around him. Almost like a hug.

He hadn't had one of those since the last time he saw Valee Girl.

Decker's daughter always squeezed him tight. He wasn't sure if the big man told her to do that or she did it on her own because she sensed he needed it.

He mentally shook himself back to the meeting.

"My husband was an officer with the Pittsburgh PD. Some of you might remember, almost sixteen years ago, when a group of neo-Nazis marched downtown and created havoc. My husband was one of the first responding officers. Two were killed and three critically injured when they clashed with the group."

A murmur went through the participants.

Nox remembered that riot in the city and how much damage was done between loss of life, injuries and property destruction. A bunch of bystanders standing up to the marchers were also badly injured. It was a dark day in Pittsburgh.

"Not only did I lose my partner and husband, I was pregnant at the time."

Nox's lungs seized, every muscle locked, and his fingers dug painfully into his thighs.

"Mark never got to meet his son. And my son never got to meet his father. All due to a group who didn't believe what's stated in our country's Declaration of Independence," she pointed to the floor, "signed right here in this very state... that 'all men are created equal.'"

When Aaliyah paused, she used that time to look at every person in the group. One by one, she met their eyes. Before she made it to the back row, he yanked his baseball cap lower and tipped his face down so she couldn't do the same with him.

Despite that, he knew the exact moment she reached him, because he could feel her eyes boring into him. He kept his head down until she continued talking, then he lifted it enough to see she had captured and held hostage everyone's attention.

The woman was bold, beautiful and very well-spoken.

In truth, he could listen to her talk all night. He only wished it was on a different topic.

"Even though a lot of time has passed since that day and the pain has dulled somewhat, that deep ache of loss has never completely gone away. While you never want to forget your loved one—or your friend or coworker—you also need to learn to function and move on with your life. You can't let someone else's death turn *you* into a ghost. I'll admit it... It's work to get past the grief and live life again. And to go back to enjoying that life without guilt."

She caught him then, when he had dropped his guard. Her dark eyes locked with his over the rest of the small group.

They might as well be the only two in the room as she

continued. "We can't only focus on the sadness. We need to focus on the good parts of their lives. Of ours, too. Grief can be overwhelming, and everyone handles a loss of an important person in their life differently. The bottom line is, there's no right or wrong way to grieve. However, the person we loved and lost would not have wanted our lives to stop at the same moment that theirs did."

Damn.

His throat narrowed and he struggled to swallow.

While Bonnie was annoying, Nox now regretted she was leaving. Maybe he'd have to find another group that Jamison would approve of since he wasn't sure he could stay in this one. He worried that the woman standing at the front of the group could somehow get past the armor he wore.

After her story, she opened the floor for anyone and everyone to speak. Anything could be shared. From feelings to a funny story, to just tears.

Sometimes Nox listened. Sometimes he didn't.

And he never once shared.

Nor did he plan to.

He was doing his time. If he was going to open up to anyone, it would be his therapist, not this group. He didn't want anyone looking at him with pity.

Or with tears in their eyes.

Or worse, wanting to give him a hug.

When everyone else had their say and the hour and a half was almost up, she turned her eyes toward him.

Fuck.

"You, in the back. Yes, you, in the baseball cap. Do you have anything you want to share tonight?"

He shook his head.

Her perfectly shaped eyebrows rose. "Nothing at all? Not about the weather, or traffic, or about your job?"

"No."

"Do you want to tell us about the person you lost? Even if it's simply his or her name?"

Her name was Jacqueline Lennox, and she was my everything. We didn't expect our vow of "'til death do you part" to come sooner than later.

"No."

Her eyes remained on him, trying to read his body language, trying to read his expression. Trying to get inside.

He locked all that shit down.

Finally, with a nod and a slight flare of her nostrils, she announced, "Thank you again for your warm welcome and I look forward to seeing you all again next week. Same time, same place. Please stick around for the refreshments that Bonnie so generously provided tonight. She even brought cupcakes!"

Nox was out of his chair and taking long strides toward the door when he heard, "Hey!"

Whoever she was calling out to couldn't be him and if it was, he was going to pretend he didn't hear her.

He slammed the push bar on the door with both hands and before it was even done opening, he rushed through it and down the hall to the exit that led to the parking lot.

"Hey!" joined the quick clicking of heels as she followed him.

He did not slow down, he did not stop, he didn't even glance over his shoulder.

His Harley was waiting, and his ass needed to be on it.

He didn't hold the door for her, instead he let it slam behind him and picked up his pace. Not quite a jog but it was damn close.

But, *damn*, the woman could move.

He moved faster.

One second, he was still hearing the clicks of her heels on the pavement, the next, he wasn't.

Thank fuck she gave up.

With his eyes focused on his bike at one end of the community center's parking lot, he sighed in relief when he got there. But before he could swing his leg over, he heard an out-of-breath, "Hey," behind him.

Christ.

Taking a deep breath, he closed his eyes. When he opened them a few seconds later, he turned to face her.

Her high heels were hanging from her fingers. He let his gaze roll down her to see her feet were bare.

What the fuck?

Her, "Nice bike," had him pulling his gaze back up to her shadowed face.

She was checking out his custom Softail with what looked like real interest.

"What do you know about bikes?"

Did her lips twitch? What the fuck was funny about his question?

"Enough to know a nice one when I see it."

He almost asked how but caught himself. That would open him up to conversation. He didn't want to talk, he wanted to walk.

Speaking of walking... "You shouldn't be out here barefoot."

"You were hard to catch."

That was the point.

"It was pretty obvious you didn't want to be caught," she concluded from his silence.

But here you are, anyway.

"I've seen group participants closed off like you before.

Not willing to share. Not willing to talk. Not willing to listen." Her head tilted as she waited for him to respond.

He didn't since that would be an invitation for her to continue.

She did, anyway. "My guess is your loss is fresh and you're still going through the early stages of grief."

She couldn't be more wrong about him going anywhere. He was stuck.

"At least you're taking an important step by coming to group meetings. That shows you want to help yourself."

"I was forced," he muttered.

"What?"

"I had no choice," he said louder.

"No choice in what?"

"Coming to this fucking group."

"Ah. So, that's your issue. You have a chip on your shoulder."

"The only thing on my shoulder is my head."

"I bet you have a really thick skull."

Chapter Two

AALIYAH WAS USED to dealing with pig-headed men. But because of her father and his extended "family," she couldn't escape them. He was a man who liked to share his opinion loudly and didn't care what you thought about it.

So, yes, she was used to dealing with stubborn people.

It had to be in the blood, since her teenage son was taking after his grandfather and not after his own even-tempered father, who he never got to meet.

Devyn had this mistaken idea that his opinion was the only one that mattered in her household.

He was wrong.

A fifteen-year-old didn't dictate her life. Neither did a fifty-seven-year-old.

Luckily, she wasn't afraid to tell that to either of them.

Since the tall man before her didn't react at all to her comment, she tried another tactic. "You never shared your name in the meeting."

"I gotta go." He turned back toward his Harley.

"Since you already know my name, can you at least give me yours?"

His broad shoulders stiffened. "Why?"

This guy... Was it even worth trying to break through? If she pushed, would he lock himself down even tighter? "I guess the question is, why not? Is it a secret?"

"No."

"It would be the first step to opening up."

He spun on her. "That's the problem."

Damn.

Because of how he resisted her attempts to get him to talk, she was surprised when he asked, "Why here?" Actually, it wasn't really an ask but more of a demand.

She'd allow it. *This* time. But she wasn't going to tolerate a one-sided conversation.

"When Bonnie decided to move south for her retirement, she asked me to take it over." She raised both hands along with her shoulders in a shrug. "So, here I am."

"Here you are," he repeated. "But Bonnie said that already. I mean why *here*. In Shadow Valley? Don't you live in Pittsburgh?"

She shook her head. "Not anymore. Once I had my second child, my place was too small, and I wanted to move closer to my father and his family."

"*His* family? Isn't his family your family, too?"

Interesting how he picked up on that particular detail. It smelled as if he was a cop. He actually looked like one, too.

She was pretty good at sniffing out cops.

Another topic her father had a loud opinion about since he hated them and wasn't afraid to let them know what he thought about them to their face.

"Sure they are. They are definitely all my family." Whether she wanted them to be or not.

"You have a big family," he surmised.

"I'd say. My parents married when they were teenagers after ending up pregnant with me. Not long after, they had my brother Malcolm. Then their relationship went to hell. No surprise since they were too young for life commitments, be it a marriage or children. About fifteen years ago, my father remarried, and he ended up having two more children with my stepmother. Her family is extremely large, too." And not just with blood family. "My brother also has two kids. That means holidays tend to be busy and noisy." She smiled. "Truthfully, I wouldn't have it any other way."

Though, after any big gathering, she was glad to go home to peace and quiet. She also ended up hitting a bottle. Of aspirin.

"So now that I've shared more about me, what about you? Can you at least give me your name? You don't have to give me anything else." When he didn't answer, she asked, "You *are* coming back next week, right, Allen?"

His head twitched.

"It would be nice to at least have a way to address you, Bob. If not, I'm going to go down the alphabet and call you every name I can think of until I get to the letter Z. Then I'll start all over again, Calvin."

His chest visibly expanded when he inhaled deeply. Was he battening down his armor or loosening it up?

Time would tell.

"Just so you know, Deepak, I'm a lot like my father. I'll warn you now that I don't give up easily. My advice is to save yourself by telling me your name before I drive you to the brink with my persistence."

"I could just ride away."

"You could, but you haven't yet, Edgar."

"I'm tempted to fucking stand here until you get to Z."

Even though his stony expression didn't change, could he possibly have a sense of humor buried deep inside him?

"I've got all night, Fabio." She really didn't. She needed to get home to her kids and before she did that, she wanted to go back inside the community center and help Bonnie shut things down.

"Lennox," he mumbled.

"What?"

"Lennox," he repeated more clearly.

"Is that your first or last name?" Most likely his last since law enforcement usually called each other by their last names.

"Bradley Lennox."

Holy shit. She was actually making headway. Even if it was only a smidge. "Well, Bradley Lennox, nice to meet you." She jutted out her hand.

His gaze dropped to it, but he kept both of his down by his sides. "Nobody calls me that," he grumbled.

"I just did. Tell me, what do people call you?"

"Nox."

"How did you get that nickname?" She knew full well it was short for Lennox, but she wanted to keep him talking.

"Got shortened in the Army."

Having served in the military could sometimes be a sticky subject with people so closed off. She decided to ask something safer. "Do you live here in Shadow Valley, Nox?"

"Work for the PD. Live in Rockvale now."

"Shadow Valley PD?" She knew a few people who worked for the local police department because they were tied to the Dirty Angels MC. And her father's MC was tied to the Dirty Angels because they were close allies. However, that wasn't her only connection to the DAMC... Her stepmother was another one.

"Yeah. But I've been... On other assignments."

He left that vague for a reason. She'd respect that.

It was time to let him go while she was ahead, anyway. She needed to chip away at him slowly, not try to break him open with a sledgehammer from the start.

"Well, Nox, I need to get back inside. Not only to say a final goodbye to Bonnie but to help her clean up. I look forward to seeing you next week."

He grunted.

She stood there for a few moments longer to watch him swing a long leg over his "sled," what her father and the rest of the bikers she knew all too well called their rides.

His Harley roared to life and the rich rumble of the exhaust vibrated deep in her chest. The very familiar sound tended to get her heart pumping.

Even though she wasn't raised in the MC life, like it or not, she could no longer avoid it. The day she reconnected with her father, she automatically got sucked in and it never let her go.

She got no response when she called out, "Be safe out there."

Instead, he shot out of his parking spot and onto the road like the devil was chasing him.

Huh. Was she the devil?

She smiled.

––––––––

"Welcome!" Aaliyah greeted at the top of the hour. "Thank you to whoever came early and set up the chairs. However, we're going to switch things up from here on out. I prefer we all sit in a circle and that I don't stand at a lectern. I want to be considered one of you since we're all here for the same reason. To share. To support each other. To even give advice."

"For fuck's sake," Nox grumbled under his breath.

"Sorry? Did someone say something?" She glanced around the room and when no one fessed up, she looked at him.

He kept his expression masked.

"All right, I see how excited you all are," she said dryly, "so let's move our chairs."

The group was small tonight. At most a dozen people, including the woman who haunted his gray matter since last week.

He'd been right when he thought she was bold. That exchange out in the parking lot after the meeting had proved it.

She seemed willing to take on any challenge, including him.

He needed to make sure she knew that wasn't an option. He wasn't a challenge for her to conquer.

He didn't want to pretend to be at the meeting for "sharing and caring."

He didn't want to share.

He definitely didn't want to care.

He just wanted to be left alone.

He remained seated as everyone rose and moved their chairs into a large circle. Aaliyah slid the dais away from the group and grabbed an empty chair for herself.

She wanted to be "one of them."

He hated this whole circle concept. It made him face other group members and he couldn't hide in the back. It would also be harder to sneak in with seconds to spare and rush out immediately after.

So, *yeah*, this new setup sucked ass.

As Aaliyah's very observant gaze circled the group, it landed on him again. "You're messing up our circle by making it lopsided."

All eyes turned toward him.

Fucking great. "I'm fine where I'm at. I'll stay in my row."

One perfectly shaped eyebrow rose. "One chair does not make a row. How about you join us." It wasn't a suggestion; it was an actual order.

She mentioned she had two kids. She just used her mom voice.

On him.

For fuck's sake.

When he didn't move, she rose from her chair and came over. What was she going to do? Wrestle him into compliance?

She might get a rude awakening.

She lowered her voice to assure him, "Change is good."

"That's your opinion."

"And in this room, my opinion matters."

"Mine doesn't?"

"Only if you express it. With actual words. Do you plan on sharing tonight?"

"Is that another change you're making? Is sharing now a requirement to attend?" Because if it was, he'd either find another group somewhere else or pretend he was attending by finding somewhere to hide for two hours once a week.

The only problem with the second option was that Jamison lived and worked in Shadow Valley and Nox wouldn't put it past his sergeant and BAMC president to check the parking lot for his bike or truck to make sure he was holding up his end of the agreement.

Attend counseling and these meetings or lose his Shadow

Valley PD badge and get kicked off the Tri-State Federal Drug Task Force.

Neither which he wanted.

He pulled in a breath through his nose.

She had him by the damn balls. All she had to do was squeeze hard enough to bring him to heel.

Setting his jaw, he quickly surged to his feet, causing her to stumble backwards in surprise.

"Those heels almost made you trip. Try orthopedic shoes next time. I'm sure Bonnie can suggest a good place to buy them."

She pressed her lips together and narrowed her eyes on him as he lifted the metal folding chair and set it down with a loud clatter in line with the rest of the circle.

He glanced at her. "That good? Is your circle perfect now?"

"It's not perfect yet," she said, "but it will be soon." After delivering that warning, she strode across the circle and back to her chair, quickly planting her ass in it.

He tried not to notice how good her ass looked in her dress pants. He failed.

Tonight she wore what he thought were called capris, pants that were short for her long-ass legs. They exposed slender ankles and revealed a delicate gold chain decorating one of them.

The woman sure liked jewelry and dressing up.

She had to be high maintenance.

Nox was the exact opposite. Give him a pair of comfortable jeans, a pair of broken-in boots, a T-shirt, slap a baseball cap on his head and he was good.

When he worked the road, he wore his uniform.

He owned three suits. All in black. He only pulled them

out of his closet for weddings, funerals and court appearances.

He owned no jewelry except his wedding ring. And that was a plain gold band.

He drove an older Chevy truck without all the bells and whistles, owned a Harley *with* all the bells and whistles and second-hand furniture filled his apartment.

Currently, his bike was his most prized possession.

Before that, it was his wife.

He would give up everything he owned to have her back.

He would do anything to speak to her one more time.

He would sacrifice all his material possessions—past, current and future—for the chance to say one last goodbye.

But the harsh truth was...

Nothing he did would bring her back.

Nothing he did would give him even a few more minutes in her presence.

And nothing... *Absolutely* fucking nothing would give him back the child they created together.

The one he never got to hold.

Or name.

Or see who she took after.

Their unborn, unnamed daughter now kept Jackie company in her grave.

At least his wife had that.

While Nox was alone.

The woman and child he lived for, gone in a single moment.

The overpaid therapist couldn't bring them back.

This fucking group couldn't bring them back.

And neither could the woman forcing them to sit in a goddamn circle like that was going to make everything fucking better.

It wasn't.

Nothing would make any of it better.

Nothing would dull the fucking pain.

His fingers dug into his thighs, and he squeezed his eyes shut.

He was struggling to breathe.

Struggling to move on.

Everything was a goddamn struggle.

The only way to be a family again would be to join them.

But if he told anyone he wanted to be placed with Jackie and his daughter in their casket, they would lock him away. Far away from them.

Probably in some locked, padded room. With a mattress and no sheets. No metal utensils.

No shoelaces.

Nothing. Because they knew what was better for him than he did himself.

That was the excuse they'd use.

When it wasn't true.

"Brad."

Chapter Three

WHEN HIS NAME whispered through his head, his eyes opened and he glanced around looking for the owner of that voice.

Jackie.

She was calling out for him.

Just like she probably had on that day.

Someone to his left droned on about the loved one they lost. Reminiscing about a core memory that made them both laugh and cry at the same time.

He didn't give a shit. But he damn well bet *she* did. She was probably blubbering, too.

He glanced across the circle, surprised to find that *she* wasn't listening to that person at all.

She was watching him.

His heart began to race, and his eyesight began to narrow. His ears rang so loudly, it drowned out the person talking.

He needed to get the fuck out of there.

She was going to break him open and turn him inside out.

She was going to make him feel again.

And he couldn't risk that.

Not again.

He jumped out of his seat and beelined toward the door.

Not hearing anything.

Not seeing anything but escape.

He made it out the door and down the hallway. But before he could shove his way through the double glass doors leading outside, his elbow was grabbed and squeezed hard.

He jerked his arm free and spun to confront the person.

Of course.

It was *her.*

Once again chasing him down.

Determined to help.

Despite him not wanting that.

He had no good reason to crack himself open because he already knew what was inside.

Nothing.

Emptiness.

Darkness.

"Nox..."

Without a word, he spun again, shoved open the door and headed outside.

Where he could breathe a little easier.

Where he didn't feel so boxed in.

"Nox," she called out.

He cursed under his breath but kept walking, making a break for his bike.

"Bradley Lennox! You stop right there!"

He slammed on the brakes and spun, surprised to find himself face to face with her. The woman could move. "Stop talking to me like I'm a goddamn child!"

"Then stop acting like one!" she yelled back.

His head jerked back.

She glared at him with her chest heaving.

His was doing the same.

He could see her mentally shake herself and her next words were much quieter. "You're going to destroy my self-esteem if you keep trying to avoid me. Is it my breath? Do I have an extreme case of halitosis?" She cupped her hand over her mouth and huffed into it. "No, just a little bit of garlic from my lunch."

Was this woman for real?

"Listen... I know change can be difficult, but you shouldn't have such a meltdown over something as simple as going from sitting in rows to a circle."

"I didn't have a fucking meltdown."

She tipped her head to the side. "No? Then, I guess I should clean my glasses."

"You're not wearing glasses."

"That's right. Because I have perfect 20/20 vision and I know what I saw."

Holy shit, this woman. She might be able to out-will him. If he let her. Which he wouldn't. "Your group is waiting for you."

"You're a part of the group." She flung a hand toward the community center. "Let's go back inside."

If he insisted that he didn't want to sit in a circle, he *would* sound like a damn child. But then, storming out hadn't been very mature, either.

Christ, this whole thing was a lose-lose situation. "I gotta go."

As he turned, her hand shot out and snagged his forearm. Why did she keep touching him?

He stared down at her tight grip.

"I've been thinking about something you said last week. You mentioned you were forced to be here. By who?"

43

Her question made him raise his eyes back to her face. It was so strikingly fucking beautiful.

He grimaced at where his thoughts went.

That grimace deepened when he answered her. "By the people I answer to." Why the fuck did she have the power to get info out of him?

You have the right to remain silent.

Her eyebrows knitted together. "What do you mean?"

Anything you say may be used against you...

"People I report to at work," he answered.

He wasn't going to get into details. He certainly wasn't going to tell her about the task force or the Blue Avengers. He didn't want to give her any more than what he had to.

And even that was too much.

"Your police department," she surmised.

She could take his answering grunt however she'd like. He didn't care.

"Then I bet they wouldn't like you leaving before the meeting even begins."

He met her gaze head-on. "Who's going to tell them?"

"*Ah.* Is that the ol' 'snitches get stitches' threat?"

He grunted again.

She could take that answer however she'd like, too. Because, once again, he didn't care.

"Just so you know, I don't scare easily. Only two people exist on Earth who're scarier than my father. And one isn't you."

He frowned. Now he was curious about who her father was, as well as those two other "scary" people. Who the hell was she hanging out with?

"Look, you told me where you work. I know your name. I can easily find out who your immediate supervisor is. It's not some secret. Don't make me tell them you're skipping out on required meetings."

Damn, that was a low blow.

"But if you want to bow out tonight, fine. Do that. It'll give you a whole week to mentally prepare to. Sit. In. A. Fucking. Circle. Next. Week." She bit every damn one of those words off.

This woman was not fucking around.

He sneered, "Like in kindergarten."

"That's a fitting comment since you're acting that age. Maybe I'll bring carpet squares next week. We can all sit criss-cross applesauce on the floor. Maybe clap hands while we sing the song *If You're Happy and You Know It*. I'm sure you know the words."

"I don't know the words."

"Figures you don't." She sighed. "Leave tonight if you must, but I want to give you something first. Can I trust you not to hightail it out of here before I do?"

He grunted.

"That sounded convincing." She flipped a hand toward a small sporty Mercedes parked only a few spots away from his bike. "It's in my car and I'm parked right there."

Of course she'd drive a damn Benz. Just as he thought, high maintenance.

"If you wait here, I promise not to narc on you. This week, anyway. But if you skip out on next week, no promises."

"Hurry up. I'm sure the group is wondering where you are."

"They know where I am. They couldn't miss me sprinting after you in the middle of Tina's story. Stay here."

"Stop giving me orders."

"Then stop making me give them," she countered as she pulled her key fob from her pocket and unlocked her car. When she opened the passenger-side door, she bent over to dig in her center console, giving him another good look at her ass.

And the way her hips rocked as she searched for something in the car's interior.

He quickly dropped his gaze to his boots as she straightened and turned with something small and light-colored in her hand.

The door slammed shut and the car beeped when it was relocked. The clicks of her heels as she approached had him lifting his eyes again. This time they got hung up on her chest.

"You're not as dead inside as you think. You staring at my ass and tits is proof." She raised a palm. "Don't even deny it. Mothers have eyes in the back of their head."

Damn. She wasn't lying.

She extended her hand and tucked between two fingers was what looked like a business card. "All my info is on that card. Please reach out if you need to talk to someone."

"I don't need that."

She slapped the card against his chest with her palm and held it there. "Take it."

"I don't want it."

"I don't care. You're going to take it, anyway."

Reluctantly, he held out his open hand.

She peeled the card from his chest and slapped it into his palm. "Like I said, if you need to talk—"

"I don't need that since I'm not only forced to come to this group, but I have to see a therapist."

"And I'm sure you turn into Chatty Cathy while in his or her office. Anyway, the offer still stands. Any time. Any place. We could talk over coffee instead of in a stuffy office.

I've done my time sitting in those offices in front of therapists. Some helped, some did not. Some sit there and listen, but most likely are secretly judging. What I can promise you is, I won't judge. I've been in your shoes. I've felt the same pain. I will truly listen to whatever you have to say and keep my mouth shut while you say it. Even if it's simply about the weather."

"I don't think that's possible with you."

"What isn't?"

"The ability to keep your mouth shut."

"You're wrong. The key is knowing when to shut it and when to keep it open. If I had kept my mouth shut, you'd be gone and would never come back. Because I didn't, you'll be back next week. You'll also call me when you need to talk."

"You're so damn confident I'll do that."

"You're right, I am. And the reason I am is because I know you, Bradley Lennox. I know you because I used to be you."

———

HE'D DONE SOME RESEARCH. By pulling up the news articles and skimming through them. By searching for any mentions of the Pittsburgh officer named Mark.

He looked at pictures and watched videos of the march-turned-riot.

He had no idea if Aaliyah kept her late husband's last name since she said she had a second child. She could have married again. In reality, she still could be married to the father of her youngest child.

Then he found it on a fallen officers' page. Pittsburgh PD Officer Mark Alan James was on the list. At his end of watch, he only had five years on the job.

Using his name, Nox dug deeper to find James arrived on scene after a 911 call. Since the so-called march wasn't planned and didn't have a permit, he hadn't gone prepared by wearing any riot gear. His only protection was most likely his Kevlar vest and the weapons found on his duty belt.

He arrived thinking it was only a group of white supremacists marching without the city's permission or planning. Once on scene, he quickly discovered they were using spray paint to tag buildings with hate symbols, like swastikas, the iron cross, SS bolts and the number 88.

The group was not only gathering illegally, but they were also destroying property and intimidating citizens.

When Mark James tried to stop a member of the group from breaking out the windows of a business, he was struck in the back of the head with a flagpole. As he lay stunned on the sidewalk, another group member walked up and shot the man while he was down.

Aaliyah James's husband bled out before anyone could get to him.

Even though the photo in one article was blurred on purpose, it was easy to see just how large the pool of blood was that surrounded a lifeless Officer James.

How many of those photos had Aaliyah seen?

Did she stand in a courtroom and face his attackers while giving a heartfelt victim impact statement? Possibly while still pregnant with her late husband's child? Or by then had she been holding that baby in her arms?

Did she wish her husband's attackers to die the same violent death?

Nox wouldn't blame her if she did.

It was only natural to wish "an eye for an eye."

Nox grabbed a beer from the fridge, skirted around the counter and headed over to where Roland North, Mike

Miller and Crew were playing poker at the card table. Smoke spiraled toward the ceiling from their lit cigars and classic rock filled the first floor of The Plant, the Blue Avengers' church.

"You want in on the next hand?" Crew asked around the cigar jammed between his teeth.

Nox shook his head. "Too rich for my blood."

Crew coughed out what sounded like, "Bullshit."

"Like you don't have spare cash lying around," North huffed. "You sold your damn house, moved upstairs and pay dick for rent."

"Spent money to fix up the second floor."

"And you did all the labor yourself. Sit the fuck down and we'll deal your ass in for the next hand, cheapo."

He wasn't there to play poker, he was there for some answers. He pulled out one of the card table chairs, flipped it around and settled into it backwards. "You guys remember the neo-Nazi riot in the Burgh about sixteen years ago?"

Crew frowned. "I do. It was ugly as fuck."

"I don't," Miller answered, "but then I wasn't with the PD sixteen years ago. I mean, it's hard to avoid hearing about it by simply being a Pittsburgh officer. It's talked about to this day, but I don't remember the actual event. I'm just a baby."

North snorted loudly. "A baby making babies. You need to get the ol' snip-snip before you populate the Earth all by yourself, my man."

Miller shrugged. "My ol' lady loves being pregnant. And it's fun making her pregnant." He grinned.

"You have to be able to afford all those kids, asshole," Crew said. "If you weren't aware, you can still have the fun part without knocking her up. Did you miss that class in Sex Ed?"

"I think he's got a breeding kink," North announced.

"That makes sense," Crew said on a laugh. "That's one fucking expensive kink."

"Anyway," North continued, "unlike Mr. Young and Horny over there, I'm not only old enough to remember it, I was there. Mullins was, too, but he was a rookie when it happened."

Don Mullins, a task force member, was also a narcotics detective for Pittsburgh PD, so that made sense.

It was also a reminder of what a damn small world it was.

Crew narrowed his gray eyes on Nox. "Why are you asking about that riot?"

Shit. "It came up in conversation the other day."

"That shit doesn't come up in casual conversation," Crew insisted.

"I met the widow of Mark James," he admitted.

Silence circled the table and all eyes rose from the playing cards in their hands to land on Nox.

"Aaliyah James? Where?" North asked, dragging a hand down his dark cheek.

Nox ground his hand back and forth against the back of his neck. He wasn't sure how much he should reveal. His brothers tended to turn any info into ammo.

"Met her in passing."

"Nah, that's bullshit," Crew said. "You don't strike up conversation with random strangers."

Nox shot him a frown. "How the fuck would you know?"

"Because I know you."

I know you.

Chapter Four

I KNOW YOU.

I know you because I used to be you.

"I remember her," North said. "She was pregnant when her husband was killed. A damn shame."

"Damn," Crew whispered.

"I had heard that," Miller said next.

"That had to hit harder than normal," Nox risked saying. He hoped North would share more details without him having to dig.

If he showed too much interest, red flags would begin flapping in the breeze.

"I would recommend staying clear of her," North warned.

That was the last thing he expected out of the man's mouth. Nox frowned. "Why?" That would be difficult if he continued going to the grief group as required.

"Because of the company she keeps."

Nox opened his mouth to ask North what he meant but noticed Crew watching him too closely. He slammed his trap shut since the man was really damn good at figuring shit out. One of the reasons he was a senior agent with the DEA and the leader of their federal task force.

But it wasn't only North's comment making Nox wonder about her connections. On Wednesday night out in the parking lot, Aaliyah had also mentioned something along that line. Her words had stuck with him.

Just so you know, I don't scare easily. Only two people exist on Earth who're scarier than my father.

While he had been curious at the time about who those people were, including her father, North's warning now made him want to know even more.

His BAMC brother knew something Nox didn't.

And Nox didn't like being unprepared.

Aaliyah had given him her card, but he had shoved it deep into his front pocket, pretending he didn't want it. Even though it had burned a hole through his jeans that night, he hadn't looked at it. In fact, the pair he'd been wearing still hung over the back of his couch.

Tempting him.

He was afraid if he saw her phone number, he might text her.

To meet up.

To have conversation.

And get busted again for staring at her tits and ass.

But now... Those discarded jeans called to him like a damn siren song. Urging him to run upstairs. To grab that business card.

To find out her connections.

He almost jumped out of his skin when Crew's cell phone rang. The volume of his ringtone had to be turned up to the max.

Miller winced. "Damn, old man, are you deaf or something?"

"Maybe Cabrera is right, and you do need hearing aids," North ribbed Crew.

"Eh?" Crew curved a hand around his ear before snagging the phone off the table. "It's Fletch."

"Yeah, we know, since his mug is filling your screen. Do you have all of our pics on your phone?" Miller asked.

"No, just the pretty ones," Crew answered dryly. "You don't qualify." When he answered the call, he immediately put the BAMC vice president on speaker phone. "Yo."

"*Boss,*" Fletch greeted, using the nickname their newest task force member called Crew to get under his skin.

"Fuck off." Crew warned, "I'm at church with North, Miller and Nox and you're on speaker phone."

"What's up, fuckers?" Fletch asked on a laugh. "Believe it or not, I miss you assholes. Hopefully, our time being undercover is coming to an end soon. Right, Crewser?"

"I know you want to be free of that assignment, but I need you two to stick it out for as long as possible."

"We should have enough shit on them to bring the whole MC down."

"Yeah, for the most part, but that's not the only reason I want you to stay under with the Demons. We need someone on the inside to make sure we're one step ahead of them."

"Group one has two members within the Demons," Fletch reminded Crew.

"Yeah? And now so do we."

"For fuck's sake. I didn't want to be under for more than a few months and here it is going on year two."

"Jesus, have you been gone that long?" Miller asked. "I didn't miss you at all."

"It hasn't been two years," Crew insisted.

"It will be by the time this is all wrapped up."

Fletch was right. It had been about a year and a half since the Tri-State Federal Drug Task Force was formed. But they all knew going in that it wouldn't be a quick investigation. Too many players were involved. And their part of the investigation didn't even include the Pittsburgh Cosa Nostra or the Mexican cartel.

Hell, their part only included the Deadly Demons in Pennsylvania. Two other groups covered that outlaw MC in West Virginia and Ohio.

All three groups had to work as a team and coordinate. None of them could wrap up their investigation until they all could. Planning and communication would be key.

Nox was glad he was only a grunt in this case. No different than during his time in the Army. He kept his head down and simply did what he was told, then did what he wanted to do when no one was looking.

He just couldn't get caught.

Nox lost track of the conversation between Crew and Fletch but he didn't miss that the task force leader ended the call while Fletch was still bitching.

Typical Crew. The man didn't end calls like a normal human.

But then, he wasn't normal.

North shuffled the deck of cards. "You want in on this next hand, Hard Nox?"

No, he wanted to head upstairs, grab that business card and make a call of his own.

Instead, Nox pulled in a breath and dug for his wallet. "Yeah, deal me in."

————

NOX PACED BACK AND FORTH, counting each step he took. He strode all the way to the front of his apartment before spinning on his heel and following the same path back.

His apartment was pretty damn big since it took up the whole second floor of The Plant. When he started working on it, it was mostly all open floor space and a blank canvas. He now had a kitchen, a nice sized living space, a spacious bathroom and two bedrooms, as well as some closet space.

He did the framing, drywall, painting, electrical work and plumbing all himself. Skills he learned while in the Army. He also sanded down the scuffed and scarred wood-planked floors and refinished them back to their original glory by giving them a high gloss finish that made the wood grain pop.

The place was perfect for him. Big enough to not feel closed in—especially with the front windows still being boarded up—but small enough for him to manage on his own. The only thing he didn't have, and wished he did, was a washer and dryer so he didn't have to haul his dirty clothes to the nearest laundromat.

Every time he trekked across his apartment, he glanced at those damn jeans in passing. Normally, he tossed dirty laundry in the portable hamper he kept in his bedroom.

Both the Army and the instructors at the police academy drilled into him to be "squared away." Dropping clothes on the floor or throwing them over furniture went against his grain. But it wasn't the jeans being discarded over the couch that bothered him.

It was that fucking business card.

He slammed to a stop, pinched his nose and dropped his head back. "Fuck!"

Even though he kept putting it off, he already knew what he was going to do.

He *knew* it.

Because the woman had managed to get under his skin.

She had gotten into his head.

Jesus Christ, he needed to evict her.

The only way he might be able to do that would be to find out who she was connected to. The way North made it sound, they were bad people.

"I would recommend staying clear of her... Because of the company she keeps."

Was she a part of a criminal enterprise? Is that how she could afford those fancy clothes, the gold jewelry and expensive Mercedes sports car?

She'd been married to a cop so it wouldn't make sense if she switched over to the dark side. However, a lot could change in sixteen years. Desperation could make the most lawful person turn bad. Especially since she had been a single mother and could've been struggling to provide for herself and her son.

Most parents would do anything to keep a roof over their children's heads, as well as food in their bellies.

Holy shit. Why the fuck was he letting his imagination run wild? All he had to do was look at her damn card and see what it said. Then he needed to contact her and find out the damn truth instead of making up wild and unfounded accusations in his head.

He was a man who preferred facts over fiction. And right now, his brain was making up stories.

"For fuck's sake." He took long strides over to his sectional and snagged his jeans off the back.

He shoved his hand in the pocket and... found nothing.

Shit. Did he lose it?

He just put himself through all that bullshit and he lost her damn card?

He closed his eyes, shook his head at his own dumbass-ness and then pulled in a breath to slow his speeding heartbeat.

Maybe it was in the other pocket. He opened his eyes and checked. It wasn't there, either. It also wasn't in the back pockets.

What the actual fuck?

He threw the pair of jeans back on the couch and pulled out his wallet to dig through it. Not there, either.

He pinned his lips together and stared at the tossed-aside jeans. He'd have to wait to talk to her until next week. Maybe he could go early and pull her aside.

Wait...

Something cream-colored peeked from between the couch cushions. He jammed his hand into the crevice and grabbed it.

His mouth twisted into an almost-smile.

With his thumb brushing back and forth over the back of the card, his mouth twisted again, but this time in a frown. It wasn't his damn business whose company she kept. Her personal life didn't have anything to do with him.

He didn't want to be friends with her. He didn't want anything from her at all.

So, why the fuck did it matter?

That didn't stop him from flipping the card over to read it.

Aaliyah M. James
Owner/Broker
Exclusive Realty, Inc.

The card also included her office and cell phone numbers as well as the company's website address.

Now it made sense. The way she dressed professionally, even at a casual grief support group. The way she presented herself. The way she was outspoken and outgoing. The type of vehicle she drove, a likely choice to impress clients.

He skimmed her title again.

Owner.

A successful real estate agent could make a shitload of money. But an owner of a real estate brokerage firm... He had to assume she got a cut of every sale her agents made.

He was now damn sure she out-earned his ass. By a lot. Most local cops lived paycheck-to-paycheck. He'd be doing that too if he hadn't sold his marital home and moved into The Plant.

He no longer had a mortgage. With the equity in his home, he paid off the remaining balance on his Harley. His labor and the materials he purchased to turn the second floor into an apartment had been in lieu of rent. He was better off financially now than he had been previously. However, he was sure his bank account looked anemic compared to hers.

When he thought about Aaliyah's attitude, he easily believed that she had no problem running a successful business, as well as supervising a bunch of agents.

Heading over to the kitchen counter where his laptop sat, he opened it and typed in the website address. Within seconds, a very professional website filled his screen.

In the top left was Aaliyah's professional head shot. Whoever took the photo knew how to highlight her rich, dark skin tone and make her glow. He couldn't deny she was fucking gorgeous, and her wide smile looked genuine, open and not forced.

He made himself stop staring at her photo to skim over the rest of the page. He clicked through the site to discover she'd had opened the agency over ten years ago and when she started, she was the sole agent. Two years later, she became a licensed broker and over the years expanded her business until she supervised over a dozen agents and associate brokers.

None of what he read surprised him.

If someone was going to kick ass and take names, Aaliyah M. James seemed to fit the bill.

He flipped her business card over and over within his fingers as he checked out a few more pages on her website.

The sales listings were top-dollar homes owned by upper-middle class and above. Mansions, expansive estates, guarded, gated communities and high-end condos filled the multiple pages of homes available for sale.

The woman wasn't playing and most likely used the word *Exclusive* in her business's name to target her preferred clientele.

Bottom line, high-dollar homes equaled high-dollar commissions.

But still… North's warning made him wonder if she lived a secret life other than the one portrayed in public.

He slapped the business card on the counter next to his laptop, plugged her information into his contacts and sent her a text.

Need to talk. When are you available?

She didn't need to know what he wanted to talk about. He'd let her assume.

He stared at his phone for the almost five minutes it took for it to ding with an incoming message. *Who is this?*

Apparently, in his rush to send the text before he changed his mind, he omitted an important detail.

Nox.

His pulse thumped in his temples as he waited. Was she in shock? Is that why it was taking her so long to respond?

Finally, a message popped up on his screen. *Who?*

Before he could answer, she texted: *The man who avoids talking like the plague?*

She followed that immediately with: *The man who made me chase him down—TWICE—now wants to meet up?*

He knew this was a fucking mistake.

Nox shook his head and his fingers moved quickly over the keyboard as he typed out a short and to the point message. *Forget it.*

Before he could put his phone down, it rang. He was not expecting to talk to her right now. He needed to mentally prepare himself first. Instead, he quickly sent: *Can't answer where I'm at. I'll just see you next week at the meeting.*

Oh no, sir, you aren't backing out now. That message was followed with: *Name the time and the place. I'll be there.*

Shadow Valley Community Center, Wednesday at 7 pm.

Try again. Apparently, she could be short and to the point, too.

He should've known she wouldn't accept that answer. When he had opened the damn door, she jammed her foot in it to prevent him from closing it. The only way he'd be able to achieve that would be to let her in and shut it behind her.

He needed to come up with somewhere to meet that would be both quiet and not in Uniontown, Shadow Valley or Rockvale. Last thing he needed was someone he knew, especially anyone wearing a badge—more like a "busy-bee" badge—seeing him with a woman. That gossip would spread like a brushfire during a drought and high winds.

Do you know Above the Ground in Knoxville? he asked.

A long pause proceeded her answer. *Did you pick that place because of the town name?*

Picked it because no one will know us there.

She came back with: *I know a lot of people.*

Unfortunately, she wasn't the only one.

Are you worried about being seen with a woman?

Instead of answering her question, he texted: *Tomorrow night at 7:30?*

The coffee shop wouldn't be busy then. That meant less chance of getting busted by someone he knew.

See you there. Make sure you show up. Don't make me chase you down for the third time, because believe me, I will. I need to get my daily steps in somehow, even if I'm wearing heels.

Chapter Five

Two cars and one familiar Harley were the only vehicles in Above the Ground's parking lot. If she didn't already know it was a coffee shop, she would consider the name a bit morbid.

With their connection, why the hell he picked a coffee shop with that name...

She sighed.

After slipping her Benz into the open spot next to his sled, she stared at it for a few seconds, surprised he actually showed up. In truth, she expected to be stood up on this little coffee "date."

Before heading to Knoxville, she fed her boys dinner and told Devyn he needed to keep an eye on his little brother. She assured them she'd be home soon, before giving them both a kiss on the forehead.

Keenan still loved her kisses and hugs. Devyn, not so much. He got them anyway.

Her sons would only be children for a short amount of time, and she wanted to cherish their childhood while she could.

Her childhood wasn't the best and she was determined to do better with her own kids. While she wanted to give her boys everything, she also didn't want to spoil them. She tried to find a happy medium.

But she wasn't meeting the man calling himself Nox to talk about her kids, she was there to listen.

Heading into the coffee shop, she spotted him sitting alone at a corner table and facing the entrance. She was aware that law enforcement avoided sitting with their backs to the door whenever possible. For a valid reason.

Instead of approaching him, she ordered an iced chai latte at the counter and as she waited for the employee to make it, she turned and stared at Nox's broad back and shoulders.

She realized every time she'd seen him, he wore a baseball cap. It made it easy to hide his eyes and his thoughts.

But tonight, he wanted to share them. With her.

If he was ready to talk, she was ready to listen. If she could help him, she would. The main reason was, people had been there for her when she lost Mark. She wanted to pay it forward. The same reason she decided to get back to leading a bereavement group. It had helped her, she hoped it would help someone else.

She grabbed her drink and went to the table, rounding it to face him.

She stood there waiting until he lifted his head and asked, "Are you only going to stand there?"

"I'm waiting to see if you sprint for the exit before I sit down."

He sat back in his chair and raked his gaze over her from head to toe. Before making her family dinner, she had changed into a pair of jeans, sandals without a heel and a pastel pink embroidered V-neck top. She also had her hair pulled back from her face with a rolled pink bandana.

"Surprised you didn't wear sneakers, then."

"I can run in these sandals," she assured him.

When he lifted his coffee cup to his lips instead of springing from his seat to make a quick exit, she pulled out the chair across from him and settled into it. "I take it by your semi-relaxed posture, I won't need to chase you tonight."

"I invited you."

His grumble reminded her of a Harley with straight pipes.

"And you shocked the shit out of me when you did," she admitted truthfully. She took a sip of her iced chai and sighed with how good it was.

"I have questions."

Well, look at that, so did she. Though, Aaliyah doubted he'd answer any of them. "I thought you wanted to talk."

"I want you to talk by answering my questions."

She sat back with a frown. "Like an interrogation?"

"No. Just simple questions that need simple answers."

Her eyebrows pinned together. "I don't understand. Why?"

"I heard you have some questionable connections."

Okay, now she was getting annoyed. Mr. Unsocial wanted *her* to answer *his* questions. She only came to be a sympathetic ear. She didn't like this turn of events. "Heard from who?"

"Roland North."

She ran that name through her mental Rolodex. "That name sounds familiar."

"It should. He's a lieutenant with the Pittsburgh PD."

She racked her brain to put a face with the name but couldn't.

She didn't have many connections with that police department anymore. For a while right after Mark's death, she heard a lot from them. They checked in with her constantly while she was pregnant and right after Devyn was born. Then slowly people became caught up in their own lives and forgot about hers.

While that was to be expected, it was sad they lost touch. At the time, she was swamped with raising a baby by herself and trying to pick up her life after it came crashing down. Add in the fact she began studying for her real estate license to have a more flexible schedule.

She stared at the man across from her. "What does this have to do with our group?" When he didn't answer, she asked, "It doesn't have to do with our group at all, does it?"

"You said you know three very scary people, one being your father."

Well, at least now she knew he'd been listening. "So?"

"Who's your father?"

This was a very odd line of questioning. "Why?" She didn't know this man and she didn't owe him any answers about her personal life.

"I'm curious."

She shook her head. "No. *Uh uh*. It's more than that. This was why you wanted to meet tonight? Not because you needed to talk?"

"We're talking," he stated simply.

"Again, this feels more like an interrogation." She should go. She was wasting her time with him. He didn't want help.

"Is it a secret?"

"It's irrelevant."

"Not to me."

"Why?"

He didn't answer.

She raised her chin and met his eyes. "Because Lt. North

planted a seed about the people I call family and because you're curious as to who those people are, you invited me to meet you so you can dig. Even though my personal life is none of your business since it doesn't in any way touch yours."

"It does now that you lead the support group."

That was a stretch. A long one. "Bullshit." When she shot to her feet, her chair was shoved back abruptly, causing it to scrape the floor loudly.

His nostrils flared and his mouth got tight. "Sit down."

"Oh no, Bradley Lennox, you don't get to give me orders. No one does." She snagged her cup off the table since the hell if she was going to leave her chai latte behind. No man got between her and her chai.

When she turned to hightail it out of there, his, "I checked out your website," made her stop.

She glanced over her shoulder to see him sitting back with his arms crossed over his chest. Doing so pulled the worn cotton of his T-shirt snug over his broad shoulders. *Don't get distracted, Liyah, this man's a fucking mess.* "And?"

"You're very successful."

She turned back to the table and narrowed her eyes on him. What was he about? "I am. I built that business from the ground up and I'm proud of what I accomplished."

"As you should be. Please sit down." At least it was a soft request this time instead of a sharp order.

"I don't understand the point of this meeting if you didn't need to talk. I also don't like being lied to."

"I didn't lie. I needed to talk to you."

"About my personal life."

He got up and moved around the table to stand in front of her. Her pulse sped up as he searched her face. A few seconds later, he put his hand on the back of her abandoned chair and said, "Please sit."

Holy shit. She just figured out what he was "about" tonight. The reason for this meeting.

The reason he didn't want anyone seeing them together.

He wasn't only interested in her connections, he was interested in *her.*

Since he didn't want to be interested in any woman, he found reasons to push them away. He planned on using her connections as a reason to do that with her.

By finding faults with any woman he may have even the slightest interest, he used those faults as an excuse to not let that woman in and continue to keep himself closed off.

He looked for problems to avoid finding happiness.

To him, being alone was safe. And painless.

She wondered how long ago his wife or partner—she still didn't know who it was—died.

If it had been years, this man needed more help than what she, and maybe even the average therapist, could give him.

But she was willing to take a shot at it.

She closed her eyes and pulled in a breath. Why would she even consider getting herself involved in his emotional mess?

She was busy with her career. She had two young men to raise. She had family to deal with. Not to mention, all the extra people who came along with that family.

And now she had the weekly group to lead.

A murmured, "Please," had her opening her eyes and meeting his.

She had two options. She could leave and wash her hands of him. Or...

She could sit and feel him out. See what "faults" he could uncover.

Would her father and his family be a fault? Her being a single mother? The fact her two sons were fathered by two different men?

The fact that she still loved her first husband with all her heart? And always would?

She truly believed that Mark had been her soulmate.

She found out the hard way that Jason had been a soul crusher.

Every day she wished Mark was still alive. Every other day she wished Jason was... not.

Maybe she judged Keenan's father more harshly than she should. Even so, she knew better than to ever say that occasional thought out loud. Because if it passed her lips, she was afraid the wrong ears would hear it and it might actually happen.

She held onto the thinnest thread of hope that one day Jason would change and see how he was missing out on his own son's life. But if he didn't change, then Liyah didn't want him anywhere near Keenan. Her boy would be better off without him.

She made a mistake, and her youngest son didn't need to pay for it.

With a single nod, she moved to sit down and was surprised when Nox did the gentlemanly thing and moved her chair into place once she did so.

The man had manners. It was possible he only dusted them off when he wanted something.

And what he wanted from her was information.

Chapter Six

AALIYAH WAITED until he rounded the table and retook his seat before saying, "I'll consider giving you what you want but only if this is an actual conversation. Not just you lobbing questions at me, expecting answers and not giving me anything in return." When he didn't respond, she asked, "Does the thought of that scare you?"

"No."

Maybe scared wasn't quite the right adjective. The more she dealt with him, the more she realized, like her, he probably didn't scare easily, either. "Make you uncomfortable?"

Again, he didn't answer.

"You lied to get me here. Because of that, I have no problem making you squirm a little. Get you out of your comfort zone."

Holy shit, the man was like a blank wall. So hard to read.

But then, she'd been right where he was. Not wanting to go on. Thinking life wasn't worth living anymore. Thinking all the hopes and dreams she and Mark made together would never come to fruition.

71

Devyn had been her reason not to give up. Not to bury herself under the covers and pretend the world didn't exist.

In truth, Devyn had become her world. Her world was only a little smaller without Mark in it.

With every step, every breath, every heartbeat, it got easier.

She didn't have to forget Mark to move forward, she only needed to learn how to live without him.

The man across from her needed to learn how to do the same.

"I will tell you what you want to know, but only if you do the same. Don't mistake this as a negotiation. Since you lured me here by telling me you needed to talk, that's what we're going to do. But like I said, this won't be one-sided. If I give you what you want, then you'll give me what I want. That's the deal. Take it or leave it."

His lips thinning proved he didn't like that deal.

Too bad.

"We'll start off with a simple question..." She was making an assumption with her next question, but she was pretty confident that her guess was correct. Because every time she looked at him, it was like looking at herself in the mirror sixteen years ago. The only loss he could be this devastated over was a child or a soulmate. And because he came to the group alone, she narrowed it down. "What was her name?"

His heart was trying to knock a hole in his chest. If it succeeded, nothing would be left but a big, gaping wound.

A wound he couldn't close.

"We're not doing this."

"Does it bother you to say her name?"

"We're not doing this," he repeated, his eyesight

narrowing when it darkened around the edges. The walls of the Above the Ground starting to box him in.

He wasn't ripping himself open in a fucking coffee shop. *Fuck that.* Especially with a woman he'd met only three times.

He hadn't even shared the details with his therapist.

His only stipulation was to go to a counselor and the grief support group of their choosing. He was doing that.

Not once was it said that he needed to actually talk.

He didn't want to relive that day voluntarily. It was bad enough when he relived it involuntarily.

Over and over.

Talking about it wouldn't change anything. All it would do was draw it closer to the surface.

Make the pain more unbearable.

Underscore his deep-seated loneliness.

Put an exclamation point to that deep loss.

"I'm only asking her name, that's it. By not saying it, you think you're keeping her contained inside you. You're afraid if you say it, she'll escape, and you'll lose her forever. Take it from me, you won't. The more you talk about her, the stronger your memories will become. She will live on because you are helping her memory do that."

Some memories he wanted to keep, some he didn't.

On one hand, he was glad he was the one to find Jackie. On the other, he wished he hadn't. Because seeing her that last time would forever haunt him. That was the memory he wished he could forget.

Unfortunately, the exact moment he realized the reality of the situation would be seared into his memory forever. It always rose to the top and buried all the good ones.

"Okay, then. We're not doing this. That means you should've let me leave. So, now I will go and stop wasting any more time here. I have two sons at home who need me. You apparently don't."

This woman didn't sugar coat shit. She told it like it was, like it or not.

He might not like it, but he respected it.

Even so, he had a difficult time un-welding his jaws to answer her as her dark eyes met his across the table.

With her lips pressed tightly together and her fingers choking her drink, she scooted back her chair and rose to her feet.

She was going to leave him sitting there in that coffee shop. Then he'd leave without the information he wanted because he refused to give her the simple answer she asked for.

It was one damn word. One name he couldn't push past his lips.

He watched Aaliyah head toward the door, her spine stiff, her shoulders pulled back and her head held high.

His brothers had ambushed him with an intervention because he needed help.

He was broken and unless he did something about it, he'd never be fixed.

A therapist couldn't fix him.

A group of people meeting once a week to share laughter, tears and memories couldn't fix him, either.

Only he could fix himself.

The same person holding himself back.

"Jackie!" burst from him, causing her feet to stutter to a stop just as she pushed open the door. "Jackie," he repeated again, not so loudly this time. "Her name was Jackie."

She didn't turn around. She didn't come back.

As the seconds ticked off in his head, he thought he'd uttered his wife's name for nothing. That he'd been too late.

"C'mon," she said loud enough to catch his ears before walking out into the spring evening.

He stood, pulled out his wallet and tossed some ones on the table, then followed her out to the parking lot to see her waiting by her Mercedes Benz. When he got there, she jerked her chin toward the passenger side. "Get in."

He stopped and stared at her. "Where we going?"

"Nowhere. What I have to tell you I don't want to say inside. Without any other customers, the two employees have no one to watch or listen to except for us. I prefer to keep what I'm about to tell you between us."

He continued closer. "Is it that bad?"

"I don't think so, but others may not have the same opinion. My car is more private."

She clicked a button on her key fob and as soon as the doors unlocked, she slid in behind the steering wheel and placed her drink in a holder after taking a long sip.

Once she slammed the door shut, she powered down the window. "It's now or never, Nox. I don't have all night."

He jerked into motion and rounded the car, folding his body into the passenger seat. The deep maroon four-door AMG GT was top quality. Not to mention, way above his budget.

But that wasn't the only thing he noticed. The interior smelled like a combination of vanilla and chocolate.

"A car like this has a mortgage, not a car payment."

"Or, if you're successful enough, it has neither. Years ago, I learned the hard way not to buy things I can't pay for outright."

He just about choked on his own spit. "You bought this with cash?"

"You're sitting in it, aren't you?"

He pressed his lips together because her question almost made him grin.

Now that he gave Aaliyah his wife's name, he expected her to press for more details. How did she die? When did she die? How old was she? Where was she?

When she turned in her seat to face him, he ran interference so that didn't happen. "Why does your car smell like chocolate chip cookies?"

"One, I love to bake. Pies are usually my go-to. Two, I bake cookies a lot and bring them to open houses. The smell of freshly baked cookies makes a house smell more like a home. It helps the buyer envision themselves living in the house. Three, somehow, I always get stuck making something for the school bake sales. So, if it isn't cookies, it's brownies. If it isn't brownies, it's Rice Krispie treats. And if it's for my father, it's his favorite... Sweet potato pie."

"Sweet potato pie?"

Her eyes widened. "You've never had it?"

"No."

"Think pumpkin pie but better."

"Nothing beats a homemade pumpkin pie."

"You're wrong. But then, you haven't had my sweet potato pie."

And he doubted he ever would.

"But we're not sitting in my car to discuss what a baking goddess I am, are we?"

"We can't discuss it since I haven't tasted your pie." He realized what he said when her lips curved and her eyes crinkled at the corners. He opened his mouth to reword it, then simply shook his head. It was better to simply let it go. "Who's your father?"

"We're going to skip the foreplay and go right for the down and dirty?"

"I thought that's what the pie discussion was."

Her smile blinded him. "Well, Officer Lennox, I think you might have a sense of humor buried somewhere deep inside you."

It was impossible to bury it completely when dealing with his brothers. They were relentless when it came to ball-busting. A sense of humor was required, otherwise, you'd be offended. Their ability to give as good as they got was what made their bonds stronger.

"It comes in waves, doesn't it?" she asked.

He shook his head, pretending not to understand.

"Your moods. You have high points and low points. Right now you have more lows than highs. It'll change. Just give it time," she assured him.

He wasn't sure it would ever change. He seemed to be stuck. But he wasn't sitting in her car to discuss his moods. "Who's your father?"

"Malcolm Moore..."

That name sounded familiar, but he couldn't quite place it.

"But he's better known as Magnum," she finished.

He stared at her as that information sunk into his brain. That name sounded a *lot* more familiar. In fact, he knew that name pretty damn well.

"The sergeant at arms for the Dark Knights."

Aaliyah shrugged like it was no big deal. "The one and only."

Thankfully, there *was* only one of him. "You're tied to an outlaw MC."

"By blood, I guess. I wasn't raised in the club. In fact, my parents split up when I was very young and so were they. At the time, he had no involvement in any MC. That came later after he no longer had any contact with us."

"Why didn't he have contact with you?"

"That's," she sighed, "a long story that caused a lot of hurt for me and my brother. We've moved past it and have forgiven our mother for her lies. But that's what it was. We were told a story that wasn't true and, of course, being kids, we didn't know any better. That wrong has been righted thanks to my stepmother."

"What did she do?"

"She located me and made a point of making contact. She convinced me to give my father a chance. At the time, Devyn was only about eight weeks old, and Cait just had her first child with my father. If it wasn't for her, I wouldn't have mended the relationship with him. So, I owe her. And no matter what anyone thinks about my father, I'm grateful he's in my sons' lives."

"You think the sergeant at arms of an outlaw MC is a good father-figure?"

"Like I said, I don't care what anyone thinks of him. He loves his children, he loves his grandchildren, he'd give his life to protect them. If you saw him with his wife..." She sighed almost dreamily. "He'd do anything for her. That's the type of love most people are searching for. Their relationship made it, despite being a bit controversial at first and doubts from others."

"Why were there controversy and doubts?"

"Mostly because of their age difference."

"Which is?"

"Sixteen years."

That was quite a gap. "She's younger?"

"Yes."

"You said mostly... What else?"

"Her father belongs to the Dirty Angels MC." Her

mouth twisted. "Working for SVPD, I'm sure you've heard of them."

Of course he had. He had lived in Shadow Valley with Jackie. When not on the task force, he worked there, too. You couldn't live or work in that town without knowing about the Dirty Angels. Their territory included all of Shadow Valley and the surrounding area. That MC established themselves in the town back in the early seventies.

"The Angels and the Knights are close allies."

"Now, yes, but they didn't start out that way. The two clubs skirted each other for years. They didn't become allies until the Shadow Warriors began to hit the Angels hard and heavy. Decades ago, they wanted Shadow Valley for their own but the DAMC had already claimed the area and weren't giving it up without a fight. So, the Warriors created all the havoc they could. A lot of damage was done, and some lives lost. Some destroyed. But... I'm sure you're aware of that, too."

After decades of chaos, death, violence and prison sentences, some life-long, suddenly those Warriors suspiciously began to disappear. "I am. Not only because I dealt with some of that shit with work, but because Axel Jamison is my sergeant. Just like I know who your father is, I'm sure you know who he is."

"The DAMC president's brother. Axel decided not to follow in his grandfather's footsteps like Zak did. Talk about two brothers taking two very different forks in the road."

"Jamison isn't only my supervisor, he's also the president of my MC."

Her eyes widened and he knew the exact moment she put two and two together. "Holy shit! You're a member of the Blue Avengers?"

Nox tipped his head in answer. "Aiden Cross is also one of my MC brothers."

"That's right! He's the cop who married Nash from the Dirty Angels."

"He is."

"Talk about opposites attract..."

Her father's relationship hadn't been the only one controversial, so had Cross and Nash's. They hid it for a while. Not only because Cross had been in the closet at the time, but Nash had been hiding his bisexuality from his MC. Neither knew if they'd be accepted by their peers. Cross by his brothers in blue and Nash by his MC brotherhood.

"Damn," she whispered. "How crazy is that? Our lives touch and we didn't even know it."

"Six degrees of separation, I guess."

"It's not even six degrees. It's..." She shook her head. "How did our paths never cross before?"

They might have and he just hadn't been paying attention. Once he met Jackie, unless he was dealing with one in his capacity as a police officer, he really didn't notice other women. He had no reason to.

Jackie had been his everything.

"Speaking of opposites... Your father is the enforcer for an outlaw club, but your husband was a cop."

"He was. But Mark died before my father and I repaired our relationship."

"Did he mind you being with a cop? That your son's father was law enforcement?"

One side of her mouth pulled up. "Of course. He also told me I could never be with one again."

"And you listened?"

She laughed softly. "He can bluster all he wants but he doesn't get to choose who I'm with. Just because he has an issue with law enforcement, doesn't mean I do." She tipped her head. "It's the reason I took over the support group and previously ran a similar one in Pittsburgh. My father might not respect cops, but I do. Yes, some shitty ones are out there and quite a few racists ones, too, but Mark was one of the good ones. They do exist, even though they normally don't get the spotlight like the bad apples do." She shook her head. "And here I am explaining something to a damn cop sitting in my passenger seat that he already knows. Are you a good one or a bad one, Bradley Lennox?"

"I guess it depends on what side of the law you sit. If I'm there to help, you think I'm good. If I'm there to slap cuffs on you, you think I'm bad."

"You know that's not what I meant."

He did. He'd seen good and bad throughout the years. It was on the good ones to out the bad ones, but that was not always easy or possible. "Besides your father, you mentioned two other scary people you know. Who are they?"

"Well, since we discussed our ties to the Dirty Angels, it should be no surprise when I mention their sergeant at arms."

"Diesel Dougherty." She was right. That one was no surprise. "And the other?"

"Like I said, less than six degrees separates any of us. So, you might know this man as well since he's tied to—"

He cut her off with, "Ryan Mercer."

Her eyebrows shot up her forehead. "Is that Mercy's full name? I never heard it mentioned before. If it's said out loud, does it conjure him up out of the blue?" Her head swiveled back and forth as she glanced around the parking lot. "Should we duck down so we're not seen?"

She was trying to be humorous, but Diesel's Shadows were not to be messed with. Local and state law enforcement, as well as the feds, believed that group of former military special operators caused the disappearance of the Shadow Warriors. "Mercy's little band of mercenaries are aging. They aren't ghosts anymore."

Aaliyah leaned closer to him to whisper, "That's what they want you to think. Don't let their wrinkles and the scent of Bengay fool you."

Chapter Seven

"ANYWAY," Liyah continued, "aging or not, they aren't anyone to mess with. It's better not to get in their crosshairs."

"Like the Shadow Warriors did?"

"I... I'm not sure what happened to those nomads." She had heard plenty of rumors and whispers. Her father also didn't mince words when it came to that now defunct MC. Usually those words were peppered with a lot of "fucks," "fuckers," and "motherfuckers." Nothing out of the ordinary for Magnum.

Nox murmured, "They seemed to have just disappeared. One by one."

She had no doubt the Dark Knights had a hand in it. Unlike the Dirty Angels, her father's club didn't care about staying on the right side of the law. "I'm sure your department was relieved when the Warriors stopped causing problems in your jurisdiction."

"We don't like vigilantes."

Most law enforcement didn't. Vigilantes tended to be reckless. "The Angels didn't like being shot at or attacked, even killed, their property destroyed, or their women being kidnapped, abused and raped, either. They had families to protect."

"So, it *was* Diesel and his Shadows behind that club's disappearance."

Shit. "I don't know why the Warriors left the area. They could've wised up. But one thing is for sure, southwestern Pennsylvania is a safer place with them gone."

"Other MCs still exist in this area."

"I don't keep up with MCs other than the two I have ties with. I don't live the lifestyle but the people I love do, so I accept it." She overheard her father talking to his MC president Romeo about a club originally from West Virginia moving north. However, she normally didn't pay attention to the Knights' club business, so she never heard the name of the MC they were keeping tabs on.

"What about your younger son's father?"

"What about him?"

"Does he have ties to either MC?"

She laughed. "No."

"Is he still in the picture?"

Huh. Was this a way to find out if she had a man in her life? Or was he being nosy in general? "Unfortunately—or fortunately, depending on how you look at it—he's long gone."

Even under his baseball cap, she saw Nox's brow furrow. "What do you mean gone?"

"Like skipped town once he decided family life wasn't for him." But by that time, it was too late. "I thought Jason would be a good father figure to Devyn. I also thought he'd be a good father once I realized I was pregnant with Keenan. I was so damn wrong."

"Was he a cop, too?"

"No. About eight years ago, I met Jason at the support group I was running in Pittsburgh. His brother had been a Baltimore officer killed in the line of duty and Jason was struggling to deal with it. They'd been extremely close, and it hit him pretty hard."

"So, he began coming to the group."

"Yes." She sighed. "I certainly wasn't looking for anyone, but one night after a meeting, he struck up a conversation with me and we ended up talking for hours. It quickly moved into dating, then living together, and eventually a proposal."

She regretted letting him in. She didn't think anyone could live up to Mark. Unfortunately, she'd been right.

"Even though it wasn't planned and despite taking precautions, I found myself pregnant. I figured he'd be happy since, once we got engaged, we had discussed building a family together." She pulled in a breath, and released it with, "Boy was I wrong. When I surprised him with the news, he reacted with shock instead of excitement. After he recovered, he only pretended to be happy about the news because a week later when I got home from the office, he was gone. All his stuff was gone, too. No note was left. Nothing. He totally ghosted me, leaving me to go at it alone with baby number two."

A muscle jumped in Nox's cheek. "Damn. You never heard from him again?"

She shook her head. "No."

"Did you look for him? To at least have him help out financially?"

"I didn't need his money. And if I chased him down to get child support, he would have a say in Keenan's upbringing. He gave up that right the second he scooted on down the road like a scared little shit."

When she was five months pregnant with Keenan, she

got an unexpected call from Kiki, the Dirty Angels' attorney and the VP's wife. She asked Liyah to stop in at her office to sign some paperwork. Apparently, Jason couldn't give up his parental rights without Liyah's consent.

Liyah couldn't sign that paperwork fast enough.

Kiki didn't have to tell her who got that ball rolling. It certainly wasn't Jason. Not only did Magnum have Kiki prepare the paperwork, but her father somehow got Keenan's sperm donor to sign.

Her best guess was that he went to the Shadows to find Jason.

She told her father she didn't want to know the details. She was damn sure they weren't pretty. But then, karma could be ugly at times.

In truth, she lost no sleep over it.

However, she'd be sharing none of that information with the police officer in her passenger seat. Instead, she said, "I'm so damn lucky to have my family's support." And have connections to people who could get things done, whether legally or otherwise. "Widowed, abandoned, I'm batting a thousand when it comes to finding my happily ever after. Maybe I'm not meant to find it."

"You have your boys."

She smiled softly. "You're right. They make me happy and give me a purpose. My boys are my life. Everything I do is for them and their future. To make sure they grow up to be good, responsible men."

"With a grandfather who's the muscle in an outlaw MC."

She shrugged. "Everybody isn't perfect."

"Why'd you lose contact with him?"

"It's a long story, but basically, my mother lied about him. She told me and my brother that Magnum abused all of us. It turns out, she lied to the police, lied to the judge to get a protection from abuse order, she even went as far as showing us photos with fake bruises. Who the hell does that?" The anger that subsided years ago was coming back to the surface. This was why she didn't like to talk about it. She loved her mother but didn't love what her mother did. "I didn't find out the truth until much later, but my father said he never gave up. Once he had enough money to hire a good attorney, he fought for visitation. Unfortunately, by that time, MJ and I were old enough to make the decision whether we wanted to attend supervised visits with him or not. Because we believed our mother's lies and saw the so-called proof with our own two eyes, we both decided we wanted nothing to do with him."

Once her stepmother Cait convinced her to meet with her father, he didn't admit he'd been devastated when his kids refused to see him, but she could clearly see it on his face. That made her feel so much damn worse.

Once she found out the truth, Liyah didn't talk to her mother for about a year. In the end, she felt terrible for keeping Devyn from her. However, her mother's actions had kept Liyah from having a relationship with her father. They got robbed of spending years together.

Years.

Was her mother perfect? Far from it. She had really screwed up big time in her quest for them to live a better life.

But then, Liyah wasn't a perfect mother, either. Guilt gnawed at her that neither of her boys had a father in their lives. The only real father-figures were their grandfathers and her younger brother, Malcolm Jr.

Since MJ didn't live close by, Liyah decided to move closer to her father. Magnum wanted to help as much as possible and she hoped he'd teach her sons how to respect and protect women. He might be the sergeant at arms for an outlaw MC, but he was the perfect example when it came to how he treated his wife and the mother of Liyah's two youngest siblings, Asia and Caleb.

And Liyah witnessed what a great father he was with his two youngest children. Sometimes seeing that made the bitterness resurface when it came to her and MJ missing out on his time and attention. She now spent a lot of time with her father to make up for the time they lost.

Both of her parents doted on Liyah's sons. So did Mark's, despite Keenan not being related to them by blood. They had accepted her youngest son with open arms. Keenan even called them Grandma and Grandpa. She was thankful to still have them in her boys' lives.

Now that Nox knew a lot more about her, it was only fair she learn more about him. She didn't want to push him but maybe she could risk asking him one more question.

He gave up his wife's name when she didn't think he would, so anything was possible. "Since you now know a lot about me and my past, can I ask you one more thing?" He was going to tell her no, so she hurried to ask it before he denied her. "Did you and Jackie have children?"

His nostrils flared and his jaw flexed. "I gotta go."

He shoved the door open and, before she could say another word, Nox bolted from the car.

"Damn. I guess it was something I said," she whispered as she watched him, within seconds, mount his sled, start it and ride away. Once again, like the devil was chasing him.

If it wasn't the devil on his tail, then ghosts sure were.

———

SILENCE GREETED him when he opened the front door. He was getting home later than normal since he had to work overtime to finish processing a man he arrested. Nox wouldn't even call him a "man," as real men didn't commit violence against women.

The motherfucker had punched his wife three times in the head and knocked her out cold. And it wasn't the first time Shadow Valley PD officers had visited that home.

It wasn't even the second.

But hopefully it would be the last.

Unfortunately, knowing how domestic violence cases typically went, it most likely wouldn't be.

Despite that depressing thought, slapping cuffs on the abuser and reading him his Miranda rights at least gave Nox a little satisfaction. But it would have been a lot more satisfying if Nox could deliver similar blows to the asshole's head to provide a short but effective lesson on how not to treat women.

He glanced at his cell phone. Since it was almost eight, he was surprised Jackie wasn't curled up on the couch under her favorite blanket watching one of her cooking shows. She tried to watch those when he wasn't home, so he didn't have to suffer through them.

"Jackie," he called out, "I'm home!"

The house was too damn quiet. Lately, she'd been falling asleep at the drop of a hat, so maybe she went up to bed early.

He did a quick detour through the kitchen and checked the fridge to see if she made him a plate. She did. Once he touched base with her and made sure everything was okay, he'd come back down to reheat his dinner.

Three cups of black coffee and a protein bar hadn't cut it.

He took the steps two at a time up to the second floor, the only sound besides his own footsteps came from the cool air blowing through the vents.

When he pulled into the garage, he had parked next to

her car, so she had to be home, unless a friend picked her up. But normally, Jackie wasn't leaving the house after eight o'clock and she would have at least texted him to let him know if she was.

He headed down the hallway and when he stepped into their bedroom, he was taken aback by how quiet the room was. The lights were off, but the curtains remained open. The streetlight outside illuminated the room enough so he could see her in the bed.

No, not *in* the bed. She was asleep on top of the comforter.

He frowned. "Jackie," he called out softly, not wanting to scare her. He sat on the edge of the bed and gave her thigh a light squeeze. "Jackie..." Why the fuck was she so damn tense? "You okay?"

He shook her gently, but she was stiff.

What the fuck? Something wasn't right.

Leaning over to the nightstand, he switched on the light...

When Nox shot up on the couch, a bead of sweat slipped down his temple and dripped off his jaw. His chest pumped frantically as he glanced around.

He spotted the book he'd been reading, now on the floor.

He pulled in a deep breath, trying to slow his rapid breathing.

This time he woke up just as he turned and was about to look at the bed.

Thank fuck he woke up in time. Even though he knew what came next.

He'd never forget it.

Going to therapy, attending those fucking group meetings and now dealing with Aaliyah trying to crack open his armor...

All of it was bringing to the surface what he had buried deep almost two years ago.

The nightmares were once again getting worse and coming more often. To the point he no longer wanted to sleep.

Something needed to change if he was ever going to survive.

Because, *for fuck's sake*, he couldn't live like this anymore.

He. Was. Done.

Chapter Eight

THE CHAIRS WERE in a goddamn circle again, so as soon as he sat down, he focused on a spot on the floor so he wouldn't have to make eye contact with the members across from him.

He didn't care if it made him look anti-social. He was doing what he needed to do to get through it.

He hadn't had a decent night of sleep for days. His ass was dragging so badly he struggled to think and function. His patience was non-existent and his temper sharp.

With how he left the other night from the coffee shop's parking lot, he avoided the group leader as she finished setting up cookies next to the coffee and water on the table near the door.

Near the fucking door.

He was sure she had set up the refreshments in that location on purpose. The food and coffee were always where people gathered—and chit-chatted—before the meeting and after.

Bonnie used to set up the table along the opposite wall. Out of the way. Where it was easy for Nox to avoid.

His goal was simple. He came, he sat, he left.

He didn't share. He didn't cry. He didn't socialize.

He tugged his baseball cap lower. What the hell was taking her so long? She needed to get the meeting started before someone tried to strike up a conversation with him.

Throw the cookies on the damn platter, and let's fucking go!

This wasn't an open house where she needed to impress home buyers. She wasn't even getting paid to be here. The longer she futzed around, the longer this meeting would last.

A cookie tucked in a napkin appeared in front of his face. "Chocolate chip."

"They're so addictive, Liyah!" someone near him gushed. "You should open a bakery."

Nox snorted softly. He doubted the woman would give up her lucrative real estate business that had her rolling in the dough to actually roll in dough.

Aaliyah shook her hand, encouraging him to take the cookie from her. "This is why my car smells so good," she said under her breath.

He hoped like fuck no one else heard her. He didn't want anyone in the group thinking something was going on between them. "I don't want it."

"I don't care," she countered and balanced it on his thigh before heading across the circle to her seat.

He stared at the precariously perched cookie for a few seconds before lifting his gaze to her. And as soon as their eyes met, she shot him a blinding smile.

The woman sure knew how to get under his damn skin.

"All right," Aaliyah called out. "Let's start off tonight's meeting by going around the circle, introducing yourself and letting us know where you're at tonight. In other words, how you're coping."

For fuck's sake, did that mean she expected everyone to participate?

When his knee began to bounce, the cookie tumbled to the floor and broke.

"That was a waste," said the woman next to him. "There are starving children in—"

"Then ship it to them," he responded before she could finish.

Her mouth fell open as she looked at him.

"Don't worry about the cookie, Nox, you can clean it up after the meeting," Aaliyah said. Using her fucking mom voice again. "Okay, Linda, can you start us off? Then we'll continue around the group."

Great.

One by one, the members introduced themselves—even if they'd been attending for years—mentioned the name of the person they lost and how they were connected, then shared how they were doing emotionally.

Nox went back to concentrating on the spot on the floor. His eyes drifted from it to the broken cookie next to his boot.

Then he snuck another peek at Aaliyah.

She was watching him.

He did not drop his gaze this time, but instead met hers full on. He wasn't going to break their locked gaze; he was going to make her break first.

When her eyes narrowed, so did his.

When one side of her mouth pulled up, his flattened.

She lifted a single eyebrow, her expression smug. "Your turn."

Whose turn?

Damn it. He was the one who broke when he glanced around the circle to find all eyes were on *him*.

It was his turn.

Shit. He really missed Bonnie and her damn orthopedic shoes. She never forced anyone to participate.

He only needed to say something brief, then they could move on to the next person. "Nox. Fine." A noise came from Aaliyah, but he ignored her. Other than that, the group was silent. To make sure they knew he was done sharing, he added, "Next!"

He breathed easier when the person to his left began to speak.

He snuck a glance at the time on his cell phone. They'd only been there less than ten minutes. Tonight was going to drag on and he would need to hang on to his seat by his fingernails to remain there the whole time.

Aaliyah's smooth-as-honey voice filled the space between them. "Next, we'll go around and share one good memory of your loved one. It doesn't have to be long; it can be short and sweet. Simply a memory that makes you smile when you think about it. Maybe it'll make us smile, too."

She was purposely torturing him, wasn't she? Her whole motive was to break him down and break him open.

She wouldn't succeed. She couldn't succeed. If she was declaring war, he was ready to go to battle. She wasn't going to win. He would fight until he had no fight left in him.

Once again they went around the circle, but this time, Aaliyah started.

Normally, he either half-listened or blocked out the stories completely, but this was one story he wanted to hear.

"This is not only a good memory, it's my favorite. We'd been trying to get pregnant..."

He tensed. Maybe he didn't want to hear it after all.

"...and month after month, the test was negative. Every time I took one, thinking this was it, we were disappointed. Then it happened. The second the test turned positive, Mark grabbed the test stick, ran out of the house and into the driveway, yelling at the top of his lungs that he was going to be a dad. I'll never forget his face and the way he waved that damn stick above his head. He was so excited and happy."

Even from where he sat, even though she smiled softly, he could see the sheen in her eyes.

Nox remembered being disappointed, too, once they started trying. He was worried they'd never get pregnant. Jackie cried every time it was negative, even though she tried to hide her disappointment from him.

As each group member shared their good memory—some were short, others long-winded—his chest got tighter as it came closer to his turn.

Then he was in the hot seat.

"Nox?" Aaliyah prodded. "Tell us a good memory. In more than a couple of words this time, please." Again, she was using her mom voice.

Only, he wasn't a fucking child.

"I have too many." That was four words.

"I need you to pick one."

His favorite memory was similar to hers, but he would not voice it out loud.

He closed his eyes and watched that moment play out all over again like a movie on the back of his eyelids. His reality. His nightmare.

He could see it plain as day.

He shook that memory free. "Sunday mornings in bed," he lied.

"What about them?"

"Snuggling under the covers." He made sure to keep his expression masked when she searched his face.

She didn't believe him.

The woman was too damn astute. "That sounds sweet."

He wasn't the only one lying.

He tipped his head to the side. "It was." He yelled, "Next!" before she could ask another question.

The look she shot him was most likely similar to what she gave her sons when they were being bratty.

If he was going to lose sleep, it wouldn't be over that.

Ten minutes later, everyone had answered her question. Apparently, it was time for a new one when she announced, "Now... What do you miss most about them? Name one thing. Nothing's too small or insignificant to mention. It could be the way they smiled. Laughed. Their bad jokes. Anything. I'll start... Mark cupping my cheek and kissing my eyelids. The first time he did it, I thought it was weird. Now, I miss it."

Nox used to cup Jackie's cheek, stare into her eyes and whisper, "Love you."

She'd come back with, "Love you more."

He'd finish by saying, "Impossible."

He waited with dread as all attendees to his right shared what they missed most about their late spouse, parent, sibling or even best friend. The reason they were in the group.

His chest tightened when he was next.

When he was a kid, he wished his superpower was being invisible. Tonight was no different.

"Nox? What do you miss about..."

He had held his breath, waiting to see if she would say Jackie's name. He had never told the group who he lost. Not her name, not who she was to him.

He had kept all of that to himself.

"Your loved one?" she finished.

He thought she was going to throw a curve ball at him. She didn't. Even so, he didn't want to take part this "go around the circle" game she was playing tonight.

On purpose.

To get him to participate.

Another reason not to come back next week and find another group. Even if it was more than an hour away.

He dug his fingers into his thighs to keep his emotions under control. "Everything."

"Could you be more specific?"

No. "There's nothing I don't miss about her. It's impossible to narrow it down."

And that was true.

Aaliyah could accept his answer or not. He didn't care. The same way she didn't when he told her he didn't want the damn cookie.

As she opened her mouth to push him, he yelled, "Next!"

Her mouth snapped shut and she shook her head, shooting a glare across the circle. Then like magic, her voice became soft as she encouraged the person to his left to continue.

He won the battle.

Once they got back around to her, instead of coming up with another question, she opened the floor to anyone wanting to talk.

One side of Nox's mouth pulled up as he crossed his arms and sat back in his chair and let his muscles loosen.

He'd no longer be in the hot seat.

All he had to do now was escape the second the meeting was over.

"All right," Aaliyah called out. "Thank you for coming tonight and to everyone who shared. Don't forget to stick around for refreshments. Nox..."

Oh fuck.

"Do you mind sticking around afterward to help me clean up and put everything away since you haven't done it yet? I think it'll be fair if everyone takes a turn." She was really something else by guilting him into staying.

He did mind. Not the helping clean up part, but the sticking around part.

But he would do it so he didn't look like a complete dick.

Though, that ship had probably already sailed.

Chapter Nine

LIYAH STOOD by the refreshment table, half-listening to the conversation around her. She wasn't paying attention to what was being said so she hoped no one asked her a question. She was too busy watching the man with the jerky movements as he folded up chairs and stacked them in the storage closet.

She needed to make sure he didn't sneak out when she wasn't looking.

Because he would.

And their conversation from the other night in the coffee shop parking lot wasn't over with.

He thought it was.

He was wrong.

One by one, the group members sticking around long enough to snag a couple of her cookies, a bottle of water or a coffee to-go left until only Linda remained.

"Do you want me to help, Liyah?"

Liyah shook her head. "No, Nox and I have it under control." She patted the woman's shoulder. "Why don't you head home and catch your little ones before they fall asleep?"

Linda laughed softly. "I wish they *did* fall asleep. I'm sure they're sitting up with my mother watching a sitcom. Do you mind if I bring them a cookie?"

"Help yourself to the rest." She was planning on sending some home with Mr. Grump, but she had another container in her car she could give him.

Who could be moody while eating chocolate chip cookies? Well, if anyone could, it would be Bradley Lennox.

She set her jaw as she made eye contact with the man standing on the other side of the room. He was as far as he could get from the refreshment table as he waited for Linda to leave before approaching.

After Linda gathered what cookies remained on the platter, she said, "See you next week. The new format is a nice change."

She doubted the man with the jawline able to cut glass would agree.

The second she heard the door to the room click shut behind her, she turned and began to gather what remained on the table so they could fold it up and put it away.

The man could move as quietly as the ghosts that chased him since she felt his presence before she heard him.

He grabbed the almost empty box of coffee and lobbed it into the large rolling trash can sitting next to the table. She did the same with the disposable platter before tucking the remaining reusable items back into a plastic storage bin.

When she was done, she went to pick up the bin to put it away and he practically body-checked her to take it from her. Once he had a hold of it, he took long strides across the room and disappeared into the large closet.

While he put that away, she began to fold up the table next. Before she was through, he was there, again, nudging her out of the way. "You wanted me to help, let me fucking help."

She threw up her hands. "Fine." She was also tempted to yell, "Next!" but bit back that response. She shouldn't lower herself to his level, but her frustration level with the man was high.

Really, she shouldn't care enough to get frustrated. He shouldn't be treated any differently than the rest of the group members.

If he didn't want to participate, that was on him.

If he wanted to wallow in his own misery, she should let him.

If he never wanted to get better...

Shit. His brothers wanted him to get better. They cared.

Somebody loved him even if he didn't love himself.

"You owe me an explanation," she started.

He heaved the table up under his arm and began to beeline across the room. The man was impressively strong. "I don't owe anyone anything."

She followed with her lips pursed, checking out his bulging biceps and thickly-veined forearms as he carried the table. He'd be much more attractive if he had a personality to match. "You are always running from me."

"Take that as a sign."

"What, that you don't like me?"

"Is this a popularity contest?"

"No. I run a group to help people like you. People like me. You're too fucking pig-headed to let it do what it's meant to do."

"Boo-hooing about bullshit doesn't help."

She followed him into the large closet. "How would you know if you don't let yourself deal with your loss?"

After he leaned the table against a shelf, she stumbled a

step back when he spun on her. "Weren't you the one who said that everyone deals with loss differently?"

Oh, he was getting angry? "You're not dealing with it; you're keeping it buried."

"So fucking what? How does it affect you?"

"It doesn't affect me. It affects you."

"Then let me worry about it. Being a single mother with two boys probably keeps you busy. You don't need to take on another project."

"You're a human with emotions, not a project."

"You got the first part right, at least."

"Oh, you have emotions, because you're clearly annoyed right now. If you didn't have any, you'd be a sociopath."

He took a step closer, crowding her. "Maybe I am."

She was tall for a woman, but he was taller. But when wearing heels, like she was tonight, she was basically eye-to-eye with him. "No, you're not."

"I thought you sold real estate, not did psychological evaluations."

"You mask the pain. I know that because I did the same thing. I did it so I wouldn't have to deal with it. You think you do it for self-preservation, but eventually it'll backfire."

"I already have a therapist. I don't need another one."

She was definitely not a therapist, but she could speak from her own experience. "And do you actually talk to this person? Or do you sit on the couch closed off with your arms crossed over your chest and your mouth pinned shut?"

His sharp jaw shifted. "Again, my life doesn't affect yours."

"Not mine, no. But despite what you think, it's affecting the people who love you."

He blinked, then pulled in an audible breath.

Ah, maybe that was a way to convince him to work on

dealing with his grief. Not for himself but for everyone else. His family, if he had any, his BAMC brotherhood and maybe even his coworkers at Shadow Valley PD.

"If you don't care about yourself, then what about everyone else around you? Don't you care about them?"

"I gotta go."

"Of course you do." She blocked his way out of the closet. Could he push past her? Sure, if he really wanted to. "Like I said, always running from me. You don't want to hear the truth."

He leaned in and went practically nose-to-nose with her, grinding out, "Here's some truth for you... I don't like the new format for the group."

She shrugged. "Then I suggest you start your own group. You can stand at the lectern and scowl at everyone who shows up. Then you can continue standing there for an hour not saying a damn thing. Good luck with that."

"Why do you feel the need to push me?"

If she didn't, who would?

Yes, some of the people who cared about him forced him to attend therapy and the grief group. However, only attending—and not participating—did him no good. So, yes, he had taken the first step by showing up, but now he needed to take the next. Even if he was forced to take it by being pushed.

Or being shoved hard. Sometimes tough love was more effective than gentle persuasion.

"You know, you're right. I'm wasting too much energy on you. You have made it abundantly clear that you don't want help, so... Have a nice life, Bradley Lennox. With the way you're going, that life might be short-lived." After dropping that harsh wake-up call, she spun on her heel to leave.

She didn't even finish taking a step before his hand

snaked out and grabbed her arm, swinging her back around to face him.

The man was no longer annoyed, he was pissed. "You don't know shit about me."

"You're right, I don't, but I was willing to listen. I offered an ear, and you didn't want to take me up on that. I'm done, Nox. Especially after what you pulled at the coffee shop. You don't want help; you want to wallow in your misery. So do that. But when you do, you need to look the people who love you in their eyes and tell them you don't care about them the same as they do you. Tell them you don't give a fuck that they worry about you. Tell them you couldn't care less about being happy and you prefer to be a miserable asshole for the rest of your life. Poor Nox, he's such a victim."

She tried to pull her arm free, but he only tightened his grip.

"No matter how short that life is?" he growled. "It's been almost two years, and I haven't offed myself yet, so maybe you don't know shit."

Holy shit, was he aware that he just gave her a tiny piece of info? Did he do it on purpose? But what floored her the most was the revelation that he lost his wife almost two years ago.

Two fucking years and he was still swallowing his grief.

More like choking on it. That couldn't be healthy.

"I think the problem you have with me is, I do know shit. I can see through that wall you've constructed around yourself, and you don't like that."

"And you think you can break down that wall."

"I can, but I can't do it alone."

"And who's going to help you?"

"I need your help," she said softly. "You need to want it, too, Nox."

"That's the problem. I do want it. I never expected to want it again but by you being all up in my goddamn face, you've forced me to pay attention. I did."

What the hell was he talking about? "You want me to help you?" Was he finally giving in?

"No."

What the hell? She shook her head. "You're not making any sense."

"Because none of it makes sense to me," he ground out.

Well, that was as clear as mud. "So, explain."

"No need to explain, I can just show you."

His voice had turned gruff and if she thought his eyes were dark when he was pissed, they were even darker now.

The way he was looking at her...

Should she be afraid?

It was possible he wasn't a threat to himself but to others. Like to her. Had she pushed him too far?

She forced down the lump wedged in her throat.

Why did she leave her purse with her knife locked in her trunk? Her father regularly drilled into her that she should always be prepared by having a weapon within reach to protect herself.

If she died in this fucking closet at a community center in Shadow Valley, he'd be pissed. At her at first for not listening, then he'd go on a damn rampage. Magnum was scary when he was angry. He turned into the Black Hulk.

Hulk! Smash!

She was so damn distracted by her own crazy thoughts, she was caught off guard when Nox clamped his hand around the back of her neck and squeezed hard, holding her in place as he dropped his head and smashed his lips to hers.

Holy shit. What was happening right now?

What the hell was happening?

Maybe she did drive him over the edge. Not to do violence, but...

Damn, he was a good kisser.

She was so freaking confused since this was so unexpected. Did she even want him to kiss her?

She fisted his T-shirt and melted into him. *Oh hell yes,* she wanted him to kiss her. This was no sloppy-ass kiss, either. He was kissing her like he meant it.

As his lips moved over hers, she opened them and invited him in.

She figured that move would send him sprinting out of the closet and far away from her. But it didn't. Instead, he accepted the invite with gusto. With his fingertips digging deeper into her neck, the fingers of his other hand splayed over her cheek as he deepened the kiss.

For not having kissed anyone for over two years—and she had no doubt that was true—the man certainly wasn't rusty. Or timid about it. He was leaning into that kiss with everything he had.

She had no complaints as their lips moved against each other, their tongues tangled, their breaths mingled and the tiny sounds coming from the back of their throats were in harmony.

They ignored the fact his baseball cap had been knocked off his head.

They ignored the fact they were eating each other's face in a closet in the Shadow Valley Community Center.

But more importantly, she ignored the fact that kissing a cop would drive Magnum on the same type of rampage as if Nox killed her.

To her father, hooking up with a cop was just as heinous as being murdered by one.

It didn't matter that she was thirty-nine years old and

quite capable of making her own life choices. The drawback of reestablishing her relationship with her father was that he thought he had a say in everything she did.

In everyone she did.

His opinions were both strong and loud.

But this was only a kiss and nothing more. A knee-jerk reaction by Nox and most likely a way to release some of his frustration with her pushing him to the breaking point.

However, this kiss most likely didn't only stem from frustration. Not with the way she kept catching him staring at her tits and ass. Plus, being a cop, he probably noticed that she had been checking him out, too. But visually checking each other out was a whole lot different than actually getting physical.

Though, she was enjoying it and not discouraging it.

Despite Nox being moody and closed off, his thorough kiss made just about everything on her tingle. Including one spot that had been ignored for longer than she'd like to admit.

She hadn't even done any self-help in a while. Working long hours, running the group, dealing with family and raising two boys on her own kind of put a crimp in that. Even if she locked her bedroom door, either Kee or Dev would be pounding on it and asking where the peanut butter was. They'd still ask even if it was hanging from a fishing line in front of their faces.

The "unable to find the most basic stuff" gene was deeply embedded into the Y chromosome.

The individual with a Y chromosome sharing the closet with her was also making her nipples ache and stand at attention. Her pussy kept clenching and getting slicker by the second.

But she wasn't the only one the kiss affected. The steel

rod in his jeans was proof it was stirring him up as much as her.

Huh.

Just as quickly as the kiss started, it dropped from a hundred miles per hour to zero in a second flat when Nox ripped his mouth free, released her and took a step back.

With his eyes a bit wild, his chest pumped and his nostrils flared as he sucked in oxygen. The lips she recently enjoyed now no more than a slash.

The man was not happy. All because for a moment there, he had let himself *want*. He let himself be human. Let himself remember what it was like to be attracted to someone other than his late wife.

Whether that kiss came out of frustration or desire, he *felt* something and had been driven to take action.

That terrified him.

That disappointed him.

That made him feel like he was cheating on his late wife's memory.

He was doing his best to hide it, but she recognized the signs because for the longest time, she also had been scared to move on. She'd been afraid to give her heart to someone else, worried it would get beaten and bruised all over again.

And, like she feared, it did. Badly.

The relationship she hoped that would last, ended up being destroyed.

Luckily, she was older, more experienced and stronger when it happened, so she was able to handle it differently.

Like Mark's death, she survived Jason abandoning her and leaving her to raise their son on her own.

Nox drug the back of his hand across his mouth like that would magically undo the kiss, his erection and Liyah's damp panties. Since it wouldn't, she had no doubt he'd beat himself up for giving in to the urge to kiss her.

He flinched and jerked his head back when she reached up and wiped a spot of lipstick off his bottom lip. "Missed a spot."

"I gotta go," he grumbled. Bending over, he snagged his fallen hat and slapped it back on his head, pulling the brim low.

Disappearing once again into his shell like a turtle protecting itself.

"Of course you do," she said dryly, trying to keep up as he shot out of the closet and across the room toward the exit. "You don't want to talk about what just happened?"

Of course he wouldn't, but that didn't mean she wasn't going to ask. She had a point to make.

"Nothing to talk about."

"I disagree." She stopped in the center of the room. "Avoidance is your middle name, isn't it?"

He avoided that question, too, of course.

Just as he reached for the door, she called out, "See you next week, Bradley Avoidance Lennox. Have a good rest of your night."

He stopped with his hand on the push bar. She waited as he stared at the door for a few seconds. Then he glanced over his shoulder. "You're not leaving?"

"I need to finish in here first."

Chapter Ten

Nox TURNED to face the woman standing in the center of the room.

The woman he just fucking kissed.

In a closet.

Like he was at some late-night high school party, where they were all getting smashed and playing Seven Minutes in Heaven.

He had lost his goddamn head for a few minutes.

He needed to go. To get out of that community center before he was tempted to kiss her again.

Maybe do even more.

He hated the fact that he was attracted to her. Not because of who she was or related to. But because she was the first woman to draw and hold his attention since meeting Jackie all those years ago.

Unfortunately, Aaliyah was so damn pushy.

You need to do better, Nox.

You need to get over it, Nox.

You need to move on, Nox.

Maybe the woman didn't say any of that directly, but when it all boiled down to it, that was exactly what she meant.

The more time he spent around her, the more he was afraid she'd break through. The kiss, along with his hard-on, proved she had caused a crack in his armor. And it wouldn't take much for her to wedge herself in even farther.

She was proud, strong and unafraid. He found that a fucking turn-on.

He liked bold women.

He liked independent women.

He liked intelligent women.

He liked a woman willing to meet challenges head on.

Aaliyah was all of that and more.

To him, she was as dangerous as meth to an addict.

He needed to go. Get as far from her as fucking possible and never come back to this weekly meeting.

Lose her business card and delete her number from his phone.

Forget he ever met her.

But what he wouldn't do was leave her at the community center by herself. He couldn't leave yet. Not until she did. "I'll wait while you finish closing up."

Her head tilted to the side and one eyebrow hiked up. "Why? You don't think I'm capable of turning off the lights and locking the door by myself?"

He sucked on his teeth. "You can't simply say thank you?"

"No. Because I don't need you to protect me."

"You're going to get it, anyway. Just so you know, I can be just as pushy as you. Let's see how you like it."

He noticed most of the lipstick she'd been wearing was

now gone. He glanced at the back of his hand and saw exactly where it went.

Fuck.

He asked, "What do you need to do yet?"

For a second, nothing but air escaped her parted lips, then she directed a huge smile at him.

He didn't like that smile, nor the gleam in her eyes.

"To close up," he added, his pulse speeding up once again.

Oh yeah, this woman was dangerous. Because he wanted nothing more than to make short work of walking to where she stood with her hand planted on her hip, so he could take her mouth again.

She had woken something deep inside him.

Something that had been sleeping.

He didn't like it, but he couldn't deny...

He wanted her.

"I already told you," she started, her honey-smooth voice now husky, "turn off the lights and lock the door. I don't need your help for that."

"You're right, you don't. I'll walk you out to your car, then."

"I'll be fine."

"I'll walk you out to your car," he repeated more firmly.

"Fine, Officer Lennox, since you feel the need to protect and serve." She jerked into motion, walking toward him.

What was she up to?

She kept coming straight at him, her hips rocking smoothly with each step she took.

Jesus Christ, she was sexy as fuck. All curves and smooth ebony skin. Her dark, observant eyes held a mischievous spark more often than not. Full, soft, kissable lips. Long legs made even longer due to the high heels she wore.

He held his breath as she stopped toe-to-toe with him, leaned in and raised a hand...

Then the lights went out and the room turned pitch black, all except for the slightest red glow from the lit exit sign above the door.

"See? I could do that all by myself." Her words whispered over his lips.

Christ, she smelled good, too. Better than those damn chocolate chip cookies. "I'd give you a cookie for your effort, but they're all gone."

"Well, look at that," she murmured, "your sense of humor does exist. It was just shoved all the way up your ass, along with that stick." Her nails scraped lightly along his jawline, then her thumb swept across his bottom lip.

"Aaliyah..." He curled his fingers into his palms to avoid reaching for her.

"*Hmm?*"

"I can't do this."

"You already did."

"I can't do this," he insisted again.

"Then don't. The exit's right there. However, it sounds like you're trying to convince yourself more than me."

She was right.

He swallowed in an attempt to loosen his tight throat. "You're in the way."

She took a step back, giving him enough space to get around her. "We can leave. I'm done here."

For fuck's sake. "I'm not."

He reached for her and pulled her into him, digging his fingers into her hips to pin her against him.

"Nox—"

He smothered whatever she was about to say next when he slammed his mouth against hers. Those lost words became

116

a moan, and she wrapped her arms around his back, embracing him tightly.

Christ, he didn't realize how much he missed holding someone and getting held in return.

By an adult.

He appreciated and accepted every hug Valee Girl gave him, but it wasn't the same. The hugs between a four-year-old he considered his niece and a mature woman he was attracted to was definitely nothing alike.

With Aaliyah's breasts smashed against his chest and their lips locked together, their tongues played with each other.

She looked delicious, smelled delicious and tasted delicious, too.

She could quickly become an addiction.

An addiction he needed to avoid.

Fuck, he wanted this woman, but his head and his heart continued to war with each other. His head said, *"Go for it. It's time to move on."* His heart...

Ached.

It also told his brain he should feel guilty for finding pleasure in touching and kissing Aaliyah. For wanting more. For wanting her in all the ways two adults wanted each other.

Was this a turning point for him, or strictly a stumble?

Would his guilt compound later when he was alone? When he thought back on these kisses?

He could end this mistake right here and now.

He turned his head to break their kiss. But before he could put space between them, he couldn't stop himself from turning back and taking her mouth one more time.

Fuck. Just what he was afraid of... she *was* addicting.

It was only a kiss.

It should mean nothing.

Simply a moment of weakness.

And that right there was a lie because the only thing saving him from taking it further was the fact they stood in a public building.

A fucking public building.

In a town where he still worked and had previously lived and knew just about everyone.

Fuck.

He pulled his head back enough to say, "I can't do this."

"Too late."

When he took a step back to put some space between them, he bumped into the wall.

He couldn't continue standing there in the dark because he was afraid they would end up doing a lot more than kissing in a room where anyone could walk in at any time.

"So... Do you want to talk about *that?*"

He shook his head and skirted around her, heading to the door and holding it open for her. "You got a key to lock up?"

"No. The night janitor will lock up once I text him."

He frowned. "You said you lock up."

"Yes, by texting him."

He shook his head at her answer.

They stepped out into the hallway, and he shut the door behind them.

"Are you still going to walk me out?"

"Why wouldn't I?" Gripping her elbow, he steered her toward the building's outer doors.

"Because you might be afraid you'll trip and your lips will accidentally get stuck to mine again?"

This woman certainly knew how to push his damn buttons.

Apparently, she wasn't done yet. "You're always wearing a hat. It not only hides your eyes, but it also makes it more difficult to suck face. I guess you use it like a force field."

"Suck face?" He pushed open the door and escorted her out into the warm spring night.

"Yes, kissing. That's what my fifteen-year-old calls it."

"I know what it means. It was a bit jarring coming from you."

She shrugged. "Unfortunately, I pick up a lot of their vernacular. Only, I have to be careful not to use it around my clients."

"But you don't need to be careful around me?"

"No, because a little slang isn't going to hurt you," she answered, "since you need to loosen up."

"Your opinion."

"And a pretty good one, if I say so myself," she quipped.

"Of course you'd think that."

When they stopped in front of her Benz, he waited for her to dig out her key fob and unlock the doors.

"You can go now," she announced.

"I'm not leaving the parking lot until you do."

"Such a gentleman," she murmured and slid into the driver's seat.

He pressed his arm along the top of the door frame and leaned in. "Hey..." As soon as she was settled in her seat and glanced up at him, he continued, "Just to be clear... This can't happen."

"I don't know what you're talking about."

She was purposely being obtuse. "This."

"This what?"

She was really going to make him spell it out. "Whatever this is between us."

"Nox, we only shared a kiss. Not *a* kiss, three to be exact, if we're keeping score. But it would've ended after the first one if I hadn't enjoyed them. I'm assuming it would be the same for you."

He did enjoy them. Too much.

Her lips curled slightly. "I guess you plan on being celibate for the rest of your life, then."

"I never said I'm celibate."

Her husky laugh had him straightening and taking a step back from her car. "You didn't have to say it. You're having a complete meltdown over a kiss."

"I'm not having a fucking meltdown."

"Okay, you're wrought with guilt over it."

"You're imagining that."

She clicked her tongue. "You're not a good liar, Nox. You might want to practice."

"I lie just fine."

Her peel of laughter got his heart pumping a little faster. When she was done, she asked, "Are you going to tail me to make sure I get home safe, too?"

"No."

"Then, you have a good night, officer." She pulled her door shut and the rich rumble of her engine filled the air.

With a shake of his head, he strode over to his bike, parked only a few spots away.

After throwing a leg over his seat, he got ready to ride by turning his baseball cap around and slipping on the protective glasses he wore to keep suicidal bugs from taking out an eye.

When he pushed the start button, he realized just how good his bike sounded versus a car. Unless it was a classic muscle car with a big block engine, a Harley with straight pipes couldn't be beat.

Her Benz might be fast and sound decent, but he'd always prefer two wheels over four.

He twisted his head when he heard, "Wait! I have something for you," over the gravelly purr of his beloved ride.

For fuck's sake, now what?

He was worried she'd break her damn neck as she trotted over to him on those high heels, carrying something square in her hand.

He squinted, trying to see what it was. A container?

"I'm surprised you didn't shoot out of here like a rocket when you saw me coming."

"It crossed my mind."

"Again, you're a horrible liar."

"I'm not lying. I couldn't get it in gear fast enough."

"Then, maybe you need one of those bikes with an automatic transmission."

"Blasphemy."

She smiled. "You should let your sense of humor out to play more, it makes you seem a little more human."

"I wouldn't want people to mistake me as human."

She rolled her eyes. "Obviously. You work very hard at coming off as an emotionless piece of driftwood."

She jammed the container she was holding into his chest.

"What's that?"

"What's it look like?"

"A plastic container," he answered with the obvious.

"Why would a genius like you ever want to be a cop?"

"For the fortune we make."

"Now I *know* that's a lie. Will you take it... please?"

It sounded like she was getting irritated. Welcome to the club. "I don't want those."

"Yes you do, but it's your life mission to be difficult. Who the hell turns down homemade chocolate chip cookies?"

"I don't have any way to carry them."

"Sure you do." She pulled the container from his chest

and jammed it between his thighs, instead, making him jerk when her hand came dangerously close to skimming over his crotch. "There you go. Bikers know all the tricks to hauling shit on their sleds. I'm surprised you don't."

Sleds. She might not live the life, but she sure knew the language.

She must have a vast vocabulary between being around her two sons and her biker father.

She smiled. "Have a great night, Officer Lennox. See you next week."

The way she purred that made his dick jump in his jeans. "You too, Ms. James. And I might not be here next week." Not if he could find another group within an hour's drive.

"*Uh huh.* See you next week." She gave him a little salute and headed back to her expensive car.

One she left running and unlocked in the dark parking lot. Good thing Shadow Valley wasn't a crime-ridden town.

He shook his head and waited for her to leave.

Once her taillights disappeared in the distance, he remained there staring in that direction for a few more moments, going over the evening in his head from all her pointed questions during group, to the kisses they shared.

The woman would be perfect if...

If he was looking.

He wasn't.

Chapter Eleven

His COMMUTE to work was short and sweet. Only one flight of stairs stood between his apartment and the task force's office space.

The feds leasing the top floor of The Plant from the Blue Avengers had fattened the club's coffers. The monthly payments weren't a huge windfall but certainly helped keep the lights on and prevented the BAMC treasurer, Mike Miller, from jacking up the members' dues.

Once the DEA shut down the task force, they'd be back to doing a bunch of fundraisers and trying to recruit more members to help fund their clubhouse.

Nox punched in the security code and as soon as he heard the lock release, he walked in to find that quite a few of the task force members had already arrived for the meeting.

Today's meeting should be a pivotal one. They were nearing the end of their investigation and had gathered enough evidence between the three task force groups to get indictments on the Deadly Demons MC. The Tri State Federal Drug Task Force group leaders, including Crew, had submitted their damning reports to the Assistant US Attorney.

He was sure Crew would be giving them an update on where the investigation was heading next.

"Hard Nox!" Rez called out.

"How the fuck are you here before me?" Usually, his BAMC brother sauntered in at the last minute.

Rez shrugged. "Guess you're a slacker."

With a shake of his head, Nox dropped the container of chocolate chip cookies in the center of the conference table next to a ravaged box of donuts. Not much remained except for powdered sugar residue, chocolate smears and crumbs.

He tucked the last cruller between his teeth and headed over to the coffeemaker for some much-needed black gold.

Thank fuck someone had made a pot of coffee, even though the full carafe would be kicked soon enough. The whole team drank it like it was crack.

As Nox filled his mug, Torres asked, "What's in the container?"

He glanced over to see some of the guys already crowding around the cookies.

Rez leaned in to inspect the contents. "What is it?"

"Is it food?" asked Crew.

"Chocolate chip cookies." It was hard to understand Torres since he had already shoved a whole cookie into his mouth. Once he swallowed, the plant manager exclaimed, "Damn, these are the bomb! You make these?"

"Have I ever baked for you fuckers before?" Nox asked around a mouthful of the sweet, airy donut.

Torres shrugged. "You could've found a new hobby, asshole. How the fuck would I know? It's not like you share a lot."

The "share" comment had him thinking about Aaliyah.

And he was trying not to think about her.

It was a losing battle.

He hadn't thought about anyone else since the other night at the community center. *Hell*, he hadn't thought about much of *anything* else, either.

The woman had somehow embedded herself in his brain.

He had told her that he wasn't going back to her group.

But he already knew that was a lie.

He'd be going back.

He shook himself mentally to return to the conversation happening around him. That was when he realized the herd of hungry, hungry hippos circling the table had emptied the container within seconds.

He hadn't eaten one damn cookie since he didn't need another reason to be attracted to the woman who baked them. "Jesus. I swear you're all feral. Don't any of your significant others feed you?"

"Are you saying it's a woman's job to feed her man?" Cabrera asked, taking a bite of a cookie.

He glanced over at their newest task force member. "Is that what you heard?"

"Yes, that's exactly what I heard. If you're unaware of this fact, men are perfectly capable of cooking and/or feeding themselves."

He jerked his chin toward the table. "Not those men, obviously."

Cabrera grinned. "You might have a point."

"Look, you dropped a container of homemade cookies on the table and now you're complaining that we're eating them?" Crew asked. "Wasn't that the point of putting them on the table?"

Nox ignored the task force leader by taking another sip of his coffee.

"Who made these, anyway?" Crew's eyes narrowed on Nox. "They didn't come from a bakery."

"Maybe I bought them from a bakery and only put them in the container to keep them fresh."

Rez coughed out a "Bullshit." He lifted the container high enough so everyone could see the bottom. "Who's James?"

Fuck. Aaliyah had used a black marker to write her last name on the bottom.

Nox kept his expression neutral. "You don't know Jim?"

"Know plenty of people named Jim, but none of them bake cookies."

"Then you don't know the right Jims," Nox told Rez.

"Did you," Decker started carefully, making Nox brace, "switch teams? I mean, there's nothing wrong with it, if you did."

"We won't hold it against you," Finn assured him with a smirk.

"Yeah, everyone deserves to be loved," Rez added, also with a damn smirk.

"Cross can give you some pointers, if you need them," Crew suggested, definitely wearing a smirk.

"Fuck you all. Are we having a meeting or not?"

Finn plopped his ass in a chair at the conference table, cradled his chin in his palms and batted his eyelashes. "Once you tell us all about James. He sounds dreamy if he can bake like that."

"Why? So you all can ride my ass?"

"Is that what James does? Are you the bottom in the relationship?" Torres asked.

"When you're coming, do you cry out James, Jim or Jimmy?" Decker asked, now also wearing a smirk.

Crew took his seat at the head of the table. "Or Jam Jam?"

"Is Nox taking some Jam Jam up the yam yam?" Luke Rodgers dropped into the seat next to Finn.

"This is putting a new meaning to the nickname Hard Nox." Decker took the chair next to Cabrera.

Nox scowled at Crew. "Do I need to be here for this meeting?"

"Yes. Everyone does. Anyone not here physically is calling in."

"Tell us... Is he tall, dark and handsome?" Rez wiggled his eyebrows.

No, but *she* was tall, dark and gorgeous.

"How about we stop busting on Equi-Nox and get this meeting started?" came from the phone in the center of the table.

"Wilder with you, Fletch?" Crew asked the undercover task force member.

"I'm here," Wilder answered, "but I agree with Fletch. Let's get this meeting started because the ol' ladies expect me to meet up with them later to help clean the Wolf Den."

Finn snorted. "That has to be a shitty job."

"It could be," Wilder said, "if they didn't make the sweet butts scrub the bathrooms."

"Yeah, they're so fucking gag-worthy," Fletch confirmed. "Showers, toilets... everything. They're a bunch of filthy pigs."

"No, according to them, *we're* a bunch of pigs," Rez said on a laugh.

A bunch of oinking circled the table.

"That licked-clean cookie container and decimated donut box kind of proves they're right," Nox muttered.

Finn slapped the table. "Oh, look at that... Fort Nox told a joke."

"Isn't a joke if it's true," Nox responded.

Crew rapped his knuckles on the table. "Okay, let's get started."

"Thank fuck," Ken Proctor mumbled under his breath.

"Proctologist, you're stuck here all fucking day transcribing wiretaps. Are you in a fucking rush to get back to it?" Torres asked him.

Proctor shot a grimace at Nox. "Tell more jokes, Annie Lennox."

"Comedy hour is over," Crew announced. "Time for serious business..."

A few of them booed or hissed.

"It's all fun and games until a Sicilian puts out a hit on an outlaw biker," Crew reminded them. "Okay, if you've been keeping up with the meetings, you know that we—by we, I mean the group leaders—have been submitting our reports to the Assistant US Attorney. In turn, she has pulled together a grand jury and has begun to introduce the evidence to them."

"Holy shit. This is good news," Fletch said. "I finally see the light at the end of this long damn tunnel."

Nox glanced over at Cabrera since she currently living in Fletch's house. As soon as Fletch and Wilder were finished with their undercover assignment, they'd be moving back into his home, and she'd have to find a new place.

Nox's eyes slid from Crew to Cabrera and back.

Though... something was off between those two.

Or something was on, more like it.

They could pretend that they annoyed each other, but to Nox it couldn't be clearer...

Crew and Cabrera were fucking.

Even though those two were pretending nothing was

happening between them, Nox had a feeling Cabrera wouldn't have a problem finding a new place to live. In Crew's condo.

"For those a bit dense," Crew hesitated and cocked his eyebrow at Rez, "let me explain how this will work and our part in it. That means, pay attention. This grand jury can last weeks or even months, depending on how much evidence the prosecutor decides to present. Even though Pam, the AUSA, is starting the proceedings, we're still not done collecting evidence and won't be until we're told to shut things down."

"Soon?"

"Yeah, Fletch, my guess is soon," Crew answered with a shake of his head. "Pam—"

"The old stud muffin is on a first name basis with the AUSA. Makes you wonder, doesn't it?" Decker snuck a glance at Cabrera to see if she reacted.

She didn't. She had an expert poker face.

Crew ignored Big Deck and continued, "*Pam* decided to convene the grand jury to get the indictments rolling, hopefully before war breaks out between the Demons and the Russos."

"I guess some of us could be called for testimony?" Finn asked.

"If the grand jury requests it, yeah," Crew said, "and again during their trials."

"Once the indictments are handed down, do you think this AUSA will let them turn themselves in or do a *wham, bam, thank you, ma'am,* round up?" Decker asked Crew.

"My guess? The second one since they'll all be considered flight risks. They're going to handle the MC like they would any other RICO case, since our evidence proves their criminal activities went further than only trafficking drugs."

Wilder's voice came from the speaker. "Money laundering is certainly part of a RICO charge. And I agree that they'll want to do the shock and awe maneuver to arrest everyone at the same time. Otherwise, they'll scatter the same way roaches do once a light's turned on."

"Speaking of the Mafia, what's happening on that front?" Nox asked Crew. "We haven't heard much about the Russos from you or anyone else when it comes to what the feds are doing on that end." And something should be done, especially after they tried to off Wilder when they ambushed her at her condo. La Cosa Nostra needed to be annihilated the same as the Demons.

"I've been concentrating on the Demons and our part, but I can check on that. But the feds always have their finger on the pulse of any criminal organization like that. Right, Wilder?"

"That's true," she answered. "Usually more than one agency will have eyes on an enterprise like them."

"If the feds are going to wipe out the Russos—legally, of course—they really should do it at the same time as they do the Demons. Otherwise, they might get squirrelly when they hear that their drug mules are being corralled."

"Not my call," Crew told Decker. "Let's get back to our own investigation. The word is that the AUSA will request that the Demons are held without bail until trial. Of course, that's due to them being flight risks. And also to prevent that war we're all worried about."

"Once this goes to trial, our part should be done," Rodgers said.

"For the most part, except for any questions that might need answered or if we're called to testify in either the grand jury or at the trials. No matter what, the task force will be dissolved after the indictments and arrests go down."

"We get to take part in the round up, right?" Finn asked. "I have cuffs with Saint's name engraved on them."

"Well, damn, so do I," said Rez.

"Any of you can volunteer to be a part of serving the indictments and arrest warrants, unless you're still undercover," Crew told them. "Or plan to do future undercover work within your own agency."

Fletch groaned. "Nova and I will be stuck staying undercover to the very last fucking second, won't we?"

"I told you before, brother, it's good for the investigation to have eyes and ears in each chapter. If the Demons get a heads up that arrests are coming, we need to know that and move more quickly. We don't want another ambush like what happened to Wilder, even though that had nothing to do with our particular investigation."

"A-fucking-men." Rez made the sign of the cross.

"Anyway, helping with the round-up is voluntary. No one's required to do it, since we all know how dangerous that shit can get."

"But fun," Torres added.

That was true and Nox wanted to be a part of the team serving up those indictments and arrests. Unlike some others on the task force with significant others or families, he had nothing to lose if an arrest went bad.

Of course, with the Demons, he was pretty fucking sure some of the arrests would go bad. None of those outlaw bikers would go easily. They were going to do their worst by fighting back or trying to run.

Not only did it need to be a coordinated effort, but the teams would also need to hit them when the bikers least expected it.

"All right, so that's the main shit I needed to share. Like I mentioned, questions will most likely arise that we'll need to answer for the AUSA or the grand jury. Or even the judge. And if they request any of us to testify, you'll be notified of the details. But for now, we're going to keep on keeping on until we're told differently by the individuals paid a much higher salary than mine. Side note: even if you don't have to testify in front of the grand jury, don't assume you won't have to do it at trial. That means you need to make sure your reports are spot on. You don't want to get jammed up on the witness stand because of shitty notes. Don't forget, whatever you have written down can and will be used as evidence by both sides. Bottom line, whatever you do will be reflected on me as your leader. Let's keep that in mind."

A few snorts and bursts of laughter circled the table.

"We done?" Fletch asked.

"As long as no one has anything else."

"Keep your mouths shut, fuckers. Talk to you all later." And with that, Fletch and Wilder were gone.

"I guess we're done," Crew announced, then added, "For now. I'll keep you all apprised of any updates from Pam."

Nox assumed, like Fletch, the rest of the task force members on the line had all hung up, too.

He liked meetings that were short and to the point.

Chairs scraped the floor and groans and sighs could be heard as everyone got up from the conference table and either headed to a computer or a wiretap station or to grab more coffee. Or even leave.

Cabrera was the first out the door to head home to catch some shut eye since she had been working undercover almost every night at the Hawg Wild Saloon.

Nox did not miss Crew tracking her as she left.

Oh yeah. They were fucking.

Crew's dick now had a collar around it and Cabrera held the leash.

That almost made Nox want to smile.

He also wanted to bust on the professional ball-buster about it, too. But Nox didn't want to out their relationship to the rest of the team. Not because of Crew, but because of Cabrera.

Nox went shoulder to shoulder with Crew and elbowed the man in the ribs. That was enough to pull Crew's gaze from the now closed door to him.

"What's up?" Crew asked him.

Nox raised his eyebrows and jerked his chin toward the door. "You tell me."

"Nothing to tell." Crew's masked expression didn't even slip an inch. He managed to keep it securely in place.

Crew knew better than to show any sign of weakness in the sea of circling sharks that included both the task force and the BAMC. Falling for a woman, especially one Crew wasn't happy about joining the team and one much younger than him, would be a weakness.

"All right, well... put me on the list for the round-up. I want in."

Crew pursed his lips as he considered Nox. "Are you sure?"

"Yeah."

The task force leader sucked in an audible breath. "Nox..."

"Make sure I'm on it."

"I'll keep that in mind when we get to that point."

"Do that." With that, he headed over to his computer station since today he planned on watching some of the camera feeds, both live and recorded.

Chapter Twelve

Nox glanced over his shoulder for the fiftieth time to make sure no one was paying attention to his computer monitor.

Or to what he was doing.

Because what he was doing, he shouldn't be. He shouldn't be running anyone's information through the law enforcement databases unless he had a valid reason to do so.

He wasn't digging deeper into Aaliyah James, successful business owner and single mother, for Shadow Valley PD or for the federal task force, he was selfishly doing it for himself.

He first pulled up her PennDOT info, including her driver's information. While he had that up on the screen, he snapped a quick photo of her address with his cell phone, but not before once again making sure no one was watching. He purposely sat at the desk on the end to keep his records search under the radar.

Already this morning he experienced shit handed to him simply by a name written in black marker on the bottom of a fucking container. If any of the team saw him running a records search on a woman that had zero to do with the investigation?

It would be brutal.

Not because they knew he shouldn't be doing it, but because they would come up with the craziest scenarios about who Aaliyah James was to him.

Even though the truth was, to him, she was no one.

Only a thorn in his side.

A participant in his wandering thoughts.

As well as the leader of a grief group he would no longer be attending.

If he was smart.

He skimmed down her driving record and over the few speeding and parking citations she received over the years. They were nothing more than summary traffic offenses and not out of the ordinary for someone spending a lot of time in her vehicle when showing and listing homes, as well as meeting with clients.

After a few more keystrokes, he moved on to check for a criminal record and breathed a sigh of relief when that came up clean.

Scraping a hand down his jaw, he stared at the screen.

She might not have a criminal record but someone she was related to certainly did. With another quick glance around first, he quickly typed in the name Malcolm Moore next.

Two came up in the system. A junior and a senior. When he checked their dates of birth, it was obvious that junior was Aaliyah's brother, leaving Malcolm Moore, Sr. to be her father.

That was confirmed when he saw the nickname Magnum listed under the man's aliases. Then there was his extensive list of identifying tattoos.

The tattoo that caught his eye was the one mentioned on the man's back. His Dark Knights MC colors. Typical of bikers living the true MC life. To show their loyalty to their brotherhoods, they permanently tattooed their club rockers and patches onto the skin of their backs.

Nox didn't even bother to check his driving record. He was damn sure it wasn't spotless. Magnum most likely no longer had a valid driver's license, either. Despite that, a dedicated biker like her father would continue riding his "sled" even if suspended.

Riding was life for these MC members, an element needed to survive and as important as air and water.

Nox decided to dive right to the meat of things...

The Knights' sergeant at arm's rap sheet.

For fuck's sake. Nox shook his head while he scrolled the long and extensive list. Aaliyah's father was also no stranger to taking involuntary vacations in a locked concrete box.

Funny how these outlaw bikers always spouted the saying, "ride free or die," but ended up spending big chunks of their lives behind bars.

He dug a little deeper and discovered an expired PFA. The protection from abuse order had not only covered Aaliyah's mother but also the two children.

Had the PFA been granted on a lie or the truth?

Had he gotten violent with his children?

Nox couldn't imagine that Aaliyah would've agreed to repairing their relationship if Magnum had done so.

She also trusted her boys with him.

If the PFA had been issued due to false information, no wonder Aaliyah had been angry with her mother. It was a bullshit way to keep a father away from his own children. It was both scheming and manipulative. And a good way—once the children became adults and discovered the truth—to turn your own kids against you.

It sounded like Aaliyah forgave her mother for the most part, so Aniyah Moore was a lucky woman. Nox wondered if Moore was still the woman's last name, or she had changed it after the divorce or if she'd remarried. Aaliyah hadn't mentioned either scenario.

Approaching footsteps had him minimizing the site so whoever it was couldn't be a nosy fucker.

The empty plastic container was dropped on the desk in front of Nox. "Thank James for us," Rez said. "And don't forget to bring him by. We'll need to approve of him just like Monty's man Clark."

Nox spun his office chair around to face his brother. "We can't approve of Clark since we don't know shit about him."

"That means we won't have that same issue with James, right?" Rez asked with raised eyebrows.

"If he existed."

"Someone made those cookies."

"The Keebler elves," Nox suggested.

Rez snorted. "Bullshit."

"Mrs. Fields."

"Doubt that."

"It could've been Famous Amos."

"These were better. They tasted like they were made with *loooooove*." Rez batted his eyelashes and made a heart with his fingers over his chest.

Nox shook his head. "No love was involved. Just sugar, flour and..." He had no idea what was in the cookie recipe.

"And?"

"And whatever other ingredients are needed to make fucking chocolate chip cookies."

"Like chocolate chips? Since you don't even know the basic ingredients, it proves you didn't make them."

"I said I didn't. Clean out your fucking ears, Rez-ervation."

"Hey," Rez dropped his voice lower, "you think Crew and Cabrera are fucking?"

Nox gave him a pointed look.

Rez hooted, "I knew it!"

Nox glared at him. "Keep your voice down, asshole."

"What did you know, Rez-dispenser?" Crew asked from where he sat.

Nox and Rez's eyes locked for a second before Nox warned him under his breath, "Let it go for now. It'll come out soon enough."

"I'm all-knowing," Rez answered Crew. "So, the question is, what don't I know?" He lowered his voice again so only Nox could hear him. "Damn. I don't know if I can keep that secret. I might explode."

"Like your ass does after you eat your mom's black beans?"

Rez smirked. "They're worth it."

"To you. Not to anyone else. I don't know how Sapphire puts up with you or your ass."

"The tongue and hip action." With a grin, Rez wiggled his tongue and humped the air. "Gets them every time."

"Christ almighty. Thanks for that visual."

Rez winked at him. "You're welcome." As the man wandered away, he threw over his shoulder, "Say hi to James for me."

———

It turned out she lived just north of the Dirty Angels' territory. That club's area now butted up against the Dark Knights'. The two ally clubs had technically closed "ranks" to prevent any other MCs from trying to take over the previously unclaimed area between them. After decades of dealing with the Shadow Warriors, they didn't want any other club wedging their way in between their territories to try to divide and conquer them.

Nox wouldn't put past those idiot Deadly Demons.

The DAMC and the DKMC, along with the Blood Fury MC, pretty much ruled western Pennsylvania. That was why it surprised Nox that the Demons had expanded north from West Virginia into Pennsylvania.

It had been a risk. One that most likely paid off as long as they didn't step on the other two clubs' toes.

But the Demons were not a club to step carefully. Especially when it came to making money.

Even so, Nox wasn't pulling his Harley into Aaliyah's driveway to discuss the politics of the area's motorcycle clubs. His visit had another purpose.

Yes, he had her number and probably should have called first—to at least see if she was home—but riding over to her place had been a spur of the moment decision.

Sort of.

After removing his goggles and bandana, he dismounted from his bike, glanced at the empty container in his hand and considered the lie he just told himself.

Having a reason, other than the true one, lessened the guilt. Somewhat.

He should leave.

He should set the container on her porch and roll the fuck out of there before she spotted him.

It was a mistake looking up her home address and then

showing up like a fucking stalker. He could get booted off the task force and canned from Shadow Valley PD for doing so.

If he got fired, he could no longer be a part of the Blue Avengers. He might even have to move out of his apartment. Between the two, he'd lose his brotherhood and truly be alone.

He'd have no one left.

He'd have nothing left.

All because of his interest in the woman opening her front door and stepping out onto the porch with her forehead creased in confusion. "What are you doing here?"

She didn't stop on the porch but kept coming. Her long, dark sleek legs, exposed from wearing tan shorts, quickly ate up the distance between them.

He curled his fingers of his empty hand when the urge to run them up her well-defined, glistening calves and thighs came over him.

Instead of physically touching her, he visually skimmed her from her maroon-painted toenails to her curly hair, pulled away from her make-up free face with a cream-colored, paisley-patterned bandana. Her olive green, short-sleeved shirt was loose enough to drop off one shoulder, exposing a black bra strap.

She most likely wore the outfit around the house for comfort, but it was still sexy as fuck.

At least on her. He didn't give a fuck what it would look like on anyone else.

When she stopped in front of him, she tipped her deep brown eyes, full of curiosity, up to his. Since she was barefoot, she was only about three inches shorter than his six-foot-two.

He'd never been into tall women.

Until now.

He didn't get it. He hadn't been attracted to any woman

—sexually, physically or even mentally—since Jackie died. That was not the case with the woman in front of him. And he had no fucking clue why.

She's still waiting for an explanation on why you're standing in her damn driveway, dumbass.

He shook himself mentally and finally remembered the object he was close to crushing in his hand. "To drop off your container." He held it out to her.

Instead of looking at it, she kept her eyes locked with his. "It could've waited until this coming week's meeting."

"I won't be there, remember?"

"*Mmm hmm.*"

He jammed it into her chest the same way she did to him the other night. "I figured you wanted it back since it has your name on it."

"If I don't label my containers when I take them into the office, I never see them again."

"Then, I don't want to be accused of being a container thief like your coworkers."

She finally took it from him, and he jerked when her fingers brushed over his.

That touch was no accident.

She lifted the empty container. "Apparently you must have liked the cookies since they're all gone. Or did you toss them out?"

"They were eaten." That wasn't a lie.

"I have more if you want."

He shook his head. "No." What he wanted from her wasn't food.

His head twitched at that realization. It happened again with what she said next.

"Hey, just a warning... My father's supposed to show up here at any moment. When I heard your sled, I thought it was him." She rolled her eyes. "Of course it wasn't. I swear the man will be late to his own damn funeral."

He preferred not to deal with the outlaw biker whose daughter he was stalking. "I'll leave."

"I didn't tell you that so you could—" She whispered, "Fuck."

He heard the reason for the curse and her frown... The roar of straight exhaust pipes.

"Your old man?"

"Yes," she answered. "Tell me quickly... You never arrested him, did you? He's the kind of man who doesn't forgive and forget."

"Are you telling me that I'm taking my own life in my hands by simply standing in your driveway?"

"I didn't have to tell you that, you figured it out on your own. Don't tell him you're a cop."

Nox wasn't planning on it. He knew better than that. "I'll just go."

"Too late."

Malcolm Moore, Sr., aka Magnum, motored his Harley next to Nox's. What surprised him was the Dark Knights' sergeant at arms had a sidecar attached to it.

The rest of what he saw did not surprise him. While he never met the man face to face before, he'd heard plenty about him at his police department. The biker was well-known in Shadow Valley. Not in a good way.

Magnum was a big fucking dude. Nox could see where Aaliyah got her height. The Black biker had a solid inch over him and probably a good thirty pounds, if not more.

Even in his late fifties, her father was intimidating. His massive fists could be used as lethal weapons. Though, Nox figured he was packing some other kind of weapon besides the ones attached at the end of his arms. Despite being a felon and forbidden to own or carry any weapons.

After shutting down his bike, Magnum's bald head turned to take in Aaliyah and Nox, standing closer together than they should be.

But if Nox stepped back now, he would seem guilty of something.

Like being interested in the man's daughter.

Instead, he stood his ground. Aaliyah actually shifted a bit closer, as if she was going to protect Nox from her father.

Nox swore the Knights' enforcer moved in slo-mo when he dismounted, fussed with something on his bike, then adjusted his cut. When he was finally done, he lumbered over to where they stood, keeping his eyes glued to Nox.

"Who this?" he asked in his deep, rumbly voice.

Nox lifted his chin and met his gaze head-on. "Are you asking her or me?"

"You a man? You got balls?"

Nox shouldn't be surprised the man said whatever crossed his mind. "Last I checked."

"Then you fuckin' answer, 'less you always let a woman speak for you. If you do, you definitely ain't got any fuckin' balls."

"Dad!" Aaliyah hissed. "Stop it."

Magnum kept their eyes locked, trying to make Nox look away. He didn't.

He wasn't one to scare easily.

Magnum jerked his chin up at Nox. "How d'you know Liyah?"

"I—"

"He's a member of my group," Aaliyah said before he could.

Nox grimaced since a woman answered for him.

For fuck's sake.

Even though Magnum turned his head enough to scowl at his daughter, he still kept his eyes turned toward Nox. "What group?"

She sighed. Loudly. "The grief group."

The man's thick brow furrowed, and he finally looked at his daughter. "You ain't sad."

"I know I'm not sad. Jesus. You don't have to be sad to join the group."

"Ain't grief sad?"

"Grief is a whole bunch of things, Dad... I," she shook her head, "I'm not explaining it to you again. You should've paid attention the first dozen times I told you why people attend that kind of group."

"You fuckin' moved on."

"Yes, I moved on," she agreed.

"No reason for you to be in that kinda fuckin' group."

"I'm not *in* the group. I *run* it. Remember?"

"If you need scratch..."

"I don't need money. I don't get paid to run it. I volunteer." She didn't hide her impatience in her voice.

"Why the fuck wouldya wanna do that?" he bellowed.

Aaliyah glanced at Nox and bugged out her eyes.

He kept his expression neutral since he should stay out of it.

"Because I like helping people?"

"You can do that and make plenty of fuckin' scratch like with your house sellin' gig."

"I do more than sell houses. I've also explained that to you at least a dozen times." Instead of bugging her eyes out this time, she rolled them.

"What's he do?"

"Minds his own business," Aaliyah answered. "You should try that sometime."

"If it's gotta do with my girl, it's my business."

"Not in this case. Why don't you go in and get the boys and their things together?"

"They ain't ready?" Once again, the man's voice carried through the neighborhood. Magnum's volume setting must only have two settings: loud or silent. Nothing in between.

Nox could imagine both were scary as fuck if you were on the biker's bad side.

Aaliyah lifted one dark eyebrow. "What do you think?"

"They knew what time I was gonna be here."

She shrugged. "They also know you're never on time."

"Gonna smash those fuckin' gamin' systems," Magnum grumbled.

"Did you forget who bought them?" Aaliyah asked.

"Didn't realize they wouldn't be able to fuckin' function without 'em."

"Next time run their Christmas wish list past me first before you go on a spending spree."

Magnum grunted his response and, with one more glare at Nox, turned on his boot heel and headed inside.

Both Nox and Aaliyah waited until the front door shut, then she turned toward him. "Sorry about that. He's a bit... protective."

"I see that. But I was going to say he's like a bull in a china shop."

She sighed. "That's true, too. Do you mind waiting out here while I go deal with the testosterone currently under my roof?"

"I can go."

She grabbed his forearm and squeezed. "No, don't. My father isn't staying. He's only here to pick up his grandsons."

Now the sidecar made sense. "You got your container. No reason for me to stay."

"There are plenty of reasons for you to stay."

Did he detect her voice getting husky? "I gotta go."

"You say that a lot."

"Because it's true."

"Where do you need to go?"

Nowhere. "Home."

"What's waiting for you there?"

Absolutely fucking nothing was waiting for him there. Everything he wanted currently stood right in front of him.

Because of that, he said, "Go. I'll wait."

He only hoped he didn't regret it.

Chapter Thirteen

LIYAH CLOSED the front door behind her and saw her father standing with one hand on his hip at the front picture window, holding the curtain to the side as he peered out.

No surprise.

She loved her father, and he was actually a great grandfather, despite being an outlaw biker, but, *damn*, he liked to be all up in her business.

With a shake of her head, she asked, "Are the boys getting ready?"

"Better be. Went in, unplugged their fuckin' game systems and told 'em their asses better be the fuck out here with their shit in five minutes. Or else."

"Was that how you said it?"

His dark eyes flicked to her. "Yeah."

Of course.

Luckily, her boys were now at an age that they understood they couldn't go around cursing in school like their grandfather. But when they were younger, she was always getting calls from the staff in regard to their foul language.

Her father had the uncanny knack of making the word "fuck" the most versatile word in the English language. If it could be used in a sentence as a noun, verb, adjective, or even as an amount of something, he used it.

Generously.

Because of that, it rolled out of her sons' mouths too easily. Along with the rest of her father's biker lingo.

While she might let the cursing slide, what she would not tolerate was Magnum bad mouthing cops in front of her sons.

Especially since both Devyn's father and paternal grandfather had been one.

"Woman, want the truth... Who's that fucker?"

To Magnum, every woman was "woman" and everybody he didn't know personally was a "fucker" or "motherfucker."

"He really is a member of my grief group." She had no idea if that answer would slide, but she certainly was going to give it a shot.

"Why's he standin' in your driveway?"

She answered, "He needed to drop off something."

"His dick?"

She lifted the container to show him. "This. I didn't check inside but I doubt his dick's in it." She shook it. "If it is, he's got a pretty damn small one."

"He's a white boy. Course he got a small one."

A laugh managed to spurt from between her pinned lips. "That stereotype isn't even true."

"The fuck it ain't."

In her lifetime she had dated more white guys than Black. She knew for a fact that wasn't true. *Hell*, both the fathers of her children were white. "I'm not going to discuss white men's penis sizes with my father."

He grunted and turned his eyes back out to the driveway. And Nox. "Rides a sled."

Well, at least they'd moved on from talking about dick sizes. "That's how he got here."

"But no colors."

"I didn't notice any, did you?" Good thing Nox wasn't wearing his Blue Avengers cut. She knew they had them since Axel Jamison, Cross and other members of the BAMC had worn theirs many times at multi-club fundraisers for Ellie Walker's foundation, a charity for amputees providing prosthetics and care for those who couldn't afford it.

Still holding the curtain open, Magnum pursed his lips as he continued to stare out of the window.

"He can see you staring at him."

"Yeah," Magnum grunted.

"You have no shame."

"Don't give a fuck. If he's interested in my baby girl, I'm interested in him."

"Asia's your baby girl. I'm far from a baby."

"Know what I mean. Always gonna be my baby. Always gonna look out for you. Always wanna know who's sniffin' around my girl."

"Like I said, he's only dropping off the container."

"Container's in your hand and he's still standin' out there. He's sniffin'. So you're either lyin' to your old man or he's lyin' to you." Magnum finally dropped the curtain and turned toward her. "He a pig?"

Holy shit, her father had the scary sixth sense of picking out cops.

She carefully schooled her expression since he purposely asked that question when he could watch her face. The man was far from dumb.

In fact, he was a hell of a lot smarter than most people gave him credit for.

"He's a man," she answered. "You think anyone who's

151

buff and has short hair is a cop. He could be military. Army reserves or something."

"You don't know, and you plan on havin' him in your fuckin' house when you're alone?"

She rolled her eyes. "I know you missed out on most of my childhood, but please remember, I'm now thirty-nine and have two children of my own."

"That you're raisin' by yourself."

"And?" she asked sharply. They weren't having that conversation again. Jason might have been a mistake, but Mark was not.

And no matter what, both her sons weren't, either. They were both loved and wanted. Even when they were talking back and being difficult and she threatened to put them both up for adoption.

"Gimme his name. Gonna have one of Diesel's Shadows run him. Don't want you hangin' 'round someone you don't know fuck about."

"Maybe I do know 'fuck' about him. Anyway, I know who he is, and I know where he works. I don't need you being Sherlock Homie."

His head jerked back. "Think you're fuckin' funny. I take your goddamn safety serious. After that last one..."

She sighed. "Jesus. We all make mistakes, *right?* You've certainly made your share of them."

A muscle ticked in her father's cheek.

"Boys, your Grumpa is waiting!" she yelled. Where the hell were they? She was afraid if it took too long to get her father out of her house, Nox would leave.

"He ain't gonna fuckin' be here when I bring them back on Sunday, right?"

She wasn't going to explain yet again about the damn

container. Magnum obviously didn't believe that excuse. Again, the man wasn't dumb.

"I didn't realize I had to get approval from my father for my sleepovers." When she saw Magnum gearing up to roar about what she just said, she quickly raised her palm to stop him. "He won't be here on Sunday. He's still grieving."

"Maybe the fucker's here for you to comfort him, if you get what I'm sayin'."

"Could be."

Her father shot her a look.

"But that doesn't need to take all weekend." She smothered her grin. She *loved* to get her father going. Mostly because it was so easy to do.

"Grumps, did you bring your sled?" Keenan yelled as he ran down the hallway, his over-stuffed backpack gaping wide open and banging against his leg. The kid liked to overpack.

"Yeah. Why?"

"I wanted to bring my games—"

"No."

"But—"

"Said no. Mean no. No back talk."

Her son's face fell. "But Grumps..."

Magnum raised his eyebrows at her seven-year-old son. That was all it took.

Keenan's mouth twisted.

Liyah advised him, "Close your backpack so your stuff isn't spilling out all over the road. Be more responsible about your things."

"Yeah, 'cause I ain't turnin' the fuck around to get it. You lose it, you lose."

"You hear that?" Liyah asked. "Your loss will be some other boy's gain."

While Keenan secured his backpack, her fifteen-year-old meandered down the hall like he had nowhere to go.

"Let's fuckin' go, boy!" Magnum yelled at him. "Actin' like you got your whole damn life ahead of you."

"That's because I do, Grumps," Devyn answered with a roll of his eyes. "Can I bring—"

"No. Got my sled. No room."

"You bring your bike on purpose," Keenan whined.

"Yep," Magnum agreed. "Let's go. Unlike you two, don't got my whole goddamn life ahead of me. Time's a tickin'."

"Where are your helmets?" Liyah asked them. "You're not going anywhere without them."

"Garage," Devyn grumbled.

"Go get them and meet us outside," she told them.

With a grumble, both boys headed into the garage as she and Magnum went back outside. She stuck like glue to her dad so he wouldn't harass Nox, who, amazingly enough, still waited.

Even so, she did not miss the stink-eye that Magnum shot Nox's way. Before she could tell her father to behave, the boys came barreling out of the house.

"I'm riding shotgun!" Keenan yelled and ran over to the sidecar, now wearing both his backpack and his helmet with the face shield up.

"No, you ain't. You're ridin' behind me. Your brother's in the sidecar. Ain't ridin' nut to butt with someone over the age of ten."

"Dad!" she scolded.

"What happens when I'm over ten?" Keenan asked.

"Givin' you back to the stork," her father answered.

"I didn't come from a stork!" her youngest son yelled. "I came from Mom's pussy!"

"Keenan!" *For fuck's sake*, the whole neighborhood just heard that.

"That's what Grumps said about Grandma Cait. He said Asia and Caleb came out of her pussy."

Her head spun toward her father. "You did not."

Devyn was practically folded in half, laughing his ass off. He wasn't the only one amused.

"Not what I said," Magnum told her, failing at keeping a straight face.

"Yes you did, you said—"

"Keenan!" Liyah scolded. "Stop right now or you'll be grounded for a week. What did I tell you about repeating everything Grumps says?"

"Damn, kid, what'd I tell you 'bout bein' a snitch?"

"That— Wait... Who's that, Mom?" her youngest whispered loudly, finally spotting Nox where he leaned back against the monster oak tree in her front yard. He had one boot propped on the tree trunk and his baseball cap pulled low to hide his eyes as he waited.

He might act like he wasn't paying attention, but she was damn sure he did not miss any of the family chaos or what Keenan belted out at a volume level of one hundred.

She wouldn't blame the man if he sprinted across the yard, hopped on his bike and split the same way he did at the coffee shop.

"Some white boy who shouldn't be here," Magnum answered for her. "Figured he'd get tired of waitin' and be gone by now."

"You all should be gone by now. I'm supposed to be enjoying some peace and quiet this weekend and you're already messing that up."

Magnum grunted again and turned to her boys. "Devil, get in the side car. Keeper, you ride behind me."

She hated the "road names" Magnum gave her sons. However, they loved them since it made them feel a part of his MC without actually being members. If she could, she would strongly discourage them from ever joining the Knights.

She didn't have anything against her father's club, but she'd prefer her sons didn't live that lifestyle and that was what it was... a whole damn lifestyle. Unlike Nox's club, the Blue Avengers, which was more of a social club.

She stood off to the side and watched her family get situated on the Harley. Once the sled roared to life, Magnum gave her a chin lift, scowled one more time at Nox and managed to do a U-turn in her driveway without striking the cop's bike.

She sighed loudly and squeezed her forehead as she watched them disappear down the street. Once she could no longer hear the bike's exhaust, she knew the coast was clear and headed over to Nox. "You stayed."

He dropped his boot to the ground and straightened. "Who can resist free entertainment like that?"

"I can with no problem. Especially since it involves my household."

He shook his head and... *Holy shit.* Was that an actual chuckle she heard? If so, it was worth the chaos and embarrassment.

If it was anyone else, she'd wonder how he figured out where she lived, but he wore a badge, making it easy for him to find her information. The only question she had was why he looked for that information in the first place and then followed through by showing up.

The container excuse was bullshit.

She didn't want to spook him, so she needed to proceed carefully. "The boys won't be back until Sunday night."

"I guess that's a nice break for you."

Why was his voice such a damn turn-on? "Sure is."

"Your father take them a lot?"

"He does. My sister Asia is the same age as Devyn and they're two peas in a pod. Asia might officially be Dev's aunt, but since they grew up together, they're close like siblings. Despite our problems in the past, our family is now very tight."

"What about your husband's parents?"

"Mark's dad was also a Pittsburgh PD cop. He and my mother-in-law moved out to Arizona to enjoy the retired life a few years ago. I fly the boys out there a few times a year."

"Both of them?"

"Yes. Keenan might not be their blood, but he might as well be. They accepted him as their own."

"You said Keenan's father split, but what about his family?"

"They're no better than Jason." She sighed. "Anyway, family doesn't have to be blood. I'm grateful my sons have three sets of grandparents."

"Three?"

"My father and stepmother. My mother and her husband. Mark's parents."

"How much does Keenan know about his father?"

"Not much. I keep it vague since he's only seven. If he asks questions, I answer them as carefully as possible without actually lying. When he's older, I'll tell him the complete truth. I wouldn't put it past the kid to go search for his father once he turns eighteen and I want him to be prepared that he will most likely be rejected."

"Damn," Nox whispered.

She glanced back toward the empty street before swinging her gaze back to the man standing in her yard.

"Anyway, now that my house is empty, why don't you come inside?"

"I should go."

"You keep saying that but you're still here. You could've left while I was inside, you didn't. You came here for a reason, and it wasn't to return a cheap plastic container. Especially when I can easily buy a whole pack of replacements at the dollar store. So, are you going to keep lying to yourself on why you dug up my address and stopped over?"

Chapter Fourteen

LIYAH WATCHED HIS CHEST EXPAND, hold for a few seconds and finally collapse. "I don't know why."

"Yes, you do. We both do."

His hazel eyes turned toward her. "What's the reason, then?"

"To take me for a ride."

His eyebrows pinched together. "On my Harley?"

"Not unless you named your cock Harley." So much for not spooking him. She wanted to word it more carefully but half the blood running through her veins came from Magnum.

The king of not being subtle.

Nox's head twitched. "What?"

If he started running, she might have to trip him to give her enough time to plead her case. "Well... The boys aren't here, but you are. I feel like I should be taking advantage of that."

"By taking advantage of me?"

"I figured it would be mutual. You can't deny we're

attracted to each other. Or that we have a connection. If you do, you'd be lying."

"Do you normally proposition men in your yard?"

"Only when my milkshake brings all the boys to it." At least she didn't sing that catchy song.

"I..." He seemed to glitch again. "What?"

She laughed and shook her head. "Nothing. It was a joke that didn't come off quite as I'd hoped. This is why I'm in real estate and not on stage doing standup. Anyway... Since you're here, you might as well come inside."

"I... can't."

"Oh, you can. You just don't want to."

"No, that's the problem..." He once again pulled in a deep breath. "I want to."

At least he recognized that he was interested. She could work with that. "Then, what's stopping you?"

He stared in the direction her father disappeared.

She frowned. "My father?"

"Not afraid of him."

Liyah kept the fact that he probably should be to herself. She was damn sure he knew all about her father. The same way he knew her address.

"You're allowed to enjoy life, Nox, without feeling guilty when you do. It's not heartless, it's human and, despite how empty you feel, you *are* human. We all need time and attention from others. Since your person is no longer able to give it to you, you need to get it from someone else."

"My person?"

"Yes, it's clear that your late wife was 'your person.' What others may call a soulmate. Mark was mine."

"Was it difficult?"

"Was what difficult?"

"Moving on. Having," he jerked up a shoulder, "relationships—sexual or otherwise—with others. After."

"It took a while. I had to remind myself I wasn't cheating on Mark. Or even cheating on his memory. That was the most difficult. One night in bed, I couldn't sleep because I was missing him so damn much that my heart ached unbearably. I knew I couldn't keep going on like that. Life had turned into a chore. I wouldn't let myself have fun or open up to other people. That night it hit me... If the roles had been reversed, if it would've been me who died first... what would I have wanted Mark to do?"

Nox already knew where her speech was headed because his extremely tight jaw shifted, but that didn't stop her from continuing.

"Live. I would've wanted Mark to continue living his life to the fullest. I wasn't doing that. When Mark died, I died, too. Yes, I was still standing and breathing, functioning as best as I could, but I was dead inside. I knew I had to break free of that before Devyn was born. Did I still grieve? Of course. But I actually finished going through the stages instead of remaining stuck.

"That's not to say I still don't feel sorry for myself on occasion and wonder what our life would've been like if he was still with us. But the reality is, he isn't. He's gone and never coming back. Wallowing in my grief will never change that. But I have a different outlook now. I try to live a life that would make Mark proud. Maybe he can see that from wherever he is, maybe he can't. We don't know what's on the other side. But why not live the best life you can in the short time we have on this Earth? Because as you and I both know all too well, life can be very, very short for some of us."

With his hands on his hips, he now stared at his boots, his chest pumping after she hit him with some hard truths.

Still, she wasn't done.

"And because life is so damn short, we shouldn't waste even a minute of it."

"Is that what you think we're doing by standing out here?"

She didn't because she got to share some wisdom with him, but she didn't want to say that. She only hoped she was getting through to him.

Her heart bled for the man standing in front of her. She'd been in his shoes and knew it wasn't easy.

"My father said something to my boys earlier that stuck with me. He told them they have their whole lives ahead of them and that he didn't. He said time is ticking. He's right and we need to make the most of that time."

"By having sex."

"By going after what you want."

"You want me."

"And you want me, even if you find it difficult to admit." She curled her fingers around the T-shirt fabric at his stomach and whispered, "What could it hurt to lose yourself for a little while? I'm not asking for anything more than... you."

He finally lifted his head again. His hazel eyes were now sharp. "You see me as a project. Something broken to be fixed."

"No."

"Then what?"

"How about the simple fact I find you attractive and intriguing? And sometimes I see the smallest glimpse of the man you used to be, even though you take great pains to hide it."

"That glimpse you see... How would you know that was

162

how I was before..." He pulled in another audible breath and instead of finishing that sentence, he left it like that.

"Am I wrong?" When he didn't answer, she released a stilted laugh. "I've never worked so hard to convince a man to sleep with me. You're going to put a hurting on my self-esteem."

"Can't imagine anything would mess with your self-esteem."

"All right..." She released his shirt and took a step back. "My intention wasn't to pressure you and I don't want to do that, so... You have a nice weekend, Nox. I hope it's a peaceful one for you." It was difficult, but she managed to keep the disappointment from her tone. "Be safe."

Without waiting for a response, she turned and strode across the yard, keeping her ears open in case he called out to stop her.

He didn't.

When her father told her he was taking the kids for the weekend, she had looked forward to some alone time.

Between her family, immediate and extended, her business and the group, she rarely got time to herself unless the kids went to visit their grandparents, be it Mark's parents, her mother's home or her father's.

Unless an emergency came up at the office, she didn't plan on going in at all this weekend. Instead, she looked forward to kicking her feet up, drinking a glass or two or even a bottle of wine and watching some movies the boys refused to watch with her. Or she'd lose herself in a good book.

She wasn't going to do any chores around the house, either. This weekend was supposed to be a little staycation.

But then Nox showed up out of the blue and it made her think a change of plans were in order. Her *stay*cation could potentially turn into a *play*cation.

163

Because of her boys, she never invited men over. *Hell,* she rarely even went on dates. Jason had left a sour taste in her mouth when it came to men. Now she was extremely cautious.

Some women followed the "I don't have sex on the first date" rule. Liyah was more like, "I don't have sex on the first ten dates."

That weeded out most men.

Actually, it weeded them all out.

She loved sex. She did.

But because of the policy she set into place, she rarely got to date number eleven.

Despite his issues—which she had a good understanding of—she *liked* Nox.

He was different than the rest and, for some reason, she felt completely comfortable around him. It wasn't because of anything he said or did.

It was just how it was. She couldn't explain it.

And crazy enough, she had felt the same way the first time she met Mark.

She knew Mark was "her person" within minutes. Of course, she didn't tell him that because he probably would've thought she was crazy. Even though she was ten years younger than him, she had asked him out for a drink.

He was not only amused by her boldness but impressed. Because of that, he said yes.

The rest was history.

But Mark was now gone, and she no longer had anyone to be intimate with.

No one to share those special moments.

Or to text when she thought of something funny.

To call simply to tell him she loved him.

To bake for.

To love.

Fuck. Nox had stirred up something she thought she had gotten over.

Her loneliness.

Because she was constantly surrounded by people, the deep loneliness that came after losing your soulmate was drowned out.

After all these years, she thought she was okay.

She was not.

She needed a connection.

Not with her children. Not with her family. Not with her friends or employees.

With a man.

Someone to touch her, kiss her, whisper into her ear. Make her pussy clench, her nipples pebble, her lips part, her breathing shallow, and goosebumps to break out all over her skin. Make heat swirl through her. Cause her to moan.

Make her come.

Someone she would miss when he was gone. Content when he wasn't.

Deep down she knew that person wasn't Nox.

But that didn't mean they couldn't share a moment.

With the way he acted, she knew he hadn't had sex in at least two years. It was close to the same amount of time for her.

So, what harm would there be in enjoying each other's company? For a night? Or a few hours? Even for thirty heart-pounding minutes?

None.

It wouldn't involve deep conversations and sharing of secrets.

It would strictly be about sex.

They would both get something out of it.

And maybe it would spur him to realize there *was* life after loss.

She risked a quick glance back before she closed the door.

He was still standing next to the tree. He hadn't headed to his bike to leave. He hadn't even moved.

He only stared toward her house. At her.

His head and heart were once again warring with each other.

She had no doubt that he wanted her. Only he was trying his fucking damnedest to resist it.

He no longer needed to resist. She would make the decision easy for him.

She closed the door.

And locked it.

Chapter Fifteen

LIYAH CHEWED on her bottom lip as she pressed her back to the door. She didn't want to move until she heard the roar of his Harley while he rode away.

Only, all she heard was silence.

She was tempted to peer out and see if he still stood by the tree. However, if he could resist, so could she.

Her interest in him was a waste of time.

He didn't want help.

He didn't want to move on.

He was fine with remaining wedged between anger and depression. And maybe teetering on disbelief.

Being stuck like that for two years wasn't healthy. His brothers must recognize that, since they strong-armed him into attending weekly group meetings and therapy. But what they could not force him to do was open himself up to that help.

He preferred to protect himself by remaining closed like a goddamn pistachio nut that was impossible to open. Eventually you had to use a hammer or risk your teeth to crack it open. Or simply give up and throw it out.

She tried the hammer. Now she was throwing out that stubborn nut.

She couldn't help someone uninterested in being helped.

She couldn't even have a friendship with a man who closed himself off to others.

If she truly wanted a physical relationship with someone, she needed to accept the fact it wouldn't be Bradley Lennox.

He was lost.

And didn't want to be found.

For some reason, that not only disappointed her, it hurt.

"Aaliyah." It was not yelled through the door. It wasn't even spoken.

It was nothing but a tortured whisper.

One she never would've heard if she hadn't been leaning against the door.

Did he whisper in hopes she wouldn't hear him?

Probably. Because he was so damn unsure about what he wanted.

No.

Wrong.

The man knew what he wanted. He was only conflicted about letting himself have it.

Because of that, he made an effort that wasn't much of one. This way he could tell himself he tried to take a step forward without actually putting his foot down and taking it.

Whether he realized it or not, it *was* a step. Because he hadn't left, he stayed.

How long could she wait before he left? It would be smarter on her part if she let him do so.

Her fingers curled around the knob but didn't turn it. Instead, she hesitated.

If she opened the door, would he actually take the next step to come inside?

"Aaliyah."

Hearing her name whispered like that again cracked open her heart.

"I might regret this," she said under her breath before turning the knob and pulling open the door.

Nox leaned forward with his hands braced on either side of the door frame. His head was tipped down and it took him a few seconds to lift it.

Oh yeah, the man was fighting with himself.

Even so, she refused to mince words with this man. If he couldn't handle it, too bad. Someone needed to knock him upside the head and since he was currently standing on her porch, she guessed it was up to her.

"You hoped I wouldn't hear you. You hoped I wouldn't open the door. But I did. Now what?"

"Now you invite me in."

She couldn't deny that his deep rumble did things to areas on her body currently covered in cobwebs. "I already did."

"I figured that invitation was revoked."

She opened the door wider, stepped back and swung an arm toward the interior of her home. "You're making me think you're a vampire with needing an invitation to cross my threshold."

"I don't know shit about vampires," he grumbled as he stepped inside.

She closed the door behind him. "Yeah, well... I was on a bloodsucker kick for a few years there. Books, movies, even documentaries. I know more about them than any sane person should."

"Lock the door."

Her heartbeat sped up. "It's locked."

"Your father have a key?"

"Yes." Since having sex hadn't been on her to-do list today, should she take a quick shower and do a little maintenance?

When was the last time she shaved her legs?

Or other places?

Did she smell okay? She fought the urge to lift her arm and sniff her armpit.

Was she fresh *down there?*

Shit.

"Does he just come over unannounced?"

What? He who?

Oh, that was right. He was busy worrying about her father barging in while she was worrying about hygiene issues. "Sometimes."

"Does your bedroom door lock?"

Were they really going to do this? Or would he back out at the last second? "Of course it does. I have two male children who struggle to function without asking me fifty questions first. They can't even find their socks in their sock drawer. But funny how they have a sixth sense when it comes to their game controllers—"

"Bedroom."

Did he just bark an order at her? "What did you say?"

"Bed... room."

Well then...

He was a cop after all. She was well aware that they tended to be bossy but that didn't mean she had to like it.

She was her own boss.

And that had nothing to do with her business. She was in charge of her own destiny, despite what anyone else might think.

Apparently, Nox thought otherwise when he grabbed her wrist and plowed down the hallway.

"Do you even know where you're going?" she asked, trying to keep up. She was afraid if she stumbled, he'd keep going, dragging her in the process.

The man had apparently made up his mind.

For now.

Again, will he suddenly change it once reality hit him?

"I have no doubt you'll tell me if I'm headed in the wrong direction."

That was true.

"How big is this fucking house?"

"Pretty damn big." Even though it was two-stories, her bedroom suite was on the first floor in the rear of the house.

She loved her bedroom. It was her sanctuary, at least when her boys weren't invading it.

French doors with plantation shutters led to an oasis-like backyard consisting of a large covered patio, an outdoor kitchen and large kidney-shaped pool with a basketball net and slide for the kids.

She had purposely bought a house with a pool. Due to financial circumstances while growing up, her father never had the opportunity to take swimming lessons. She didn't want that for her boys, so she enrolled them in classes as soon as they were old enough.

After she bought the house, Magnum also learned to swim in that same pool. Even though his stubborn ass refused to take classes, between Liyah, MJ and Cait teaching him, he was now pretty decent at it. He wouldn't be competing for any gold medals, but he wouldn't drown, either. Her father and his wife also made sure Liyah's younger siblings, Asia and Caleb, were proficient at swimming.

They came over to use the pool often during the summer months.

Her little slice of heaven also included a massive bathroom with a large shower with multiple heads, a deep, jetted soaking tub and an extensive walk-in closet.

Her closet was bigger than her childhood bedroom. Every inch of it was full of designer clothes, shoes and accessories, including her impressive amount of purses.

Despite shaking his head at her self-indulgence, Magnum was proud she was as successful as she was. He had grown up poor and since Liyah's parents were only teenagers when they had her and her brother, they didn't have shit, either.

Everything she had, she worked hard to earn it. Her success hadn't been easy, but it was so damn satisfying.

She used what she received from Mark's life insurance policy as the seed money to start her real estate agency, but it wasn't until she began hiring a team was when she started making real money.

Over the years, her business continued to grow. She hoped to one day pass it on to her sons, but she wouldn't push them in that direction. It was there if they wanted it, but if their heart wasn't into it, she'd rather they not get into a career they'd eventually hate.

She loved the industry that helped people find their dream home. Nox was currently using his long damn legs to stride through hers.

Suddenly, he stopped dead. "Upstairs?"

"No, keep going."

He did.

"Make a left," she directed.

He did that, too, then charged into her room and immediately stopped again. "Damn."

One side of her mouth pulled up. "Are you going to release me?"

Once he was done taking in her bedroom, he turned, glanced at where he held her wrist and let her go. "Sorry."

"Nothing wrong with a little enthusiasm." She went over and shut the bedroom door, turning the lock. After heading over to the French doors to make sure those were also locked, she flipped the shutters closed.

Last thing she wanted was to be buck naked in bed with a cop and have her father press his face to the glass wondering what she was doing.

The only thing worse would be her sons seeing their mother doing the "deed."

She'd have to pay for a lifetime's worth of therapy. Times two.

It was much cheaper to close the shutters.

When she turned, she found that Nox had moved so quietly, he now stood right behind her.

His baseball cap was still pulled low on his head and, despite still being fully dressed, she had no difficulty noticing the miniature baseball bat making an impression against his jeans.

Her father believed that white men had smaller penises. From what she could see so far, Nox was going to blow away that ridiculous myth.

However, she wouldn't judge his size until she could see it for herself.

Not that size mattered. For the most part it didn't. A man with a small cock with some wicked skills was a much better sex partner than one with a decent size unable to get the job done.

"Turn around."

"Why?"

He repeated out the order again. "Turn around."

She pursed her lips and stared at him. She wasn't sure she liked this bossy shit.

However, here was her dilemma... She really didn't think they'd get far enough to actually have sex, anyway. She expected him to bail before that.

Guilt would weigh heavily on him, and he'd have a change of heart. Then he'd be running for the door.

She worried if she took her eyes off him, that could happen sooner than later. She still might have the harness and leash she used on Keenan when he was a toddler and was always bolting away from her. She got tired of chasing him.

Using that get-up on Nox was extremely tempting.

"Are you having second thoughts?"

He was asking *her* that? She bit back a burst of hysterical laughter.

She raised both eyebrows at him and slowly turned to face the French doors.

Oh yes, she was glad she closed the shutters.

"Hands on the door frame."

"What are you going to do? Frisk me? I'm not hiding any weapons."

"You sure?"

Whoa.

"Hands on the door frame."

"But, officer..."

"I wasn't planning on frisking you, Liyah. But if you're into that..."

Wait, she had to unpack what he just said. First of all... "Did you actually ask a Black woman if she's into being frisked?"

"You brought it up, not me."

True. She couldn't argue with that. With a sigh, she

planted a hand on each door, careful to avoid the glass panes and the wood shutters. "Just a warning... I hadn't planned on anyone seeing me naked, so—"

"No one's getting naked."

They weren't? "What are we doing, then?"

"Apparently, having a conversation. You like to talk, don't you?"

"Last I checked, it's a form of communication and the easiest one once you're over a year old." A rush of breath moved the hair on her neck, sending a shiver through her and making her nipples stand at attention. "There *are* ways to stop me from talking..."

"A gag?"

She didn't bother to fight her grin, since she was turned away from him. He definitely had a sense of humor somewhere inside him. It gave her some hope that all was not lost when it came to Bradley Lennox. His true self only needed to be coaxed out from wherever it was buried.

She jerked when his knuckles slowly brushed down the side of her neck. She tipped her head to the side to give him better access. Unfortunately, she was too late, since his touch was there and gone in a flash.

Or so she thought.

His knuckles grazed along her jawline next before quickly disappearing.

Holding her hair to the side, his very short nails skimmed down the back of her neck. His long, warm fingers then curled around to the front of her throat, where they remained for a few seconds before moving on to explore the hollow of her throat and the length of each collarbone.

His touch reminded her of an artist using a paint brush. Long, smooth strokes followed the lines and curves of his human canvas.

He was not rough, but gentle, as his fingers continued to whisper along her skin causing more goosebumps to break out. She didn't bother to contain her shivers or her ragged breath. She wanted him to be fully aware of what his touch was doing to her. The same as him making her fully aware of every spot he touched.

Stepping closer, he pressed his hard-on into her ass. Skipping her breasts entirely, he slid his palm down her belly and breathed her name into her ear. "Aaliyah."

Holy shit. She could listen to him say her name like that all damn day. All night, too.

Who was this freaking man?

Certainly not the same man she met that first night at group.

Or the second night.

Or even at the coffee shop.

This was the real Bradley Lennox. The one he kept locked away.

He squeezed her hips and pressed his soft lips to her shoulder, causing another shiver to shoot through her. When she reached behind them to curl her hand around the back of his head, she realized somewhere along the way, he'd gotten rid of his hat. She brushed her fingers over hair not long enough for her to get a good grip.

Just when she thought he was continuing on to the apex of her legs, he reversed course and circled his arms around her waist and pressed himself from chest to cock along her back.

He had totally avoided the areas she wanted him to touch the most. "You missed the best hiding spots, officer. You might need to do a strip search."

Holy shit, did she sound breathless, or what? They hadn't even kissed yet and she was melting simply from his touch.

Was it because of him or because she was that desperate? Or both?

It didn't matter. What mattered was, he hadn't run scared... yet. She mentally prepared for it so she wouldn't take it as a personal slight.

"You have condoms?"

She nodded. "*Mmm hmm.*"

"Where?"

"In the bathroom closet, behind a stack of towels." Hopefully they weren't expired. Or covered in cobwebs like her vital parts that were now pulsing from his attention.

"Why there?"

"It's so I don't have to explain..." She shook her head. "It doesn't matter. I'll grab them."

When she tried to pull free, his arms tightened around her. "No. Stay here. I'll get them."

Normally she wouldn't let some stranger go through her closet, but Nox wasn't quite a stranger at this point. And she didn't want to get into a discussion about why she didn't let anyone go through her things. She didn't want to give him any kind of opening to leave.

He peeled her hand from the back of his head and planted it on the door frame. "Don't move," he demanded.

With a sexy as hell, rumbling cop voice like that, she wasn't planning on going anywhere.

Chapter Sixteen

SHE WAITED IMPATIENTLY while listening to him rustle around her bathroom and dig through the closet.

She should've expected that he didn't carry condoms in his wallet since it was a safe bet that he hadn't had sex since his wife died. Before that, he was married and most likely had no reason to wear them.

"Check the date on the box," she called out, then whispered, "it's been a while."

Did he grunt an answer?

Good thing she was fluent in grunt-speak because of not only her father, but from being around the rest of the Dark Knights, as well as the Dirty Angels.

She jumped when he said right behind her, "They're good."

"How the hell do you walk so quietly when wearing boots?" She rolled her eyes when he grunted again. "Words are crucial in communication."

"Here are some words for you," he said dryly, "no one would ever doubt you're a mother."

"I can't help it. Sometimes you're as frustrating as my sons."

"Can we not mention your kids right now?"

Probably a good idea, considering the circumstances. She added her father to that list.

Okay, so he now had both intent and condoms. The next step would be them getting naked. Right?

Wrong.

While she half-expected him to bark out an order for her to get undressed, he didn't. Instead, he encircled his arms around her waist again.

In a sliver of glass not quite covered completely by the shutters, she could see the condom tucked between his teeth.

She was really going to be disappointed if, after not having sex for so damn long, her first time back in the game, he skipped the foreplay.

The hug was nice, but...

Oh, never mind. She shouldn't be rushing the process...

The shorts she wore had an elastic waistband, making it easy for him to push those and her panties down far enough until they could drop to her feet on their own.

With one hand cupping her throbbing mound, his other slipped under her baggy T-shirt. The heat of his palm practically seared the skin on her stomach as he slowly pushed the shirt up... up... up... until he reached her bra.

She'd admit that her sturdy bra was a fortress not easy to breach since she was naturally large. Having kids only made them bigger and heavier. And of course, droop more than when she was eighteen. They also tended to be annoying, but not enough to get a breast reduction.

Nox took the easy path and managed to free her breasts by simply shoving her bra up and over them. It wasn't the most comfortable for her, but it got the job done.

He continued to get it done by giving her mound a squeeze, then releasing it to cup both her breasts and test their weight. He kneaded them with his strong, firm fingers.

Yes, yes, yes! That was more like it.

She dropped her head back until it rested on his collarbone. "Nox..."

She realized he couldn't answer because of the condom still held between his teeth. Or at least, he couldn't answer with words, but actions, on the other hand...

When he tugged and pulled on her nipples, she swore there was an invisible line directly connected from where he was touching to her clenching pussy. Every tweak and twist caused her to become even wetter.

Not to mention, more eager to have sex with the man behind her.

Since she was now at the point where she'd be extremely disappointed if he bolted, she needed to move this along so he would be past the point where that might happen.

Because if he ran now, she'd chase him down and tackle him. Her neighbors might get an eyeful, but, *hey,* they'd deserve it for not minding their own damn business.

Pulling one of his hands free, she slapped it back on her mound. Her breasts and nipples weren't her only parts needing attention.

A loud, relieved sigh escaped her when he finally slipped a finger between her slick folds and stroked her gently.

Unfortunately, it still wasn't enough for her. He was being too gentle. Too tentative. Like he was working his way back into the groove.

He very well might be.

She'd give him some leeway, but... "Can we move to the bed?"

When she heard a muffled, "No," it made her suck in a breath to keep her patience.

Damn. It hit her then, why he didn't want to move to the bed and wanted her to face the door. He didn't want her to face *him.*

This moment was a major step for him, and she understood why he wouldn't want to look her in the eyes while taking it.

Making eye contact during sex was a very intimate action, so she shouldn't take it as a personal insult. How he was handling this wasn't because of her but because of himself. It might be the only way he could get through it.

This time he'd be "breaking the seal." Maybe next time he had sex, it would be easier for him.

The next, even easier. Until he could be intimate with a woman without guilt weighing him down or making him question his choices.

When she thought back, she realized it had taken over three years after Mark died before she even considered accepting a date. Even longer before she had sex with anyone.

Then, she met Jason...

Fuck Jason. He didn't even deserve a thought. That asshole wasn't in the room with her, Nox was.

Of course, thinking about Jason made her more determined than ever to avoid accidentally getting pregnant during this encounter. Even though she was on birth control, she should have him wrap it twice to be safe...

She really didn't want to raise three kids on her own...

"Liyah..."

She shook herself mentally. "Yes?"

"Am I hurting you?"

"No?" Why would he think that?

"You're tense."

She needed to get out of her head. To do that, he needed to get busy. "What happened to the condom?"

"Tucked it in my pocket so I can concentrate on you."

Well, then...

"Hands back on the door."

Okay, fine. She'd play.

With both hands back on the door, she closed her eyes and let him sweep her out of her own head and wandering thoughts.

He pressed his lips to the side of her neck, twisted a nipple and without any fanfare, slid two fingers inside of her.

Oh, yesssss, she'd definitely play.

Thick, long fingers plunged in and out of her as he sucked on her skin.

"Nox," she breathed.

"You really need to talk right now?" he murmured against her neck.

No, she didn't. She zipped her lips shut.

Well, not really. What he was doing to her was making her pant a little and she needed her mouth open for that.

He might be a little rusty but, *damn,* the man was quickly proving he knew what he was doing. The more he played with her clit and fucked her with his fingers, the more her thighs quivered. She had to lock her knees to prevent them from giving out.

Because, *holy shit,* she was about to come.

That quickly. That easily.

Her orgasm turned out not to be an explosion that rocked her, but rather a nice, easy one that rolled through her, curling her toes and causing her to moan in satisfaction.

And when she did, his rock-hard cock thrusted against her.

He had to be uncomfortable.

Most other men would've had their pants dropped down around their ankles by now. But from the moment she met him, Nox was proving not to be "most" men.

That was most likely the reason he still mourned his late wife. The man could be intense and that led her to believe he loved intensely, too. Intense enough that his wife's loss hadn't left a mark, but a deep, gaping wound instead.

Even so, he needed to let it heal enough to scar over. And that scar would be a reminder of what used to be...

A love gone but never forgotten.

Liyah had her own scars. One she cherished. One she regretted.

She'd like to avoid a third.

When he slipped his fingers from her, she lifted her head from where it rested against his shoulder. As his hand disappeared behind her, she noticed his digits were shiny from her response to his attention.

What was he going to do? Wipe them on his pants?

Her motherly instinct kicked in and she turned her head only to find him sucking on the same fingers that had been inside her.

Damn, if that didn't make her pulse race and her pussy clench all over again.

Watching him finish sucking his fingers clean, she recognized the indisputable fact, while the cop was hot in a baseball cap, he was even hotter without one. Since he also had a full head of hair, it proved he didn't wear that hat to hide a bald spot, he used it to simply hide.

"Nox, can we move to the bed now?"

"Face the door, Liyah."

She both hated and loved when this man gave her orders. On one hand, it annoyed her, on the other, it turned her on.

Obviously, she was very confused, so she shouldn't even bother to try to make sense of it.

With a slight shake of her head, she faced the door again.

When he stepped back, she heard his belt being unfastened and the sound of his zipper. The slide of denim along his skin. The tear of the foil condom wrapper.

"I thought you were kidding when you said no one was getting naked."

With another answering grunt, his heat was once again at her back.

He clamped a hand on her hip and tugged. "Tip your ass up."

She was A-okay with that particular demand.

She shivered when he pulled the back of her shirt higher to completely expose her bare ass.

Should she worry about what it looked like? Cellulite, stretch marks, the list could be endless...

Hell, did she remember to lotion this morning?

Or... should she simply not care?

Really, it was out of her control. Either he liked how she looked or he didn't.

She could be wrong, but he didn't seem to be the type to nitpick over a little extra weight, loose skin, or even scars.

The truth was, nobody should judge unless they were perfect themselves.

Obviously, Nox was far from perfect. Though, she wouldn't mind seeing him naked so she could do her own thorough assessment.

Unfortunately, that wasn't going to happen—today, anyway—since the man was determined to have sex with her while standing up, with her facing away from him and by only dropping his jeans far enough to whip out his cock.

While in contrast, she was naked from the waist down and her breasts hung free.

Not fair.

But at least she was getting some action, right? And from a man who was fine as hell.

Awkward or not, doing this today might lead to more sex with him in the future. The next time might not be as awkward, on an actual bed and when she wouldn't be worried he'd get spooked and sprint for the exit.

Normally, she'd say this was a baby step. But for Nox, it had to be huge.

While she needed patience and understanding, she also needed his cock. What was he waiting for?

Ohhhh. That.

His hand skimmed over one ass cheek before doing the same on the other. His touch was feather-like until he grabbed a cheek and squeezed. Hard.

Slipping a hand between her legs, he once again tested her wetness.

She could confirm, she was ready for him to proceed.

He withdrew his hand to draw the head of his cock down through her crease before reversing course and sliding it back up.

His scorching temperature radiated against her skin, even where they didn't have direct contact. He was burning up and she was burning up for him.

Having sex would either help him move forward or hurtle him back down into his dark space, where he retreated to feel safe. Time would tell if this would help or hinder him.

"Ready?" His gruff voice shot a shiver through her.

Oh hell yes, she was ready. She nodded to let him know, even though it was unneeded.

"It's been a while," he said softly.

"It has."

"I meant for me."

"You're in good company."

He stilled behind her. "You haven't been... dating?"

Was "dating" his alternative way of saying "fucking?" Because she hadn't been doing either.

"Who has time for that?" she half-joked.

Not only did she not have the time, she didn't have the mental energy to deal with a dating scene that consisted of slogging through lumps of coal to find an elusive diamond.

Plus, after Jason, she now looked at all men with tinted glasses. And that tint was far from rose colored. It would take a lot for her to ever trust a man enough to give him her heart.

Not only that, but she wasn't one to have sex with a random stranger.

She glanced at the man she didn't know very well standing behind her with his cock in his hand.

At least Nox wasn't random. Or a complete stranger.

That was her story, and she was sticking to it. Sometimes a girl had to do what a girl had to do.

And she was about to "do" Nox.

"You didn't need to warn me. I figured."

"I don't want to disappoint you," he whispered.

"I'm only disappointed that you're taking so long to—"

Chapter Seventeen

WITH ONE HAND on her hip and the other grabbing her shoulder, he drove into her hard, causing her to jerk forward and eat the rest of her words. She braced her arms so he didn't smash her face into the door with how hard he was thrusting.

She adapted quickly to his thickness. He was definitely the perfect size to clean out her cobwebs.

She forgot how good it felt to have a man fill her completely. While her toys got the job done, using them was not quite the same as sharing mutual satisfaction with another person. Of her choosing, that was.

Nox was definitely that.

Intimacy was lacking when she only used a vibrator. With Nox, all her senses were being utilized.

Well, except for taste. They hadn't kissed yet. And she wasn't sure if they would, given the circumstances. She hadn't even touched her lips to his skin like he had with her. But as for the rest...

Her ears picked up his harsh breathing and the sound of

their skin slapping together. Her nose got a whiff of his heady masculine scent, as well as the aroma of her own arousal. And as for her eyes... She glanced down at his hand between her legs.

For the moment, he had taken possession and claimed her pussy as his.

She'd rather him be more forceful than tentative.

She wasn't breakable. She was horny. Along with a dash of impatient. "Nox, you're not going to hurt me. Don't hold back."

After answering with another deep grunt, she felt a switch, and something break free inside him.

He was no longer tentative. No longer cautious. He was finally caught up in the moment and with what they were doing.

And what they were doing was worth everything that had come before. Her frustration with him began to wane while her hope increased.

As he continued to thrust forcefully, he alternated pinching, circling and flicking her clit. Occasionally his long fingers would brush where they were intimately joined. He would use the wetness he gathered there to lube her clit before going at it even more intensely.

She was about to encourage him to continue the way he was but caught his reflection in the sliver of glass.

Were his eyes closed? Was he pretending she was someone else?

Should she be offended if he was?

Short answer: no.

The longer answer: If it helped him moved forward, she was fine with it. Grief was a clingy beast, and you could only move past it when ready. No matter how much everyone around you wanted differently.

Some needed a slight push. Some a powerful shove.

But either method didn't always work.

Just enjoy the moment, Liyah. Don't sweat over the rest right now. You'll have plenty of time later to worry whether this will end up being a step forward or a step backward for Nox. He wouldn't be doing this if he didn't want to.

He's responsible for his own mental health. Not you. Not his brothers. No one else.

The man's hip action did not let up even for a second. Every powerful pump was now accompanied by a hiss of breath.

As his cock continued to piston in and out of her, she had to be soaking him because her inner thighs had become slick.

She originally thought she wouldn't be able to come in this position, but she was wrong. And she was only wrong because Nox was determined to make her orgasm again.

Good thing she was just as determined.

This wasn't ending until she had a second one.

She'd also be perfectly fine with a third, but she wasn't pushing her luck.

As he continued to spear her over and over with his cock, he pulled an unexpected move. He slid his middle finger through her folds and plunged it inside her, causing an odd sensation and for her to stretch around him even further. She never had anyone do that to her before.

She certainly wasn't complaining, and she was always game to try new things.

With Nox's right arm pinned across her chest, he grabbed her left breast and rolled the aching nipple between his fingers before pinching it hard enough to make her cry out. Not for him to stop, but to do it again.

When he did, his cock thickened even more inside her and his pace turned more erratic. With not having had sex in so long, his stamina was actually impressive, but he had to be getting close.

Everything in and on her was now quivering as her own release got within reach.

Slipping his finger from inside her and releasing her nipple, he grabbed her hips with both hands and slammed his against her over and over. Driving her to that sweet edge of total abandonment.

With her heart trying to burst from her chest, she had a difficult time pulling in her next breath as her lungs seized and her muscles locked. Not even a second later, an orgasm ripped through her that was so intense, it knocked her for a loop.

Yes.

Yes.

Yes!

"Nox!"

He didn't falter at his name being yelled, but instead dug deep and continued to drive into her, almost desperately. His soft grunts vibrated against her neck where he'd hidden his face. His warm, ragged breath beat a pattern against her skin.

With one last deep thrust, he stiffened against her, his cock pulsed and pulled a little aftershock from her as he came.

When they both stilled, he pressed his damp forehead to her shoulder and her thoughts became as loud as their breathing.

He did it. He didn't run. He stayed and persevered.

He even got her to the point of orgasm without much effort. That meant if he really put in the work, sex with him would be some of the best she ever had.

That made her more determined than ever to have sex with him again.

In a bed.

Facing him. Kissing him. Exploring him with her eyes, mouth and hands.

Making it more of a two-person sport.

More than a hurdle for him to overcome.

And while she was proud and hopeful that he had taken this step, she wouldn't be surprised if his thoughts were spinning, too. He was most likely coming up with an escape plan.

One she wouldn't take as an insult.

WHAT THE FUCK did he just do?

He swore this woman would be his undoing. She pulled him in in a way he couldn't explain.

But why her?

What was it about Aaliyah that drew him? And why couldn't he resist?

She was outspoken and pushy. Stubborn and, without a doubt, could easily outsmart him. If he let her.

Every time he tried to expel her from his thoughts, he failed.

He said he wasn't going back to the group's weekly meetings. That would turn out to be a lie. He already accepted defeat on that front.

But that wasn't what was eating at him...

He just had sex with a woman who wasn't his wife.

Just had sex with a woman he didn't know very well.

He. Just. Had. Sex.

It had been so long...

Too damn long.

Despite that, how could he want another woman as much as his wife?

That pull he couldn't explain... It was the same as when he met Jackie.

That realization sent a bolt of fear and confusion through him.

He didn't understand the unmistakable pull then. He didn't understand it now.

Back then he didn't question it. He didn't fight it.

Now he did. *For fuck's sake*, he had no choice but to fight it. Ignore it. Pretend it didn't exist.

Because the truth was, Aaliyah wasn't for him.

No woman was.

He couldn't risk making a connection again like he had with Jackie.

As the panic rose, he pulled in a breath and caught Liyah's unique, subtle scent. Whatever she wore. Her lotion or a perfume. Maybe her soap.

Mixed with her arousal.

From her orgasm.

No, *orgasms*. She had more than one.

Even as awkward as this whole thing had been, she managed to find some satisfaction. However, he was damn well sure she was still disappointed.

As was he.

Not only for his less than stellar performance, but in himself.

For not being strong enough to resist.

For wanting this woman as much as he did.

Gritting his teeth, he secured the condom at the root of his cock and pulled out. He kept his head down as he removed the prophylactic and yanked up his jeans to secure his cock.

"Going to clean up," he muttered and spun on his boot heel. Striding across the room, he paused only to snag his hat from where it fell before continuing into her bathroom and shutting the door behind him.

He tossed the spent condom into the trash and turned to use the sink...

Only to be met by someone he didn't recognize.

"What the fuck just happened?" he asked.

That stranger didn't answer.

He set his jaw and washed his hands, unable to look that person in the eyes.

He couldn't face the judgement.

He also avoided Aaliyah's when he left the bathroom.

Instead, he simply grumbled, "Gotta go," and rushed out of the room, not waiting to hear her response.

Like a goddamn coward.

Because that was who he was.

A goddamn broken coward.

The hallway had become a narrow tunnel funneling him toward the exit.

He saw nothing around him except his escape.

The burn in his chest spread to his gut.

It wasn't heartburn.

It was guilt.

He was unable to get rid of that burn by swallowing and choked on it, instead.

He burst out of the door and down her porch with his eyes glued to his bike.

His means of escape.

After straddling it, he didn't look up because he was afraid she'd be standing in the doorway.

If he saw her there, he might go back inside.

And he shouldn't. He couldn't.

He didn't belong at this house.

He didn't belong with her.

This couldn't happen again.

He needed to go. Get the fuck out of there because he wouldn't put it past Aaliyah to chase him down.

To make him face whatever he was feeling.

He needed to leave before she stopped him.

Only, he had one thing to do first.

Slipping his cell phone from his pocket, he pulled up his message app, and added one more text to the long string.

I made a mistake. I'm sorry.

Chapter Eighteen

THE HOUSE HAD BEEN EERILY quiet after Nox rushed out like that pesky ghost had been chasing him. So quiet that she considered heading into the office on Saturday to be around people who valued her. People other than her family, that was.

Instead, she stayed home and took advantage of her empty house by blasting some classic rock while cooking and baking. All without any interruptions or having to smack grabby, grubby fingers when they tried to steal food.

She even managed to meal prep lunches and dinners for the week ahead. For both the boys and herself.

She kept herself so busy in the kitchen, she no longer had room in the fridge and freezer to store anything more.

For now.

The second the bottomless pits walked through the door, they would head directly to the kitchen, then sniff out and eat half of what was supposed to last all week. Her own stomach hurt simply remembering Devyn inhaling a large meat-lovers pizza all by himself a few weeks ago.

Like it had been a damn snack.

Her hips and ass would be twice their size if she ate like that. That was, if she didn't throw up first.

Of course, she hadn't heard from the elusive Nox since he'd sprinted out her door. But then, she didn't reach out to him, either. She figured she'd give him time to process what occurred. And to forgive himself for whatever sin he thought he committed. Most likely the sin of cheating on a memory.

The quiet weekend quickly came to an end when she heard the roar of Harley straight pipes pulling in her driveway.

She frowned. It was hours earlier than they were expected. Even though she didn't get a call or text first, something had to be wrong.

She rushed to the front door and flung it open to see two bad-ass Harleys instead of one. She groaned at who was straddling that second bike.

Romeo.

The Dark Knights' president.

And the MC's resident horn-dog.

If a woman was wearing pants, he'd do everything in his power to get down them. If she was wearing a skirt, he'd turn on the charm to get up it.

Hence his road name.

The man didn't stick with a woman for more than the time it took to pull his jeans down, stick his dick in, shoot his load and pull his jeans back up.

For Romeo, that was a long-term relationship.

The man thought he was "all that" and a bag of fucking chips.

A bag of chips filled with mostly air.

She sighed as she slipped her feet into the flip flops she kept near the front door and headed out to greet her sons.

And those other two.

Tweedle-Do and Tweedle-Don't.

She had her invisible flirt-resistant armor locked in place by the time she reached the testosterone-filled driveway.

"Hey, Ali-Cat," Romeo purred with his deep brown eyes raking over her from head to toe.

She gave him the "palm" and a sharp, "No."

Now she needed another shower.

He raised his eyebrows and donned a faux hurt expression. "Only sayin' *hey*."

"*Mmm hmm*. Not interested, Romeo. Sniff elsewhere."

"But you smell so damn good."

Her eyes flicked to Devyn. Her oldest was grinning. She really didn't want Romeo rubbing off on him. She wasn't thrilled that he'd been on the back of Romeo's bike, either.

She glanced at her father. Magnum knew all of that and masked his own expression.

She shook her head. "Boys, go in the house. I need to speak with Grumpa."

Romeo snorted whenever she called Magnum that.

"But, Mom—"

"No lip. Get inside like your momma told you," Magnum grumbled at Keenan.

Her youngest's face twisted and he dragged his feet all the way into the house.

"You, too," Liyah told her oldest when he continued to stand next to a man he should not be emulating.

"See ya, Rome, Grumps."

Romeo shot Devyn a huge grin and gave him a two-finger salute. "Got a prospect cut ready for you. Just don't grow too much more or it won't fit."

"Devyn..."

"I'm going, Mom!" he yelled and jogged to the house.

Once both boys were inside and the door shut behind them, she turned to face Magnum. "Had to bring backup, didn't you? Just in case my visitor was still here? I also noticed that you brought them back earlier than normal."

Her father wanted to catch Nox still at the house.

"Just wanted the fucker to know who's got your back."

"He's not a fucker and he already knows you're protective of me, Dad. Anyway, I don't think he's afraid of you. And for the millionth time, I'll remind you that I'm almost forty and not a teenager only starting to date."

"So, you're fuckin' datin' him," Magnum growled.

"No, I'm not. He stopped by to drop off that container."

"That takes a fuckin' minute. The fucker was still hangin' around when I left."

"He sure was."

"Who you got doin' you, woman?" Romeo asked. "Whoever it is, I can do better."

"No, you can't."

"You give me a chance, I'll fuckin' prove it to you." Romeo wiggled his eyebrows.

"You can keep your cold sores and crabs to yourself, thank you very much."

Liyah stifled a laugh at seeing his indignant expression.

"Don't got crabs or cold sores."

"Maybe not today. Tomorrow's another story."

"Man, Ali-Cat, you're always playin' hard to get."

She ignored him and leaned in to plant a kiss on her father's cheek. "Thanks for taking the boys this weekend."

"Romeo's interested," Magnum mumbled as she pulled away.

Liyah rolled her eyes and shook her head. She turned to give Romeo her back and kept her voice low. "Romeo is interested in every woman. Period. And I can't believe you're encouraging me to hook up with him. Forget the fact that he's the president of the Knights, he's a damn dog who sniffs every hydrant. He's not selective. Or loyal. And as you well know, I already had one man skip out on me."

The man in question probably heard everything she just said, but none of it was a lie. So, he could simply deal with it.

"Somethin' wrong with bikers?" her father asked, even though he already knew her answer since this wasn't the first time this conversation had come up.

"Yes. A lot of things. Do you want me to start listing them?"

"Lotta shit right with us, too."

For her, the cons outweighed the pros. "Anyway, thanks for your concern with my love life and my safety. It's unneeded when it comes to Nox."

"Nox," Magnum growled. "What's the rest of his fuckin' name?"

Shit. "It doesn't matter. I doubt he'll be returning any more containers."

"But he's in that damn group of yours, so you'll be seein' him again."

She shrugged. "Maybe."

"Liyah, want the truth. He a pig?"

"He's a human, Dad. And you know how I feel about you calling cops that. I asked you not to do that around the boys."

"Boys ain't out here. And your fuckin' answer is makin' me think he is."

She looked directly into his eyes and said slowly and carefully, "Whether he is or isn't doesn't matter. We are *not* dating. We're not anything. Got it?"

Magnum grunted.

She jerked when Romeo came up and dropped his arm around her shoulders, turned his cheek toward her and tapped it. "Me next."

Liyah grimaced and pulled away. "Not going to happen."

"Then a hug."

"No."

"Why don't you like me?"

"I like you plenty, Romeo. But I don't want you in my *business*, if you get what I'm saying."

"Bet I got a bigger dick than the white boy Mag said was here the other day."

"I don't care if you do."

Romeo reached for his belt. "Lemme show you."

She turned to Magnum. "Dad..."

"Rome, knock it the fuck off. You ain't gonna whip out your fuckin' dick in front of my baby girl."

Romeo grinned. "Just tryin' to make my case, brother."

"She don't need visual proof. I don't, either. Keep your dick in your pants."

Liyah shot Romeo a smile. "Your sergeant at arms has spoken."

"And I outrank him."

"Not over me, you don't," she reminded the DKMC president.

"Next time," he murmured.

"No," she said. "All right, I'm sure they're putting a dent in all the food that's supposed to last for the next week, so I need to go inside."

She headed for the house and stopped on the porch. "Dad," she called out.

He paused before starting his sled and glanced over at her.

"Thanks for taking the boys this weekend. I love you."

He gave her a chin life, and his Harley roared to life.

She waited until both bikes disappeared down the street. Then with a shake of her head and a sigh loud enough for the neighbors to hear, she turned to go inside and hear all about her sons' weekend.

Chapter Nineteen

"HEADS UP, I think the Russos caught wind of the Demons' dick move of cutting them out."

Nox's head twisted to see Crew bursting through the door to the third floor of The Plant.

"What the fuck? Already?" Finn asked. "Not good."

"Yeah. Just got a call from Fletch. He thinks the Pittsburgh Mafia has someone planted in the club."

"Holy shit," Torres grumbled the same as what Nox was thinking. "That could get messy."

Decker spun his chair around. "Messy. Bloody. A whole shitload of things."

"*Let the bikers hit the floor...*" Finn sang, changing the familiar song's lyrics to fit the situation.

A chorus of groans rose since Finn thought he was an expert singer when that was the farthest from the truth. The man got an A for effort, but an F for execution.

Nox's brow furrowed. "How the fuck is a Sicilian fitting in with that MC?" Most—if not all—of those bikers were pasty white. He was surprised that someone olive-skinned would pass the Demons' scratch and sniff test.

"Not sure if he's Sicilian," Crew answered. "He could be half or none at all. They could be paying some random asshole off the street to be their eyes and ears."

"Right. He could be some druggie they're paying with meth," Cabrera suggested from across the room.

"Doubt that," Decker told her. "Meth-heads are unreliable. They'd want someone able to pay attention and report back all the little details. They're either paying this dude in cold, hard cash or he's one of their goons. Sicilian or not."

"Did Fletch sneak a photo so we know which one he is?" Torres asked. "If we know what he looks like, we can scan the footage to see how long he's been around and if he looks sketchy."

"He texted it to me," Crew answered. "The pic sucks and is a bit grainy since he had to do it on the down low. I'll email it to everyone on the team, so you all have it. Torres, if anyone spots him on video, maybe snag a few still shots if they're clear, so we have something to tack up on the board with the rest of them."

Cabrera snagged the keys to one of the pool cars off the hook. "All right, I'm off to go sling some drinks and dodge some sticky fingers at Hawg Wild."

"I'll walk you out," Crew announced.

Nox shared a glance with Finn. One side of his redheaded brother's mouth pulled up. Then he made an "O" with his fingers on one hand and plunged his index finger from the other in and out several times in the universally known hand motion for fucking.

As soon as the door shut behind Camilla Cabrera and the task force leader, none of them bothered to be quiet about it.

"They're fucking, aren't they?" Torres asked.

"My guess," Nox answered.

"Of course they are," Finn agreed. "Don't you notice how tense he gets around her sometimes? Like he's working hard not to say the wrong thing around us? Something that'll give away that Cabrera has seen his tiny pickle?"

Decker laugh-snorted. "He's also struggling not to touch her in front of us. He knows he'll be flayed open if he does."

"If he *is* doing her, her father being one of the top dogs at the DEA must keep him puckered twenty-four-seven," Finn said.

"No doubt," Torres answered. "You couldn't pay me enough to touch one of the top brass's daughters."

"Good call since you're married," Nox reminded him.

Torres huffed, "I meant if I wasn't, Fort Nox. In fact, I'd have more than a puckered asshole. I'd have heartburn, indigestion and diarrhea."

"You sound like a candidate for Pepto Bismol," Finn laughed. "Should I sing the jingle?"

As he opened his mouth to belt it out, everyone yelled, "NO!" in unison.

Nox's mouth twisted into a half-grin.

"You don't sing to Mel, do you?" Torres asked.

"Every night," Finn boasted and puffed out his chest.

"And she hasn't smothered you with a pillow yet?" Decker asked.

"Guess not, since I'm sitting here still breathing."

"Damn shame," Torres muttered.

When Crew came back through the door, his eyes held a gleam. He looked as guilty as fuck.

They all made kissing noises.

"Fuck off," he growled.

"You never walk me to my car," Finn complained.

"Anyway, back to business," Crew started.

"Speaking of business... You're giving it to her, aren't you?" Finn pounded his fist into his palm. "You can tell us. We promise not to tell anyone else. It'll be our little secret."

Crew released a loud sigh.

"Why don't we have security cameras around this place?" Torres wore a mischievous smile.

"Because it would come out of the MC's funds and the club's account is still at rock bottom after refurbing this building. We can barely scrape together enough money every month to keep the damn lights on and the water running. *That's* why we don't have fucking security cameras. And you only want them to spy," Crew accused Torres.

"Of course. We all do. Right?"

"Yep," Finn answered. "We want to see you sucking face with our newest member."

"I don't suck face," Crew muttered.

"Suck dick?"

"Why are you such a fucking child, Pippi?" Of course Crew had to add a childish nickname to his accusation.

"Nothing wrong with being young at heart." Finn blinded everyone with a huge smile.

"Anyway, on a more serious note... After Fletch's call, I'm now wondering if they have anyone installed in the other chapters."

"I wouldn't put it past them. La Cosa Nostra tends to be paranoid. I highly doubt they ever trusted an outlaw MC named the Deadly Demons," Decker said. "Those two organizations aren't best buddies, they're business partners. Lots of business partners end up shafting the other."

"All for the mighty dollar," Nox mumbled.

"So, what's our next step?" Finn asked. "How do we prepare for the fallout, J. Crew? Because we all know the Russos aren't going to simply let it go."

"I'll let the AUSA know that they need to hurry the fuck up with these goddamn indictments."

Torres blew out a breath. "Won't happen. I have a feeling they plan on hitting the Demons with RICO charges. For that, a grand jury will take a while. Then add on trial time with endless ridiculous motions to dismiss or delay. With dozens of defendants, it'll also take finesse and top-notch organizational skills."

"You know Pam's got the skills to keep shit organized, Torres," Crew told him, "but time is the issue none of us can control. Not only do we want the grand jury to indict every one of those fuckers—or at least enough of them to scorch the MC to the ground—we want those charges to stick when it comes to the trials. Hell, we need the indictments to *make* it to trial."

Decker nodded. "I doubt any of them will flip, either. They know that would be a death sentence."

"True that," Finn muttered. "And I agree... Time will not be our friend on this. What happens if shit hits the fan before the teams can go in and sweep them all up?"

Crew frowned. "Then we wait until the dust settles and see who's left."

"It'll be a bloodbath," Nox grumbled.

Decker shrugged. "No loss."

Nox agreed. Those Demons needed to be removed from society in one way or another. It would really be a damn shame if it was a permanent removal.

"How much will the taxpayers save if the AUSA drags her feet, the Russos massacre that whole damn club and then the feds concentrate on taking down La Cosa Nostra instead?" Finn asked.

"If that happens," Crew began, "less Sicilians will be strutting around Pittsburgh, too, since the Demons will fight back. The problem comes in with innocent bystanders getting caught in the crossfire."

"Yeah, that wouldn't be good," Nox said. "Law enforcement already has enough black marks, we don't need more."

"A-fucking-men," Torres muttered.

"Yeah, well... Doesn't matter what we do, someone is always going to hate us. Some for valid reasons, some not. We still need to do our job," Crew said. "All right, so I'll email that crappy photo and if you get a better one, let me know, Torres. And I'll give the other group leaders a heads up about the Russos possibly having plants among the Demons."

"Sounds like a plan, Stan," Torres joked.

As soon as Nox got the photo from Crew of the planted "prospect," he took a good look at it and then began to scan footage from the Wolf Den, the Demons' Uniontown clubhouse.

He saw the hidden camera got plenty of shots of Fletch and Wilder hanging out there, since "Ghost" had been patched over along with his ol' lady "Kitten" into the Demons from the Angels. They didn't hide from the cameras, but the possible Mafia plant made sure to stay inconspicuous. Nox had a hard time getting a good look at him.

He reversed some of the digital footage, looked closer, blinked a couple of times to clear his vision, then reversed the recording again. He hit the pause button and leaned toward the monitor, squinting this time as if that would make the black and white footage clearer. It didn't.

Even so, he had to be seeing things.

No fucking way was that asshole prospect still a member of the Demons. No fucking way was T-Bone still breathing.

No goddamn way.

"Yo," Nox called out to Finn and Decker. "Come look at this."

It sucked Rez wasn't around to ask his opinion, too. But between Decker and Finn, they should be able to recognize that jag-off, if it was T-Bone.

The last time any of them had seen the prospect, it was in a dark field out in the middle of nowhere. Where they left him tied up.

Planting the seed that T-Bone had been skimming some meth off the top should've been enough for the Demons to strip the piece of shit of his colors and even bury him deep enough so that his remains would never be found.

Nox had to be getting this wrong. It had to be someone who looked similar. Another scumbag wearing a Demons prospect cut. They all had shaggy hair, unkempt beards and looked like they took a bath only on Saturday nights.

Finn came to stand behind Nox's chair. "What?"

"Fletch said they gave T-Bone's room at the Wolf Den to another prospect. He also said he hasn't seen him or heard his name being mentioned. If that's true, who the fuck is this?" Nox pointed to the person caught in the stilled footage.

Finn leaned over Nox's shoulder to get a better look.

Decker joined them. "What's up?"

"He look familiar, Double Decker?" Nox asked, pointing again.

Decker elbowed Finn. "Move out of the way, Carrot Top."

"I'm trying to get a good fucking look. Because if that's T-Bone..."

"T-Bone?" Decker bellowed. "That motherfucker still can't be upright."

"Not sure if it's him, but if it is..." Nox left the rest unsaid. He picked his cell phone off the desk and texted Fletch: *If you can, call.*

Not even thirty seconds later his phone vibrated. Nox put him on speaker phone immediately.

"What's up?" Fletch asked.

"When's the last time you've been at the Wolf Den?" Finn asked.

"Last night."

"You see anyone we all know and love?" Decker asked.

Only silence came out of the phone for a few heartbeats. "If you're talking about T-Bag, I haven't seen him."

"Anyone mention him in the last few days?" Crew asked. Nox hadn't even heard him approach.

"No, but I hadn't had any meaningful conversations with any of those fuckers."

"But you're keeping your ears open?" Decker asked Fletch.

"Always. How the fuck do you think that I figured out the Russos had someone inside that club?"

"Not by listening to any conversation," Finn huffed. "They're not going to say, 'Hey, have you heard that the newest prospect's last name is Russo?'"

"No, but I pay the fuck attention, *Blaze*."

"That means we're just seeing things, then," Nox said.

"My guess. A word of advice, don't go Sasquatch hunting. You'd suck at it."

"That's more than one word," Finn countered.

"I don't know, brother, that guy caught on the camera feed sure looks like that asshole we all know and hate," Decker said. "Keep an eye out, Fletch. I want to know if that fucker's still breathing."

"So do I," Finn said.

"Rez would also like a word," Nox added.

"Let's not forget that T-Bone isn't our main focus," Crew

reminded them. "Personal vendettas could screw our investigation."

"Says the man who didn't have his woman kidnapped," Decker grumbled.

"Or have his woman battered around," Finn added.

"Again, Rez would like a word," Nox repeated.

"That's because Crew doesn't have a woman," Fletch explained.

Finn snorted.

"Wait. Why is Ginger Snap snorting like that? What am I missing?" Fletch asked.

"Nothing," Crew rushed to answer. "They're just being their normal dick selves and making shit up."

"What shit? This doesn't have to do with the new team member sleeping in my bed, does it?"

Crew leaned over and ended the call before anyone could answer Fletch's last question.

Finn smirked. "Why'd you do that? You don't have anything to hide, right?"

"We have work to do." Crew raised his eyebrows and repeated more firmly, "We *all* have work to do. So, let's get it done."

"The lady doth protest too much," Nox quoted.

"Where's that from? I've heard that before."

"It's called Shakespeare," Nox told Finn.

"*You* are quoting Shakespeare?"

"Unlike you, I read," Nox answered.

"You read Shakespeare?" Decker asked.

"Damn, you're weird," Finn said as he headed back to where he'd been working.

"I'll take that as a compliment," Nox called out.

"You do that."

Decker also wandered away, but Crew remained.

"Do you think that's him?" Nox kept his question low.

"I don't know. They want numbers on their side, especially if they have to take the Russos or one of the other MCs head on, so I don't put anything past those bikers. Maybe he begged for forgiveness, and they were generous with him. Maybe he lied his ass off and they believed him over a stripper. Or it's more than likely not him and it's someone who looks similar. Sometimes those scumbags all look alike. Who fucking knows? Fletch will find out."

"And if it is him?"

Crew glanced over his shoulder before answering. "I'm going to tell Fletch to let me know first. I'll decide what to do with that information once I have it. I really don't want our brothers getting involved in vigilante justice."

"Well-deserved justice," Nox reminded Crew.

"Not arguing that. I know they want their pound of flesh, but we need to do this above board and not fuck up almost two years of work."

"Hear that," Nox murmured.

"If you can positively ID him in the footage, let me know first."

"Will do." He didn't like it, but Crew *was* the task force leader. And both of them didn't want their BAMC brothers doing anything that would put them in a jam. Or fuck up all the hard work—not to mention, long hours— they've put into this investigation.

The AUSA wouldn't be happy about that, either.

"Don't you have a meeting tonight?" Crew asked.

He *mmm*'d.

"Everything going good with them?"

Nox *mmm*'d again.

"Are they helping?"

He stopped scrolling through the video and shot him a look.

Crew threw his hands up. "Fine. I won't ask, Hard Nox. As long as you're going," and headed over to Torres.

Nox hadn't planned on going tonight.

Or next week.

Or even the week after.

Actually, he planned on never going again.

Not only because he couldn't face her.

Not only because he was struggling to accept what he did.

But because he didn't want to be tempted to do it again.

Unfortunately, he'd thought of nothing but her since Friday night.

When he closed his eyes, he pictured her beautiful ass as he fucked her. He heard her as she came. He remembered the scent of her arousal and how slick she became.

Once again, he heard her saying that, like him, it had been a while since she'd had sex with anyone.

At one time, they had worn the same shoes. Only Liyah had hers resoled, while his still had gaping holes. He knew he needed to repair his so he could get back to walking comfortably. But he avoided handing them over to be fixed because he was afraid that, by the time he got them back, he'd forget how they used to feel.

When they had been comfortable and fit perfectly.

He closed his eyes and breathed.

But when he did so, a replay of what happened in Liyah's bedroom against her French doors once again played on the back of his eyelids.

He knew fucking her would be dangerous.

He was right.

215

When his phone vibrated on the desk, he opened his eyes and saw his alarm going off.

If he was going to go tonight, he would need to head out now so he could grab something to eat on the way.

If he was going to go.

If.

He shook his head and frowned.

Chapter Twenty

HE WAITED until the meeting had already started before quietly slipping through the door and finding the nearest empty seat.

Unfortunately, that seat was next to Liyah.

The person talking only hesitated for a second, then continued as Nox rounded the circle to the other side and slid into the hot seat.

He cleared his throat and ignored the woman burning a hole into the side of his face simply by using her eyeballs.

Yanking the brim of his hat lower, he spread his knees, set his boots flat on the floor and slid down until he slouched in the metal folding chair. Then he crossed his arms over his chest and half-listened to whatever story the guy across from him was rattling on about.

Memories.

That was what—What was his name? Jack, maybe—was droning on about.

The same as what most members of the group talked about every week.

Memories that made them sad and cry, or happy and smile.

Unlike Nox's memory of last Friday night.

Of touching Liyah, tasting her skin, tasting her arousal on his fingers, breathing in her scent.

Of sliding in and out of her.

Of coming hard.

Goddamn it. The last thing he needed was a damn hard-on in the middle of a grief group.

He was a fucking mess.

He slid his eyes to the right and snuck a glance.

Yep, she was still staring at him and totally not paying attention to Jack talking about his honeymoon trip to Maui that happened twenty years ago.

Aloha.

Once the next person began to talk, he snuck another glance and saw she was back to paying attention to the stories being told.

Thank fuck.

He let his gaze roam over her, from the way she wore her hair pulled back tonight, to the empathy softening her eyes, to her slightly parted lips. His eyes slid over her chest and down her arms to where she had her hands folded in her lap. How the narrow black skirt she wore, along with the way her legs were crossed, showcased her smooth skin on her endlessly long legs. Tonight she wore strappy, open-toed, high-heeled sandals in a peach color that complimented her dark skin tone and matched her silk blouse.

The little of her he saw the other night made him wonder what she looked like totally naked. His imagination was good, but he was damn sure the reality was a fuck of a lot better.

When her head spun toward him, his spun, too, so she wouldn't catch him staring. He focused on the floor in the center of the circle instead of the woman sitting next to him.

His nostrils flared just enough to pick up the light scent of her perfume. He had no idea what it was but knew whenever he smelled it in the future, he would think of her.

"Nox, you're up next."

His head jerked back, and his eyes widened. "Next for what?"

Fuck, he should've been paying better attention.

"Since you missed the discussion because of coming in late, I'll clue you in."

Jesus. She was using her mom voice again and might as well be scolding him.

"Tonight, we're going around the circle and sharing a favorite trip with your loved one."

"Denial," he said under his breath.

"Did you say the Nile?"

He sucked on his teeth and thought about his favorite trip with Jackie. "I don't have one."

"Sure you do. We all do. It could be as simple as going to the movies or the park. It doesn't have to be some exotic trip like climbing Mount Everest. Or traveling down the *Nile*." Her lips flattened into a thin line.

He opened his mouth to ask, "Do I have to?" but then realized that would make him sound like she was correct in using her mom voice with him.

He needed to stop acting like a miserable fuck. He hated when he heard himself, but despite that, he couldn't stop it.

Since the day he found Jackie, happiness seemed to stay just out of reach.

In the rare times he laughed or smiled, or cracked a joke, he felt guilty for enjoying life. Even for those fleeting moments.

"Nox?"

Shit.

"I don't have one," he repeated automatically, then cursed himself for being such an asshole.

The one trip that rose above the rest, he couldn't share because he couldn't force it past his lips.

Fuck, he'd been so goddamn happy that day. The day they went to the imaging center to get a 3D ultrasound. The day he was able to see his daughter for the first—and last—time.

The day he was clueless about the train barreling around the corner about to hit him at full speed.

Knocking him right out of those comfortable shoes.

"Nox?" finally penetrated his brain.

He turned to look at Liyah. Her brow was furrowed, and she wore a concerned expression. "There's nothing you're comfortable with sharing?"

"I," the weight bearing down on his chest quickly became unbearable, and he finished on a whisper, "can't."

Her throat undulated as she swallowed, gave him the slightest nod and went on to discuss their next activity.

Thank fuck she didn't push it.

He said he wasn't coming back to these meetings. He should've stuck with that declaration. What was the point, if he didn't share anything? If he got absolutely zero out of attending?

He glanced at the woman next to him.

Originally it was because his brothers forced him to attend.

Now?

He only had one excuse.

Her.

To see her. To hear her voice. To be near her.

She also gave him the hope that he'd eventually be able to move on and to push past the guilt for doing so.

Mark James had been a love of a lifetime for her.

The same as Jackie had been for him.

The difference was, once Liyah got her footing, she continued to live the life she was meant to have. Only without her husband and father of her child.

Did she hit some speed bumps? Of course. Life never went as smoothly as anyone hoped. Despite that, she kept her head up and marched forward by raising her two sons, running a very successful business, and helping others. Even stubborn fucks like him.

The woman was impressive.

And he was simply a dick.

A hand clamped around his forearm, making him jerk back to reality. "Can you stay and help me put everything away?"

What? The meeting was over already? Had he been that lost in his head?

He glanced around and noticed everyone getting to their feet and collecting their belongings.

"Nox?" she whispered.

He nodded. "Yeah."

He continued to sit as everyone gathered by the front door in front of the refreshment table, stuffing baked goods into their mouth or grabbing a couple of whatever she brought tonight to go.

He stayed where he was as the group slowly funneled their way out the door until only one or two people remained, talking to Liyah.

They were all smiling and joking, unlike his miserable ass.

For fuck's sake, he just wanted his life back.

The way it had been.

Even though that was impossible.

His life would never go back to being what it used to be because one major piece of it was missing.

He studied the woman standing there, being kind and encouraging to others...

She could do more for him than any fucking therapist.

Because she *wanted* to help. She wasn't doing it because she was being paid. She was genuine and not only going through the motions.

When the last two group members finally left, he unfolded himself from the chair and headed over to where she surveyed what remained on the table.

Mostly nothing but crumbs and a couple of empty plastic containers.

"I saved you one."

"One what?"

She held up a Rice Krispie treat tucked in a napkin.

His mouth watered. *Damn it.* "Your boys must love them."

"I've found that all boys love them. Including adult boys."

He pressed a hand to his stomach. "I had a big dinner."

"Stop being so damn difficult." She shoved the treat at him.

Of course, that meant he had no choice but to take it. So he did. She stared him down until he took a big bite.

He blinked as the sweet treat hit his taste buds. "What did you do to them?" he asked around a mouthful.

"If I tell you my secret, you'll have to sign an NDA."

"NDA?"

"Non-disclosure agreement," she explained.

"I know what an NDA is, Liyah. But we're talking baked goods here, not NASA secrets."

She grinned. "I was just seeing if you were paying attention, unlike during the group meeting. I add a dash of vanilla and cinnamon."

He wasn't any kind of baker but now that she mentioned it, he tasted those flavors. Nothing overwhelming. She added the perfect amount.

After she watched him inhale the rest, they got to work cleaning up the room and putting away the table and chairs.

As they carried the last of the folding chairs to the storage closet, she said, "You told me you were no longer coming to the meetings."

"Did I say that?"

"I heard it and actually believed it. I was completely shocked when you walked through that door. I figured you couldn't face me."

"Why's that?"

Inside the closet, she stacked a chair and turned toward him, settling her hands on her curvy hips. "You tell me."

He put the chairs he was carrying with the rest, making sure they wouldn't fall over like noisy dominoes. "I've got nothing."

"Oh, I'm sure you have plenty, but you don't like to share. Like in the group. I'm also sure you aren't spilling your guts during your sessions with your therapist."

"Maybe you should stick to baking and selling houses, instead of accusations."

"Accusations? What did I say that's wrong?"

"That I couldn't face you. Me being here dispels that notion."

"You probably wouldn't have shown up if your job wasn't threatened," she countered.

"You'd be wrong."

"And why's that?"

"Because I only came here to see you." *Shit.* Did that just tumble out?

An audible breath slipped from her lips as her hands dropped to her side and her head tilted. "You came here to see me?" she repeated softly.

Her reaction made him immediately stop regretting his slip-up. "I certainly didn't show up tonight to hear Jack's honeymoon story for the third time."

Her perfectly shaped eyebrows knitted together. "Jack?"

"Isn't that his name?"

She smothered her laugh with a hand. "No. It's—"

"I don't care what it is." He grabbed the hand from her mouth and pulled it into his chest, effectively pulling her closer. "Liyah?" he murmured.

"Yes?" she whispered.

He stared down into her deep brown eyes. "I'm sorry about the other night," came out on a breath.

"I'm not."

"It couldn't have been great for you."

"I came, didn't I?"

"That's not how I normally..." He wasn't sure how to finish that. "Fuck" sounded too crude. "Make love" was far from what it was.

The truth was, it had been embarrassingly awkward.

"When's the last time anything has been 'normal' for you?"

Jesus, this woman certainly knew how to peel away his layers. "Too long," he admitted.

"It takes a while to get back to what you think is normal." She reached up and cupped his face. "It also takes someone willing to work at it."

He would love to get back to normal. His normal, anyway. "You're a good motivator."

"That's the point of our group. For us all to motivate each other."

"No." He shook his head and gently squeezed her fingers. "Not the group. You."

"You're giving me too much credit. Like I said, you have to be willing to change and it seems as though you're now ready for that."

"You mean I've reached my limit of self-pity."

"No, you're tired of being sad about a situation that will never change because it can't. But no matter what you do, you can't move on until you accept that situation. Are you ready?"

"Do I have a choice?"

"No, you don't. Unless you want to continue to wallow in your grief, anger and bitterness. Let's not forget... make everyone around you continue to worry."

"I like that you're bold enough to smack me in the face with the truth. You don't tiptoe around me, worried that I'll spiral even lower than I already am."

"Someone needs to be upfront with you. Normally that would be your counselor, but, again, you're not sharing shit with him or her. Instead, you're holding everything inside."

She hadn't been wrong yet and apparently, she wasn't finished.

"You're a ticking time bomb unless you begin to release that built-up pressure. Friday was a start to that release. So, don't apologize for it. You're moving forward whether you took a step, or you stumbled."

"You're saying I stumbled with the way I fucked you?"

She locked eyes with him. "Yes."

"Do you ever lie?"

"All the time. I have two kids."

When he burst out laughing, she leaned back as far as his

hold would allow, with her eyes wide and her mouth gaped. "Holy shit."

For the first time in a long time, he didn't feel the need to smother a laugh or his grin, or to cut it short. He let it go. It was that release she was talking about.

"The sound of that..." she breathed.

"It's rusty."

"No, Nox, it's... the most amazing sound I've heard in a while."

And it was all due to her.

Chapter Twenty-One

THE JOY on her face was genuine and all it took to put it there was for him to laugh.

A fucking laugh.

Jesus Christ. That was how much of a sad fucking sap he'd been. "I'm sorry."

She frowned. "For what?"

Of course, now he just killed her joy. "For making everyone worry."

"You need to tell them, not me. But if you ask me, I don't think you need to apologize to them, either. If they are your true brothers, they understand. And whether you grieve for two months or five years, they would be there to help and support you for however long it takes."

Again, she was right. This woman was so goddamn bright, it was blinding.

She pulled her hand from his grip and planted both palms on his pecs before sliding them up to his shoulders and squeezing him there. "You're going to be okay."

It was a simple statement, but he believed it now.

He would be okay.

He slid both hands along her jawline and tipped her face up even higher. She stared up at him as he brushed his thumb back and forth across her soft cheek. There wasn't a big difference in their heights, since she was naturally tall and wore those heels tonight.

She could almost look him right in the eye.

Almost. But he still had to dip his head a little to meet her soft gaze.

She dragged her fingers from one shoulder, up his neck and the side of his face, making the fire in his gut burn even hotter. She popped his hat off his head and tossed it on the shelf behind her before turning back to face him.

She had a heated look in her eyes that continued to stoke that fire. "Liyah..."

"*Hmm?*"

He was about to tell her that they shouldn't continue.

But why the fuck not?

She was single. He was single. He needed to get it through his thick fucking skull this was not cheating.

Not on Jackie. Not even on her memory.

The only thing stopping him from kissing her—and more —was himself.

He was his own damn cockblock.

In reality, his world hadn't gotten darker, or spiraled out of control, when he fucked her the other night. If anything, everything around him had become brighter.

At the time, he didn't want to see it for what it was...

Liyah was a spot of color in his grayscale world.

He dipped his head further, until his lips were a hairsbreadth away from hers, until their breaths melded.

Since they were now too close to focus on each other, he

closed both the small gap between them and his eyes until his lips briefly touched hers.

Soft, warm and inviting.

She curled her fingers around the back of his head and pulled him down for another light lip touch.

"Liyah," he breathed as he dragged his lips over hers once, twice... before that gentle kiss turned hungry.

Because he was fucking starved.

For touch.

For attention.

For anything and everything this woman could give him.

And what she was giving him, at the moment, was an erection.

Wrapping one arm around her back and the other around her hips, he pulled her closer, proving to her just how much she turned him on.

In case she had any doubt.

For fuck's sake, he wanted her.

That realization fucked with his head because he never thought he'd want *any* woman as much as he had wanted Jackie. It also made guilt circle the outskirts of his brain. He did his best to shove it away so it didn't take over and ruin this moment.

Because this kiss *was* a moment. *Their* moment.

He wanted it to be all about them and no one else. Not Jackie. Not Mark. Not her father or his brotherhood.

Only Nox and Aaliyah.

In a closet. In a community center. After a grief group.

The group created to help people move on.

He originally didn't think attending would help.

But in reality, it was. Just not in the way it was intended.

Her long nails dragged through his hair before she dug

them into the back of his neck, returning him to the moment. And her.

She also caught his attention when her teeth scraped across his bottom lip. And when her tongue twisted with his.

This woman was not shy. She went after what she wanted.

She apparently wanted him, and he had no idea why. He figured it would be in his best interest not to ask.

But if she had only wanted to use him for sex, last Friday would've been a good enough reason for her to look elsewhere. Because there was no fucking way this woman was desperate and would screw any Tom, Dick or Harry.

Or Brad.

Christ, his cock was a steel pipe in his damn jeans. They should move this elsewhere before it went any further.

He turned his head enough to break the seal on their lips. "Doing this here is not smart."

"Kissing?"

"Is that all you want?"

She didn't hesitate to answer, "No."

"Right."

"In that case... My kids are home, so my place is out. How about yours?"

The fuck if he was bringing her to his place. At. The. Plant. Where his brothers or his fellow task force members would see her.

And possibly hear them.

Ask prying questions.

Rib the fuck out of him.

Maybe even want to give him a fucking high-five.

No, *fuck that*. That wasn't going to happen.

He was not bringing her to his place.

The little peace he got would be destroyed. He loved his

brothers, would have their six until the day he died, but they were assholes.

"Nox?"

He shook himself mentally. "Can't go to my place."

"Why?"

He decided to tell her the truth. Partially. She didn't need to know about the task force since that wasn't public information. "I live above the BAMC's church."

"Your room isn't big enough for both of us?"

Shit. "It's not the size of my place that's the issue. It's—"

"Dealing with your brothers," she finished for him. "I get it because I've seen it. They can be nosy shits and you want to keep anything between us private."

Damn, it was nice dealing with a woman who accepted an answer, understood why it was answered in that way and didn't argue. "Yes."

"Well, then... Close the door, Nox."

Next issue... "I don't have a condom." *For fuck's sake*, he needed to tuck one or two into his wallet. Of course, after he went out and bought some first, since he stopped using them years ago.

Not carrying protection just derailed this whole thing.

"I do."

She what? "You do?" He frowned. "Why?" The other day she admitted, like him, she hadn't had sex in a while, so why was she carrying condoms?

"On the off chance I had the opportunity to have sex in a community center closet with a member of my grief group. In fact, I think one of those condoms is labeled for that particular use."

The fact that she managed to say all that with a serious expression...

"That's pretty damn specific."

She shrugged. "I like details."

"How about the detail on the location of that earmarked condom?"

With her full bottom lip snagged between teeth, she lifted a finger and two seconds later was gone.

He blinked.

Someone acted extremely enthusiastic about having sex with him again. Maybe she was the one needing the therapist.

Within a minute, she was barreling back through the door and shutting it behind her. She carried a large purse that was brown and tan and had some sort of gold symbol printed all over it.

Whatever designer it was, Nox had a feeling that accessory cost almost as much as his Harley.

"While you were out there, did you lock the door to the meeting room?"

"No," she answered with her head down as she dug through that overpriced bag. "It would be futile since the janitor has the key."

"Does the closet door have a lock?"

"Not that I saw," she murmured, still digging.

How much shit did she have in there? He didn't want to know.

Every time Jackie had handed him her purse to hold, it almost strained his arm. A woman could probably survive a month lost in the wilderness as long as they had their purse.

Glancing at the door, he noticed no lock, so he grabbed the easiest tool to keep people from walking in on them. He jammed a folding chair under the doorknob.

"Smart." When he turned, she was holding up a foil wrapper in her hand. "See? Just like a Girl Scout. I came prepared."

"But you didn't think I was ever coming back to group."

She lifted her eyebrows in answer.

This woman was too damn smart, as well as intuitive. "You knew I would."

"I've been doing this for a while, Nox."

"So, you figured I'd come back. But did you really plan on having sex in the closet?"

"Look, stop asking questions and just be happy that I thought ahead." She shook her head and placed her purse next to his hat.

"You planned on using that with me?"

"I sure as hell didn't plan on boinking some random guy on the street."

"Boinking?"

"Do you need to look that up?"

This woman. "No. I know what it means." She probably picked that term up from her kids, too.

"Good. Then let's boink. But I have one requirement first..."

He braced, unsure what the hell was going to come out of her mouth next.

"We're not doing it standing up again."

"We're not?" Was there a cot in the closet that he didn't know about?

She shook her head and grabbed one of the metal chairs, unfolded it and set it in the center of what little empty floor space existed in the storage area. She pointed to the seat. "Pants down and sit."

His mouth gaped for a second before he snapped back into his former military self. "Yes, ma'am!"

"So, you *do* know how to take orders..."

"Of course I know how to take orders—I'm an Army vet—but that doesn't mean I always follow them."

"You just gave me another piece of your puzzle."

"That wasn't a secret. But I'm warning you now, my puzzle does have a few missing pieces."

"I'm good at finding them."

He didn't doubt that.

"You're still standing there," she observed.

"So are you," he countered.

"I have nowhere to sit until you do."

His gaze hit the chair, then flicked between the two of them. "I really don't want to die while locked in a storage closet in a community center."

"I'm not going to fuck you to death."

He was impressed by how seriously she said that. "I was more worried about that chair holding us."

She studied it. "I won't ride the chair. I'll only ride you."

"I guess that'll work."

"No guessing needed."

"You've done this before."

"Not on a metal folding chair."

"That's my worry."

"My legs are long enough that I don't need to put all my weight on you."

His gaze skimmed her endless legs. "That they are. Do you need to remove the skirt, or can you shimmy it up?"

"Shimmy it up over my hips? I'm going to have to remove it." She turned and gave him her back, then only stood there. "Well?"

"Well?" he repeated.

"You want to help a girl out?" She pointed to the hidden zipper on the back of the skirt.

He jerked into motion and dug around until he found the delicate zipper tab, then pulled it down.

She turned and wiggled out of the skirt. "Heels on?"

He stood there like an idiot simply watching her.

"Nox."

The question finally permeated his brain. "If it's not uncomfortable for you."

With a nod, she folded her skirt neatly and placed it next to her purse.

Her ass was fucking amazing. He wanted to lick every inch of it, as well as her legs.

"Now you."

Chapter Twenty-Two

Now you...

Nox lifted his gaze when she turned to face him again. "Me?"

She jerked her chin toward his jeans.

Apparently, seeing her undress made him stupid. Most likely because all of his brain cells had rushed into his dick along with his blood.

But she didn't continue removing her clothes. She now stood before him still wearing her heels, panties and blouse. With her hands on her hips, she also wore a stern expression. "Nox. Do we want to have the janitor join us for a threesome, or do we want to keep it intimate and only between the two of us?"

"If I was going to have a threesome, it wouldn't be with a man." A second after that claim, he realized what she was hinting at... the possibility of them getting caught.

The corners of her lips twitched, and her eyes sparkled with amusement. "I never said the janitor was a man."

It was a logical assumption when she previously called the janitor a "him." Maybe he misheard her.

"Well, if that's the case..." His brain glitched and he frowned. "Hold up. You'd have a threesome with another woman?" This was an interesting turn of events.

"It took you over a year and a half to have sex with one. Do you think you're up for sex with two?"

Damn. "You know how to hit a guy when he's down."

"That guy needs to drop his drawers and sit down so we can boink."

"Jesus Christ, if I accidentally say boink in front of my brothers..."

"I'm sure they've heard it before."

"Not from me." He unfastened his leather belt, popped the button out of the loop and unzipped his cargo pants.

Her watching him closely made his cock kick in his now very snug boxer briefs.

As he began to drop his cargos, she said, "All the way off. I want to see what I'm riding first."

"Yes, ma'am," he responded again, but not as forceful as the first time.

"We're also going to face each other."

"Yes, ma'am."

"You can stop calling me ma'am now."

"I'm trying to be respectful."

"What we're about to do isn't close to respectful. And if it is, I don't want to do it."

He snorted and shook his head.

"You need to take your boots off first," she reminded him since, apparently, his common sense was down in his dick hanging out with his brain cells.

"Good call." At least someone's brain was functioning. He dropped to the chair and unlaced his boots, pulling them off. He glanced up as he was tucking the laces inside the boots. "Socks on or off?"

"Do you have cloven hooves you're hiding?"

"Not at all, but I'm sure the floor isn't the cleanest."

"We're back to the janitor joining us, are we? Socks on, socks off, I'm not in this closet for your feet."

He decided to keep his bare feet off the floor and left his socks on. "Shirt on or off?"

"When did sex turn into a damn quiz?" she teased. "If we were both twenty years younger, we'd be ripping off each other's clothes and not caring about the details."

"Got it. No questions, only boinking."

He paused to watch her when her husky laugh hit his ears. Laughter really *was* the best medicine. Especially when it came from Liyah.

Because of her, the black cloud that had been hanging over his head for so damn long was beginning to clear.

He got to his feet but hesitated before pushing his pants down. "Where's the condom?"

"I have it under control, don't worry."

"Do I look worried?"

"You look like you're still dressed."

"Easy fix." He shoved his cargo pants down and they dropped to his feet. "Good?"

She shook her head.

He hooked his fingers in his boxer briefs next and as he pushed those down, they got hung up on his erection. After fighting to free it, he finished shoving them down his legs and stepped free. "Better?"

When she didn't answer, he glanced at her to find her staring at his cock. And that caused it to flex and a pearly bead of precum to form at the slit. "Liyah?"

"Oh yes, much better." She pointed a finger at the chair again. "Now sit."

He sat, but he almost jumped back to his feet since the metal seat was shockingly cold against his bare ass and balls. He should've put something between him and a chair that was probably as clean as the floor.

Too late.

"Now you." She still wore panties and they needed to go.

She shook her head and glanced around until she spotted his cargo pants. She snatched them up and folded them.

"You don't need to do—" He swallowed the rest when he realized she was folding them up to put them on the ground between his feet. What was she doing?

With a wicked look in her eyes, she shoved his knees apart even farther.

"Liyah?"

"Do you really want to ask more questions right now?"

"I'll figure it out on my own."

"Good call." She braced her hands on his knees to help lower herself to hers.

"You don't have to do that." His throat tightened at the sight of her kneeling between his legs and his heart raced with anticipation on what would happen next.

"You're right. No one forces me to do anything I don't want to do."

"I don't imagine they do," he murmured.

He jerked when she wrapped her hand around the base of his cock. He held his breath as she lifted it at the same time she lowered her head.

This could be dangerous.

"Liyah... If you want to have sex—" His words were stopped when she smashed a fingertip against his lips at the same time circling the crown of his cock with her warm, wet mouth.

He groaned and forced himself to keep breathing when she just about swallowed him whole.

Holy shit.

Hoooooly shit.

His head dropped forward, and his eyelids slid shut as she worked his cock with her mouth by sucking his length and twirling her tongue around the tip.

His fingers flexed with the urge to grab her head and guide it up and down. Instead, he dug his fingers into his bare thighs... because she stated that no one forced her to do anything she didn't want to do.

More importantly, she was doing just fine without any guidance.

"Liyah..." came out on a ragged breath.

Her fingers at the root squeezed tighter, making his cock even harder.

He wanted to lift his hips and thrust deeper into her mouth, but if he started doing that, he might not stop until he came. And as much as he was enjoying her giving him head, he really wanted to be inside her when he did so.

After a few more bobs of her head and strokes with her tongue, she released him with a wet pop.

Even though it was over too soon, in reality, it wasn't. Sucking him had been a very risky move on her part. But he'd keep that fact to himself since he managed not to blow it. Literally. *Thank fuck.* If he thought the other night had been awkward, coming prematurely would be worse.

"I would take the time to take you to that sweet but sharp edge but if you haven't noticed, we're in a community center closet like two naughty teenagers."

"Thanks for that reminder," he muttered.

241

With one side of her mouth pulled up in a semi-smile, she stood, pulled the condom from her bra and ripped the wrapper open, sliding out the latex disc.

"Time to boink?" he asked.

"Time to boink," she confirmed with a nod.

He was doomed. He just knew he was going to slip and use that stupid term in front of his MC. Or the task force. Then they'd incorporate it into some ridiculous nickname for him.

She grabbed his cock, making him groan, and did the honor of rolling the condom down his hard length. When she was done, she stepped back and surveyed her work for a second, before sliding her panties down her luscious thighs. He tracked them falling to her feet and her stepping out of them before he took his time lifting his gaze, following the long lines of her legs all the way to her sweet, sweet pussy.

Fuuuuuck.

His mouth watered when he remembered the taste of her arousal when he sucked it off his fingers the other day.

With a sly smile, she straddled his thighs but remained on her feet. When her hands landed on his shoulders, he automatically grabbed her hips in preparation.

"Look at me," she ordered softly.

He pulled in a breath.

"Nox... look at me."

He took his time lifting his gaze until he reached her gorgeous face and found her focused on his. With their eyes locked, she held the base of his cock in one hand, curled the other around the back of his neck, then sank down slowly.

A satisfied sigh slipped from him when he was enveloped in what felt like warm velvet. And when her pulsing pussy squeezed his cock, a groan worked its way up his throat next. She caught it in her mouth as she pressed her lips to his, kissing him long and hard as she did what she said earlier... She kept her weight off both him and the chair as she slid up and down his length.

His hands slipped from her hips to her ass where he dug in his fingers, getting a good grip and feeling her muscles work as she continued to ride his cock at a steady, sensual pace.

With their tongues doing the Tango and her nails scraping along his skin, he lost himself in her.

For the moment, everything was wiped clean. His life a completely blank slate.

Nothing else existed outside of the two of them. Not her family. Not his. Not even any distant memories.

Memories that could derail this moment, if he let them. He needed to prevent that. So, despite the kiss, he opened his eyes and concentrated on the woman willing to have sex with him in this storage space.

Willing to deal with his issues, for some unknown reason.

The second he fisted her hair, her mouth popped open, and the kiss ended abruptly.

Did he fuck up? He remembered hearing something about Black women not liking their hair touched. He figured any woman, no matter who, wouldn't like to be touched by a stranger, but someone they were having sex with? He wasn't sure...

"Nox..."

"Sorry."

She pressed her silky soft cheek to his. "No, don't apologize... I want you to be yourself and to do what comes naturally. I'll tell you if you step over a line."

He had no doubt she would, but... "I don't want to fuck up."

"If you do, you'll learn from it and do better next time."

Next time... He liked the sound of that. "It's okay, then? You're okay?"

"I'm good. And so are you."

"Good," he murmured and used her hair to tug her head back and expose her arched throat. A vulnerable area that called to him.

He pressed his lips to the hollow at the base before working his way higher, nibbling lightly along her taut skin. Her groan vibrated his lips as he went. He drew his mouth under her chin and along her jawline. He did not release her hair even after he captured her mouth again...

Chapter Twenty-Three

Nox couldn't get enough of her mouth. Her smooth skin. The way her pussy fit his cock perfectly.

Her strength was impressive as she kept her word about not putting her weight on him or the chair, even when she lowered herself until he filled her completely and she circled her hips, driving his cock deep, before rising again. All the while, she kept their lips connected as they played tongue tag.

He lost track of time in their little cocoon. He assumed it was the same for her.

Neither had an urge to rush. Instead, they used those moments to appreciate one another. To appreciate their unexpected connection.

Despite this location not being the most ideal for what they were doing, it was a hell of a lot better than in her bedroom the other day when he was struggling to wrap his head around the idea of having sex with a woman other than his wife.

On Friday, he had flip-flopped back and forth. Questioned himself. Felt guilty. Unsure if he should even be doing what he was doing.

But he powered through it and Liyah was the perfect, patient woman to help him break through that mental block.

Tonight, though... The difference was clear. He wanted this. He could fully appreciate the woman riding his cock.

Not only for helping him, but for her simply being who she is.

It all made him realize it was time to take back control of his life. To return to living it the way it was meant to be lived. Because Liyah had been right...

Jackie wouldn't want him to continue wallowing in his grief. The same as he wouldn't have wanted her to, either.

Prior to Liyah, he couldn't even see a blip of light at the end of the long, dark tunnel. Now he could.

It might not be a blinding spotlight, but it was there... Flickering. Encouraging. Allowing him to see enough so he could make his way further through that narrow tunnel.

The end was finally in sight. It might not be perfectly clear, but it was visible. It gave him hope. Whereas before, he had none at all.

He thought his life was over the day he found Jackie.

He had been wrong. And for once, he was okay with being wrong.

Now he was more than okay with what was happening in that closet and with whom it was happening.

His therapist would be fucking thrilled with this news. *If* he shared it.

When Liyah's thighs began to quiver and her fingers drove deeper into his flesh, it yanked him out of his head. He figured she was either getting weary from her workout or getting close to coming.

He hoped it was the second, otherwise they'd have to ditch the chair and come up with another solution and he certainly wasn't putting his bare ass on the floor.

He pulled his lips from hers. "You're shaking."

"Yes," she breathed.

"Are you going to come?"

"Soon."

Good. "What do you need to get there?"

"Just you."

You have me, whispered through his head.

He drove one hand between them, finding her sensitive clit, and with the other, he swept his thumb back and forth over the curve of her breast, even though he wasn't sure how much she could feel over her bra and blouse.

They really needed to do this again while fully naked. He wanted to see all of her.

He wanted to explore every damn inch.

He also wanted to taste her completely. Sucking his fingers clean the other day had only been an appetizer. He was ready to dive in and enjoy the rest of the meal.

He was fucking hungry. For her. For more of this.

For the unexplainable connection they had.

In truth, he didn't need an explanation. He didn't need to know why. He only needed to accept what he didn't understand.

A sudden sense of peace came over him, despite his heart pounding, his pulse racing and his cock hardening even more as she clenched tightly around him.

Was that an orgasm?

He opened his eyes and saw her head thrown back, her eyes closed and her mouth gaping as her breath rushed in and out.

Her pace didn't falter for one second.

No, she hadn't climaxed yet.

Not yet. Soon...

"Nox!" burst from between her lips and she crashed onto his lap. For a second, he worried that the chair would be unable to handle their combined weight. But in the next second, he didn't give a shit.

Because he was too busy watching her orgasm.

He got swept up along with her.

She was gorgeous.

Absolutely fucking gorgeous.

She didn't come close to the beauty he'd seen in his life-time. The fiery sunsets. Soaring mountains. Crystal clear lakes. Turquoise seas.

She blew them all away.

None compared to Liyah.

As soon as her climax tapered off and the pulsing of her pussy waned, she lifted her head and opened her eyes to lock them with his.

She began to move again, lifting and lowering. Keeping her weight off him and the chair as she worked to bring him to orgasm, too.

Grabbing his face, she made sure he couldn't look away as she rode his cock until he was at his very limit.

And when he was, her mouth crashed into his, his hips shot off the chair and he slammed up into her. His balls tight-ened and he came with an intensity that he swore made his soul leave his body for a few seconds.

When it returned, he slowly lowered his ass back to the chair, taking her with him. His cock continued to twitch, and his heart kept trying to break free from his chest.

"Liyah..." came out on a pant. He pressed his damp fore-head to hers, using that time to collect himself.

Until time slowed and his focus returned.

Until he came back to the reality that they just had sex on a metal chair in a closet in a community center.

In a community where he normally worked.

Where he was damn sure, she also did real estate transactions.

He could see the headlines now...

Local cop caught boinking the area's top real estate broker at the Shadow Valley Community Center.

News at five.

For a few seconds, she lazily combed her long nails through his damp hair. And, *damn*, did that feel good.

He tightened his arm around her waist to keep her there for a little longer. But as soon as she began plucking at her own hair, he realized it had not fallen back into place like he thought it would after he fisted it.

Proving he knew nothing about Black women's hair.

He should take the time to learn because he didn't want to fuck up. Especially if they ended up having sex again. "Sorry about messing up your hair."

A soft, satisfied smile crossed her face. "It was worth it."

LIYAH HAD no idea what her hair looked like after he grabbed a handful of it in the heat of passion. But no matter what, it was fixable, and she hadn't been lying... It had been worth it.

Especially since there was an obvious change with Nox. He seemed to be more into it tonight than on Friday when he was trying to break down some barriers.

Tonight was proof those barriers have started to crumble.

And that was a good thing.

Her hair would survive.

Anyway, she really didn't want to tell him not to do what came naturally for him because she didn't want to discourage him in any manner. He was taking the necessary steps forward. She didn't want to be the reason for him retreating to where he'd been previously.

He gave her hips a squeeze. "I need to pull out before there needs to be a cleanup on aisle five."

Oh, yes. This man was making progress, for sure. Was it all because of her? Liyah doubted it but she hoped she at least had a hand in it.

Helping people came naturally for her. Making the people around her happy— whether she helped them buy their dream home or helped free them of crippling grief— made her happy. It also gave her a sense of worth.

Some people fed off others' misery. She was not one of them.

With one exception. She hoped Jason stepped on Legos with bare feet every night for the rest of his miserable life.

Once she gave Nox a nod, he secured the condom as she stood, breaking their connection and stepping back.

She really needed to clean up. So did he. As a mother, she was in the habit of carrying tissues and hand-wipes. But as she turned to grab her purse, she heard, "Liyah... Is that a wig?"

Her head jerked back, and she glanced over her shoulder. "I'm sorry?"

Did he just ask her if she was wearing a wig?

"I..." He winced. "Shit... No, I'm the one who's sorry. I hope that question didn't offend you, but I'm pretty ignorant when it comes to Black women's hair. I assumed most wore a weave or a wig. Or..." He grimaced, most likely from her expression. "How about I just shut the fuck up now?"

"First, I'm not most women. Second, if you ask the wrong woman a question like that, you'll learn real quick about Black women and their hair."

"I take it, not in a good way."

"It's like asking a woman her age. Actually, it's worse."

"I know your age."

"That you do." Liyah grabbed her purse and took the two steps back to him to poke him in the chest. "Stick with me, mister, and you'll learn a lot about us beautiful Black queens."

"How am I going to learn if I can't ask questions?"

In all honesty, she was pleased he was interested and wanted to learn. "Good point, but all you have to do is observe."

"Not a hardship."

"What isn't?"

"Watching you."

She traced a fingernail along his jawline. "Same, Nox. I don't have to blind myself with a hot poker after looking at you."

The corners of his eyes crinkled. "I guess that's good."

"Very good. You are one fine male specimen. And not just down there." She raised her eyebrows and tipped her head toward his now wilting cock.

"I aim to please." One side of his mouth rose. "Those beautiful curls are all you, then."

"It's all me, baby," she confirmed. "All natural."

"Do you ever change it up?"

She lifted one eyebrow. "Do you?"

He scrubbed a hand over his short hair. "I keep it basic. Going from the Army right into the police academy didn't give me a lot of opportunity to grow it out."

"But you could now."

"To an extent."

"And to answer your question... I've worn wigs in the past—especially fun, colorful ones—as well as weaves. Honestly, it just depends on my mood and the time I want to spend on it. But mostly, I go natural. I actually prefer it like this."

"I'm sure you look gorgeous any way you style it."

"Here's a secret... You don't need to work hard to convince me to sleep with you. In case you missed it, you just got laid."

"I'm not complimenting you to get laid and I don't bullshit. The style fits you perfectly."

"Should I ask why you think that?"

"It says you're both a professional but also aren't uptight."

"Yes, I take my business seriously but I'm not overbearing. Now... Are we done discussing my hair?"

"Is it in my best interest if I say yes?"

"Yes..." She found a travel pack of tissues in her purse and handed them to him so she could dig around again, searching for wet wipes. She found a few at the very bottom of her bag. She pulled them out and gave him two, keeping two for herself.

After they cleaned up as best as they could, she pulled on her panties and grabbed her skirt off the shelf, stepping into it. "You know, sex in a bed when we're both naked would be even better than in a closet."

He glanced up from pulling his boxer briefs up his long, muscular legs. "Okay."

"Okay?" That answer could mean anything, and she didn't want to misinterpret it.

"That's me agreeing with you, *in case you missed it.* I want to see you naked."

She grinned at his smart-ass comment. *Oh yes,* the man

definitely had a sense of humor. And he was finally letting it out to play. "That makes two of us. I mean, I've already seen myself naked too many times, but I'd love to see you in all your glory."

He shrugged. "Not much to look at."

The man acted like didn't know he was a damn snack. She preferred that over someone cocky and vain. "Officer Lennox, you are something to look at when you're fully dressed so don't play with me when it comes to you being buck naked. Your mental health might need a few tweaks but from what I've seen so far, your physique is top notch."

He shrugged again. "Need to keep in shape for my job."

She snorted out a little laugh. "I know plenty of cops who couldn't point out a treadmill in a lineup. Their physique was created by Krispy Kreme donuts and Big Macs."

She turned and gave him her back. Without her even asking, he zipped her up.

When he was done, she turned and planted her hands on his T-shirt covered chest. "I'm assuming you want to do this again."

"No reason to assume. What about you?"

"Let's just say, tonight was a huge improvement over the last time. That said, even after how it went Friday, I was interested in having sex with you again. We only need to find a better location."

"Like a motel?"

"Or your place," she suggested, watching him carefully.

"I told you that won't work."

"Because you don't want anyone to know."

He gave her a single nod. "Sorry. I'm not ready for them to—"

She lifted a palm, stopping him. "I understand. Then we'll play it by ear." She sighed. "All right, since my boys are

253

home alone, I need to get home to make sure I have a house to go home to."

"That was a mouthful."

She dragged a finger along his sharp jawline and gave him a smile that caused his pulse to speed up again. "So were you."

Chapter Twenty-Four

SHE TEXTED him while still in her car and parked in her mother's driveway. *Boys spending the weekend with my mother. Want to boink?*

She couldn't wait there until he answered since she had no idea if he had plans or not. So, after putting her Mercedes in reverse, she began the trek home, hoping to hear from him either way.

She wanted to plan her child-free weekend.

After a few minutes, her phone dinged and her car read the incoming message through the speakers. *I could boink.*

She did a giggle-snort at the robotic female voice saying the word "boink."

She used the text-to-voice feature as she drove. "I'm heading home now from dropping them off. My place in a half hour?"

Four more traffic lights later, his response came through: *Can't get free for another hour.*

"Have a date?" she asked.

With some criminals.

"Are you close enough to home to pack a bag?"

It was a few more miles before he answered. *Are we going on a trip?*

"Something like that," she purred and, in anticipation, so did her pussy.

K.

She rolled her eyes at that last message. It was the same kind of answer she got from her boys. Apparently, it was too much trouble to say or spell out "okay" since the word was extremely long and complicated.

She quickly did a mental inventory of her refrigerator and pantry. If he actually ended up staying the night and didn't sprint out of her house immediately after having sex, she would need to have something for breakfast.

Something other than Fruit Loops, Cocoa Pebbles or strawberry Pop Tarts.

For her own breakfast, she normally stopped at a locally owned coffee shop on her way to the office to fill her over-sized travel mug and grab a breakfast sandwich or wrap.

She should've planned this better and had a French toast casserole already assembled and waiting in the fridge, so it was ready to pop in the oven—

Wait. Why was she trying to impress him by making him a nice breakfast? He was only coming over to boink—she shook her head—to have *sex*. Like two full-grown adults and not naughty teenagers.

She sighed at herself when she automatically pulled into a grocery store.

One hour, fifteen minutes and ten bags of groceries later, she pulled into her driveway to find a Harley parked in it and a very hot and handsome man parked in one of the rockers on her front porch.

Sitting by his left boot was an olive-green rucksack.

The man had understood the assignment.

Of course, he wore his signature baseball cap tipped low enough to hide his eyes.

Out of the corner of hers, she saw him rise at the same time the garage door did. By the time she was done pulling in, shutting off her AMG and getting out, he was waiting for her in the garage.

"Sorry I'm late," she started, climbing out. "I had to pick up something for breakfa—"

Before she could even finish her excuse or close the driver's door, the rucksack was dropped to the floor, and she found herself shoved against the car when he latched onto her neck and took her mouth.

Damn. Somebody was hungry, but not for the groceries in her trunk.

His tongue swept through her mouth, then began a deep exploration. She clutched his T-shirt like a lifeline when he very successfully turned her bones to liquid with the intensity of his kiss.

Not soon after his cock turned rock solid, he released her by taking a step back.

"Well, then..." she breathed, surprised but pleased with his greeting.

He held out his hand and when she took it, he pulled her upright.

"Hello to you, too," she finished.

He picked up his baseball cap that had fallen to the floor during the kiss, beat it against his thigh, folded it in half and shoved it into his waistband at the small of his back.

Funny... Mark used to do that, too. If she had to guess, they must have been instructed to do that as cadets in the police academy.

Or in Nox's case, he might have gotten into that habit in the Army.

Either way, it didn't matter. His hands were now free to help her carry in the groceries. "I wasn't expecting you to beat me here."

"I wasn't, either. You said a half hour."

"And you said an hour, so I did an unscheduled stop at the grocery store."

His hazel eyes swept the interior of her car before slicing to the rear of her Benz. "Pop the trunk."

She was thrilled that she didn't have to even ask for his help and knew what was expected and appreciated. She had to ask Keenan and Devyn twenty times to help and by the time they finished considering it, she already hauled all the groceries into the house herself and would find them digging through the bags she had already dragged inside and stuffing food in their mouths.

She really needed to train them better for their future spouses. She put that on her mental to-do list.

The second she pressed the trunk release on her key fob, he was opening it and grabbing bags.

When she came around, he shook his head. "I got it. You can unpack them as I carry them in."

"I can carry a couple in with me."

"Take your purse, I got the rest."

Huh. There was no point standing there and debating it, so she headed inside and toward the kitchen with him on her heels.

"On the island?" he asked as he followed her through the house and into the chef's kitchen that was one of her favorite rooms in the house.

"That's fine," she answered and dumped her purse on the counter. When she turned, he was already gone.

Damn. The man was on a mission.

Maybe he figured the sooner she got the groceries put away, the sooner they could get naked.

She could get on board with that plan.

She took him in when he returned to the kitchen and dropped off the last four bags on the counter. The man's outfit tonight was a pair of jeans, boots and a T-shirt.

No thousand-dollar suit. No shined dress shoes. No jewelry except for the simple gold band he still wore on his left ring finger. Not even a drop of hair gel.

Simple. But still hot as hell.

Though, she was damn sure he looked like fire in his uniform.

She frowned when it hit her that not once had he mentioned working a shift at Shadow Valley PD, his place of employment.

She opened her mouth to ask him about it but was derailed when he said, "This can't be all for breakfast."

She shrugged. "Well, I wasn't sure what you liked."

"I like anything not labeled 'ready-to-eat.'"

It took her a moment to realize he was talking about the MREs served in the military. "Damn. I knew I should've had that tattoo removed from above my pussy."

With a low, soft chuckle, he came up behind her, circled his arms around her waist and pressed her into the counter. "I guess I can make one more sacrifice for my country," he murmured against the side of her neck, his erection pushing against her ass.

She reached back and cupped his face. "That's the spirit. But if you keep doing that, I won't finish putting away the groceries and the sacrifice will be the perishables."

With a last brush of his lips along her jaw, he released her and stepped back. "Can I help put anything away?"

Damn, maybe *he* needed to train her sons. Either his mother did a good job teaching him manners or his late wife did.

"No, it'll be faster for me to do it myself than taking the time to explain where everything goes. Grab a cold drink out of the fridge, if you want, and take a load off." With a now empty bag in her hand, she turned and pointed toward a stool at the large center island. "So tell me, Officer Lennox, do you get every weekend off? Don't they have rotating shifts at SVPD?"

"They do." The deep baritone of his voice was so damn delicious.

She tipped her head and regarded him closely when she stated, "But you have no problem getting off for the Wednesday night meetings, either."

He dragged his thumbnail across his forehead and as he stared at the counter, she could see him making up an excuse.

"You're about to lie to me."

He lifted his head. "Why do you think that?"

"A mother's instinct."

"You're not my mother."

"But I *am* a mother. We tend to develop certain skills to deal with our offspring."

"A sixth sense," he surmised.

"More like a woman's instinct on steroids. Or hormones, more like it."

He pulled in a breath as he considered her. "I'm currently on a special assignment."

Or was he on temporary leave because of his debilitating grief? "A secret squirrel assignment?"

"Something like that."

Interesting. "I'll respect that and not dig any further."

She caught the relief in his eyes before he hid it. "Thanks."

"You can thank me with something besides words once I'm done here."

———

THE FIRST TIME was while they were standing.

The second while sitting.

While she didn't mind variety, she was glad this time it would actually be in a bed. Most likely lying down.

The blood hummed through her veins in anticipation. For both the sex and finally getting to see the man naked from head to toe.

Her head jerked. That meant he'd get to see her completely naked, too.

She'd been aware of that when she invited him over for the night, but now it was actually hitting home as he leaned his rucksack against the dresser in her bedroom.

She was thirty-nine. She had given birth twice. She had stretch marks, cellulite and loose skin. Her breasts were heavy and the opposite of perky. Gravity had done a number on her ass, too.

She sure as hell hoped his expectations were realistic. If they weren't, reality was about to smack him in the face.

She normally wasn't self-conscious. She had accepted the changes having babies did to her body, as well as getting older. But, for some reason, she was worried she might disappoint Nox.

When she was young and not as wise, she worried about impressing men. As life went on, she stopped worrying. They either accepted her as she was, or they could hit the road if they didn't like the way she looked, acted or her success.

However, she didn't want the police officer currently standing in her bedroom hitting the road, or rushing to leave, because he was no longer attracted to her.

"No possibility of your father bringing your boys home early?" he asked with his broad back still turned to her.

"They're with my mother, remember? And that would only happen if an emergency came up. Don't worry, they'd call first."

He turned and bent over to unlace his boots. "Your mother remarried?"

Liyah swore she mentioned that fact previously but maybe he was a bit distracted with what was about to happen. "She's on her third husband."

"Damn," he whispered, setting his boots aside and tucking his socks inside.

"She said third time's the charm. I agree with that since my current stepfather is great. He's also lasted the longest."

"He's good with the boys?"

"He's excellent with the boys. Another reason I hope this marriage sticks."

"You said your father and her were really young when they had you."

"In their teens."

"That had to be difficult."

She nodded. "Especially after they had my brother a year later."

"Being overwhelmed with responsibilities broke them up?" he asked.

"It contributed to it, but the main reason was my mother wanted a better life for herself. She was tired of being poor and my father never being home because he was working hard to provide for his young family."

"So, instead of working toward making their life better with your father, she kicked him to the curb?"

Damn, the man got it. "She did, then set out to find husband number two."

"Did the second hubby have more money?"

"He did. But she quickly found out that money didn't buy happiness or stability. However, she walked away with a nice divorce settlement, so she did benefit in the end."

His expression turned troubled. "You said she wanted a better life for herself. You didn't say she wanted a better life for you and your brother."

She was impressed that the man picked up on that, too. "Because my mother was very selfish when she was young. It was all about what she wanted. Not what was good for her family."

"Do you think it would've been better for you if she had stayed with your father?"

"I can't say. But what I can is, she shouldn't have lied to the authorities and also to us about him. Once I found out the truth, it took me a long time to forgive her." And to this day, she still occasionally had to beat back the bitterness.

"But eventually you gave her a second chance."

Liyah held it against her mother for a long time. In truth, it was both Magnum and his wife Cait who convinced her to forgive her mother. She forgave her but didn't forget. And never would.

What her mother did hurt her and her brother's relationship with their father. It also critically wounded Magnum.

"She's different now. If she wasn't, the boys wouldn't be there for the weekend."

He nodded and when he began to pull his T-shirt free from his jeans, she yelled, "Wait!"

He froze and his brow furrowed. "What? Too soon?"

"Definitely not too soon... But go slower."

The creases deepened along his forehead. "Why?"

Liyah wiggled her eyebrows.

Did the man actually roll his eyes?

She grinned. "Do a girl a solid and go *slooooow*."

"So you can ogle me?" he teased.

Oh yes, his true personality was beginning to re-emerge. Those little glimpses gave her hope that he would soon shed that heavy blanket of grief.

Of course, he'd still have moments of sadness when he remembered Jackie. She experienced those herself. Especially when she saw Mark in Devyn. In his features. In a look. In the way he smiled or laughed.

Her fifteen-year-old might never had met his father, but he sure took after him in many ways.

And sometimes that caught her off guard.

But it wasn't Mark peeling off his T-shirt and exposing a body that was drool-worthy.

It was Bradley Lennox.

Her eyes weren't drawn to his hairless chest. Instead, she focused on his club colors tattooed on his left pec above his heart.

She rose from where she was perched on the edge of the bed and approached him. "Is that your only tattoo?"

"It is."

If the man was going to have tattoos, she expected him to have one of his wife's name or one in memory of her. "Most MC members have their club colors inked onto their backs." She stopped only inches from him and slowly traced the lines of the top and bottom rocker, as well as the center patch lightly with her fingernail.

"Were not an average MC."

"That's true. Do most of you have a BAMC tat?" She

dragged her fingernails over his warm skin. First across his chest and one nipple before heading south.

"I don't know. I don't inspect my brothers' bodies."

She grinned. "Well, if you need a volunteer..."

"They all have wives or girlfriends."

She thought of Cross and Nash. "Or husbands."

"True. We also have a female member with a boyfriend."

"Sounds like more of a melting pot than an MC."

"Definitely diverse. Unlike your father's."

"Can you blame them? It's not like most MCs accept anything other than lily white members."

"Ours does," he murmured as she worked on unfastening his belt.

"That's good to know. So do the Dirty Angels, if you weren't aware."

"I was. Also, the Blood Fury up north."

She didn't know too much about that club. "My knowledge about the Fury is limited to them being an ally of the Knights and Angels. That's it." She slipped the top button of his jeans free and slowly worked the zipper down, the backs of her knuckles brushing against his erection.

When she glanced up, she saw Nox had his head tipped down and was watching her.

She worked his jeans and boxer briefs over his muscular ass and down his lightly furred thighs. Eventually they fell to the floor with a jingle, from both the change in his pocket and his belt buckle.

Stepping back, she slowly took in every inch of him since he was now completely naked.

Finally.

She had to admit, it was worth the wait.

His hands hung by his sides with the fingers loosely curled.

His thick, hard cock jutted out from a dark patch of wiry hair.

A pearly bead of precum clung precariously to the smooth tip.

His balls hung heavily.

"Liyah..."

She glanced up to see his throat working, his nostrils flared and his jawline sharp. His hazel eyes were heated as they met hers.

He demanded in a gravelly voice, "Now you."

Chapter Twenty-Five

Since she had a good look at him, Nox was now more than ready to see her.

All of her.

Every last fucking inch.

"Do you want to do it for me?"

He shook his head. The offer was tempting but he had all night to touch her. Instead... "I want to watch."

"No pressure, right?"

For the first time since meeting her, she lost some of her confidence. He needed to fix that. "I've touched you, tasted you, inhaled your sweet scent... Now I want to see all of you."

"I hope you like what you see," she murmured.

"I doubt anything you reveal will change my opinion."

"You say that now..."

"Liyah..."

She lifted a hand and shook her head. "I don't care how confident a woman is in her everyday life, we still have moments where we question ourselves, our decisions or how we look."

"That doesn't only apply to women."

She lifted one eyebrow and gave him a pointed look. "Obviously."

With a sigh, she worked the buttons free on her sleeveless blouse until it hung open, exposing her very generous breasts and a bra that did a lot of the heavy lifting.

With a shrug, the blouse slipped off her shoulders and fluttered to the floor behind her. Reaching behind her back, she unclipped her bra and shrugged again. It fell forward, freeing her breasts.

She caught him licking his lips and squeezing the root of his cock. At least his throbbing erection proved he liked what he saw.

He cleared his throat. "Keep going."

Since she had kicked off her shoes while in the kitchen, she now stood in front of him only wearing shorts.

Since she seemed to be in no rush to remove them, he asked, "Didn't you suggest that we should have sex in a bed while totally naked?"

"Did I?"

He tipped his head to the side. "Second thoughts?"

"No. But getting naked for the first time in front of someone can be a little nerve-wracking."

"Keep going," he urged again, stroking his cock. Every time he got to the head, he squeezed it, forcing out another bead of precum.

"Keep doing that and my panties will be soaked before I can get them off."

"Then that's a good reason to remove them."

Today's shorts, like the pair she wore the other day, had an elastic waistband, so she easily pushed them and her panties down in one shot. But when she straightened, her hands covered her lower belly.

She was too late. He had already seen what she was now attempting to hide.

Anyway, she wouldn't be able to hide it when she was spread naked on the bed. And that was where they were headed next.

He understood the hesitation of her wanting him to see it, but she had no reason to worry.

He really did like everything he could see.

Besides the fact that she was the daughter of an outlaw biker with a hatred for cops, she was perfect. *If* he was looking for more than the reason he was there.

He wasn't.

He'd been barely ready to have sex with another woman. He certainly wasn't ready for any kind of relationship, even a casual one. However, being in her bedroom tonight wasn't about the future, it was about right now.

He stepped up to her and gently peeled her hands off her lower stomach. "Don't hide yourself from me."

"My stretch marks..."

"What about them?"

"They're ugly."

"They're not. They were caused from creating life. They're the mark of a warrior."

"Well, that's a nice way to put it."

"Because it's true. Women are special because they are built to create a whole other human."

Grabbing her hips, he lowered himself to his knees and brushed his lips over the long scar-like lines. Lighter than the rest of her skin, they stood out like reverse tiger stripes, but they were far from ugly. They told the story of how her body accommodated the life inside her. "Your womb grew those children."

"Nox," she whispered, combing her long nails through his hair.

He grabbed her hand and pressed a kiss in the center of her palm before rising. And on his way, he lightly kissed each breast, also decorated with stretch marks. "These nourished those children." When he straightened completely, he brushed his lips across hers. "Your kisses comforted those children. And still do." He then kissed her forehead. "You protect and guide those children." He ran his hands down her arms until he interlocked his fingers with hers. When he stepped back, he held her arms up and to the side. "Women are amazing. *You* are amazing.

"Not every woman wants to be a mother."

"No, and that's to be expected. More importantly, not every woman should be a mother. But on that note, every man shouldn't be a father, either."

"Well, that's so damn true. I've got the receipts to prove it," she said dryly.

"Despite any setbacks, you still managed to be a great mother and human in general."

Her face softened. "You give me too much credit."

"I don't bullshit. If I say something, I mean it."

"In my business there are plenty of slick salesmen. It's a turn-off for me. I wouldn't have given you the time of day if you were some bullshit artist."

"Well, damn. I figured you were attracted to my sparkling personality."

"I have a feeling your personality only needs a bit of polishing to get it back to where it was before—" She sucked in a breath.

Before...

The day that divided his life to the time before and the time after.

Before this evening got derailed, they needed to end this line of conversation and get back to business. He didn't want thoughts of one woman in his head while another stood before him.

That wasn't fair to Liyah. She deserved all his attention.

When she moved, it yanked him out of his head and back to her bedroom.

With a smile and her confidence back, she kept walking backwards away from him. When her legs bumped into the foot of the bed, she crooked a finger at him, beckoning him to follow.

He continued to stroke his cock as he closed in on her, but right before he reached where she stood, she climbed onto the mattress and continued to scramble backwards toward the headboard.

As he followed her onto the bed, he dragged his fingers along her smooth, soft skin, starting at the tips of her toes, up her calves, over her knees, along her thighs...

"Wider," he urged.

He didn't have to repeat himself. She didn't hesitate to spread her legs, giving him plenty of room for what he planned next.

After dropping to his stomach, he brushed his nose over the patch of hair above her pussy, then he lightly touched the tip of his tongue to her clit.

Her breath caught.

Then he dove in like a man lost in the desert for a week without a drop of water.

She was his water.

Maybe even his lifeline.

She was what he needed exactly when he needed it.

As much as his brothers wanted to help him, they couldn't.

As much as his therapist should be able to help him, he couldn't.

Deep down Nox knew... This woman was the one capable of putting him on the path to healing.

Simply by being herself.

When he dragged his tongue down between her slick folds, she stroked his hair. When he drew it back up and swirled it around her swollen clit, her nails dug into his scalp. Her hips hopped off the bed when he scraped his teeth over the sensitive nub.

And when he plunged a couple of fingers inside her and sucked on that clit, she jammed her pussy right into his face.

He loved every fucking second of it.

He couldn't eat her fast enough. He couldn't get enough of her.

She was sweet. Tangy. Delicious.

When she slammed her hand on the mattress, he almost jumped out of his skin. His heart tumbled a few times but quickly settled once he realized it wasn't a threat.

As long as it wasn't her father busting in the door, he was good. The hell if he wanted to go head-to-head with that man, especially while naked.

It hit him then... He was about to turn forty and was worrying about a father catching them in the act.

It would be humorous if it wasn't true.

But then most fathers weren't Magnum.

When she cried out Nox's name, any thoughts or worries about the big man were quickly washed away.

Her trembling thighs now squeezed his head as tightly as earmuffs as she bucked against him. He fucked her faster with his fingers as his tongue and lips teased and tortured her clit. Until finally he heard it... A gasp, then a long, drawn-out moan as an orgasm ripped through her.

He stayed where he was, slowing his pace but still licking and tasting the result of her climax. Still gliding his fingers in and out of her as she experienced a couple of aftershocks.

When she finally melted into the mattress, he came up for air, peering up her luscious body to see her head thrown back, her eyes closed and her lips parted with a slight curl at the corners.

He was pleased to see her chest pumping and her pulse pounding in her neck.

Proof he hadn't lost his touch.

For fuck's sake, he had missed the taste of a woman's essence on his tongue. He hoped like hell it wouldn't be almost another two years before he got to savor it again.

As long as Liyah didn't get into a serious relationship with anyone else, maybe she wouldn't mind doing this with him again in the future.

If it was up to him, the very near future.

She didn't seem the type to push him toward anything serious. She understood what he was dealing with and had the patience to deal with it, too. Plus, she was independent. She owned her own house, raised her kids as a single mom, as well as started and grew a very successful business.

She did not need anyone to give her a sense of worth.

She did that all on her own.

He couldn't imagine this woman would be clingy, would demand constant attention or would need a man to make her life complete.

Liyah bent her knees and reached out a hand, encouraging him to move over top of her. "Condom?"

Fuck.

He shook his head. "Need to grab one." Either the one in his wallet that was still in his discarded jeans or one from the box hidden in her bathroom closet.

If they did this again, he needed to plan better.

"Luckily, I thought ahead and moved the box from the closet into the nightstand."

"So, your invitation wasn't off the cuff."

She pursed her lips for a second before her lips twisted into a naughty smile. "I mean... as soon as my mother asked if the boys could stay the weekend, I thought about how I could take advantage of an empty house."

"By taking advantage of me."

That smile grew blinding. "One hundred percent. I expect you to take advantage of me, too."

"Think I just did that."

Reaching for the drawer, she told him, "But you're not done yet." She removed the open condom box—open because he was the one to actually open it for the first time a week ago —and pulled out a single condom.

"Open it," he ordered.

As soon as she ripped it open, he plucked the latex disc from inside the wrapper.

"Hey, maybe I wanted to put it on you."

"How many are left in the box?" Unless she used some in the last week, which he doubted, ten should remain.

She made a big show of peeking into the box. "Plenty for tonight."

"How about for in the morning?"

"Someone has some lofty ambitions. I doubt we'll burn through what will be left."

"Maybe. Maybe not. We'll see."

She wiggled her eyebrows. "I like your enthusiasm."

He offered her the condom. With a grin, she sat up, took it and whispered, "Come here."

He shuffled closer on his knees and when she grabbed his

throbbing cock, his hips jerked. But she made short work of rolling on the condom and then inspecting her handiwork.

"Now..." she started.

"You good with me being on top?"

"Absolutely."

"Good." He pushed her shoulder gently and she flopped back onto the bed with a giggle.

That giggle actually made him smile.

In truth, it wasn't just her giggle. It was everything about her.

Chapter Twenty-Six

With a groan, Nox rolled onto his side and opened his eyes.

Only to find Aaliyah gone.

So much for his plans on having sex with her again this morning.

Then it hit his nostrils.

A pork product. Possibly sausage.

Some sort of carbs. His nose twitched. His best guess was pancakes.

And of course, coffee.

She was making breakfast.

He rolled again and snagged his cell phone off the night-stand to check the time.

Holy shit. It was already nine. He hadn't slept that solidly in...

A long time.

His gaze caught the knocked-over condom box. Nine remained after using two last night. Depending what time she kicked his ass out the door today, they might have time to use another one.

If he could convince her into giving him one for the road.

After yanking on his jeans, he hit the bathroom to do his business, wash his face, and utilize the toothbrush he brought along in his rucksack.

Once he was somewhat awake, he followed the delicious scents to the kitchen.

When he got there, he leaned a shoulder against the wall just outside the kitchen and watched Liyah putter around. She wore a black and gold slinky robe that clung to her curves and a matching silk scarf was still tied around her hair. When he asked about it last night, she explained that wearing it while she slept protected her locks.

He had so much to fucking learn.

His ears picked up soft music.

A radio?

He listened more carefully. No, she was humming softly while she worked, but he couldn't identify the song. He wanted to get closer to figure it out but was afraid that if she spotted him, she'd stop.

He also wasn't ready for her to know he was there. He was enjoying the view too much. Especially with the way she rocked her hips back and forth while she continued to hum, adding in a word or two here and there.

He pinned his lips together to keep from making a sound as she danced around the kitchen, totally oblivious to his presence.

When she turned to grab something out of the fridge and spotted him, her dark brown eyes went wide, she released a squeak and slapped her hand over her heart. "Holy shit. How long have you been standing there?"

"Long enough. Don't let me interrupt you."

Instead of grabbing what she needed from the refrigerator, she changed course and approached him, raking her gaze down him from his bedhead all the way to his bare toes. "Damn, Officer Lennox. Seeing your sexy self wearing nothing but jeans is enough to get my motor running this morning."

Did she really just purr?

"I would've gotten it running in a different way if you hadn't let me sleep in."

When she stood bare toe to bare toe with him, she dragged her fingers along his jawline, a reminder that he needed to shave. "It looked like you needed that sleep."

He couldn't argue that fact. "What can I do to help?"

"I have something super easy for you to do. Simply keep looking more delicious than the breakfast I'm about to serve you. I have it under control." She tipped her head toward the coffeemaker. "Help yourself to some coffee. I set out a mug for you. There's creamer, milk or half and half in the fridge, if you use it." She pointed to the counter. "Sugar's in that jar there."

"Black is good for me."

She stopped dead on her way back across the largest residential kitchen he'd ever been in and glanced over her shoulder. "I'm glad you like your women the same as you like your coffee."

He snorted. "You're the first Black woman I've been with."

She laughed. "Even if I didn't already know that, you make it pretty damn obvious."

He slapped a hand over his heart. "Wow, you wound me."

With a smile, she shrugged. "I'm glad you ask questions instead of making assumptions."

"I'm glad you have the patience to answer them instead of kicking my ass out the door."

On his way over to the coffeemaker, he detoured to step behind her, grab her hips and pull her into him, pressing his nose against the side of her neck. "How do you smell so damn good this early in the morning?"

"A dab of vanilla behind the ears. A baker's secret and a man's downfall."

He slid his nose up to the tender spot behind her ear. "You don't need vanilla to be a man's downfall."

She bumped her ass into his crotch. "Is that a good thing or bad thing?"

He tightened his hold. "Depends on the man, I guess."

"Since you want to remain emotionally detached, my guess is, if you fell madly in love with me, I'm sure you'd see that as a downfall."

If you fell madly in love with me...

With a frown, he released her and stepped back.

Something inside him twisted. Began to swell.

Filling him. Taking over.

He rubbed at his pounding temple and pulled in a deep breath, trying to beat back the thick, sticky guilt creeping in again.

It wanted to ruin the moment.

Ruin the possibilities of moving on.

Prevent him from going back to living a life worth living.

In truth, he had concluded being by himself was safer. He couldn't risk falling in love again and then possibly losing that person. He barely survived the first time, and he still hadn't fully recovered.

"I'm not ready to move on," slipped from his lips, despite it being a lie. Even so, it was a knee-jerk answer to protect himself.

"Nox... First, I was only teasing you. Second, you standing in my kitchen this morning means you *are* moving on. Whether you realize it or not, being here, staying the night, is a huge step. If anyone understands how hard it is to heal from losing the love of your life, it's me. Mark and I were supposed to spend the rest of our lives together. Loving each other. Building a family and our home. Raising our children. Also like you, I felt cheated when that didn't happen, when his life, as well as ours together, was brutally cut short."

She was right. Fate cheated him out of a lifetime of loving Jackie.

She continued, "I asked the universe what I did to deserve it. I'm sure you did, too."

Too often.

"I understand it's difficult to simply accept it and move on like it never happened. Because it *did* happen. It's obvious you two had a strong connection. You both fell head over heels in love with each other, you planned your future... Hell, you planned on growing old together. But now... What other choice do you have? Besides to continue to wallow in bitterness and grief?"

Fuck. While he didn't want to have this kind of discussion this morning, he knew Liyah was only trying to help. "As much as I don't want to wallow, I can't seem to stop. Sometimes it feels like I'm stuck in thick sludge and, no matter how hard I try to break free, I can't. I get dragged back down into that pit to the point I feel like I'll be swallowed whole."

"Sometimes?"

This woman did not let him gloss over anything. She wanted details, even if they were painful. He understood why. He needed to face those details head-on. His therapist had already explained that. It was also one reason he didn't share much during his sessions.

281

"More often than not," he admitted.

"When don't you feel that way?"

"When I'm around my brothers' kids." When her eyebrows stitched together, he quickly asked, "Does that sound weird?"

"Noooo..." she drew out.

He quickly explained. "It's like they don't yet know the evil that lurks. They see life through unburdened eyes."

"Does being around the kids help you see life like that?"

He shrugged. "Sort of. If I could, I'd capture that innocence and hold onto it. I know I can't but sometimes I hope a little of that rubs off. When I'm around them, the chains restraining me in that heavy sludge feel a lot lighter. They give me hope that I'll be strong enough to escape."

"That makes sense. And I can see what you mean about the innocence of children. At least until they hit puberty." She leaned back against the center island and studied him. "Do you want some of your own?"

His chest tightened. He didn't want to go down that rabbit hole with her or anyone else. It wasn't only one chain that held him down. It was two.

However, if he was going to discuss that second loss with anyone, she would be the one. She wouldn't give him a bunch of emotionally empty "sorries," or try to slap a Band-Aid over a gaping wound.

"Nox," she prodded.

"I used to."

"And now?" she asked.

"That opportunity died with Jackie."

Liyah frowned. "No, it didn't. You have plenty of time."

"I'll be forty soon." Since some men had babies in their eighties, that wasn't even a good excuse, but it was the one to

keep from going down this path. He was afraid if they continued, their breakfast might be ruined.

"When?"

"In three weeks," he reluctantly admitted.

"Then, we'll have to celebrate your big 4-o."

He shook his head. "That's not necessary."

"I'll bake you a cake."

"It's not a big deal."

"You're right, it won't be. It simply gives me an excuse to
bake. I already told you..."

He didn't want to celebrate. Life's milestones no longer
had the same meaning as they used to.

He closed his eyes and lost track of what she was saying
when he remembered the last time he celebrated his birthday.
It was the day he turned thirty-eight.

At the time, he received what might be considered the
best birthday present a husband could get...

Finding out he would be a father.

Jackie had purposely held off telling him she was pregnant because she wanted to surprise him on his birthday.
That had to be so damn difficult for her since she had a hard
time keeping news like that to herself.

He forced his eyes open because he was *determined* not
to go down that path. Not today. Not now. Not in Liyah's
kitchen.

This was why he kept this shit buried deep inside.
Because when it came out, it was like an avalanche, dragging
him along, not caring that he got bloodied and bruised while
he was hurtled down that mountain.

His throat closed, making it difficult for him to swallow.

For fuck's sake, he was heading to the place he was trying
desperately to avoid.

The last time this happened was when he stood outside

an open motel room door in Ohio. The day they found Sloane's sister on that bed. Lifeless.

Seeing Sadie like that had dragged him back to when he found Jackie.

His heart thumped furiously, and a band tightened around his chest when he no longer stood in Liyah's kitchen. He was once again walking through the garage door into the house he and Jackie bought right after their honeymoon.

He had come home from working the day shift and once he went inside, he called Jackie's name like he normally did. In fact, he called it a couple of times without an answer, despite her car being in the garage and her keys and purse on the table by the door.

Since he got no response, he dropped his keys on the kitchen counter and his duty bag on the floor and headed upstairs.

Where he found his wife on their bed.

At first, he thought she was sleeping since it wasn't uncommon to find her in bed. The pregnancy exhausted her, so she napped a lot.

Only this time, she wasn't resting. Because when someone slept, they still breathed.

Jackie was no longer doing so, and her skin was a shade of pale that he recognized from working as a cop.

It wasn't only that, everything about her appeared... *off*.

With his heart racing and vomit threatening to rise up his throat, he checked for a pulse.

He found none.

He opened her eyelids to see them sightless.

He couldn't wrap his head around the situation. None of it made any sense.

He had no fucking idea how long Jackie had been like that.

He jerked into action and dialed 911, insisting that they send EMS immediately due to the slim possibility that the baby might still be alive. But if she was, she wouldn't be for long.

Maybe he could remove the baby himself. He could find a knife sharp enough...

A howl escaped from deep inside him as he placed a trembling hand on the swell of Jackie's stomach, sliding it around to check for any signs of movement and found none.

None.

He was too late.

Too goddamn late.

Jesus Christ. He had no idea how she even fucking died!

What the fuck happened?

He inspected her from head to toe. He didn't have to go far to find what he was looking for.

A large knot above her left ear.

It wasn't open or bleeding, but the area was swollen. However, it couldn't be the hematoma that killed her, could it? It had to be whatever caused that internal bruise.

She must have struck her head. He had no idea on what. He had no idea what time. He had no idea why she hadn't reached out to him if she had slipped and fallen.

While waiting for the ambulance, he glanced around for any signs that might explain what happened.

But all he found was a garbage can full of vomit next to the bed and a Ziploc bag full of water next to her pillow. He assumed it had been full of ice that melted.

He sat on the edge of the bed, picked up her cold hand, squeezing it tight and he leaned over to press his forehead to hers.

"What the fuck, Jackie? What the fuck?"

Goddamn it! He would've come home immediately if she

reached out to him. He would've either taken her to the hospital, if warranted, or at least kept an eye on her for any changes.

Instead, they both slipped away while he went through his day like it was any other fucking day.

Unaware that his life was being flipped upside down.

Unaware his life would be changed forever.

Unaware that his wife and baby girl were gone.

Things might have turned out differently if he had been home taking care of his own family instead of staying later than normal to process some motherfucking wife beater.

A simple text was all it would've taken.

He would've rushed home and had someone else finish processing the arrest.

He might have been able to save them both.

He should've fucking been there!

"Goddamn it! I should've been there!" burst from him, slamming Nox right back into Liyah's kitchen.

"Where?"

Liyah's question barely penetrated his brain. His world was spinning out of control and he couldn't get it to stop.

"I found her!" He slapped at his chest. "Me. I came home and fucking found her like that."

"Holy shit," Liyah whispered, putting her fingers to her gaping mouth. "Nox..."

"And not just her..." He ground the heels of his palms into his eye sockets. An attempt to keep from getting sucked back up into that memory. "Not just her."

"I don't understand. Was she with a lover?"

He dropped his hands and his brow furrowed. "What?"

"Did you find her with a lover?"

A lover?

"She wasn't cheating on me," he spat out.

"Then, who did you find her with?"

Jesus fucking Christ. She wanted him to say it.

"I didn't just lose Jackie that day."

"I don't understand."

He didn't want to say it. "Don't make me say it."

"Say what? Who was she with? Who else did you lose?"

Chapter Twenty-Seven

AALIYAH HAD no idea what the hell was going on. Was this a breaking point or a breakthrough?

Either way, Nox was unraveling right before her eyes.

Not in their grief group.

Not in his therapist's office.

But in her kitchen.

She wasn't sure what to do. Whether to encourage him to keep talking and make him face the unfaceable, or simply comfort him. She hesitated to push him, but maybe that was what he needed.

While she was thankful he felt comfortable enough around her to finally discuss his wife's death, she also worried his breakdown—if that was what it was—might spur one of her own.

It had been a long time since she was in that same dark headspace. She desperately wanted to avoid returning there.

On the other hand, she also wanted to be there for Nox.

He needed her.

Everything about him was as stiff as the Tin Man. The tendons in his neck were strained. His eyes unfocused. His hands were curled into fists.

He was stuck in his head. Most likely back on the day he lost his wife.

He'd never forget it, just like she never forgot the exact moment she was informed that Mark had been killed in the line of duty. At that moment, someone might as well have done a leg sweep and knocked her off her feet.

But the difference was, she wasn't the one who found him. If she had...

She couldn't imagine finding the love of your life dead. Especially if he'd been by himself.

When they came to tell her about Mark, she was surrounded by three other Pittsburgh PD officers. Officers she personally knew. Co-workers Mark had been close with.

They were there to pick her up off the floor. To listen. To hold her as she went through the initial stages of shock and denial. And they remained with her until the reality of the situation hit home and until her mother and Mark's family came to take over.

But Nox said Jackie wasn't alone when he found her. Why didn't that person contact him? Warn him first?

None of it made sense.

"Who was with her, Nox? Somebody you knew?"

A muscle jumped in his cheek. Once again, he pressed his fists into his eye sockets. Most likely to try to stifle the visions in his head. "I didn't have a chance to get to know her yet."

That did not clear up her confusion, but the tortured tone of his voice caused dread to fill her chest.

Whatever it was, wasn't good.

Lord no. It was really bad.

She was afraid to hear what he would say next. She wanted to know but also didn't. So, she braced herself for the worst.

"She was seven months pregnant with my daughter."

Her blood turned to ice in her veins. Her lungs struggled to pull in air. Her heart stopped beating for a few seconds. She had to fight the wail that threatened to burst from her.

For her, Mark's loss was excruciating enough, but to lose one of her sons?

No wonder his wife's death hit him so hard and for so long. It wasn't one loss.

It was *two.*

And the second one hadn't had the opportunity to live even a minute of life.

Gone before she even arrived. Before the world got to meet her.

With her stomach twisting, Liyah wanted to puke.

Breakfast would end up tossed in the trash. She lost her appetite, and she was damn sure Nox would no longer be in a mood to eat.

She closed the space between them. When she stopped in front of him, she didn't pull his hands away from his face, but instead, wrapped her arms around his waist and pressed her cheek to his bare chest. For a moment, she listened to his thumping heart. His muscles were still as hard as concrete.

He was struggling to keep from breaking down.

Maybe that was what he needed. A release.

To stop holding everything inside.

"What happened?" she asked gently, squeezing him even tighter.

His words sounded thick when he answered, "Cause of

death was determined to be an acute subdural hematoma from a fall."

"And do you believe that diagnosis?"

"Yes, I found... Yes, that's how... I..."

He suddenly jolted against her and before she knew what was happening, he slipped from her grasp and landed on his knees at her feet.

He was no longer holding anything in. No longer trying to wear a brave face.

He was letting it all go.

Finally.

Even so, her heart cracked in two as he hugged her legs and hid his face against her lower belly...

But it was when she heard his broken sobs...

Tears welled up in her own eyes while she clutched the back of his neck with one hand and gently combed her fingers through his hair with the other, trying to soothe and support him without words. She wanted him to know she was there for him.

For as long as he needed her.

She swiped at the hot tear rolling down her own cheek and locked her knees so she wouldn't collapse into a puddle on the floor next to him while mourning the loss of, not only Nox's wife, but his unborn baby girl.

A daughter clearly and completely loved by her father, despite the fact he never got to the chance to see or hold her.

"Is this the first time you've let yourself cry?" *Lord*, tears thickened her voice, too.

His lack of answer was answer enough.

Smothering a sniffle, he wiped at his eyes and nose. But he didn't move away, he remained at her feet with his face pressed to her stomach. Most likely waiting for the stirred-up, deep emotions to pass.

Some men, especially cops, had this mistaken idea that crying showed weakness. But the truth was, everyone cried at one point or another. And Nox had every reason to do so. No one would ever judge him for it. If someone did, that person had a dried up, wrinkled heart and zero empathy.

Or never experienced a loss as tragic as Nox.

Once his breathing was somewhat normal and the sniffling subsided, he held onto her hips and got back to his feet. But he still didn't move away. Instead, he circled his arms around her waist again and tucked her head under his chin, holding her close.

She rubbed his back and lost track of how long they stood there connected, sharing both their energy and sadness.

Eventually she asked, "What was her name?"

It took him forever to answer and when he did, he had to take a deep inhale first. Most likely to keep from falling apart again. "I never named her."

Holy shit. She was not expecting that answer. She couldn't just ask, *"Why not?"* She needed to handle the questions that popped in her head carefully. "She wasn't buried?"

"She was with Jackie."

Her brow furrowed. "In the same coffin?" Was that even allowed?

"I didn't need to get her one. She couldn't be... saved, so they never..." He pulled in another deep breath. "They never..."

It hit Liyah what he was trying to say. The baby remained in the womb. She stayed tucked safely within her mother.

Two souls remained connected for eternity. While another became lost, trying to figure out how to survive without them.

Good God, his situation was so much worse than she originally thought. And she had no words that would make it any better.

It wasn't true that time healed all wounds. Eventually the pain might dull, but it would never go away completely. Nox would carry it with him until the day he was laid in the ground himself.

Just like Liyah would miss Mark until the day she took her last breath. And she'd also feel sad that her son missed out on a relationship with his father.

"You didn't choose a name beforehand?" Most parents at least had a short list once they found out the sex of the baby. And from how Nox talked, he knew the baby was a girl.

"I made her wait. I wanted to meet her first. It was my fault that she didn't have a name."

"But you can fix that by naming her now. She's still your daughter. She will be forever." And it might help with closure. Because clearly, he hadn't had any.

"I don't know," came muffled against her scarf.

He stepped back, turning away immediately and walking across the kitchen. Most likely to hide his red eyes and swollen nose. The proof he had broken down.

"Think about it. It doesn't have to be today. Or even tomorrow. Do it when you're ready. Because, Nox, she existed. And she still owns a piece of your heart."

"Sorry for fucking up your breakfast plans."

As soon as she said, "Nox, *you* are more important than breakfast," he spun and headed back to her with his eyes intense.

He didn't stop until he ran into her, enveloping her tightly in his arms and whispering, "Thank you."

Why did him thanking her break her heart even more? "I didn't do anything."

"Yes, you did. You did more than you know."

———

Aaliyah was right. He should name his daughter and add it to the headstone. He hadn't stopped thinking about it since she encouraged him to do so.

He had only "mother and child" engraved under Jackie's name. At the time, he hadn't been thinking too clearly and wasn't sure what to put. Plenty of space remained to add his daughter's name.

However, even though the thought had been on his mind since she mentioned it, he wasn't sure he was ready to pick a name. To sit down and really concentrate on it. He was afraid of what that might stir up again. One breakdown this weekend was enough.

Were things improving? Slowly. And he had to credit Liyah for that.

After spending that whole weekend at her place—only leaving at the same time she left to pick up her boys—he began to look forward to attending the Wednesday night grief group.

Not so he could share, but because he knew he'd see her.

He would tolerate the circle because that meant he could sit next to her. Being near her partially filled the emptiness inside him.

He'd been living in a bubble consisting of only work and his MC ever since he found himself a widower. So, he surprised himself by looking forward to spending time with her. Unfortunately, finding that time wouldn't be easy between her business, him being on the task force and trying to keep their connection a secret. From both her family and also his.

He didn't want her to be spotted going into his apartment. And he couldn't stay at her place when her boys were home. That would make their time together very limited, but he was good with whatever he could get.

He had no idea what it was about Liyah that drew him. Yes, they had experienced a similar loss but that was the only thing in common between them.

She was rich. He was far from it.

She had children. He had none.

She was white collar. His collar was solid blue.

She was the queen of her own empire. He was only a grunt in the trenches.

He used to be satisfied with his life. He never needed much, only a roof over his head, the love of a good woman, his loyal brothers and a steady income.

He didn't need a hot sports car, a mansion, designer clothes and a fat bank account.

People and close relationships were more important to him than things. But then, that was the way he'd been raised. Love and family had always been more important to his mother than objects.

Like Liyah, his mother had raised him by herself. She was another loss that made his heart break. His mother had been a hard-working, good woman who unfortunately made bad choices when it came to men.

The same way Liyah had with the father of her youngest son.

Maybe Keenan's father turned out to be a piece of shit, but at least the man hadn't caused major emotional or physical damage to Liyah. The last man his mother had a serious relationship with still sat in prison to this day. He would die in prison if Nox had anything to do with it, while his mother rested eternally in the cemetery plot next to Jackie and his daughter.

All because she had put her trust in the wrong man.

That bastard rotting behind bars might not be karma but it was damn close.

He sneered. Kevin was lucky that the police grabbed him before Nox did. The asshole left Nox motherless at eighteen. The whole reason he joined the Army and afterward became a cop.

His career goal became to put away monsters like Kevin. Men who pretended to love and respect women on the surface but at their very core hated them. They were pros at faking it until it was too late.

One day it became too late for his mother.

The difference between losing his mother and losing his wife, was the fact what Kevin did pissed Nox off so badly, he could kill that motherfucker with his bare hands. Jackie's death was an accident. His mother's wasn't.

Thinking about what that motherfucker did was not the path he wanted to be on today. Not after his breakdown in Liyah's kitchen yesterday morning.

After pulling his bike through, he closed The Plant's back gate and drove it around to the side lot where he normally parked. He noticed a few other bikes parked there.

Most of the time the task force left their four-wheeled vehicles in the bigger lot directly behind the building, leaving the side lot open for any two-wheeled rides. But being Sunday evening, the only task force members up on the third floor would be anyone assigned to listen to "dirty talk." That meant some Blue Avengers were hanging out downstairs.

He could go up to his apartment and be anti-social or he could stop in and hang with them. Or at least say hello.

He noticed the more time he spent with Liyah, the less he was tempted to hide.

Once he shut off his bike and covered it for the night, he pulled open the side door and stepped inside the club's meeting room. As he rounded the conference table—not as long as the one on the third floor—he spotted a piece of trash on the floor. When he paused to pick it up, he heard voices coming from the common area.

Chapter Twenty-Eight

Nox straightened after picking the balled-up receipt off the floor and continued toward the open doorway, only to slam on the brakes when he heard Crew ask, "Have you noticed the difference in him?"

Was that about him?

Nox heard Axel Jamison next. "Do you think it has to do with the ultimatum?"

Jesus. They were definitely discussing him. And without him present. Of fucking course.

"What else could it be?" Crew asked.

With a shake of his head, Nox leaned a shoulder against the wall.

"I don't see him as often as you, Crew," Cross said, "that makes it easier for me to see the difference. You see him every day."

"How about you, Prez? You don't see him as much, either. What do you think?"

"I agree with Cross. It's seems like he's improving a little more every week. Something is shifting for the better," Jamison answered Crew.

"That's a fucking relief," the task force leader mumbled.

"Let's hope it continues in the right direction," the BAMC president continued. "We thought he was improving before and then finding Sadie derailed him again."

"Well, we can't keep him fucking bubble wrapped. He's not only a cop, he's a member of my task force team. He's going to see shit. People are ugly to each other every goddamn day. If he can't handle it, he needs to get a job at McDonald's or something."

Crew always had a way with words.

"He's an excellent cop. He only needs to get over this hump."

That was a relief to hear from Jamison, since he was Nox's Shadow Valley PD supervisor. Nox liked his job and he wanted to keep it.

"Or he needs to find someone to hump. Getting some good pussy tends to help a man's outlook on life. Right, Cross?" Crew chuckled.

For fuck's sake. Nox had heard enough.

"I'd have to take your word for it, since—"

Stepping out into the common area interrupted Cross mid-sentence and all eyes turned toward him. Jamison's widened while Crew's crinkled at the corners.

Nox pretended as if he hadn't been eavesdropping. "What's up?"

"Nothing. We're just," Jamison grimaced, "hanging out."

Sure.

"Where have you been?" Crew asked, drawing Nox's attention. "Your bike was gone all weekend."

Someone had been paying attention. Unfortunately. "Had some things to do, *Dad.*"

300

Crew, Jamison and Cross all exchanged glances.

"Should we bother to ask?" came from Cross.

"Nope."

They all shared glances again.

Crew frowned. "You're not even going to give us a hint on where you were or what you were up to?"

"The hint was when I said nope." He turned toward their president. "Did Finn get the run scheduled for next weekend?"

Jamison nodded. "He did. We should have enough members available so all the kids can go. Or at least the ones who want to go."

He glanced at Cross. "Are your kids coming?"

Aiden Cross nodded. "They'll be here, whether they want to be or not."

His daughter Bri was more agreeable about doing family activities than his son, who was more like Cross's husband. "What about Nash?"

His fellow BAMC brother stared at him. "When has he ever joined us on a run?"

The answer was never, but... "He could always have a change of heart."

Cross snorted. "Yeah, just as soon as the DAMC does and lets me join in on theirs."

"Do you even want to?" Jamison's question was colored in surprise.

"If Nash asked, I would," Cross admitted. "I'd do it for him."

Jamison's eyebrows shot up toward his hairline. "Has he ever asked?"

"No."

Crew chimed in with all his deep wisdom, "I bet if you

look up 'opposites attract' on Wikipedia, it would have a picture of you and your hubby."

Cross shrugged. "Our situation isn't perfect, but we make it work."

"And that's all that matters, brother," Jamison agreed, since his wife was DAMC born and bred, unlike Nash who joined the DAMC as an adult.

Both Jamison and Cross were in similar situations. Their spouses were part of an MC family that didn't welcome cops.

Hell, Jamison's grandfather was one of the *founders* of the Dirty Angels and he wasn't welcomed. All because he wore a badge. Tolerated? Somewhat. Welcomed with open arms? Fuck no.

Just like Nox most likely wouldn't be accepted by Liyah's family. At least the side that included her father and his club.

Crew nudged him with an elbow. "What's that look for?"

He shuttered his expression. "Just thinking how much tension it could cause."

"What do you mean?"

"The situations with the prez and Bella, as well as Cross and Nash. It can't be easy."

"But like Cross said, it might not be perfect but they make it work. As long as they're happy, right?"

Nox shot Crew a look. "You really think love can conquer all?"

Crew's face twisted. "Fuck no. Look at the disaster with me and Sasha. Anyway... I told Dylan he's riding with you on Sunday."

"He's good with it?"

"Thrilled, if you want to know the truth. Most likely because he's not stuck riding with me."

"The kids will come around." Nox sure as fuck hoped they would. For Crew's sake.

Crew's lips flattened and his jaw tightened. "Maybe."

The task force leader could be a cocky asshole, but no one would ever doubt that he loved his kids. He ended up getting the short end of the stick when it came to his marriage. And divorce. And custody of his two children.

His ex caused problems every time it was Crew's scheduled weekend, even though it was only once a month.

If Nox had kids...

He closed his eyes and breathed through the burn in his gut.

"You all right?"

He opened his eyes and answered Crew with a, "Yeah. I'm good."

"You seem to be heading that way. What changed?"

"What do you mean?" He noticed that Jamison and Cross were now standing over in the kitchen area grabbing beers from the fridge and not paying attention to his and Crew's conversation.

"Is it the therapist? The weekly group meetings?"

Nox answered with a simple, "Yeah."

"Yeah? Which one?"

It was time to change the subject. The fuck if he was telling Crew about Liyah. He'd never hear the end of it. "Any word on the indictments?"

"The AUSA is working on them. Are you still up for busting in some doors... And heads?"

"Always." Especially after what those fuckers did to Sloane, Sapphire, Mel and Sadie.

They needed more than their heads busted in.

"Okay, I'll make sure you're on the list."

"You on that list?" Nox asked the task force leader.

"I haven't decided yet. I might leave it for the young-ins."

"You're not much older than me, Crewser."

303

Crew's head tipped to the side. "Isn't your fortieth coming up soon?"

"Yeah."

"Wanna celebrate it?"

Actually, he'd prefer to ignore it. "By doing what?"

Crew shrugged, then got a look that made Nox brace for whatever came next. "I'd say strip club but the fuck if we're going to The Peach Pit. Mel needs to get hers open soon so we have a decent place to go."

"Decent? Strip club? Does that go hand-in-hand?"

Crew grinned. "When Mel's running it, it does."

That was true. Finn's woman was a class act. She had treated the dancers she managed well and with respect. Nox had no doubt the club she opened would be successful and not a sleazy dump. Her clientele would be a higher class than the customers now patronizing the Demons-run strip joint.

"There's always Heaven's Angels in Shadow Valley," Crew suggested with a smirk.

"I'll pass on the strip club."

"Maybe Jamison's ol' lady will bake you a tray of her stuffed cupcakes."

He didn't need cupcakes if Liyah was baking him a cake. "I'm good."

"But I'm not. I want some fucking cupcakes."

"Then go buy some," Nox suggested.

"Why, when we can get Jamison to bring us some for free?"

Nox shook his head. "You're a cheap motherfucker on top of being an asshole."

Crew's grin widened. "Oh good. Thought I was slipping there for a second. Thanks for the confirmation."

"Anytime. If you want, I can put a reminder on my phone

to call you a cheap motherfucking asshole once a day. Or do you want to hear it every hour? I can be flexible."

Crew laughed and whacked him on the back. "What would we do without you, Hard Nox?" He turned and yelled, "Hey, Jamison! We need Bella to make a bunch of cupcakes for Nox's birthday. He's going to hit the big 4-0 soon! He said those stuffed Tiramisu cupcakes are his favorite!"

Oh, for fuck's sake.

Chapter Twenty-Nine

AFTER LOSING JACKIE, he never thought he'd ever find anyone he'd want to spend as much time with as he did Aaliyah.

While it still surprised him, it no longer made him feel guilty.

He was allowed to live his life. It took him a while to believe that, but now he did. And it wasn't because the therapist convinced him of that. Or his brothers.

Or anyone in particular, actually.

He simply found someone he *wanted* to spend time with. Wanted to share *more* than time with.

In truth, he simply wanted her.

But, of course, Liyah wasn't an island. She had two sons, as well as a father who was a member of an outlaw MC.

That could be an issue. So, being with her wasn't actually simple.

For the last few weeks, after the Wednesday night meetings, they'd sit in her Mercedes Benz and talk. Sometimes they'd not say much of anything. Either way, afterward she'd send him home with baked goods he smuggled into his place so he wouldn't get a million bullshit questions from his nosy as fuck brothers.

But with every bite of a perfectly baked cookie or brownie, with every damn treat he ate, he thought of her. *Hell*, he thought of her even when he wasn't eating any of her food.

She was on his mind constantly.

Besides talking in the car after the meetings, he met Liyah twice for a quick dinner at a diner nowhere close to where either of them lived or worked.

Once, he even took her for a quick ride on his bike when her boys were at school, and she told the agents at her office that she had an appointment with an important client.

The ride might have only lasted forty-five minutes, but straddling his Harley, along with the fresh air combined with Liyah wrapped around his back soothed his soul.

Her smile was so damn big once she climbed off his bike, his own spread across his face. He did not miss it when she did a doubletake, then hugged the shit out of him.

And, *fuck*, did that feel good.

It took him a little longer to let go than it did her. But she leaned into it and allowed him to hang on for as long as he held her.

He appreciated that about her. She seemed to always know what he needed, sometimes before he did.

Tonight, once everyone was gone, the room in the community center cleaned up and the chairs and tables put away, he once again accompanied Liyah to her car. After she clicked the fob to unlock her luxury sedan, he opened the driver's door for her.

She paused before getting in. "Are you joining me tonight?"

Of course he was, this was his favorite part of his Wednesday nights. The chance to spend time with her was basically the only reason for him to still show up. "Yeah."

With a nod, she climbed in and shut her door while he circled the Mercedes and slid in on the other side. Once he closed the passenger door, the interior became dark and quiet.

"Music?"

"No." Nox pulled a long breath in through his nose and leaned his head back, closing his eyes to simply enjoy the alone time with her. And the peace and quiet after sixteen grief group members spilled their guts, shed some tears and shared a few laughs.

He understood that some people had to talk things out. He was not one of them.

Proof was him breaking down in Liyah's kitchen about a month ago. That had been ugly, and he never wanted that to happen again.

"Hey," she whispered. Reaching over, she snagged his hand and pulled it into her lap. After intertwining their fingers, she gave them a gentle squeeze.

Between that and hearing her pull in a deep breath of her own, he braced. Because unlike him, it meant she was gearing up for something.

Something he might not want to discuss or deal with.

"I hesitate to bring this up, but..."

Just as he thought.

"You've done a complete one-eighty since I first met you. Are the appointments with the therapist helping you?"

His brow wrinkled. "The therapist?"

She raised her eyebrows. "Yes, the one you were forced to see. That one. Remember?"

How could he forget the one he kept cancelling his appointment with? Though, she didn't need to know that.

He also hoped that Jamison and Crew wouldn't find out that Nox had been skipping out on part of his "ultimatum." The only thing they should worry about was that he was getting better. He was achieving that without going to a therapist every week. "No, he's not helping at all."

"Then what is?"

"You want the truth?"

"Of course I want the truth." She burned a hole into the side of his face with her stare.

He twisted to face her. "It's you."

She frowned. "What's me?"

"You have been helping me, not my therapist."

"You mean the grief group."

He shook his head. "No, I mean *you*."

"What have I done? I know it can't be my bomb-ass pussy."

His jaw dropped slightly before he gathered himself. "Then you don't give yourself enough credit." Though, it had been too long since he got a little of that bomb-ass pussy therapy.

"Wow. I guess I'm changing lives one cock at a time."

Since they were goofing around... "Have you ever had more than one at a time?"

"Have you?"

He chuckled. "I don't swing that way."

"Neither do I. One dick is more than enough to deal with."

"Am I a dick?"

"No, but you have a very nice one."

His head jerked back. "Hold up. Do women rate dicks?"

"Of course."

Why was he only hearing about this now? At forty. "On what scale. One to ten?" If true, he could've used this information when he was younger and on the prowl.

"Yep."

"And where does mine fall?"

She dropped her eyes to his crotch and pressed a long nail to her lips as she pretended to think really hard. "*Mmm.* I'd rate yours at a 9.435."

"Oh, I see... I merit fractions."

"Well, I haven't seen a perfect ten yet."

He fought the twitch of his lips. "Are you actively searching?"

"No."

"Will you accept a dick that's less than a perfect ten?"

"Depends on who it's attached to."

"If it's attached to someone like me?"

When she shrugged, his lips finally twisted into a grin. "I can make an exception."

"Well, thank fuck for that," he teased.

She leaned closer and brushed the back of her knuckles down his cheek. "You're not bad for an exception."

"Depends on who you ask."

"I'm going with my own opinion. I don't care what anyone else thinks."

"Then, I like the way you think."

"Though, my memory is a bit weak," she continued, "and it's been a while since I've seen it. I might have to check it out again to make sure my rating's still accurate."

"Do you want me to whip it out right here and now? Do I need to do a rub and tug first to get the best assessment?"

She laughed. "No one wants to see a deflated pink worm."

"Snake. Not a worm."

"Just be glad I didn't say button mushroom." She lifted a finger and released his hand she'd been holding in her lap, "Before you expose yourself like a pervy flasher, I have something for you..." and twisted around to grab something from the back seat.

Her ass, raised high in the air, tempted him as she stretched for whatever it was.

"That looks delicious," he murmured.

"I know, right? I spent a good amount of time on it."

"Sitting on it or doing squats?"

"What?" When that luscious rear-end plunked down in the driver's seat again, she held a large round plastic container. "No, this."

He mourned the loss of her ass practically smashed into his face. "What's that?"

"The birthday cake I promised you. I'm sorry I wasn't able to give it to you on the actual day."

Damn, she actually baked him a cake. "Liyah... You didn't have to do that."

"I'm well aware of that, but I wouldn't have done it if I didn't want to. I was hoping it would brighten your day, because when I hear you laugh or see you smile, the truth is... it brightens mine."

He opened his mouth, then closed it when he wasn't sure how to respond. He stared at her for a few seconds before asking the only thing he could think of. "It's that simple?"

With a single nod, she popped off the container's lid. "It's that simple."

The unmistakable sweet smell of frosting or icing, or whatever she used to decorate the cake, filled the car.

"I wasn't sure what your favorite flavor is because I neglected to ask. Since you liked the smell of vanilla on me, I figured the safe bet was going with a simple vanilla layer cake and French vanilla buttercream frosting."

Good call since, after smelling vanilla on her that morning in her kitchen, it was now his favorite scent. "Vanilla works."

"The most difficult part of making it was sneaking it out of the house before my boys spotted it and devoured half."

"Only half?"

"More likely it would've been a cake massacre. A smear of frosting and a few crumbs would be the only evidence left of its existence."

She was probably right. "I remember how much I ate at their age."

"I swear boys are bottomless pits."

When she went to pop the cover back on the container, he stopped her with a, "Hold on."

He might not be hungry and doubted she had brought anything along to eat the cake with, but that didn't mean he couldn't taste it. He dragged his finger through the icing along the side of the cake and lifted it to his lips.

She watched him closely as he took his time sliding that finger into his mouth and sucking it clean.

"That's damn good," he murmured.

She made a little noise at the back of her throat when he caught some more of the icing on the tip of his finger before she could stop him, but instead of putting it in his mouth, he dabbed it on her bottom lip.

"Don't!" he said sharply when she went to lick it off. "That's mine."

He cupped the back of her neck and leaned in while pulling her closer so he could drag his tongue slowly over her bottom lip, licking it clean. "Mmm. Super sweet. But I can't taste the vanilla," he lied. "Let me try again." This time, when he scooped a larger glob on the end of his finger, he ordered, "Open up."

Without a hesitation, she opened her mouth.

"Tongue out."

When she stuck her tongue out, he smeared the frosting along it, then immediately followed by taking her mouth. In truth, he didn't give a shit about the flavor, all he wanted to taste was Liyah.

Actually, he didn't care about the cake, either. While it was a nice gesture, all he wanted to eat was Liyah.

They really needed a place to go. They were both past the age of having sex in a car in some dark parking lot. Especially in the town where he normally worked.

Her tongue met his stroke for stroke, sharing the sweetness and teasing and tangling until they were both breathless and he was rock hard.

Palming his cheek, she pulled away enough to whisper roughly, "Where can we go?"

He was pleased to hear that her thoughts aligned with his. "Ms. James, are you feeling a bit spicy tonight?"

"It's been almost a month. I'd send my kids to my parents every damn weekend if they—as in my kids *and* my parents—wouldn't get suspicious." She laughed. "Does that make me a horrible mother?"

"Because you want time for yourself?"

"See, that makes it sound a little more respectable than simply saying I want to be selfish by getting naked and sweaty with a very handsome and sexy cop."

"Glad I can be of service."

"Well, you *could* service me... We just need to find a place." She glanced around. "I don't think either of us want to twist ourselves into a pretzel to have sex in my car."

"You don't like a challenge?"

"I like challenges, but I'd also like to, one, keep my leather seats clean and two, be able to walk tomorrow without having to take a half bottle of aspirin first. Oh, and I prefer not to transport my clients around in a car that smells like boinking."

"I'll give you that. Plus, I'd prefer we don't get busted by someone from the Shadow Valley PD for lewd acts and public nudity. I don't think my supervisor would be happy about that." Though, Jamison probably would. He might be thrilled that Nox was getting a little action. Even if it was in a car in the community center's parking lot.

He'd get a scowl first before an enthusiastic high-five.

He might get suspended right after he got an "atta-boy."

But yeah... He'd rather not get busted with his ass hanging out by his co-workers. He was forty now, not fourteen. "I guess the boys are home."

"Yes, judging by their five thousand texts complaining that there's nothing to eat. What about your place? Or is that still out?"

Shit. He would love to take her to his place, but he wasn't risking it. No freaking way. Not only did he not want to deal with hearing bullshit from his brothers or the task force, he didn't want Liyah harassed, either. "My place is not a good idea."

"Damn," she whispered, securing the lid on the container and handing the cake to him. "So, now what?"

Now he broke out his wallet and paid for a place. "Motel?"

"One of those by-the-hour joints?" She wiggled her eyebrows.

"I might need more than an hour."

Those same eyebrows stuck to the top of her forehead. "Oh, you think so, huh?"

Chapter Thirty

VALLEY VIEW MOTEL was similar to the diner. In a location where the likelihood of anyone spotting them together was very minimal. Being about twenty-five minutes west of Shadow Valley, it was close but also not.

Apparently, the roadside motel rented mostly to long-term residents. People with crappy credit and unable to get a lease on an apartment. Or people needing a temporary place to stay until they could find something more permanent.

Or people, like them, trying to avoid being spotted at a motel.

The sprawling one-story building might be really outdated but the room appeared and smelled clean when they entered.

Unfortunately—or more like fortunately, depending on who you asked—they didn't leave it the same way. The sheets were now in a damp, tangled mess, a discreetly wrapped, used condom sat at the bottom of the garbage can and the smell?

It damn sure wasn't the scent of vanilla lingering in the air.

He definitely got his money's worth, even though he paid for a whole night, and they only used it for a couple of hours.

Nox sat on the edge of the bed lacing up his boots while Liyah worked on getting her hair back in some semblance of order.

"Jeez," she came out of the bathroom looking, for the most part, put together, "the furniture in here reminds me of my grandmother's house."

"I'm sure it's from that same era."

"I'd call it retro but it's more like old and tired." She released a long sigh. "Well, that was fun. We'll have to do this again soon."

"I assume my imperfect cock was satisfactory enough?"

She stepped between his spread knees and drew a long nail along his jawline. "The act itself was a ten."

"I guess the action is more important than the perfection of the tool used."

"No guessing required." One side of her mouth pulled up. "But that wasn't the only tool you used."

When he rose from the bed, he grabbed her hips and pulled her into him, taking her mouth for a quick kiss. After they parted, he said, "I can meet you here every Wednesday night after you're done with the grief group."

She shook her head. "That's not going to happen."

His eyebrows rose. "You're not interested?"

She poked him in the chest. "Oh, Officer Lennox, I am certainly interested, but I'll only put out if you attend the meetings. You don't get the reward if you don't put in the work."

"Damn. Blackmail."

She shot him a cheesy grin. "No, Black female."

He chuckled and shook his head.

"All right," she continued. "I need to get home and see if my house is still standing since I've been gone longer than normal."

"Don't you trust them enough not to burn down the house while you're gone?"

Her head jerked back. "Absolutely not. These are undeveloped male brains we're talking about. They think of stupid shit like warming up pizza slices in a toaster. Not a toaster oven, mind you—an appliance that sits right on the counter and is easily accessible—an actual freaking toaster. I have an endless list of the dumb shit they do. I should hand that list over to their future wives as warning."

"Or use it as blackmail."

She *mmm*'d. "I'll keep that idea in my back pocket. Are you going to walk me out?"

"Absolutely." He planned on following her on his bike, too. At least until they were forced to split off in different directions.

The motel was located off the beaten path in an area not very populated. Twenty years ago, the two-lane road that ran past it used to be a main thoroughfare. Wider highways built to handle the increase in traffic now bypassed the area completely. The likely reason most of their occupants were long-term. Or hiding.

He tossed the room key onto the small, battered table in front of the window and made sure the door would lock behind them before following her out onto the narrow, cracked concrete sidewalk that ran in front of the rooms. About half of the rooms had at least one vehicle parked in front of them, unlike earlier when they arrived.

Movement to his left made his head turn in that direction. And when it did, he abruptly stopped and stared to make sure he wasn't seeing things.

While the lighting wasn't great out in the parking lot, it was good enough for him to swear he recognized the man helping a female, appearing drugged or ill, inside a room.

No. Fucking. Way.

Was it T-Bone? It sure as hell looked like that scumbag.

Whoever it was had a hitch in his step, but Nox wasn't sure if it was from an injury or from the half-unconscious woman leaning heavily on him. It could very well be both.

Nox continued to watch the man, not wearing a cut or any identifying club colors, open the door to the room at the very end of the motel. The farthest he could get from the office, of course.

No damn surprise if it *was* T-Bag, since remote motels without a lot of traffic seemed to be the fucker's M.O. when it came to pimping out strung-out women.

Was the woman with him high on meth? If she was, where did Bonehead get it? If the prospect had been stripped of his cut, that meant his access to an endless supply of meth disappeared the same as his club colors.

Right before ducking inside, the man with the shaggy beard and hair glanced his way and their eyes locked for a few seconds.

Holy fuck. It *was* him. It was goddamn T-Bone. Nox no longer had any doubt.

For some reason, the Demons hadn't erased that motherfucker from the Earth like they all expected. He had either escaped, or they had let him go. And if they did, why? That wasn't typical behavior for an outlaw MC.

None of it made any damn sense. It wasn't like the Demons were gentleman and would give the asshole a polite warning and send him on his way.

But still... The former prospect's eyes had widened slightly when meeting his. Did he recognize Nox somehow? If so, he had no idea how. He had never gone to The Peach Pit...

Shit. It could be from when he and Rez confronted him while undercover and doing construction at the Demons' Uniontown church. Or maybe the fucker had seen him when he and Rez found Sadie in the motel in Ohio.

It could very well be both.

Had the asshole been lurking around watching when they thought he was still tied-up in that field? But if T-Bag had spotted them in Ohio, Nox could see him using that info as some sort of bargaining chip with the Demons to remain breathing.

Had the task force been made? Did the Demons know they were being tracked?

Fuck. He should warn Crew but...

At this point, he couldn't tell anyone he spotted T-Bone because they'd want to know where. They'd also want to know why Nox was at a motel out in the middle of nowhere when he had a perfectly good apartment in Rockvale.

Unfortunately, too many questions would be asked, and he wasn't ready to answer any of them.

His best bet would be to stake out the motel on his own to confirm who he saw and document what the former prospect was up to. If he was legitimately no longer a member of the Demons, T-Bone would no longer be part of the task force's focus.

But... a few of his brothers had a bone to pick with T-Bone. Nox being one. So even if the man wasn't a target for the task force, he would be one for some of the Blue Avengers like Finn, Decker and Rez.

However, if the task force turned out to be compromised, then that was a whole different ball game.

"Is something wrong?"

Her question yanked Nox's attention from T-Bone's motel room back to Liyah, wearing a concerned expression. "No." He placed a hand at the small of her back, urging, "Let's go."

"But you look like you've seen a ghost. And you're all tense."

"Let's go," he repeated, steering her toward the driver's side of her Benz.

He really didn't want T-Bone getting a good look at Liyah. The fuck if he was bringing her back to this motel again.

What were the fucking odds he'd run into that asshole in the middle of nowhere? Slim to none, but here they were.

He needed to figure out what to do with all of this and how to handle this new snag.

For now, he'd go back to Rockvale, borrow one of the task force's pool cars and sit surveillance. If T-Bag was running his money-making operation out of this motel on a regular basis, he'd document it in case he still had ties to the Demons.

If he didn't, he'd use that info personally and share it with a select few.

The motherfucker was not getting off scot-free. Not if Nox had anything to do with it and he was damn sure some of his brothers would agree.

———

It turned out he couldn't take a pool car without either answering, or ignoring, a barrage of questions when he went up to grab the keys. Instead, he was forced to take his old

Chevy truck on his unofficial stakeout. It actually fit in perfectly with the rest of the vehicles owned by the motel's occupants. Not that he parked in the motel's lot.

He'd wait until the majority of the task force members were gone for the day and no Blue Avengers were hanging around outside, then he'd head out for the night to go sit along the long, dark farm lane that ran next to Valley View Motel.

Close enough to keep an eye out for T-Bone. Far enough that he hoped he didn't draw any attention.

In his truck he kept bottles of cold water, a Thermos of hot coffee and an empty container to piss into.

He also brought along a pair of high-powered binoculars to get a better look at the actors involved, capture their vehicle registration info and take note of any questionable activity.

He returned the same night that he and Liyah were there and wrote down T-Bones' current vehicle's make, model and license plate info, so he could do a little "research" the next day when he was officially working.

When he showed up the next night, he saw T-Bone had also returned.

And the next night.

And the next.

If he was there when the asshole arrived or left, Nox took note of the times and whether he had a woman with him. If he did, Nox recorded the description of the female the former prospect brought to the motel room on the end. He also documented as many details as possible on the "johns" showing up to use T-Bone's "services."

However, there was a pattern.

A criminal with any smarts would know not to create such an obvious one. Once again proving T-Bone was a dumb motherfucker.

The pattern was not only staying in the same room in the same motel, it was also the behavior surrounding the little "business."

The motel room door would open, what looked like cash would be exchanged, T-Bone would step outside and close the door behind him, then go sit in his piece of shit car for fifteen minutes. Some men stayed for less than the quarter hour. Some stayed—and most likely paid—for more time.

After seeing Sadie's body in the condition it was in, it made Nox's stomach churn to watch men go in and out of that room most of the night.

One after the other after the other.

The scumbag was a goddamn pimp. Only Nox doubted any of the women whose services he sold volunteered for the gig. And if they did, it was because they were addicted and were desperate for a fix.

Ideally the fucker needed to die, but unfortunately, that was illegal and the reason they had set him up by hinting to Saint that the prospect was skimming meth from the stash at The Peach Pit. Clearly, their snitching hadn't done what they'd hoped. Not if the man was still upright and breathing.

As well as abusing women.

They thought Saint—and ultimately Viper, the Demons' club president—would do the "right thing"—according to a one-percenter MC, anyway—but they should've known better. It proved the cliché that no honor existed among thieves.

While he looked forward to seeing Liyah again tomorrow night at this week's meeting and getting naked with her again afterward, he might not have the energy to give her sex worth a rating of ten. Working these unofficial "all-nighters" were taking a damn toll on him.

If he climbed in bed with Liyah, he feared he might actually fall asleep.

But T-Bone getting what was coming to him was more important to Nox than getting sex.

Though, sex with Liyah was top notch and for that, it would be worth drinking one of those energy shots, even if he ended up shaky and wired. At least he wouldn't miss out on spending time with the woman always on his mind.

Yawning, he reached for his Thermos, then silently cursed when he realized he was almost out of the much-needed caffeine.

He glanced at the time. *For fuck's sake*, it was now three-thirty in the morning. He really needed to head out soon to at least catch a couple of hours of sleep before dragging his ass up to the third floor to do some legitimate work for the task force.

Just as he reached for the key in the ignition, another vehicle rolled up to the room. Only, unlike the rest of T-Bag's customer's rides, this one didn't have four wheels.

It only had two.

Nox lifted the binoculars to his eyes to get a better view of the man straddling it. His heart began to beat a bit faster at who he saw.

Could he be so damn exhausted he was seeing things?

"No fucking way," Nox whispered, seeing that the rider wore a cut.

And that cut declared the most recent arriver was a Demon.

Nox focused intently on the biker climbing off the Harley in an attempt to identify him. He held his breath and did his best to keep the binoculars steady as he waited for the man to turn enough so he could get a better view of his face.

He would recognize most members of the Uniontown

chapter due to the endless hours of watching recorded and live feeds from both The Peach Pit and the Wolf Den, so he hoped like hell he'd recognize this one, too.

"What the actual fuck?" burst from him when he could finally see the biker's face.

It should come as no surprise, but it still had Nox's brain spinning with the possibilities since the man who just arrived was also well-known to the task force and a few members of the BAMC.

The target on this biker's back was almost as large as T-Bone's, but not by much.

Saint.

Or as Mel and Sapphire lovingly called their former boss... Saint the Taint.

Now it made sense why T-Bone still walked the Earth. Saint had T-Bone's spineless back.

Those two fuckers were most likely making money without Viper knowing it. Because if the Deadly Demons' prez was aware that a former prospect and a current member were using the club's meth to drug women, all so they could pimp them out and make money...

He doubted the president of the Deadly Demons would let that slide.

Nox could be totally wrong.

T-Bone could still be a prospect.

And maybe those fuckers weren't skimming meth from the Demons' supply.

Or Viper could be totally aware of this enterprise.

Maybe.

But Nox sure as fuck doubted it.

Chapter Thirty-One

"I'D LOVE for you to meet my boys."

Holy shit, did she just suggest that?

When Nox's head turned on the pillow, his handsome face was marred by a deep frown. "What?"

Should she pretend she hadn't suggested that? Or simply go with it?

The man loved kids—of course, not in a questionable way —so, it might do him some good to hang out with hers for a little bit. Plus, it wouldn't hurt her boys to spend some time with him.

They needed more *good* male role models in their lives. She loved her father to death, but he wasn't the best role model. However, he was good at keeping them in line and to teach them, with the way he treated his wife, how to cherish a woman. However, his cohorts were definitely not the greatest role models.

She did not want her boys following in her father's foot-steps when it came to his MC. She hoped when they became adults, they chose to follow the law over lawlessness.

Because of that, Nox hanging with Keenan and Devyn could be a win-win all the way around.

Even better, if they all got along, it could ease the idea of Nox staying over at her place.

Eventually.

If this connection between them continued.

Because so far, neither seemed to be in any rush to end things. In fact, they were settling into a routine.

At Wednesday night grief group, Nox always sat to her left. Did he ever share with the group? No. But at least he listened. Kind of.

Afterward, they'd head to a motel for some extracurricular activity.

Not the one they first went to—the motel where something or someone spooked him—but one north of Shadow Valley, on the outskirts of Pittsburgh.

It was a longer drive, but Nox made it worthwhile.

He paid every time, too. When she offered, he shot her a dirty look like she had insulted him. That made her throw up her hands and let him pay, even though she earned a lot more money than he did, and these hookups were getting costly, since they were starting to meet more than only Wednesday nights.

Every time they did, she'd hint that she wouldn't mind shouldering some of the financial burden and, like clockwork, he ignored her.

One benefit to inviting him over was, it didn't cost a dime for them to "boink" in her rent-free bedroom. Another was so she could bring him into the fold of her family and see how the boys interacted with him. See if they would accept him as a permanent fixture in their lives.

Just in case he stuck around.

"I met your boys, remember? That day I met your father."

"How could I forget? I meant come over for dinner. Hang for a little bit. Watch a movie with the family."

One side of his mouth pulled up. "That's it? A movie with the fam?"

Her head jerked back in mock offense. "Officer Lennox, what else do you expect?"

"You writhing and moaning underneath me." His expression got serious. "Have you brought any other men home before?"

"Well, that's a loaded question." One she didn't expect from him.

"I'm only asking because of your boys and if they're used to men coming over. I don't care how many of them you *boinked*."

She only invited men home if she thought they'd stick around for a while. Or forever, apparently. But in truth, there weren't too many men who came into her life worthy of meeting her sons. There had only been one so far and she obviously got that one wrong. "Keenan's father. That's it. You don't plan on knocking me up and then splitting, do you?"

When his nostrils flared, she realized that teasing might not come off as it was meant to. Especially with what happened to his wife while pregnant.

Foot meet mouth. "Nox..."

"No, I wouldn't abandon a pregnant woman," he said on a long breath.

"I was teasing."

"Yeah."

She rolled on top of him and studied his face while combing her nails through his short hair. The spark that occasionally appeared in his eyes had been extinguished.

She needed to prevent him from tumbling back into that dark hole. "How about it? Dinner with me and my boys?"

"Not sure that's a good idea."

"I guess we'll find out if it is or isn't afterward. So, tomorrow night, then?" Might as well not put it off.

His hazel eyes narrowed on her. "Just dinner and a movie?"

"I can throw in some popcorn." She grinned. "Let's see how it goes first and maybe if it goes well, we can do it again. And eventually, do *this* again."

"I don't mind paying for a motel, Liyah."

"I'm well aware. But my boys are plenty old enough to understand that their mother is allowed to date."

"I wouldn't call this dating."

"I'd rather tell them we're dating than boinking."

When it took forever for him to answer, she thought he was going to turn down her offer. She was floored when he accepted.

"Okay, I'll come over for dinner. But if things aren't going well, don't hesitate to tell me. I won't be offended if I need to leave. It's your boys' home, they have every right to feel comfortable in it."

"Well, actually... It's *my* home and I make it comfortable for them. The day they start paying the mortgage and the high water and electric bills—because they waste both—I'll consider their opinions on who I bring home."

"Damn," he whispered.

She grabbed his chin and dropped her head until they were practically nose-to-nose. "Listen, they don't want for anything. They have a lot more than I ever did at their age. They can't appreciate what they have because they've never gone without. And it's because I bust my ass for those things. For them. They are my world, but I wish they understood just how well they have it."

"They don't realize how lucky they are since most people are one missed paycheck away from being homeless."

"While that's true, it isn't due to luck, it's my hard work. I invested years of my life building my business and dealing with the bad that comes along with the good. Even with all of that, it's been rewarding, as has been raising two young men. Despite them being slobs and not appreciating everything they have."

"You're a good mother."

"I'll hold off on accepting that rating. How good of a job I did will be decided once they're grown and it's determined whether they're an asset or a menace to society."

"Most parents nowadays think their little Johnny can do no wrong, even when it's obvious they have."

"I'm not most parents."

"That, you are not. I'm sure raising two young men by yourself isn't easy. I hope one day they look back and appreciate everything you've done for them."

"Enough talk about my boys while I'm naked in bed with you."

He chuckled. "Agreed."

He grabbed a handful of her hair, pulled her head back and nibbled from the base of her neck to under her chin.

"*Mmm.* Less talk and more of that," she encouraged.

"Agreed," he repeated in a murmur against her skin.

He not only agreed, he followed through, leaving her well satisfied for the second time that evening.

As soon as her mind cleared and her breathing returned to normal, she began to plan tomorrow night's dinner.

———

"GRUMPA THINKS YOU'RE A COP," Keenan announced around a mouthful of shrimp quesadillas. A stray string of cheese clung precariously to his bottom lip.

Liyah shook her head. "Napkin!"

Kee's face twisted in annoyance, but he scrubbed a napkin over his mouth, anyway.

Nox responded, "Your grandfather's pretty smart."

Keenan's deep brown eyes went wide as did his now-clean mouth. "He was right? *Oooooh.*" He turned to Liyah. "He's gonna be *sooooo* mad at you, Mom."

"He'll get over it," Liyah informed her youngest, hoping that was true. And if it wasn't, Magnum would simply have to live being butt hurt. Her father did not have a say in who she dated. Or "boinked," for that matter. Even if he thought he did.

Even so, her father getting over the fact she was "dating" a cop would only matter if said cop stuck. And right now, it was a bit too early for that, since Nox was still on the bumpy path to healing.

Good thing Liyah had plenty of patience.

She wasn't in a rush to get in any kind of serious relationship, and she certainly wasn't worried about the ticking of her internal clock. She glanced at the males that she birthed already. Those two were plenty enough.

And her career and business was right where she wanted it. Successful but manageable.

"Where are you a pig?"

"Keenan!" Liyah scolded. "What did I tell you about calling police officers that? It's not only disrespectful to your brother's father but it's insulting to the man sitting across from you. Would you be okay with him calling you a brat to your face?"

Kee pouted. "But I'm not a brat."

Liyah's eyebrows shot to the top of her forehead. "Says who?"

His mouth gaped open. "But Mom..."

"Don't you dare 'but, Mom,' me. I told you that terminology is not permitted in this house. Ever. I guess your visits with Grumpa will need to be limited if you have to repeat everything he says."

"But Mom!" Panic filling Keenan's eyes at the thought of not being able to spend weekends with his grandparents.

"You just made it clear that you need to learn some respect and you're not learning it at his house." It was an empty threat. She'd never limit her sons' time with Magnum and Cait, or their kids, but still...

Apparently, she needed to have *another* conversation with her father and his use of that insult around her boys. She would also threaten him with limited time spent with his grandchildren.

Again, the threat might be empty but hopefully it would be effective.

"Finish your dinner and don't you ever call any law enforcement officer that again. Not under this roof and not outside of this house, either. Understood?"

Keenan's mouth tightened. "Yes."

"Next time I hear you say it, you'll be grounded, too. Now apologize to Nox."

Her youngest son turned to the man sitting quietly next to her taking everything in. "I'm sorry."

Nox gave him a single nod. "Apology accepted. And to answer your question, I work for Shadow Valley PD."

Kee's eyes lit up. "That's in the Dirty Angels territory."

Liyah mentally sighed. She didn't like the fact her seven-year-old knew so much about motorcycle clubs.

"I'm going to join them when I turn eighteen," her son declared next. "Dawg said I could."

Who said what?

"Oh no, sir, you are not." Now she had to have a discussion with Caitlyn's father, too? Dawg did not need to be encouraging her kids to join the Dirty Angels. Or any club.

"Just join the Dark Knights. Grumpa would love that," Devyn suggested, *oh so* helpfully.

"They only accept Black members," Kee informed his older brother. "I'm only half Black, like you."

Liyah smacked a hand onto her forehead and groaned. "Enough of this talk. We've had this discussion before and we're not having it again right now at the dinner table. But to be clear, half Black is still Black, and you are *never* joining an MC."

She was about to lose her shit and she wanted this evening to be pleasant, not full of drama.

Nox would never want to come back again, and she wouldn't blame him.

They somehow managed to finish dinner without Nox sprinting from the house screaming and after he helped her clean up the kitchen, the two of them moved into the family room to settle in with a movie.

Chapter Thirty-Two

AALIYAH HAD to call for her kids three times before they finally came in to join them. Of course, they dragged their feet the whole way, despite letting them choose the movie. No surprise, they picked the first Fast & Furious movie, even though they had seen it a billion and one times.

Both boys claimed the recliners flanking the center couch that Liyah and Nox were left sharing. The only complaint she had with that was, she was tempted to curl up with the man while they watched the action flick.

Instead, they kept a safe gap between them. Though a few times, Nox's fingers trailed over hers when he grabbed a handful of popcorn from the bowl they shared.

Halfway through the movie, a sound caught her ears. It took a few second to realize it wasn't coming from the television.

The loud, very distinct rumble of a Harley was unmistakable. She heard it too often not to recognize it.

With a groan of annoyance, Liyah shot up from the

couch, rushed over to the window and pulled the drapes aside to peer outside.

Holy shit. "Devyn!"

"What?" her oldest asked, trying to sound innocent around a mouthful of popcorn.

She looked for his cell phone. It was face down in his lap.

Figures. "You didn't tell Grumpa that Nox was here, did you?"

"He texted and asked what I was doing. I told him the truth because you told me not to lie."

The kid was fifteen. He lied all the time and never worried about it.

But, *holy shit,* this could be bad.

"You're lying right now! He only texts when he's forced to. He certainly doesn't text you out of the blue." Her old man preferred phone calls over typing. And emails? Forget it.

Technology was not Magnum's friend.

"Should I go hide?" A grin flirted on Nox's lips.

"Why bother? These two would just snitch on you." Unfortunately, that was true.

She dropped the curtain and, ignoring her kids' denial that they'd snitch, headed toward the door, hoping to head off her father before he came face-to-face with Nox.

Stepping out onto the front stoop, she groaned when she spotted Nox's Harley parked in the driveway. It might as well have flashing arrows pointing at it.

Her father had just climbed off his own bike when he pointed at Nox's. "What the fuck, Liyah? Whose sled's that?"

The man knew exactly whose ride it was since Devyn already told him.

So much for her nice evening introducing Nox to the boys. "You don't recognize it?"

His expression was scary when he took long strides toward the house. "He in there?"

"No, he ducked behind the bushes, Dad. Jeez." She stepped in front of him, blocking his path to the front door. "We're in the middle of watching a movie. I'll talk to you another time."

His head jerked back, and his eyes narrowed on her. Then without a word, he just about bowled her over, pushing past her and through the front door. Closely reminding her of a bull running the streets of Pamplona.

Liyah rushed to keep up as he beelined right toward the family room.

This wasn't going to be good.

Not at all.

Between Keenan calling him a pig and her father busting in to probably do the same, she doubted she'd ever see Nox again after tonight.

"Dad!" she called as the big man disappeared around the corner. Liyah sprinted down the hallway after him. "Dad!"

She came to a sliding stop once she hit the room where the boys—all of them—were.

Suddenly, too much testosterone filled the room.

She was just in time to see her father fist bump each of her sons. "Devil. Keeper."

Liyah rolled her eyes at those nicknames and pulled in a breath. "You never said why you're here, Dad."

"Can't a man visit his damn family?"

"Yes, when he calls first."

"Texted Devyn," he grunted.

Likely story. "Are you sure he didn't text you first?"

Dev and Magnum's eyes met briefly.

"*Umm hmm.* I thought so," she finished. She gave her oldest son a look of *"I'll deal with you later."*

"Was passin' by and wanted to check on my family."

Liyah held her breath when Magnum turned toward Nox. The cop looked completely unbothered by the man's presence.

Good. She was pleased to see that he wasn't easily intimidated by her biker father.

But when Nox slowly got to his feet, Liyah rushed to his side and placed a hand on his back. Just in case. "You remember Nox, right?"

Magnum grunted and stepped closer.

"Boys, why don't you go play some video games in your room?" she suggested quickly. "Or something," she added in a mutter.

"But—"

"Now!"

Both grumbled but they got up from the recliners... slowly.

"Go!" she shouted.

"I wanna visit with Grumpa!" Keenan whined.

"Another time."

They might as well be dragging their feet on their way out of the family room. "Make sure you close your doors so I can't hear your video games."

And they couldn't hear the conversation she assumed was about to occur.

Once the boys were gone, she turned to her father. "Okay, Dad, thanks for stopping by and checking on us. As you see, we're perfectly fine and would like to finish the movie we started."

Magnum didn't look at her. He was too busy eyeing up Nox. More like sizing him up. Or trying to intimidate him with simply a look. "Pig, ain't you?"

She sighed. Loudly. "Dad, we need to have a little conversation about that word. Keenan—"

"If you're asking if I carry a badge, I do."

Apparently, she was going to be ignored by both men. *Wonderful.*

"Thought I smelled bacon on you last time you were sniffin' 'round here."

Technically the last time Nox was over, they were in her bedroom and Magnum was not. But she was keeping that tidbit to herself. Especially with Nox easily within thumping distance.

"You have a problem with bacon? I'm surprised, since it looks like you can eat a whole package of it in one sitting."

Oh shit. "Okay, well..." she started, weakly. "Can we not do this?"

"Do what?" Magnum asked, still keeping his eyes glued to Nox.

Did she really have to explain? Damn pig-headed men! "Fling insults at each other."

"Guess you'd rather she be spending time with one of your brothers," Nox said next.

"Biker over a badge? Fuck yeah. Not even a goddamn question."

"Then, good thing it's not your decision."

"Okay..." Liyah stepped away from Nox, latched onto her father's tree trunk sized arm and tugged on it. "Can you come with me?"

His dark brown eyes finally landed on her.

"Yes, remember me? Your oldest daughter? The one whose house you're standing in?"

He grunted.

She went on, "The one whose decisions you might not

agree with but should respect, anyway? Just like I have to do with yours?"

"Don't like it," Magnum grumbled.

"Then don't date a cop," she suggested with a shrug.

"Datin'?" he exploded.

Oh shit. "We're not dating," she scrambled to explain. "We're f—" she swallowed that down and replaced it with, "friends."

His eyes narrowed on her.

She tipped her head in response. "Now, I don't tell you who you can be friends with, do I? And you know why I don't? Because I mind my own damn business."

"You're my business." He jerked his chin in the direction Devyn and Keenan went. "Those boys are my business."

"While I appreciate you looking out for us, this is not it, Dad." She tugged at his arm again. "Come with me." She glanced at Nox, standing with his boots slightly apart, his hands curled at his side and his knees loose.

Just in case.

"You stay here," she told him. She mouthed, "Please."

His jaw tightened but he gave her a stiff nod.

"I won't be long," she assured him.

"Take your time. I don't plan on going anywhere."

That last part wasn't to assure her, it was to stick it to Magnum.

Nice. Didn't he realize he was playing with fire by fucking with him? Or did he not care?

"Let's go, Dad," she urged.

This time her father moved. Luckily. Since it would be impossible for her to move his bulk on her own if he dug in his heels.

"Came to see the boys."

"Bullshit. You came to stick your nose where it doesn't belong."

"Bullshit," he echoed.

She stopped dead in the hallway. "Really."

"Yeah."

She pointed toward the front door. "Let's go outside."

"Not ready to leave."

"I can drop the boys off this weekend if you want to spend time with them so badly."

He grabbed her chin and met her eyes. "Maybe I wanna spend time with you, too."

Some of her annoyance dissipated. "Then we'll plan a dinner or something. Tonight is not the night."

"'Cause you got him here."

"Yes, because I have Nox here."

His nostrils flared. "He ain't for you, Liyah."

"I didn't know you had the right to decide that, Dad. You do remember I'm grown, right?"

"Still my baby girl."

"I'm thirty-nine. Your grandson will be considered a damn adult in three years."

"Not liking this."

"You've registered your formal complaint, so now can I get back to my evening plans?"

"You ain't knockin' boots with him later, right? Not with the boys here."

She grimaced. "Can we have this *discussion* outside?"

"You wanna have it outside? Gonna have it outside. But we're gonna fuckin' have it." He spun on his boot heel and strode toward the door.

She made sure the door was closed behind them after following him outside.

As soon as they hit the driveway, he spun on her. "You ain't doin' him with my grandsons here, are you?"

When the hell did he become the morality police? Coming from Magnum that was laughable. "No, I'll just wait for when they're staying over at your house."

She lifted a hand before the man exploded. She knew she shouldn't poke the grumpy grizzly but her annoyance was back in full force.

Apparently so was his, when he boomed, "You already made that fuckin' mistake once."

"Keep your voice down," she hissed. "The neighborhood doesn't need to know our business. And Mark was not a mistake! Jason was."

"Him, too."

"You better not be telling Devyn that me marrying his father was a mistake. You aren't, are you?" When her father didn't answer, she leaned in, locked eyes with him and demanded, "Are you?"

She waited for him to look away because if he did, she'd have her answer. Thankfully, he didn't. "Ain't sayin' shit."

"Good. Please don't. You never met him and have no right to judge."

"He was a pig. All I gotta know."

She sighed. "And you're pig-headed."

"Ain't gonna argue that."

Liyah shrugged. "Because you can't."

"If you're lonely, Romeo's interested," Magnum suggested.

She rolled her eyes. "As you well know, Romeo is interested in anyone with tits and at least one hole to fuck."

Magnum's head snapped back. "Better than a fuckin' pig!"

"I don't know, is he?" Liyah raised her eyebrows at him.

"You'd rather me hook my wagon to a man who can't keep his dick in his pants? Do you want a man like that helping raise my children? *Your* grandchildren?"

A muscle jumped in her father's cheek.

"I didn't think so. Now, I'm sure Cait's wondering where you are." She raised up on her toes and pressed a kiss to his smooth cheek. "Thank you for stopping by and thank you for caring. I love you, Dad, but you don't have a say in who I see."

"Don't like it."

"I know."

With a grunt, he shook his head and started toward his Harley.

She made sure her tone was sugary sweet when she called out, "Have a nice night, Dad. I'll let the boys know you said goodbye and that you love them and can't wait to see them again soon. Oh, and give my love to Cait."

Magnum grunted again.

Smothering her grin, she gave him a wave and headed back inside.

Chapter Thirty-Three

Since the night he went over to her place for dinner and a movie, he'd been spending more and more time over at her house. He was starting to be away from The Plant enough that he knew questions from both the task force members and his brothers were coming.

He was pretty damn sure they've noticed he hadn't been around as much. Especially since he'd basically been a hermit prior to the "ultimatum." They'd want to know what changed.

He could bullshit them by telling them the weekly group meetings and the therapist were helping.

Or...

He could introduce Liyah to the people who mattered the most to him...

His brothers.

He liked having her in his life and he only hoped it was the same for her. Though, if anyone was getting the short end of the stick in their relationship, it was her. It was much easier for him to deal with her than it was for her to deal with him.

And, bonus, if she was no longer a secret, they could use his place to "boink" since her sons were definitely cockblocks. He only stayed overnight on the weekends they were gone. That wasn't often enough for him, so he needed to take steps to change that.

Since her boys were staying at their grandmother's for the weekend, this weekend's club run was the perfect time for introductions as most of his brothers would be in attendance.

It would be easier to reveal the woman in his life to everyone all at once. However, he'd do it strategically. He'd show up at the last minute and do a quick intro. Then, before everyone could recover from their shock, they'd have to roll out.

His lips formed a crooked grin. That wouldn't give them much time to grill him.

Or pester Liyah.

He hoped his plan worked.

Would those questions come? No fucking doubt. His brothers would be all up in his business the same as Liyah's father liked to be with her. Nosiness was part of his BAMC brothers' nature, along with ball-busting.

Plus, with the indictments about to go down any day now, a shitstorm might be headed in their direction soon and he wasn't sure how long it would be before his life returned to "normal." He might end up working longer hours until the dust finally settled.

After having sex this morning, they rolled out of bed, shared the shower to "conserve water," ate a damn good, belly-filling breakfast before heading out. He kept an eye on his watch to make sure they timed it just right.

The club run usually started at eleven, but it never left on time. Too much chatter happened before everyone got organized and into formation. It usually took several tries by Heat Miser until everyone listened to his orders. Sometimes on purpose, sometimes because everyone was too distracted.

Today, he and Liyah were the distraction as he steered his bike through the open back gate and toward the back of the line.

He had no doubt his Harley was the only noise in the back lot since all eyes followed them and all mouths were hanging open as he pulled into formation.

He was glad he had the foresight to warn Liyah about their reaction. She might feel intimidated if she wasn't so damn confident.

She had only shrugged off his warning, covered her hair in a Diva-Do to protect it and pulled on her own helmet before throwing her leg over his bike and wrapping her arms around his waist.

No matter what the woman wore, she had a knack for always looking stylish. Even wearing a hair covering made specifically for being worn under a brain bucket. The company should use her as a damn model, she looked that good.

He swore she'd be able to pull off dressing in a gunnysack. All she had to do was add a pair of heels, some lipstick and fluff out her hair and she'd be ready to walk into a classy restaurant and order the most expensive meal on the menu.

Him? Not so much.

Proof she was so damn out of his league.

But as long as she was willing to keep him around, he was willing to stay.

They might be total opposites but for some reason they fit like two halves of a whole.

As soon as he shut down his Harley, he braced for what was to come.

Before they got bombarded, he took a quick glance around to see who all had showed up today.

He wasn't surprised to see Finn with Mel, Decker and Sloane, Rez and Sapphire along with the club president, Axel Jamison and his wife Bella. Cross, as always, was by himself since his husband, a Dirty Angels MC member, had no desire to ride with a bunch of badge-wearing "fake" bikers.

Liyah pressed her tits into his back to murmur in his ear, "Again, it's nice to see your MC is diverse."

Glancing over his shoulder, he noticed she had already removed her helmet and was now eyeing up North with his fiancé Naomi along with Frasier and his wife. Their two Black members.

"And a woman?" came next. "Is that right? Does her man normally ride behind her?"

It was hard to miss Clark sitting confidently behind Monty. Nox shook his head. He swore the bowtie wearing nerd had the biggest balls out of all of them.

His lips twitched. "Like you said, our club's diverse."

Her warm chuckle filled his ears and wormed its way into his chest.

Last but not least, he spotted Cabrera with Crew. They'd finally quit hiding their relationship and the task force leader had temporarily moved out of his condo and into Fletch's house with her because of her Irish Wolfhound.

But that would have to change soon since the task force would be wrapping up their investigation any day now and finishing the work they'd done for the past two years.

He'd miss working on the third floor with the task force and wasn't sure if he was ready to go back to Shadow Valley PD. Climbing one flight of steps to go to work had spoiled him. So did not having to deal with nuisance calls all day when he worked patrol.

He noticed the only BAMC members missing were Miller—most likely because they couldn't find a babysitter to watch their litter of kids—and, of course, Fletch and Wilder, since the couple was still undercover with the Demons and would be until the very end.

They currently had the most important roles in the investigation since they were the eyes and ears of the task force. They would contact Crew if they noticed or heard anything going down.

Because it was clear trouble was brewing.

Under no circumstances would the Pittsburgh La Cosa Nostra allow the Demon dickheads to steal their cartel contacts and the flow of dirty drug money.

Nox's head jerked back when Jamison and Crew were both suddenly standing by his bike.

"Can I help you?" he asked them dryly.

"Yeah," Crew started, "by explaining what's going on here." His gray eyes flicked from Nox to Liyah and back.

"What do you mean?"

"If you haven't noticed, there's someone on your bike besides yourself."

Nox's expression turned confused. "There is?"

Crew exchanged glances with Jamison.

"Aaliyah," the BAMC president greeted that *someone*. "How are you?"

"I'm very well. Thank you for asking, Axel. How are you and Bella?"

"*Uh.* Truthfully? We're a little confused."

Cross joined the group. "Aiden," Liyah greeted.

Frowning, Cross gave her a nod. "Aaliyah. What are you doing here?"

"She's coming along on our club run." Nox thought it should be pretty fucking obvious.

"I didn't know you two knew each other," Cross continued with his eyebrows pinned together.

"Well, we do," Liyah answered him. "We met at the grief group. I took over the one in Shadow Valley." She looked past Cross to the newcomer. "Hello, Bella."

"Hey, Liyah," Jamison's wife greeted. "I had no idea you were coming along today."

"I didn't, either, until he asked me last night."

All three men exchanged glances.

Here we go...

"Last night?" Crew asked with one eyebrow cocked.

"Yes, that time of darkness that occurs between the time of daylight," Liyah explained.

Nox wanted to fist bump her for that answer, but he refrained. Barely.

"A lot of stuff can occur in the dark," Crew said. "But for some reason, my brain is stuck on only one thing."

The corners of Liyah's lips slightly tipped up. "Sleeping?"

Jamison snorted and grabbed his wife's hand. "Let's go and get this show on the road."

"Yeah, let's," Nox agreed, meeting Crew's eyes that were full of a mix of curiosity and amusement.

When Cross, Bella and Jamison wandered away, Crew still remained.

Of course. The task force leader was looking for any reason to bust Nox's balls.

"Do you need assistance with anything else?" Nox prodded.

Crew pursed his lips.

"Cabrera's getting impatient," he warned.

Crew glanced over his shoulder at their newest task force member. "She can wait."

"Do you want to tell her that or should I?"

Crew's jaw tightened and he scraped his fingers over his short salt-and-pepper hair. "For fuck's sake," he grumbled before spinning on his heel and heading back to his bike.

"What was that about?" Liyah asked.

"He's the king of ball-busting and I think his brain glitched when he saw us together. For Crew, being rendered speechless is the same as being neutered."

"Ouch."

"Exactly. I'm sure it was painful for him."

———

About halfway through the ride, they stopped at a park that hosted food trucks on Sundays and had plenty of restrooms.

Nox watched Bella introduce Liyah, both with iced chai lattes in hand from one of the trucks, to anyone she hadn't met yet.

Nox trusted Jamison's wife to put any of their brothers in their place if they ribbed Liyah too much. Even though Nox had complete confidence in Liyah being able to handle anything thrown her way.

He had watched her the whole time she went around talking to everyone. His heart skipped a beat every time she gave someone a warm smile or she threw her head back in laughter.

From where he sat, it even looked like she cracked a joke with Crew. He didn't feel the need to worry about him saying something ignorant to her because Cabrera didn't leave his side. Nox knew the younger DEA agent would cut the older DEA agent off at the knees if he said anything stupid.

Nox thanked fuck for the women in their lives.

All had spines of steel. None took any shit. They also had no issue with speaking out and putting someone in their place when necessary.

When their thirty-minute pit stop was coming to an end, Liyah's eyes sparkled, and her hips swung smoothly as she made her way back to where he waited with his ass parked on a picnic table and his boots set on the attached bench.

When she finally reached him, he grabbed those hips and pulled her in between his spread knees. "You good?"

She practically hummed and looked pretty damn happy, but he wanted to hear it from her.

"Absolutely. It's a beautiful day. The ride has been perfect. Everyone in your club has been great."

"Everyone?"

She gave him a single nod. "Everyone. Crew's a trip but entertaining. He seems to be outmatched when it comes to Cami, despite her youth."

"He is, even though he'll never admit it. She's a lot sharper than him."

She tilted her head to the side and locked eyes with him. "A federal task force was mentioned a few times. I was told that some of the BAMC members are a part of it and working a case. Are you on it?"

Nox pulled in a breath. He hadn't told her anything about his special assignment. He really hadn't anticipated their unexpected connection would last as long as it had so far.

But here they were.

She just met his family.

Maybe it was time to tell her about the task force, even though the investigation was wrapping up. He trusted her not to say a word to her outlaw biker father.

He was damn sure Magnum knew who the Deadly

Demons were. And he was damn sure that the sergeant at arms of the Knights was monitoring what the Demons were doing, especially after they had expanded their territory into Pennsylvania.

The Demons and the Knights were now practically neighbors.

He had no doubt that the Knights were fierce when it came to protecting their territory and that they shared intel with the Dirty Angels. Though, the Angels weren't to say a word to anyone about Fletch and Wilder going undercover in their MC.

The unmistakable roar of another group of what sounded like Harleys could be heard heading in their direction.

Nox stared at the entrance to the area where they had taken their break. His spine snapped straight hoping like fuck it wasn't the Deadly Demons.

Wouldn't that be a fucking kicker.

But as the formation of bikes turned into the lot, he recognized the club's colors.

He wasn't the only one.

No one was expecting to see the MC that was about to join their party.

Chapter Thirty-Four

Nox muttered under his breath, "What the fuck?"

"Shit. Shit. Shit," Liyah chanted in a whisper when she saw him, too.

Not just him but *them*.

When it came to Nox, dealing with her father one-on-one was one thing, dealing with his whole MC was another.

Apparently, like the Blue Avengers, the Dark Knights decided today would be a great day for their club run, as well as taking a break at the same location.

Of course, they were all wearing their colors.

And, of course, so were the BAMC. Including the member she had her arms wrapped around for the last couple of hours.

This could go one of two ways...

The two clubs could ignore each other. Pretend the other didn't exist and continue on their runs.

Or... they could not.

If they didn't, she wasn't going to even begin to imagine what that would be like. Unfortunately, she didn't really know the majority of the BAMC members well enough yet. Cross and Axel and their spouses, yes. Nox, of course. But the rest? She had no idea if they would stay cool, calm and collected or make a sport out of butting heads with an outlaw MC.

Either way, it wasn't going to be any kind of Kumbaya moment. Expecting any kind of hand holding, singing and swaying around a campfire with someone playing an acoustic guitar would be laughable.

Peace, love and harmony and all that happy crap.

She only hoped there wouldn't be any kind of clashes. Or taunting.

Or, worse, bloodshed.

The Knights' formation—led by Cisco, their road captain —slowed the second they spotted the lineup of bikes belonging to the Blue Avengers. She also knew the exact moment her father spotted her. In fact, his wife was super helpful by whacking Magnum on the shoulder and pointing her way.

Thanks, Cait.

Though, she couldn't be mad at her stepmother. It was inevitable Liyah would've been spotted, even without her help. The only way to avoid being seen would be to run into the woods and duck behind a tree. She certainly wasn't doing that because, *damn it,* she had nothing to hide.

She liked Nox. A lot. She enjoyed spending time with him. She was proud that he was finally shedding his heavy cloak of sorrow.

Both at the surface and at his core, he was a good man. And nothing her father or his "brothers" could say would change her view about him.

She loved her father to death but only tolerated his biker lifestyle. She understood and accepted it was a huge part of him. As was his love and loyalty to his family. He was the most loyal man she knew, and she only hoped some of that rubbed off on her sons.

With her heart galloping like a racehorse, she asked, "Now what?"

"Now we get everyone together and get back on the road," Nox answered way too calmly.

"I'm not sure it'll be that easy."

"We don't have a beef with them. They just need to mind their own business and we'll mind ours."

"I'm not sure it'll be that easy," she repeated as the Dark Knights finished rolling through the lot and parked on the other side, leaving some distance between the two groups.

Today made it glaringly clear, their MC had a lot more members than the Blue Avengers. About two dozen Knights along with their ol' ladies, if they had one, were in attendance. Liyah knew that wasn't all of them.

Because Magnum was a beast of a man in size, he stood above the rest when he dismounted from his sled after helping Cait off first.

Even being in his late fifties, the big man still exuded strength, power and fearlessness. Was he the oldest member of the Knights? No, but he was far from the youngest.

New blood was constantly joining their MC. The club did their best to keep their numbers up by actively recruiting for new prospects. And then constantly patching-in the prospects who didn't wash out.

Besides the belief that there was power in numbers, they also wanted to remain strong and appear as a united front. That made them a good ally to both the Dirty Angels and Blood Fury MCs. It created what was known as the "Biker Army of the West." A force to be reckoned with in case any other MC, one-percenters or otherwise, attempted to fuck with any of them.

Including the Blue Avengers.

She pulled free of Nox. "I should go talk to my father before anything goes down."

"Nothing will go down."

Again, he sounded way too nonchalant for Liyah's taste. "You can't guarantee that. First of all, while they all know me, they all don't know that I've been seeing you."

"And that will be a problem," he concluded.

"They have a problem with law enforcement whether I'm involved or not."

"We're aware of that."

A thought popped into her head. "Hang on... That task force you avoided telling me about... That has nothing to do with my father's club, does it?"

"If it did, I wouldn't be able to tell you. But it doesn't, so I can assure you that they are not our focus."

Now her curiously was piqued about this "special assignment" he was on.

Even so, relief swept through her that the Knights were not their target since her father had done time in the past. She did not want him ever going to prison again. It would take him away from his family, both his own blood, as well as his club.

"Then I look forward to hearing about this task force you somehow forgot to tell me about." She sighed and turned to scan the newcomers. "Okay, I'll go settle any choppy waters, so it doesn't turn into a tsunami. I'll be back."

"You don't have to do that, Liyah. We are perfectly capable of handling anything coming our way."

"I'd prefer it if there wasn't even a risk of that."

"Want me to go with you?"

She bugged her eyes out at him. "Seriously?"

He shrugged. "If you want me with you, I'll go with you. If you think I'm scared of your father or his friends, I'm not."

You should be, she wanted to warn. "I can handle it. They'll be more tense if you're standing by my side, but I appreciate the offer."

"I'll be keeping an eye on you," she heard as she headed to the other side of the lot where the Knights were now gathering in a circle, most likely discussing what to do next.

But before she could single out her father, someone stepped in her path.

Romeo.

Of course.

The Knights' president saw she was here with another man but that wouldn't stop him from doing what he always did while in Liyah's presence.

Hit on her.

If he did it in front of Nox, he was only doing it to get a reaction.

"Get out of my way, Rome."

"Figured you were headed our way to talk to a real man."

Liyah gritted her teeth. "You'd think by now you'd get the message that I'm not interested, but here you are. Again."

The man grinned and shrugged. "Name ain't Romeo for nothin'."

He was handsome, so he had that, and he could be charming when he wanted to be. But he was still a dog.

A dirty one. Not the kind she wanted to pet.

"I know and that's one reason of many why I'm not interested."

Romeo slapped a hand over his leather-covered chest. "You know how to fuckin' wound a man, woman."

"And you wound plenty of women when you break their hearts."

"Ain't after a woman's heart."

"Then, you should tell them that upfront."

He stepped closer and into her personal space before dragging a knuckle down Liyah's cheek. "Could be a good pop to your boys."

She rolled her eyes. "Debatable."

"Can teach 'em shit."

"Like what? How to smoke pot and drink yourself into a fist fight?"

"Like be a man."

Liyah laughed so hard she almost folded in half.

When she straightened, Romeo was frowning. "What the fuck, woman?"

"Oh, you weren't joking?" She pressed fingers to her lips. "Oops."

"One day you're gonna realize what a catch I am."

"'One day' is not today. Go back to your side of the lot, Rome. I need to have a word with my father."

However, she didn't need to continue on her trek as Magnum appeared at Romeo's side.

A second later, she felt rather than saw Nox step up behind her.

This was exactly what she wanted to avoid.

Well, that and a clash between the two clubs.

Romeo jerked his chin up at Nox. "Who's this?"

"Not that it's any of your business, but a friend."

"He's a pig," Magnum announced. "Somehow my daughter forgot to tell me that he's a part of the biker wannabe club."

"Because it wasn't important," she responded. She had a feeling her father would disagree.

"You knew about him?" Romeo asked Magnum.

"Yeah," her father grunted.

"And you ain't done nothin' to stop it?"

"Excuse me?" Liyah asked sharply. "If my father wants to remain in my life then he knows not to interfere with it." No matter how much he'd like to. She locked eyes with Romeo. "And none of this is any of your business, anyway. So, *shoo*." She made a shooing motion with her hands.

"You're family, Ali-Cat," Romeo said. "Of course it's my fuckin' business. You're under the club's protection."

"Thanks but no thanks. I'm fine without that protection."

"She has me to protect her," Nox announced.

Oh shit.

She didn't care how Romeo took his declaration, but she knew Magnum wouldn't like it.

Not at all. He was super protective of his family.

Romeo sneered, and without warning, spat a hocker at Nox's feet, barely missing his boot, then acted like he didn't mean to do it on purpose.

Thankfully, Nox didn't react.

"Rome, if you disrespect him, you're disrespecting me," she warned him.

"No reason for you to be with someone like him."

Her eyebrows pinned together. "What do you mean, *like him*? You mean white?"

"Mean a fuckin' pig. But as for the other—"

"How about you keep your opinions to yourself?" Liyah dismissed him with, "Have a great run, Romeo. Dad, I'll talk to you another time." She tugged on Nox's arm, pulling him away from the Knights' president before things went sideways. "Let's go."

She could not be more aware that both clubs were watching the exchange very carefully. If things took an ugly turn between Nox and Romeo, it could get both clubs popping off. She did not want to be the cause of that.

"Aaliyah," Magnum called out.

She pulled in an irritated breath but paused and turned to face her father. "Let's keep everything between the two clubs civil, please."

Magnum pursed his lips and his dark eyes flicked from her to Nox and back. "Don't like this."

"I'm already aware but thanks for once again making that clear. I know sharing your feelings is difficult."

Nox snorted softly next to her, causing Liyah to tug at his arm again.

When she heard a very familiar female voice call out her name, she once again paused on their way back to Nox's bike. "Can you give me a minute?" Liyah asked him.

He glanced at the blonde woman hurrying in their direction. "Are you going to be all right?"

"Yes. That's my... stepmother."

"She looks our age," Nox murmured.

"That's because she is. She's only about a year older than me." And that meant she was Nox's age.

His head jerked back. "Do you find that weird?"

"I did at first. But now... Look, Cait's the best thing that ever happened to my father. He got cheated out of raising me and my brother and from seeing us grow up. He finally got that chance with Caleb and Asia."

"Your younger half-siblings."

"Yes. And to be honest, seeing how good he is with them made me even more angry with my mother for a long damn time. We were robbed out of a relationship with him. Would he have been a good father as young as he was when he had us? Maybe not the same as becoming a father again in his forties. However, no parent is perfect. You learn and grow as you go. Can you wait for me at your sled, Nox? I'll be okay. And if any of your brothers are concerned about having issues with the Knights, please assure them they won't." She sure as hell hoped she wasn't wrong with that assurance.

He stared at her for a moment before once again lifting his eyes to the woman joining them.

"Hi," Cait greeted the man standing next to Liyah.

"Hello," Nox responded in his rich, low voice.

"I'm Cait." She jerked a thumb over her shoulder. "The big man who thinks he's scary is mine."

He jutted out his hand. "Bradley Lennox. Everyone calls me Nox."

Cait took it and gave it a firm shake. "Very nice to meet you, Nox. And ignore their bluster. I'll make sure there aren't any issues between the two clubs. I don't remember seeing you before but I'm sure you know that both clubs have participated in charity events together and no one has died. And if you don't believe me, just ask Axel."

"Good to know." Amusement tipped the corner of Nox's lips upward. "I'll leave you two ladies alone to talk."

"Nice to meet you, Nox. I hope to see you again soon."

"Same," he answered before turning and heading back to his group.

Liyah kept one eye on the BAMC and one on the DKMC.

"You've been keeping him a secret."

"Not really," Liyah answered her.

"He's handsome."

"He is."

"How is he with the boys?"

"Great."

"Is it serious?" Cait asked.

"I'll let you know that answer once I know." That was the

best she could do. She had no idea where their relationship was going. They were taking one day at a time.

"Well then, in the meantime, enjoy your time with him."

"I plan on it."

"I'd invite him over for dinner, but..." Cait sighed. "These goddamn stubborn-as-hell men. Just be glad your father has mellowed with age."

"Could've fooled me."

"Oh, he has, believe me. Ten years ago, I could see him busting a blood vessel over you dating a cop. He's protective of you and always will be no matter what your age, Liyah. Telling him he shouldn't would only be wasting your breath. You know that. He's hard-headed."

"I don't know a man who isn't."

"Yes, but his skull is extra-thick. Anyway, I'm going to go back and encourage us to keep moving."

"Or we can leave so they can take a break and grab something to eat at the food trucks," Liyah suggested.

"Does anyone over there look like they're starving? The sweet butts are back at Dirty Dick's preparing a whole spread."

"I don't know how you tolerate club girls hanging all over your husband."

Cait smiled. "Because I know he will always come home to me. You'll be lucky to find anyone half as loyal as him." She looked past Liyah to where Nox was. "Maybe it'll be him."

"Maybe."

Cait squeezed her arm. "Okay, we'll talk more in depth about your new man another time. I'll want to hear all the details."

"Thanks, Cait."

"For what?"

"Being you."

"Right back at you. Thanks for being open-minded when I ambushed you in the park that day fifteen years ago." With that, she began to head back toward Magnum, now straddling his sled with a frown on his face. She stopped halfway and turned, "Do you want us to take the boys next weekend?"

Even from the distance, Liyah could see the mischief in her stepmother's eyes. "That would be great."

Cait gave her a nod and continued on back to her husband, who helped her mount the bike behind him.

After wrapping her arms around her ol' man, Cait whispered something into Magnum's ear, then pressed her cheek to the back of his cut with a soft smile on her face.

Liyah would be forever grateful for that woman. Without her, Liyah's family would look a whole lot different.

Chapter Thirty-Five

Nox wasn't sure where T-Bone and Saint were getting the women for their side hustle. Were they strippers from The Peach Pit they purposely got hooked on drugs? Or were they random women taken from the streets? Willingly or unwillingly.

Either way, he feared they would all end up like Sadie. Drugged up, physically and sexually abused and in the end, dead.

He wondered if anyone else in the Demons knew about this little enterprise.

Nox's guess? No fucking way.

From where he had sat in his truck night after night, he could see it was a lucrative business. Plus, if they skimmed meth from the Demons' supply to "pay" these women, the overhead wouldn't cost much more than renting the motel room.

After a while, if anyone got suspicious at their current location, they could easily move to another shit-bag motel.

One with staff willing to look the other way when it came to questionable goings-on.

Nox paused the recording and leaned in to take a closer look when the next dancer stepped on stage.

He cursed under his breath. While the stage lighting at The Peach Pit was on point and made it easy to see each woman, it was tough to tell if the women at the motel were one and the same. T-Bag and Saint were just smart enough to have the women keep their head down or covered for the few feet it took to get from the vehicle to the room.

Nox fast-forwarded until he got to the next dancer and routine, at the same time scanning the footage for signs of T-Bone and Saint. One thing Nox noticed while searching the footage was, the quality of dancers had spiraled toward the bottom of the barrel after Mel left. But after Sapphire was fired, the "entertainment" somehow got even worse.

Most of them danced with the enthusiasm of a wet wash-cloth. Zombies only going through the motions. Their eyes were dead, and their athletic ability was at a zero.

The Peach Pit was truly a "pit" now and Nox doubted the business would ever recover.

It wouldn't surprise him if some of the current dancers were meth addicts. Or willing to have Saint and T-Bone pimp them out for some extra cash since the audience at The Pit was as spotty as mange and only an occasional crumpled dollar bill was tossed on stage. If they were being pimped out, Nox wondered if they even saw a dime of that money, or they were fine with only getting drugs in exchange for having some stranger pumping and dumping inside them.

He closed his eyes and once again saw Sadie on that damn motel bed in Ohio. She had been nothing but a skeleton covered in a leather hide that used to be supple skin and coated in...

His nostrils flared and he pulled in a long breath to cool down his simmering rage.

Women were nothing to those motherfuckers.

Absolutely. Fucking. Nothing.

He blocked out the noise from his fellow task force members as they talked, cracked jokes and ribbed each other. He stayed out of the conversations swirling around him and, instead, concentrated on the screen in front of him.

Even though it was hard to concentrate.

Thoughts of Liyah kept filling his noggin.

Naked beneath him. Naked on top of him. Naked on her knees with his cock in her mouth as she kept her eyes turned up to him.

Naked and slick after stepping out of the shower.

Naked and curled around him as she slept.

He sensed a theme in his fantasies. In them, Liyah was always wearing his favorite outfit... None.

He shook himself mentally before he got a raging hard-on in the middle of the task force headquarters. He'd never live that down because they'd think he got it from watching the limp washrags wrapping themselves around the poles.

His mind wandered to the weekly group meetings. He only half-listened to whoever was speaking in the circle since he was too busy watching Liyah. Watching how she responded to their stories, even the ones she'd heard over and over again. Every damn time, she reacted with warmth and empathy. She always made the members of the group feel welcomed and supported.

And because of how she handled the group, it had grown to almost twice as large since Nox started attending.

He no longer came in at the last minute. Instead, he arrived early every week to help her set up. He was also always the last to leave because he stayed to help clean up. Of course, he escorted her out to her car, too.

After introducing her to his BAMC brothers on the club run, they no longer had to find a motel to "boink" after the Wednesday meetings. Now, they used his place. And used it often. Even when her house was empty because her sons were away.

Since Magnum had a key to Liyah's house, Nox wasn't risking the big man making a surprise visit. He'd rather not have to deal with her father when he was buck naked. Especially when he was about to fuck or had just finished fucking the man's daughter. The fact that Liyah was an adult would not matter to Malcolm Moore, Sr.

Crew came bursting through the door, shouting, "Time to round 'em up, boys! I got the official word. It's indictmas time! Operation Demon Destroyer is now a go!"

Nox hit pause on the footage and spun his chair around.

"My favorite time of the year!" cheered Torres.

Rez hooted. "Damn, indictmas is my favorite holiday!"

"Do we have any indictmas carols we can sing as we go door to door?" Finn asked.

"No!" everyone shouted at once.

"Do we at least get elf hats and bells on our boots?" Decker asked on a laugh.

"More like pepper spray, flex-cuffs and tasers," Crew answered.

"That'll be festive enough," Decker said. "The tasers can help light up some of those fuckers like a Christmas tree."

"Any specific fucker you plan on giving a fright by setting him alight on a starry night?" Torres asked.

Nox groaned under his breath at the lame rhyming. These guys sure getting pumped about serving warrants. On a good day it was a dangerous activity.

"Unfortunately, the one I'd love to have a crack at is no longer a part of the club."

Maybe. Maybe not. Even with all the nights he surveilled the motel, Nox still wasn't sure if the club actually ousted T-Bone or if the fucker was only laying low. "Have you confirmed that with Fletch?" he asked Decker.

All eyes turned toward Nox.

"He told us he hasn't seen him or even heard his name mentioned," Crew reminded him.

"You don't find that suspicious?" Nox asked.

"Not if they made him disappear," the task force leader answered. "Why bring up his name if they want him to remain a distant memory? My assumption is that they don't want anyone asking about him. Questions could lead to problems."

The problem was, the asshole hadn't disappeared. Now was the perfect time to tell them that discovery since Nox no longer had to hide his relationship with Liyah.

The only issue with letting everyone know T-Bone was still on the loose and up to his asshole ways, Decker, Finn and Rez might personally want to go after that prospect—or former prospect—and that could get them in a jam.

They could lose their jobs, get charged with a crime or worse.

"I can confirm he's still breathing," Nox revealed quietly, then waited for the fallout.

The whole room went into a deep freeze for a second or two. Then someone hit it with a flame thrower or something because so many of the guys were speaking at once Nox couldn't make any sense of it.

"Yo!" Crew yelled over the din. "Yo! Settle down!"

It took a few seconds but eventually, the room quieted.

Crew turned to him. "Explain."

"I spotted him at a motel—"

Nox was cut off by a slew of *wheres, whats, whens* and *what the fucks.*

Crew lifted a hand to shut everyone else up. "How long ago was that?"

"Just the other night."

"So, recently."

"Yes, recently," Nox confirmed, then reluctantly admitted, "but it wasn't the first time I've spotted him there."

Just as everyone was gearing up to pepper him with more questions, Crew lifted his hand again to silence them. "Explain. From the beginning. Don't leave anything out."

"I... *uh...* went to a motel a couple of months back..."

"Did you hire a hooker?" Rez asked.

"No, asshole, I didn't hire a damn hooker. I just happened to be in the area."

"You just said you were *at* the motel."

Damn. "Yes, I was at the motel—"

"Why?"

"Will you let the man finish, Rez?" Crew shouted. "Holy fuck."

"Continue," Rez encouraged with a smirk.

"When I was leaving, I spotted someone who looked like T-Bone. It turns out I was right. To make certain it was him and to see what the fucker was up to, I went back to do some surveillance."

Crew frowned. "Why are you only telling us this now?"

"Because I wanted to make sure it was him first." Nox would leave out the detail that he definitely knew it was T-Bone by the second night of spying on the former prospect.

"Isn't anyone else dying to know why the fuck Nox was at a motel?" Rez complained loudly.

"Are you that fucking dense?" Decker asked. "To keep Aaliyah a secret."

"So, why is T-Bag staying at a motel?" Finn asked next.

"Because he lost his room at the Uniontown church?" Torres suggested.

Nox continued, "That could be one reason, even though I didn't see him wearing his colors once. However... someone else showed up who was."

The room went still again as they waited.

"Saint."

"Are those two having a relationship?" Finn wiggled his eyebrows.

"It's a relationship, all right, but not a sexual one." Not in the sense Finn was thinking. "At least not with each other."

"Explain," Crew repeated, his expression turning darker.

Nox glanced over at Decker. "Sadie must have been a lucrative side hustle for T-Bag, because I saw several different women being 'helped' in and out of the motel room during my watch."

Decker roared, "That fucking motherfucker," and slammed his hand so hard on the desk where he sat, his mug jumped and caused coffee to spill over the rim.

"Too bad he survived that night in the..." Finn ate the rest of those words.

Only four of them knew about ambushing T-Bone and taking him out to a field to squeeze him for information on Sadie's whereabouts.

Nox and Finn's eyes met.

Even Crew didn't know all the details and the four of them wanted to keep it that way. It was safer for everyone not involved, in case it ever came to light. The concept was simple: one couldn't answer questions if they didn't know the answers.

"Okay, so now what?" Finn asked.

"So, if he's no longer a part of the club, then he's no longer a part of the investigation," Crew announced.

Exactly what Nox figured he'd say.

"But Saint's still a target," he finished.

"Targeting Saint is all fine and dandy, but what are we doing to stop T-Bone?" Decker asked. "He can't continue to get away with exploiting women like that."

Crew answered, "If we can confirm he's still a Demon, we'll include him as part of the sweep. If not, then the best thing to do is tip off the locals about him using a motel in their area to pimp out women."

"Crew—" Decker started.

Crew shook his head. "Honestly, I'm surprised he's still breathing. I figured since he disappeared, he truly *disappeared*."

"You're not the only one," Nox muttered.

"Let the locals charge him and take him into custody. He's only one minor player in the grand scheme of things," Crew said.

"He's not some minor fucking player," Finn shouted, jerking around in his chair. "Look what he did to some of our women. Look what he did to Sadie. I was okay with the Demons handling his ass but I'm not okay if they let him slide."

"You want to get jammed up? Because that's what will happen if you—or a few of you—try to handle him yourself," Crew warned with raised eyebrows. "But if he's still a Demon, I'd like to keep the locals out of it so the fucker isn't tipped off that he was being watched."

"Let's assume he's still a Demon," Rez suggested.

"You know we don't deal with assumptions," Crew told Rez. "We need facts and evidence."

"The fact is, he's an abusive motherfucker. And we also have evidence of that," Decker insisted. "He tried to abduct Val and ended up taking Sloane. He kept Sadie wired on meth and pimped her out to the point of death and, fuck, even her being a corpse didn't stop him from continuing to milk his cash cow."

"You think I'm not aware of that shit?" Crew asked. "I understand why you all want to string him up. I'm no fan of that motherfucker, either. But let's not do anything to jeopardize this investigation. We're at the five-yard line and ready to make the last play. Let's not move the goal posts and screw up our lead."

"He's not on the list to be indicted?" Finn asked.

"As far as I'm aware, none of the prospects are. They want to hit the big players. The ones that matter the most and without them around, the MC—if it survives—will be only that. A motorcycle club and no longer a criminal enterprise."

"If the Demons survive, it'll always be a criminal enterprise," Nox mentioned. "They're not going to go straight."

"Just like the Mafia," Torres said. "It's like a fucking octopus. Cut off a limb and it grows a new one."

"Or a starfish," Decker added. "Cut off an arm and a new starfish grows."

"What?" Rez asked.

"Yeah, it's true," Decker answered him.

"How do you know this?"

"Because I have a curious four-year-old," Decker answered. "She asks that Google thingy that talks back to you five thousand questions a day. I've almost smashed it a million times, but I know if I do, I'll only have to replace the fucking thing."

Nox grinned and shook his head.

"Holy fuck, is that a grin? No fucking way," Finn said.

"Way!" Rez yelled.

"You're such assholes." Nox didn't bother to hide the grin that widened.

"Oh, look what some sweet pussy can do," Crew said. "Insurance should've paid for that instead of a therapist."

"I'm sure T-Bag could've helped out with that. You'd only need to cut your dick off afterward as a safety precaution," Finn said.

"First off, Liyah isn't..." Nox shook his head. "Never mind." There was no point with this bunch.

"I figured you'd defend her," Crew said.

"She doesn't need it. All I have to do is tell her what you said, and she'll handle it the next time she sees you."

"Brothers don't throw each other under the bus," Crew warned.

"Then you shouldn't be such a dick," he told the task force leader.

"Anyway, back to the subject at hand... You guys get me proof he's still a Demon—without doing illegal shit—and I'll go to the AUSA and make sure there's a warrant with his name on it. How's that?"

Warrant and arrest, conviction or not, T-Bag was going to be handled one way or another. With Crew's knowledge or not. His gaze flicked to Decker, before sliding to Rez and ending with Finn in an exchange of silent messages.

No words were needed. They all knew what needed to be done.

"Don't pull any shit without my approval first." Suspicion colored Crew's tone. He knew his fellow BAMC brothers too well.

Decker asked, "When will the task force officially be shut down?"

"Next week was what I was told by Williams. That said,

we need to wrap shit up. Make sure all your reports are complete."

"It'll be weird seeing the third floor empty," Nox said. The executive committee would need to figure out what to do with it next. The money coming in from the lease helped keep the club's coffers in the black. Barely.

"Agreed. The task force has been in this building almost as long as the BAMC. But all good things have to come to an end, right?" Crew asked.

"You mean not seeing your face almost every damn day? That's not good, that's great!" Rez crowed.

"We should have an indictmas party," Torres suggested.

"Can we wait until after all the warrants are served?" Crew suggested. "Let's make sure everything goes smoothly first before we celebrate."

"I'd rather be celebrating convictions," Decker said.

Crew tipped his salt-and-pepper head to the side in agreement. "We can do that, too."

"I have to say," Torres started, "I'll miss working with you fuckers. This assignment has been the tits. Unlike the last one I was on."

Closing down the investigation meant anyone on the team not a federal agent would go back to their regularly scheduled programming. For Nox, he'd go back to patrol at Shadow Valley PD.

Working on the task force was a change he needed after losing Jackie. He would be forever grateful for the opportunity and the new connections he made with members not part of the BAMC.

"Now that Nox has Liyah, he can stop watching the footage from The Peach Pit for his spank bank material," Finn announced.

Nox grimaced. "You're welcome to watch it instead.

There's nothing on that stage that remotely makes my dick hard. Unlike you and Rez, apparently."

Crew burst out laughing. "Damn, the man is definitely on the track back to his former self."

Rez shot Nox a grin. "Yeah, an asshole like the rest of us. Welcome back to the dark side, Hard Nox."

Chapter Thirty-Six

"Anything?"

Fletch's voice filled Nox's ear. "Not a fucking word."

"So, can we safely assume that motherfucker is no longer a Demon?"

"Does it matter if he is or isn't?" Fletch asked.

"If he is, Crew said they can indict him. If not, we need to get the locals involved to solve that problem since the Demons didn't," Nox explained. "Or..."

"Or?" Fletch prodded.

"Or we can serve our own justice."

Since only silence filled his ears for a few seconds, Nox pulled the cell phone away to make sure the call hadn't been dropped.

"Who is we?" Fletch finally asked. "Certainly not the whole damn task force."

"No."

"Nox..."

"Again, Crew would only guarantee that fucker's indictment if he's still a Demon. Otherwise, he wants us to turn over any evidence against T-Bag to the local PD that covers the motel and let them handle it."

"Well, there you go. Problem solved. And your hands don't get dirty."

"Fletch, the man needs a reckoning."

"I won't disagree with that. But is having a *come to Jesus* meeting with one sick bastard worth your careers and possibly your freedom?"

"We would need to be careful how we handle it."

"Careful would mean going about it the legal way. I'm not sensing that here."

Nox had to admit, Fletch always had good senses. "We need to guarantee he won't pull the same bullshit over and over, destroying more women's lives."

"I won't argue the fact that he's a piece of shit who needs to be wiped. But—"

Nox interrupted him with, "There will always be buts. Life's full of them, brother."

Fletch sighed. "Listen, I haven't seen him. I've not heard his name mentioned. He's not been at any parties. He's also not been at any church meetings. Within that club, it's like he never existed. Take that information as you will."

"Okay, I'll take that as he was only stripped of his colors. Either that, or he gave up his colors willingly before the Demons could deal with him."

"It's possible," Fletch agreed. "You said he partnered up with Saint in this endeavor?"

"Yeah."

More silence hit his ears for a few heartbeats. "Okay, I'll keep a closer eye on Saint when I'm in his presence. However, I'm rarely around him since he's busy running The Peach Pit." Fletch cursed under his breath. "Could it be that Saint's telling Wolf he's tied up with the strip club when he's actually running this little side hustle with T-Bone? If so, him not being around much wouldn't raise any red flags to Wolf, Viper or any of them."

"Having a meth stash that's light might," Nox told him.

"If they were aware of it. Who controls the meth in the stash vehicle at The Peach Pit?"

Fletch's question was rhetorical since they both knew it was Saint. That meant, skimming meth from that stash would never come under the microscope as long as Saint was managing the strip club.

Nox sighed out a, "Yeah."

He yanked off his baseball cap and scraped his fingers through his hair, once again scanning the dark parking lot of the motel. While he did that, an SUV pulled up next to T-Bone's piece-of-shit rust-mobile and a second later, the former prospect got out of the driver's side to greet the newcomer.

A man climbed out of the vehicle and as the two shook hands, Nox had no doubt money slipped from one palm to the other because a second later, T-Bone jerked his chin toward the motel room door. With a nod, the customer walked through the door and closed it behind him.

Son of a fucking bitch.

This was the fifth john of the night that Nox was aware of.

It took everything in his power not to go over to the motel, kick in the fucking door and pull that woman out of there. But, one, he wasn't sure if the woman wasn't a willing participant. Two, it would be a mistake to out himself to T-Bone. And three, he shouldn't do it alone.

He had no doubt the scumbag was packing heat, and he didn't want to get involved in a shoot-out when he was officially "off-duty" from the task force and on his own time.

Hell, he didn't want to get in a shoot-out when he *was* on-duty, either. Most departments, including the feds, frowned on that.

"You there?"

Nox shook himself mentally and gave some of his attention back to Fletch. "Yeah. I'm here."

"Rumor has it you're seeing someone now."

Nox grunted.

"Brother, you don't know how fucking happy I was to hear that." When he grunted again, Fletch laughed and asked, "She a keeper?"

Was she? "It's new, Fletch."

"How new? I heard you also kept her a secret for a few weeks."

"Who had diarrhea of the mouth?"

"The list for who doesn't would be shorter."

"Fact."

Fletch chuckled again. "Look, I'm happy for you, even if it's only a fling. I only want the best for you, Opportunity Nox."

That was a new nickname.

"So let's hear it, what's she like?"

Nox pursed his lips and thought about Liyah. "Gorgeous. Well-spoken. Extremely successful. A class act, actually."

"What's she doing with you, then?"

"I ask myself that question daily."

"And what's the answer?"

"I don't have one." Nox sighed and dragged his fingers down his cheek. "She's so fucking out of my league, Fletch."

"You don't think she'll stick?"

He honestly didn't know where they would end up. They were taking it day by day. No pressure. No talk of any future together. Nothing. They were only enjoying the time they spent together. In bed and out of it, too.

"Do you want her to stick?"

Did he? "Yeah. I think so."

"Then, tell her."

"We're not there yet."

"Sounds like you are."

"Maybe. But..."

"But she has two sons, and her father is the big, bad motherfucker who's the sergeant at arms for the Dark Knights."

Nox sucked on his teeth. "Yeah, someone was running their fucking mouth."

Another chuckle filled his ear. "Of course. Have you met him?"

"*Mmm hmm*," he murmured, his eyes still glued to the motel.

"And?"

"And what? Like you said, he's a big, bad motherfucker. I'm smart enough not to tangle with him. Since I'd like to keep seeing his daughter, I need to stay clear of his bad side."

Once Fletch was done with his latest round of chuckling, he said, "I hear you, brother, I've seen him before, so I can confirm that I wouldn't want to go one on one with him, either." He paused before asking, "What about her boys?"

"She's raising them right. Typical boys, though."

"So, not hellions."

"Not yet. But I think Magnum would try to lure them over to the dark side if he could."

"And what does Aaliyah think about that?"

"She's strongly against it. She's not even close to being a biker chick. She tolerates her father's club, but doesn't embrace it."

"Good. It would suck if you had to arrest one or both of her kids down the road. That would make sitting around the dinner table a bit awkward."

He grunted again just as the door to the motel room was flung open. Even though Nox could only see a silhouette in the doorway, he knew it was the man who just paid to do whatever he paid to do with the woman inside. However, his ears picked up yelling and the man's arms were swinging wildly.

Clearly, someone was agitated.

In response, T-Bone quickly jumped out of his car and approached, stopping toe-to-toe with the man.

"Hey, I gotta go," Nox said quickly.

"All right, I—"

He hung up before Fletch could finish his sentence. Nox was sure he'd hear about it later, but he'd deal with it then. Right now, he needed to pay attention.

And what he was seeing was T-Bone's pissed-off customer jabbing the former prospect in the chest, shaking his head and returning to his car.

T-Bone waited until the man slid into the driver's seat before turning back to the motel room and shaking his head, too.

Nox was pretty damn sure that both men were agitated because of a deal gone wrong.

Not good.

The second the motel door slammed shut with T-Bone inside, Nox turned the key and, once his old pickup truck roared to life, he shoved the shifter it into Drive. He didn't bother to go the long way around, instead he made his own shortcut by driving his truck through the grass divider that separated the farm lane and motel, over a flower bed and across the motel's parking lot.

He slammed his truck to a stop in a spot near T-Bone's vehicle, threw it into Park, yanked out his key, and bolted from the cab.

After a last glance at T-Bone's customer pulling out of the lot and onto the road, Nox turned and faced the closed door.

His heart pounded as he heard the woman crying and T-Bone yelling at her through the door.

"Fuck me," Nox muttered. He didn't like the fact that he was about to expose himself to this fucker, but he was so damn done with shit. He was tired of watching and not doing anything about it.

It was time to take matters into his own hands.

He pounded on the door first but realized he should check to see if it was locked and, of course, it was, since most motel room doors locked automatically when they shut.

He didn't bother to wait for either occupant to answer, instead he planted his boot hard next to the handle. Unfortunately, the wood frame cracked a little, but the door didn't fly open like he expected.

"Shit." That failure would give T-Bone a heads up.

Fuck it. He was too invested to simply walk away now.

Just as he was lifting his boot again, the door swung open, and T-Bone stood there scowling. "What the fuck?"

"Exactly. What the fuck?" Nox pushed past him, quickly scanning the room for threats other than T-Bone.

"Who the fuck are you and why the fuck are you in my room?"

Nox tried to keep one eye on the biker as he approached the woman sitting naked on the edge of the bed with her head in her hands. "You okay?"

She lifted her tear-streaked face and nodded.

"He hurt you?"

T-Bone yanked on Nox's arm. "Fuck off, asshole. Get the fuck outta here."

Nox pulled free with a jerk of his shoulder, but kept an

eye on the man's hands. They were empty now, but that could quickly change. "Why are you crying?"

She sniffled and shook her head.

"Did he hurt you? Did either of them hurt you?"

She shook her head again.

"What happened?"

"Get the fuck outta my room!" T-Bone screamed and grabbed Nox's arm again, digging his fingers in painfully.

This time, instead of pulling free, Nox spun, used the man's grip to yank him off balance and nailed him square in the face with his fist.

Damn, did that feel good.

So, he did it again.

And again.

And one more time for shits and giggles.

When Nox's rage cleared, T-Bone was down on his knees, with his left eye already turning colors and blood rushing from his nose.

Did he also have a split lip? *Poor fucking baby.*

Nox angled himself so he could keep an eye on the former prospect as he asked the woman, "What happened?'

"The sicko wanted to shit in my mouth and for me to eat it. I ain't doing that."

Nox's stomach rolled at her honest answer. It was one time he'd prefer to hear a lie.

"Who are you?" Her eyes flicked to T-Bone cupping a hand over his busted nose and back to Nox.

Nox couldn't tell her that he was a cop. Or that he'd been watching T-Bone. Instead, he went with, "I heard the fucking commotion next door." As the former Demon prospect slowly made his way to his feet, Nox addressed him. "She said she didn't want someone making her eat his shit. Why the fuck would you let someone do that? What's going on here?"

T-Bone sounded a bit stuffed up when he responded, "Mind your own fuckin' business. She's my woman."

He glanced at the strung-out, naked woman. "Are you?"

Her wide, glassy eyes once again bounced from Nox to T-Bone and back. Her expression told him everything, even though Nox already knew the answer.

He held out his hand to her. "Let's go."

"You go with him, you ain't gettin' paid," T-Bone warned the woman.

"Get paid for what?" Nox asked, even though he knew.

"Not your goddamn business! Now get the fuck outta here." T-Bone jabbed a finger toward the open door.

"Or what? You going to call the cops?"

"Fuck no. Don't need the fuckin' pigs to handle a problem like you." A gun appeared in T-Bone's hand.

Nox froze. There it was. He figured the man was packing. He was only surprised that the weapon hadn't appeared earlier, especially when Nox was pounding him to his knees.

Did Nox rattle the asshole's brain enough so that he only just remembered he had it on him?

"Givin' you one more chance to get the fuck outta here and to mind your fuckin' business. You takin' that chance or not?"

Nox lifted up his palms in surrender, ignoring the fact he had a compact .38 revolver strapped to his ankle.

He needed to resist the temptation to pull it. He couldn't get into a shoot-out. Plus, the walls were thin in this motel, it wouldn't take much for a stray bullet to go through one and strike an innocent.

Do not pull your fucking weapon. Do not tell him you're a cop. Keep all your normal responses under wraps and handle this tactfully so you don't leave this room with more holes than when you entered.

"Do you want to stay here?" Nox asked the woman.

Her eyes again flicked from him to T-Bone before she nodded.

Nox gritted his teeth. "Fine. Have a good night. Just keep the volume down over here so the rest of us can get some sleep, got it? If you don't, I'm calling the cops."

"Fuck off," T-Bone sneered, then winced due to his busted face.

Nox lifted his hand and made a show of studying his busted knuckles. "Worth it." He took one last glance at the woman he hated to leave behind. "Call 911 if you need help."

"Get the fuck out!" T-Bone screamed, then groaned in pain.

Nox's head twitched but he slowly made his way back outside. As soon as he was clear of the doorway, the door slammed behind him. With a shake of his head, he went back to his truck, got in it and returned to his normal spot to monitor the situation.

They needed to do something about that motherfucker, and they needed to do it soon.

Chapter Thirty-Seven

Nox TURNED SLOWLY in a circle and took in the third floor of The Plant.

It was now almost empty. A couple of bare desks still remained. The whiteboard on the wall was now wiped clean. All the photos of the Demons had been removed from the cork board. Not one computer remained.

Only a dirty floor was left behind where the conference table and chairs were previously.

The task force had been dismantled piece by piece and some of the members had already returned to their regular assignments at whatever law enforcement agency they came from. The only members left were gathering at zero dark thirty to join in on today's "fun." Their last official assignment unless they were called to testify.

Though, Fletch and Wilder still remained undercover with the Demons as the task force's eyes and ears until today's early morning sweep was completed. While it was dangerous for them, in reality, serving warrants and taking unwilling bikers into custody would be risky for everyone. At least everyone about to see the results of all their time and hard work that they put into the investigation in the last almost two years.

It was a bit sad that Nox's time with the task force was coming to an end, but he was glad that the Demons would finally get what they deserved.

Or he hoped they would.

What happened next would involve judges and juries, trials, prosecutors, criminal defense attorneys, plea deals, motions and eventually appeals.

Justice wasn't simple or quick. Nor was it cheap.

Sometimes, it wasn't even served.

Or fair.

His nostrils flared as he pulled in a long breath.

Everyone in group one who wanted to help serve warrants stood around sucking down coffee because it was still considered the middle of night.

The best time to hit the Demons was after the Peach Pit and Hawg Wild closed. When a weekend long party wasn't being held at the Viper's Den. When most of those motherfuckers would be asleep in their beds or passed out on a random floor or couch.

"Where the fuck is Crew?" Finn asked on a yawn. "If we don't get this party started soon, I'm going to curl up on the cot and take a nap."

Nox glanced at the time on his cell phone. They were supposed to meet on the third floor at three AM, then head out to meet the rest of the teams at four in some parking lot that only Crew knew the address to.

Secret squirrel shit and all of that.

The less details given out about the coordinated effort, the less chance for it to get leaked. Either on purpose or by accident.

As if Finn summoned Crew by saying his name, the task force leader came barreling through the door with Cabrera close on his heels, both wearing tactical gear like the rest of them. Only, the task force leader had his phone to his ear and wore an expression that made all of them on the third floor sit up and take notice.

Actually, everyone not only stopped slouching, they all shot to their feet.

"For fuck's sake," Crew muttered into his phone. "Okay. We'll stand by until we get further word."

Further word?

That didn't sound like they were about to go bust in some doors.

Were they getting screwed out of the opportunity for some reason? Did Crew land on someone's shit list?

Crew shook his head one last time before pulling the phone from his ear and stabbing the screen with his finger to end the call. "For fuck's sake."

"You said that already. Did you forget?" Cabrera razzed him. The woman had busting Crew's balls down to a science.

And they all loved her for it.

"What's going on?" Rez asked.

"We were told to standby and wait for further word," Crew said.

"Yeah, genius, we heard that part. You want to explain why?" asked Luke Rodgers, another DEA agent like Crew, Cabrera and Torres.

"Don't mind him," Cabrera said. "Getting up this early meant he didn't get all of his beauty rest. He's a bit discombobulated."

"Pretty fucking big word for such a tiny woman," Crew retorted.

"I might be tiny, but I still pack a punch."

Behind Nox, Torres snorted. "Foreplay for the two of you must be explosive since you are always lobbing bombs at each other."

Finn grimaced. "I really don't want to think about Crew having sex. Torres, you might have to apologize to Mel when that visual makes me unable to perform."

"Don't worry, she won't notice," Rez said.

"Will you tell us what the fuck is going on?" Nox demanded from Crew, trying to get them back on track.

"They've got the state and county emergency response teams responding."

"To serve warrants? I mean—"

"Not to serve warrants. That's been put on hold for now. The Russos decided that last night was a great time to wipe out the Demons. Dead Demons are popping up everywhere. The Wolf Den. The Viper's Den. The Bear's Den. Every fucking business, every fucking clubhouse and party house that the feds are aware of, were all hit by the Russos overnight."

"It was a massacre?" Finn asked.

"Pretty damn close," Crew said.

"Now what?" Rodgers asked.

Crew shook his head in annoyance. "Now we do as instructed, stand down and wait."

"What?" burst from Rez. "Until when?"

"Until I get further word from either Williams or from the AUSA. Hard to serve a warrant to a dead Demon."

Bob Williams was the task force's supervising special agent and Crew's supervisor.

"Actually, it would be helluva lot easier to serve a warrant to someone who's dead," Finn said.

But pointless.

"They might have to rename their MC to the Dead

Demons instead of Deadly." Cabrera added, "If anyone even survives."

Of course there would be survivors. It would be impossible to pin all the Demons down at one time.

"What about Fletch and Wilder?" Finn asked.

Crew's expression caused a knot in Nox's gut.

"I've been trying to reach them since I first got word," he admitted.

"Jesus fuck, they better not have been caught up in the middle of that shit. They knew about when the good guys would make an appearance but not the Russos. They might have been caught off guard."

"Until I can talk to one of them, Pippi, I have no fucking clue. My worry was both of them getting caught up in the crossfire if this went down the way I feared."

"Maybe they were still in their apartment when shit began going down," Nox said.

"I can only hope. But they planned on being up and about for when we started kicking in doors. This way they could keep us in the loop."

"But where did they plan on being?" Rodgers asked.

"Fletch said they would be at the Uniontown church. They were going to pretend they both got too smashed last night to head home."

"Fuck," Nox muttered. Grabbing his phone, he quickly texted both Wilder and Fletch. *Check in ASAP. We need proof of life.*

With his hands planted on his hips and his head shaking, Rez bitched, "Took too long to get indictments."

The man was not happy. When it came down to it, none of them were. Getting to be involved in the arrests was like the cherry on top of the sundae. It was the finishing touch. That opportunity was being robbed from them.

Was it better for society if two criminal organizations took each other out? Fuck yes. Cheaper for the taxpayers, too. But hauling some drug-running bikers away in cuffs would be so damn satisfying.

"You know how this shit works, Rez," Crew told him.

"We get strangled by all the goddamn red tape."

"Without it, their charges would be thrown out and the indictments worthless," Crew explained. Though, needlessly.

They all were aware of that, but that didn't mean they had to like it. However, complaining wouldn't change the process.

Unlike the Demons, they had to follow rules and procedures.

For the most part, anyway.

"Look, as long as Fletch and Wilder are okay, I won't give two shits about the Demons or the fucking Russos. May they all rot in hell," Finn exclaimed. "The fewer breathing at the end, the better."

"Agreed. We were all kind of hoping the trash would take itself out, anyway. Looks like we got our wish," Torres said.

"As long as innocent bystanders don't get caught up in the crossfire," Crew said.

"Or Fletch and Wilder," Nox murmured, then asked, "But was it a true war? Sounds like the Russos went tactical. Did the Demons even have an opportunity to fight back or were they all ambushed?"

"Tactical?" Rodgers huffed. "The Russos are definitely not Navy SEALS. They don't have the training to be fucking stealth."

"But they hit the Demons when the MC wasn't expecting it. The same way we would have when we served the warrants. They're definitely smarter than those bikers."

"True. But my guess is they'll end up with casualties, too."

"No loss," Cabrera said.

"Just like in the Army," Nox started, "I'm sure they sent in the soldiers to do the dirty work and not the generals."

Crew raked fingers through his short hair. "Yeah, I'm sure the boss and underboss are somewhere safe until the dust settles."

"Or the blood stops running," Cabrera added.

"What businesses did the Russos hit?" Nox asked Crew. "Do you know?"

"All of them. All at fucking once, too. This was a planned and coordinated attack. They lit buildings on fire. They threw smoke bombs in others and took out the bikers and their women as they escaped. Pizza Town is gone. The reports I received said that the Viper's Den exploded and turned into a five-alarm fire because of the surrounding woods. Anyone inside was blown to fucking bits."

Rez did the sign of the Holy Cross. "Rest in pieces, you motherfuckers."

"The Peach Pit?" Finn asked.

"Not sure. I told you what I know so far. I'm sure I'll get updates throughout the day."

"We did all this goddamn work for the Russos to steal our thunder. I was looking forward to breaking in doors and cracking some skulls," Rez admitted. "They couldn't wait a day or two and let us have some of the fun? Assholes."

"It just makes it less for us to round up in the end, that's all. They're lightening the load for both us and the court systems," Crew assured him. "The Russos are doing what we hoped. Once the smoke clears, we'll get a better picture of who's left. I'm sure the Demons didn't just throw their hands up in the air in surrender and accept every bullet pointed their way, they probably fought back against La Cosa Nostra."

"Survival of the fittest," Nox murmured.

"That's one way to put it. Once we know who's still standing, the teams can go in and serve warrants to who remains. The bonus is, with the Russos getting involved, the feds may be able to rope in some of them, too."

"A two-for-one special?" Cabrera joked.

"It's a good way to thin the herd when it comes to the Pittsburgh Mafia. Let's not forget, they're the reason the Demons were trafficking meth into Pennsylvania in the first place."

"I figured the FBI, DEA and ATF would be all over the Russos," Nox said. He didn't know the ins and outs of how the federal agencies dealt with criminal organizations. As part of the Tri-State Federal Drug Task Force, he only followed orders.

For the most part.

"I'm sure they are," Crew said. "The FBI had Wilder undercover with the family. I have to assume they have other agents planted, too."

"Then whoever is in charge of this whole fucking thing should've gotten word that the Russos were about to go Demon hunting," Rez continued to complain.

"Are you about to shed some tears over the loss of Demons?" Torres asked him. "Do you need a hanky or something?"

"Fuck no. I was just looking forward to seeing the results of our work."

"You will. In court," Crew assured him.

"That's the boring part. I was talking about taking part in the stuff that would get our blood rushing," Rez said. "Our hearts pumping. Our adrenaline rushing."

"Can someone look out of the window to see if pigs are flying? Crew is being way too reasonable about all of this," Torres said, laughing.

"I know, it's scary, right?" Cabrera said, hip-checking her lover. "I wonder if it's the Centrum Silver vitamins I had him start taking."

"She's lying to you, J. Crew. Those little blue pills aren't vitamins," Finn warned him.

Crew made a face. "Like I need that."

"Cabrera?" Torres asked.

She grinned and shrugged. "Those vitamins are definitely working."

Rodgers gagged. "Goddamn it. Can we change the subject? I really don't need to hear about Crew's prowess, or lack thereof."

"I think you speak for all of us, Rodgers," Torres said.

"What do you want us to do, Crewser?" Finn asked. "Stick around for further word or head out?"

"No point in staying up here since this floor has been stripped down to the bare bones. We can head down to the first floor to wait, or you can leave. But if you leave, stay close to your phones in case anything changes."

When Crew, Cabrera, Finn, Torres and Rodgers headed toward the door, Rez detoured and came over to Nox to lean in close. "Hey, wanna go for a ride? If we couldn't join in the fun, we should at least get to witness the aftermath."

He'd been having that same thought himself. "Fuck yeah, I do."

"Then, let's blow this goddamn popsicle stand. I'll text Finn once we're outside so he can make an excuse for not staying. I know he'll want to go, too, and I don't want Crew catching wind of what we're up to."

"Sounds like a plan."

Rez rubbed his hands together. "I love it when a plan comes together."

"In this case, the plan fell apart," Nox reminded him.

"This will be the next best thing. Witnessing the downfall of the Demons will make me giddy. It'll just sting a little that I didn't have a hand in it."

"You did. There will still be indictments for anyone who survived, and you did have a hand in that."

Chapter Thirty-Eight

THE THREE OF them hopped into Rez's Dodge Durango Hellcat. They figured they'd scope out all the Demons-owned businesses and buildings in group one's area. Nox saw no point in heading south into West Virginia or west into Ohio to see the damage. Eventually they'd get access to view the photos and read the reports.

They did a quick drive-by of the car wash and Landry's Laundromat. Since those businesses weren't normally occupied by Demons, both still stood without any damage, proving the Russos were out for blood and not only taking out the Demons' sources of income.

When they got as close as possible to Pizza Town, where Decker went undercover for a very short amount of time, Rez pouted dramatically. "Poor Deck, he'll be sad to see his fav pizza joint burnt to the damn ground."

"He might actually shed a few tears," added Finn, sniffling loudly.

Since fire trucks and other emergency equipment

blocked the streets, they couldn't get close. Once they parked and got out, they flashed their federal IDs to the local uniforms standing guard and were told that the doors had been barred to the pizza shop from the outside before someone threw an unknown explosive device through the large front window.

Anyone attempting to escape was shot. Anyone who didn't was burned alive.

The ambush was brutal but effective.

It was one way of taking out some Demons, as well as one of the businesses where they dealt meth and pot.

"How many Demons were inside?" Finn asked the cop.

The rookie shrugged. "They've found four bodies so far. Due to the conditions of them, they haven't been identified. Right now, we have no way of knowing whether they were customers or members of that damn MC."

No surprise. Nox only hoped no civilians lost their life in the explosion.

They drove to Hawg Wild Saloon next. If they didn't already know where the bar was, it would've been easy to find. All they had to do was follow the billowing gray smoke. There was so much of it, it was easy to spot even in the early morning darkness.

Add in the acrid smell that singed their nostrils.

They pulled up as close as they could get, but once again it was surrounded by emergency vehicles and personnel still working on putting out the remaining flames and hot spots while more emergency responders searched the smoking rubble for the dead.

"Do you have a body count?" Nox asked a state trooper standing just on the other side of the yellow police tape.

The trooper shook his head. "Nothing final. Latest number is fifteen crispy critters."

Finn murmured, "I doubt fifteen Demons worked here."

Rez shrugged. "But they could've been drinking here last night."

"Either that or it was other bikers. The Mafia wouldn't care if there were more than Demons inside," Nox said. "They'd see the rest of the victims as collateral damage."

"Were the doors barred?" Rez asked the state cop.

"Yeah."

"Do you know what kind of explosive device they used?" Nox asked next.

The trooper pursed his lips. "Not yet. The feds took over the investigation."

Since that was to be expected, Nox wasn't surprised by that answer. Especially with indictments pending for a lot of the Demons. The feds would be heavily invested in this latest twist of the criminal investigation.

"Let's hope to fuck that Fletch and Wilder weren't hanging out here last night," Nox said once they were out of the trooper's hearing range.

Finn frowned and looked back over his shoulder at what remained of the bar. "Crew mentioned they were going to be hanging out at the Wolf Den."

Nox took a quick glance at this cell phone to see if either had responded to his texts yet. They hadn't.

That wasn't a good sign.

"Thank fuck Cabrera was done with her undercover work," Finn continued as they walked back to the Dodge.

"Jesus," burst from Rez, "if she would've been caught up in this shit..." He did the sign of the cross.

"Crew would've been out of his fucking mind," Finn finished.

"How far the mighty have fallen." Rez smirked.

Finn shrugged. "Look, none of us has any room to talk. We've all tripped and fallen into the quicksand."

"Speak for yourself," Nox insisted.

Both Finn and Rez snorted in sync.

"Like we don't have fucking eyes in our heads, Fort Nox. You think we didn't watch you two on the club run?" Rez made kissing noises as he hugged himself like the child he was.

"Or do you think we're blind and haven't seen her coming in and out of your apartment on a regular basis." Finn smirked. "That, I remind you, is only one floor above the BAMC clubhouse and one below where we were all working. The Russos might not be stealth but, news flash, neither are you two."

"We're going to have to start calling it Nox-ing boots," Rez declared.

Finn hooted loudly. "He Nox-es the bottom out of her."

Nox pulled in a breath. Unfortunately, the early morning air was full of smoke, and he had to smother a cough. "It's nothing serious. We're just spending some time together."

Finn and Rez shared a look before bursting out in laughter.

"You're such jackasses. All right. Where to next?" Nox asked as they climbed into the Dodge.

Still chuckling, Rez said, "I say either The Peach Pit or their clubhouse."

"If we head to The Pit first, it might give Fletch or Wilder time to respond to my texts," Nox suggested.

"With the way Pizza Town and Hawg Wild both looked, if they were in the Uniontown clubhouse when this shit all went down, they might not be identified for a while."

"Don't fucking say that, asshole!" Nox whacked the

passenger seat headrest with his hand so hard, it made Finn lurch forward.

Finn threw up his palms in surrender. "Hey, I'm only trying to be realistic. Why hasn't anyone heard from either of them yet?"

"Maybe Crew did." Nox hoped that was true.

"Check with Crew," Rez urged, meeting Nox's eyes in the rearview mirror.

Nox gave him a nod and called the DEA agent.

Crew picked up on the first ring. "Where'd you disappear to? Are you upstairs?"

"No, I had to run out. Any updates? Have you heard from Fletch yet?"

"No," Crew answered. "Not yet. I got Deck out of bed to have him go over and check their apartment."

Nox's chest tightened. "I'm not liking this radio silence."

"You and me both, brother," Crew agreed.

"Okay, let me know if they check in."

"Will do. You do the same."

The call ended in typical Crew fashion. Abrupt and without any fanfare.

"Nothing?" Finn prodded Nox.

"No."

"Fuck. This isn't like Fletch."

"Can we not think the worst?" Nox desperately urged Finn. "He'll check in as soon as it's safe to do so."

Neither Finn nor Rez responded because nothing else needed to be said.

When they got to The Peach Pit, it was a flurry of activity between the coroner, Uniontown PD, state police, and a whole shitload of feds wearing windbreakers with big yellow letters identifying whether they were ATF, FBI or DEA.

Unlike Pizza Town or Hawg Wild, the strip club had not

been burnt to the ground. It didn't even look as though any attempt was made to raze it. In fact, if the place wasn't swarming with law enforcement or surrounded with bright yellow tape, no one would expect a thing.

Rez found a spot to park outside of the taped-off area and the three of them climbed out of his Durango.

"Well, since these haven't been confiscated yet, maybe they'll get us inside." Rez held up his federal ID.

"It's a magic key." Finn pulled his out of his wallet. "Let me do the talking."

"For fuck's sake," Nox groaned.

"What? I know how to razzle dazzle."

Rez choked. "Yeah right, maybe when you're stripping on the stage as Flame."

"You mean Flare," Nox said next.

"It was Blaze!" Finn exclaimed. "Holy shit. Get it right."

Rez chuckled. "Do you make Mel call you Blaze when you're role playing in the bedroom?"

"We have a loft, not an actual bedroom. Oh, and... fuck off!"

Rez laughed way too loudly for being at a crime scene. Death and destruction was not a laughing matter.

Normally.

They approached one of the two Uniontown officers guarding the scene. They all flashed their IDs and told them they'd been on a task force investigating the Demons. They also name-dropped Ken Proctor, a Uniontown officer who had also worked on the task force.

No razzle dazzle needed. The cop lifted the tape and waved them inside the crime scene. "Just don't screw up the scene or any evidence. Keep your hands to yourself and watch where you step."

As if they didn't know that shit already.

Nox gave him a crisp salute and they headed in through the propped-open front door.

The place swarmed with federal, state and local crime scene investigators and staff from the county medical examiner's office. They were all so busy, nobody gave the three of them a second glance.

Finn elbowed Nox and pointed at two men lying in pools of blood in the lobby. One body was sprawled out with a gun still in his hand. The other, peppered with gunshot wounds, looked like he'd slid down the wall, leaving a streak of blood in his path. Once he hit the floor, he'd fallen to the side.

Both still wore their Demons cuts, only they had a few extra holes in the leather.

Finn squatted down by one body and said to the nearest federal agent, "If you haven't identified these two upstanding gentlemen yet, this one is Chubs," he jerked his chin toward the other corpse. "And that one is Popeye. Both prospects."

Since those two, being prospects, hadn't even been on the indictment list, that Nox was aware of, had the Russos done the world a service with their late-night massacre?

Maybe.

But he worried that too many innocent bystanders were involved. Especially in a business like The Peach Pit. The only positive he could come up with was that the strip club hardly had any customers anymore. And, from what Nox had witnessed with watching all the footage from inside, the few they did get usually didn't stay after midnight.

The investigator taking notes nodded. "You knew them?"

Finn showed the man his ID. "We're part of the Tri-State Federal Drug Task Force. We were investigating the Demons, so yeah, we know who they are."

"Do you have list of casualties?" Nox asked.

"Not yet," the agent answered.

"Mind if we go in and look?" Nox asked next. "This is one of the businesses we were surveilling."

"Don't touch anything. Don't move anything. Be careful where you step."

Rez glanced toward the open double doors. The center of both used to have frosted glass. That glass was now shattered and scattered all over the floor. "Any of La Cosa Nostra go down inside?"

"Two. One more was taken to the hospital in critical condition. This ended up being a shootout, but the Demons were outgunned. And some of the dancers—if they couldn't take cover—ended up being collateral damage."

Damn, that sucked since they were someone's daughter, mother, sister or aunt. With the quality of dancer Saint was pulling in, they could even be someone's grandmother.

"The three of us actually did a little undercover work in this business, so we might be able to ID some of the rest, if needed."

Nox wasn't sure if what Finn said was true. Since Mel left, the club now had a high turnover rate. Any new dancers quickly found that no money was to be had after Saint and Cookie ran the business into the ground.

Nox wondered if either of that loving couple were on location when the Russos' soldiers hit it.

Another thought popped into Nox's noggin. Due to the lack of tips, he wondered once again how many of the dancers had been convinced to participate in Saint and T-Bone's side hustle. If they had families to support, they might be lured into the promise of some extra cash. Or at least meth, if they were into that.

While Nox didn't know that answer, he was damn sure that Saint and T-Bone, if both were still breathing, needed to be stopped from taking advantage of desperate women.

Rez elbowed Nox and jerked his chin toward what was left of the doors that led into the main area of the club. With a nod, both Nox and Finn followed him.

Rez slammed to a stop as soon as he took in the scene.

He wasn't the only one. "Damn," Nox whispered, looking around.

Finn whistled softly while also taking in the carnage.

With Hawg Wild and Pizza Town, the Russos had destroyed them from the outside.

This location had been handled quite differently.

"Anyone wanna bet that they used an AR-15 with a bump stock?" Nox asked, taking in the death and destruction.

"Not just one, either. They peppered this whole fucking place with bullets," Finn murmured.

Bullet casings were strewn all over the floor, along with evidence markers, the majority of them right by the shot-out double doors. It appeared as if the Russos began firing the second they stepped inside. They didn't want to give anyone a chance to shoot back.

They seemed to be successful.

As they wandered through the crime scene, they were careful where they stepped to avoid the puddles of blood, the sheet-covered bodies, the broken glass, as well as the knocked-over tables and chairs.

A couple of customers still sat in the seats where they were shot. They didn't even have a chance to scramble for cover.

A single body remained on a blood-covered stage.

"Jesus fuck. Those fuckers didn't give a shit who they killed," Finn said in a low tone, trying not to draw too much attention to their nosy asses.

Rez said, "Maybe it was a good thing they lost a majority

of their clientele. Otherwise, the death toll would've been a helluva lot worse."

"Think they'll fix the damage and eventually try to reopen the place?" Nox asked.

"Fuck, they just need to patch a few holes and it'll be as good as new," Rez answered, glancing around.

"It would be smarter if they don't," Finn said. "Because by the time we have The Pink Pearl up and running, we plan on putting them out of business, anyway."

"Sure you don't want to buy this place instead? Just needs a bit of spackling and some paint." Rez laughed and whacked Nox on the back. "We have some experience in that department."

"Since we already bought the building and started renovations, I'd say fuck you."

"A simple no would've sufficed," Rez told Finn.

Nox headed over to the bar, only to find another body behind it, surrounded by spilled alcohol, as well as broken bottles and glassware. He squatted down and pulled back the sheet enough to expose the head.

He glanced up at his redheaded brother. "The prospect Mutt, right?" The rapid gunfire had just about decapitated the biker.

"*Mmm...*" Finn pursed his lips as he studied the body. "Used to be. Maybe his road name should be changed to the Headless Horseman."

A soft snort slipped from Rez.

Law enforcement tended to use dark humor to deal with a constant barrage of tragedies and remain sane.

"What are the odds that they took out that fucker Saint?" Finn glanced around. "Could we be that fucking lucky?"

"It's hard to kill roaches like him," Nox murmured.

"A well-placed shot would do the trick," Finn told him.

"If he was here and not at the fucking motel with T-Bone."

"We should ask if he's been identified," Rez said.

Nox spotted someone in a DEA jacket appearing to be in charge of the crime scene.

"Any survivors?" Nox flashed his ID and the agent glanced at it, then stared at him for a little too long.

"You're part of the Tri-State task force, right?"

"Yeah."

The agent then said, "I was supposed to be part of the arrest team this morning."

"You and me both."

"That would have been a hell of a lot more fun than dealing with this."

Nox couldn't argue that.

"Anyway, if there were any survivors, they took off. Everyone we've come across so far is far from a survivor. You guys had cameras set up in here, right?"

"We did, but all our surveillance equipment has already been removed. Our team's headquarters was dismantled since serving the warrants was the only thing left for some of us to do."

The agent nodded.

"Is the club's manager under one of these sheets?"

"You talking about Saint?" the agent asked.

Nox nodded. "That's him."

The man pressed his lips together and shook his head. "Didn't find anyone wearing a cut with that road name. He either wasn't here or was lucky enough to escape when shit went down."

Fuck. "That's unfortunate."

"I'm sure you're not the only one with that opinion since I heard he was a real piece of work."

"Piece of shit more like it," Nox clarified.

"That, too."

"Anyway, thanks for the info. We'll get out of your scene. But before we do, do you need us to identify anyone?"

"No, we got it covered. The dancers and customers all had IDs, and those dumbfuck bikers wear their names on their chests. We'll just cross-reference their road names to their legal names in our database."

"I'm assuming the members of La Cosa Nostra you found were foot soldiers."

"Yeah. Just some plebes willing to give up their lives for a bunch of criminal scum. You'd think these guys would know by now, no one's getting out of the Mafia alive. Hasn't everyone seen the Sopranos or the Godfather?"

One side of Nox's mouth pulled up. "Too late for them to watch them now."

The agent grinned. "A-fucking-men."

"Thanks for the info." Nox clasped palms with the agent, then returned to Finn and Rez. They were talking to a member of the medical examiner staff.

He gathered his brothers, and they headed out, but not before Rez asked, "Saint?"

Nox sighed softly. "Sounds like he wasn't here. If he was, he got lucky."

"Well, his woman wasn't," Finn told Nox. "They found Cookie back in Saint's office. News flash, she wasn't taking a nap."

"Damn. I wonder if Saint will ever get over the loss of his ol' lady?" Rez asked.

"Hopefully he'll find someone new in prison," Finn answered.

"We can only hope," Nox said. "Maybe he can be treated

in there the same way he treated women out here." As they headed outside, he announced, "Next stop, the Wolf Den."

"Any text from Crew or Fletch yet?" Finn asked.

Nox quickly glanced at his phone.

Nothing.

Now he was officially worried.

Chapter Thirty-Nine

He sent three more texts on the way to the Demons' clubhouse in Uniontown.

One to Fletch, one to Wilder and one to Crew.

"I don't like this," Nox murmured when he didn't get a response from "Ghost" or "Kitten." Crew didn't get a response either, according to his answering text.

Nox shot his BAMC brother a text back, letting him know since the three of them were "out and about," they'd check the Wolf Den for any signs of the undercover couple.

The first thing they noticed—mostly because it was impossible to miss—was that the Russos' soldiers used a full-sized SUV to ram the front entrance of the former gas station to gain access to the clubhouse.

It not only took out the front door, it also left a gaping hole in the surrounding concrete block wall. Since that SUV was an expensive way to get through a locked door, Nox figured the vehicle was stolen.

"Do you see Fletch and Wilder's assigned Harley or SUV anywhere?" Finn asked.

"No, but a lot of the members park out back," Nox answered.

"Maybe they weren't here when this all went down." Rez's voice sounded as tight as Nox's chest.

"Let's hope," Nox murmured.

Rez continued, "I would think if they were, they would've given Crew a heads up."

"If they had a chance," Nox told him.

"Or at least contact him after the bullets stop flying," Finn suggested.

"If they had a chance," Nox repeated, the dread in his gut becoming almost unbearable. He couldn't take another major loss in his life. Not right now.

If they lost Fletch...

Christ, he needed to stop thinking like that. Especially since his life was only beginning to turn around.

All thanks to Liyah.

"Look, let's see if we can get our asses inside like at The Peach Pit," he suggested to Finn and Rez.

"What are the chances that Saint was here?" Finn sounded hopeful.

"Roaches are almost impossible to kill. They'll survive the apocalypse," Rez said.

"Calling Saint a roach is insulting to roaches."

Nox agreed with Finn. "Let's go see if that boy with a badge will let us through."

Finn's brow furrowed. "Boy?"

Nox jerked his chin at the young guy in uniform standing sentry at the yellow tape while holding a clipboard. Apparently, he was tasked with keeping track of who came and went from the crime scene.

An easy, but boring, job.

Finn snorted. "Bet he can't even grow chin hairs yet."

Rez slapped Finn's chest. "Look at that, Flame, you might finally get your chance to razzle dazzle."

"Blaze!" Finn barked.

Nox dropped his head and shook it. After composing himself, he headed over to the rookie with his two brothers on his heels. When he got to the young Uniontown PD officer, he said, "We're looking for two undercover federal agents that might have been inside when this all went down."

"Not sure if all the victims were identified yet."

Victims. The dead Demons weren't victims. Anything that happened overnight was the consequences of their own actions.

A "fuck around and find out" situation.

Nox's eyes flicked to his name tag. "Mind if we go in, Johnson?"

"I was given orders not to let anyone past the tape."

Of course he was.

All three of them flashed their federal IDs at the same time, making the officer's head jerk back in surprise. However, it didn't seem as though Johnson was impressed. "Don't care who you are if you aren't on the list."

Finn pursed his lips. "There's a list?"

The rookie lifted his clipboard. "I can check it for your names, if you want, but I have a feeling that would waste both of our time."

Damn.

"Last time I did this kind of rookie shit," Finn began, "the list was to record anyone who entered and exited the scene. This isn't some party with an exclusive VIP list."

"Kid's wet behind the ears," Rez explained as if he wasn't standing right in front of the guy. "He's going to stick to the rules since he's probably still in his probation period. He doesn't want to get a spanking."

The officer frowned. "You know I can hear you, right?"

"Ready for that razzle dazzle anytime now, Flambé," Rez muttered under his breath.

"How about a little professional courtesy?" Nox asked the guy.

Johnson shrugged. "No problem, *if* your names are on the list."

Nox lifted a finger in the air. "Give me a sec. Let me ask your supervisor." He quickly called Ken Proctor, even though Nox knew he was not the officer's supervisor.

When the Uniontown PD officer answered, Nox said, "Hey, brother, me, Rez and Finn are out here at the Wolf Den. I'm sure you're aware of what went down last night. We haven't heard from two of our task force members who were deep undercover with the Demons." The whole time he was talking, he kept his eyes glued to Johnson's.

"I heard about the hit. Fletch and Wilder are missing?"

"Yeah, that's right. They were supposed to be here last night when shit hit the fan. We're on scene to search for them but we hit a little snag." Nox cocked an eyebrow at Proctor's fellow Uniontown officer.

"Okay, not sure why you're calling me?"

"Well, that little snag's name is Johnson. He's one of yours."

"*Aaah.* Now I understand what this is about. Yeah, he's one of our rookies. He started while I was on the task force, so I don't know him personally."

"You're his supervisor, right?"

"No..." Proctor sounded confused. "Wait..."

"I thought so," Nox hoped Proctor would pick up what he was putting down.

"I know who his supervisor is. But didn't the feds take over the scene?"

"Looks like it, but Officer Johnson here won't let us in, even though we're sworn federal agents." That temporary assignment was swiftly coming to an end, but Johnson didn't need to know that. Until those IDs were pried from their fingers, they were using that advantage. "He says we're not on the list."

"All right. Give me a few. I'll make a call to his real supervisor and get you inside."

"Appreciate that, brother."

"Anytime. Just remember this if I ever need a favor."

"You got it. And don't be too hard on him. You know how it is when you're new... You're afraid to break the rules."

Proctor's chuckle filled Nox's ears before the call ended.

He tucked his cell phone away. "You'll be getting a call."

While Nox had been speaking with Proctor, a flush had crept up the rookie's neck and into his cheeks. "I'm only doing what I was told."

"Like a good ass kisser should." Rez added some kissing noises.

"Don't worry, I made sure you won't get in trouble," Nox assured Johnson.

"For letting you in?"

"For keeping us out," Nox corrected firmly.

Johnson didn't even wait for the incoming call, instead he scribbled their names on the list along with the time of entry and lifted the tape for them to duck under.

"Nox has more razzle fucking dazzle than you, Fire Nuts," Rez ribbed Finn.

"Well, it wouldn't be fair if I hogged it all," Finn exclaimed as they slipped past the crushed SUV and into the Demons' clubhouse.

Inside, the building was teeming with crime scene investigators collecting evidence. A few bodies littered the floor.

Nox approached the closest person with a DEA windbreaker and a badge around her neck. "How you doing?" he greeted, jutting out his hand. "Officer Bradley Lennox."

The woman shook it but her expression was cautious. "Agent Dickson. And to answer your question, I'd be much better if I wasn't dealing with a messy Mafia hit."

"I'm sure," he murmured, then went on with, "Did you get a call from Agent Colin Crew?"

Her eyebrows knitted together. "Crew? No."

Nox tipped his head to the side. "*Aaah.* He was supposed to call ahead and let the person in charge know we were coming."

"That might be the problem since I'm not in charge."

"Maybe you can help me, anyway. Senior Special Agent Crew was in charge of the Tri-State Feder—"

The woman cut him off. "I'm aware. I know who he is."

With the way her expression closed up, Nox wondered how well she knew Crew. He might be off the market now but between divorcing Sasha and hooking up with Cabrera, the Casanova had a hard time keeping his dick in his pants.

"We," Nox hooked a thumb over his shoulder at Beavis and Butthead standing behind him, "all were members of that task force." He then showed her his ID.

She took a quick glance at it before her gaze flicked to Rez and Finn and landed back on him. "Right. I was supposed to help serve warrants this morning."

"Us, as well. But I guess the Russos had other plans for us."

"I'd say," she answered dryly. "That assignment would've been fun. This is not."

"I heard no lie in that. Anyway, we had an FBI agent and a state trooper on our team undercover with the Demons.

Their road names were Ghost and Kitten. Do you happen to know where they are?"

She glanced at the tablet she was using to take notes and pictures of the crime scene. "I don't think we've run across either of them, yet."

"Was anyone left breathing?"

"A couple of bikers were transported to the ER with gunshot wounds. One was critical, the other in serious condition."

"You know who?"

She stared at him for a few seconds before checking her notes. "Their name patches said Ringo and Stitch."

"Will they survive?"

She raised one of her eyebrows. "Do you care?"

"Not really. I'm more concerned with Trooper Shane Fletcher and Agent Nova Wilder."

"Ghost and Kitten?"

"Yes," Nox confirmed.

"Anyone alive and not injured was taken into custody," she stated.

"Were they a part of that group?"

Dickson shrugged slightly. "Sorry, I don't have that list."

"Do you know where anyone arrested was taken?"

"I don't have that info, either."

"Can you check your list for couple of Demons named Saint or T-Bone?" Finn interjected, drawing her attention.

Nox did not miss her eyeing up his redheaded brother. "Were they undercover officers, too?"

"No, just dickheads," Finn answered.

Dickson rolled her lips under for a second. "Let me see if I have anything on them."

"I'd appreciate that." Finn's voice became unexpectedly husky.

What the fuck?

Nox glanced over his shoulder to see Finn had his bottom lip caught between his teeth. *Jesus,* the man was flirting to get the info they needed. He expected his BAMC brother to wink at the agent at any moment.

There was his fucking razzle dazzle.

Rez had his lips pinned together, most likely to keep from saying shit he shouldn't and to avoid screwing up Finn's eye-roll-worthy tactic.

When Dickson finally raised her gaze, she had a sparkle in her blue eyes as she looked beyond Nox to Finn. "No, I don't see either of those names in my notes..."

She purposely left an opening and Finn didn't disappoint her. He elbowed past Nox to get closer. "Daniel Finnegan, Agent Extraordinaire."

Nox's brain glitched and Rez had to quickly turn away.

"What agency?" Dickson asked him, her voice sounding a bit wispy.

Holy shit, who flirts at a crime scene surrounded by death and destruction?

"Peckers All-Male Revue," Rez answered before Finn could.

This wasn't going to end well. Nox decided to intervene since he was the only adult out of the three of them. "He's an officer with the Southern Allegheny Regional PD. Like the rest of us, he was only sworn in as a federal agent to serve on the task force. As you see, that shit went to his head. All right, we'll get out of your hair and take a look around."

"Careful where you step and don't touch anything," she warned.

Even though he knew the drill, Nox nodded, grabbed Finn's arm and tugged. They wandered around the Wolf Den's common area, checking for any signs of Fletch or

Wilder. Of course, what they were checking were the deceased.

Every time they uncovered a face, they sighed in relief when it wasn't either of their team members.

Since there was no sign of them in the front of the clubhouse, they headed to the back where they checked every room. Even the community bathroom.

They also checked the bedroom on the end where T-Bone originally lived. They did find a body in it, but it wasn't the former prospect. It was whoever moved into that room after T-Bone got the boot.

While they were thankful not to find Fletch or Wilder, they were also disappointed not to find Saint or T-Bone.

They ended the search by heading out back to where most of the Harleys and other vehicles were parked. The only problem was, Fletch's borrowed bike wasn't anything special and none of them would recognize it enough to pick it out from the lineup.

Nox wanted to be relieved, but he wasn't since it wasn't like Fletch not to check in. He sure as fuck hoped they hadn't been made by either the Demons or Russos and taken by members of either organization.

When Nox's phone vibrated in his back pocket, he quickly pulled it out, hoping to see a text from Fletch. It wasn't. It was Crew calling him.

He braced for bad news as he lifted his phone to his ear.

"They've been found."

Nox's stomach dropped. "Alive?"

"Yeah," Crew answered.

"Thank fuck. But you could've added that to your initial sentence, asshole. You know I've been fucking worried."

"We've all been worried."

"What happened? Where are they?" Nox asked Crew.

"It ended up they were arrested because both were armed. It also didn't help that they couldn't prove who they were because of being undercover and not carrying their federal IDs. Actually, neither had any ID. They also didn't want to blow their cover at the Wolf Den while being taken into custody, just in case a Demon was watching."

That all made sense and Nox would've done the same. "Have they been released yet?"

"Yes, once their identities were confirmed."

"Where were they taken?"

"Believe it or not, the Uniontown State Police Barracks."

"Well, shit, that was convenient." Especially since Fletch worked for PSP.

"Yeah, so even though he isn't based out of that location, they knew who he was immediately."

"No surprise that he has a reputation."

Crew chuckled. "They need a ride. Wanna pick them up since you're 'out and about?'"

"We don't have enough room in the vehicle for them both. Unless Wilder wants to sit on Fletch's lap."

"Since they survived being shot at with AR-15s, let's not try to get them killed in a car crash."

"Agreed."

"I'll go get them."

"Guess you and Cabrera have to temporarily move back into your condo now that Fletch and Wilder are done being Ghost and Kitten. Better go house shopping. Or farm shopping. You'll need room for her big gray pony to run."

Crew groaned. "For fuck's sake. I guess I'll need to find a place with a pool, too."

"Happy wife, happy life. Isn't that the saying?"

"She's not my wife."

"Not yet. Maybe it should be happy wife, no knife in sight."

"I'm sure Sasha would love to stab me."

"That's why she's no longer your wife."

Crew sighed. "Are you three on your way back here?"

"Depends. I'm going to assume this morning's sweep is no longer on today's schedule and we need to wait to see who all survived."

"Bingo."

"Then no, we're not headed back yet. Hey, do you know an Agent Dickson?"

A slight but noticeable hesitation proceeded Crew asking, "Why would I know her?"

"I didn't say the agent was a woman—" The phone went dead. Nox pulled it from his ear to confirm.

There was his answer.

Shaking his head, he turned to Rez and Finn. Both wore huge grins.

"No surprise," was all Rez said. "Bastard is lucky he got snipped, otherwise he'd be paying a lot more in child support."

"I would hope most responsible men would know how to prevent accidental pregnancies." Nox climbed into the Dodge's passenger seat.

Finn got in the back. "Responsible is the key word there."

"Okay, where to next?" Rez suggested, "How about showing me where that motel is?"

Finn asked, "Do you think he's there at this hour?"

"Only one way to find out," Rez answered, starting the engine. "Point the way, Hard Nox."

Chapter Forty

A VEHICLE's high beams bouncing off his side mirrors and straight into his eyes made him wince. Did the asshole not see the Harley in front of him?

The driver could be drunk. Or clueless. It could even be that the vehicle was stolen. No matter the reason, being blinded by headlights was annoying, even dangerous, when traveling on two wheels.

He was about to twist the throttle and see how fast his girl could go to get away from the rude jackass, but when he turned onto the main street in Rockvale, the car turned, too.

Interesting. And concerning.

Since Rockvale was mostly an abandoned industrial area, it wasn't a town with a lot of traffic—not even through-traffic —making it the perfect location for the BAMC clubhouse.

He told himself he was just being paranoid.

Despite that, he purposely turned onto a street that led away from The Plant.

The car turned again.

It wasn't riding his ass but stayed close enough to keep Nox in the vehicle's headlights.

It was time to take this person on a wild goose chase. This would determine if he was being followed or if it was some random jack-wagon.

Heading north out of Rockvale, he decided to ride toward Shadow Valley in case he needed backup from his fellow officers. Since it was late, he doubted any of his BAMC brothers were at The Plant. Now that the task force had disbanded, where he lived was now pretty damn quiet and isolated.

That meant he could easily be ambushed or attacked in Rockvale, and no one would know. With what La Cosa Nostra did to the Deadly Demons the other day, it couldn't hurt to be overly cautious.

Some of those bad actors were still upright and breathing.

Was the task force the cause of the Mafia hit? Fuck no. That all landed on the outlaw MC's shoulders. Trying to cut out the Russos caused the Pittsburgh Mafia to cut the Demons off at the knees.

As the smoke hadn't finished clearing yet, the feds hadn't rescheduled the arrest teams to do the coordinated sweep. They wouldn't until they finished compiling a list of survivors.

In the meantime, Nox had gone back to donning a uniform and doing patrol. And his supervisor was once again Axel Jamison instead of Crew. While he loved his career as a cop, he already missed working with the task force.

About ten minutes north of Rockvale, the headlights stopped blinding him. Finally able to see in his side mirrors, he noticed the car had disappeared. He slowed down but didn't head back to The Plant. Instead, he continued on for a few more minutes to make sure whoever it was didn't pop out from side road and begin following him again.

When it didn't, he headed home, staying more vigilant this time. When he finally got upstairs to his apartment, he noticed he had a couple of missed calls.

One from Liyah and one from Crew.

Since he was damn sure the conversation with Liyah would take a lot longer than the one with Crew, he called the DEA agent back first.

"You rang?" Nox asked him when he picked up.

"What were you doing? Fucking?"

Nox shook his head. "Even if I was, I wouldn't tell you. But no, I was at my weekly meeting."

"With your girl."

"With a group of people," Nox corrected.

"And your girl."

"At thirty-nine, she's a woman. I don't do girls." He cleared his throat. "Unlike some people I know, I prefer women in my own generation."

Crew chuckled. "She's hot."

"Did you only call to discuss Liyah?" If so, Nox was hanging up.

"I'm happy for you."

"And I question Cabrera's mental state for choosing to be with you. And I'm not talking about your age."

"Maybe I'm just irresistible."

"Said the extremely humble senior special agent. Are you three settled back into your condo?"

"Three? Oh, you're counting the four-legged monster that shits small mountains. Yeah, but it's a tight fit until we can find the right house. That's not why I called."

"I figured you didn't call to chitchat." Should he mention to Crew that he might have been tailed? Maybe after Nox heard whatever was so important that it deserved a phone call.

"I would've sent a group text, but it was easier to call everyone individually with an update."

"Can we get to it?"

"Is she there with you? Am I interrupting?"

"No, because if she was here, I wouldn't have called you back. I'm sure whatever you have to say could wait."

"Damn, brother, I've got important shit to say."

"Then, let's hear it."

"Any Demons who popped up at ERs or medical centers have been located and arrested on scene. The feds also put eyes on all the MC's businesses that still stand. But no one has been seen. Every location is like a ghost town."

"They went underground," Nox murmured.

"Yeah. And you know what that means."

"That means we won't be serving shit. Can't serve a warrant if there's no one to serve it to."

"Right."

"Knowing there are even only a handful left out there doesn't give me the warm fuzzies," Nox admitted. "Do you have any numbers yet on who was taken out with either organization?"

"I don't have the final head count. That's going to take a bit longer and I doubt it'll be accurate."

"Head count? You mean dead count."

"Exactly. But I'm more concerned with who's breathing."

So was Nox. Especially if either the Russos or Demons were stalking former task force members. "All right, that means we won't be crashing biker parties any time soon."

"Nope. And once we know who's left, I doubt we'll even have to get teams together. At this point we're assuming the herd's been thinned enough that we can whack them as they pop up."

"Like Whac-A-Mole."

Crew chuckled. "Who knew a stupid child's game like that would come in handy when it came to our adult careers?"

"Well, since the game helped with hand-eye coordination, I'm sure it also helps you whacking off."

"Oh, look at you, telling a joke," Crew huffed.

"I was completely serious. All right, so basically, you called to tell me that you don't have any real updates."

"Did you ever consider that I just wanted to hear your voice? Now that I'm not seeing you daily, I miss your shiny, happy face, Nox." Crew sniffled loudly and dramatically.

"You'll survive."

"I'm not sure I will. I might need a hug."

"Or therapy."

"Speaking of—"

Nox swiped his finger across the screen to abruptly end the call. "Oops. Now that was a damn shame."

———

Aaliyah had left a voice message telling Nox she was on her way over to his apartment. He texted her back saying he'd be waiting.

That response made her pulse speed up and her heart thump a little faster as it always did at the anticipation of spending some alone time with him.

Despite his issues, the man had quickly burrowed his way into her heart—not to mention, how he affected some other key places on her body—whether he meant to or not.

Whenever she wanted sex, the man obliged. And, of course, did so with gusto. It was a far cry from when they first met, and he'd beat himself up over being interested in another woman.

Nox had come so damn far since she met him at that first Wednesday night group meeting. He claimed it had a lot to do with her. While she might have nudged him somewhat, he had to make those real changes himself. If he hadn't been ready to start the healing process, nothing she said or did would've made a difference since grief could not only be crippling but could cling to a person like plastic wrap.

One thing Liyah learned throughout the years of grief groups—whether she was just an attendee or she led the meeting—no one's fight to free themselves from the pain of a devastating loss was the same.

As she drove down the main street running through Rockvale, she smiled and hummed along to Usher's *U Got it Bad* as it began to play on her favorite satellite radio station.

"You definitely got it bad, girl," she whispered.

As a real estate broker, she saw a lot of potential in the ghost town where Nox lived. A lot of properties were vacant and fenced off to keep people out. The rest were full of rundown warehouses and factories, making them true eyesores. In her professional opinion, some of those buildings could be rehabbed into cute apartments and condos. Others could be demolished, and affordable housing built in their place.

When she got a chance, she could check with some of the developers she knew about building a whole community in the area, giving locals a place to live and work.

It would be a win-win for everyone.

But for now, she needed to get her mind off work. She was ready to push all real estate-related thoughts filling her gray matter out of her mind for the weekend and concentrate on the man she couldn't get enough of.

The sex was fulfilling. The conversation engaging. The man was smart, funny and caring. He also knew when to speak up and when to stay quiet. That alone was priceless.

He might not be wealthy but none of that mattered to her. She did not judge a man based on his paycheck or his success, as long he was a decent human being. Plus, she made plenty money of her own. She wasn't the type of woman that needed a man to provide for her.

She was her own woman and had her own ambitions. All she needed was to be happy and loved. Respected and appreciated. As well as stimulated, both physically and mentally.

Liyah also needed the person to love and accept her sons because, for her, they would always come first. No man would ever trump her own children.

Luckily, her boys really liked Nox. Even better, he seemed to really like them and treated them with kindness. He didn't talk down to them. He also helped them with homework if it was a subject that wasn't in her wheelhouse. One weekend, he even helped Keenan build a really cool pinewood derby car for Cub Scouts.

While they worked on it, Liyah leaned against the doorway of the garage and watched the two of them with their heads close together. If that didn't make her heart melt or cause her to fall more in love with the man, nothing would.

Yes, she admitted it—at least to herself—she had gone and fallen in love with the stubborn man. She hadn't told him yet because she worried it might affect him in a negative way. She figured she'd wait until she was sure he could handle it.

And was sure the connection they had would last.

She had loads of time and patience. Their relationship wasn't on any kind of fast track. She was perfectly okay with it traveling slow and steady. The exact opposite of when she met Jason, Keenan's sperm donor.

That experience taught her the hard way not to rush into any kind of relationship. And she was even more careful now that she had two boys to consider.

Tonight wouldn't be about the future. It would only be about satisfying sex and thought-provoking conversation. All week she was on the go, never feeling like she had enough time in the day between her business and the boys, but the time she carved out for Nox was her time to simply "be." A time to breathe and reflect, as well as bask in his attention.

As normal when she got to the building where his apartment was, the rear gate was closed and padlocked. Now that his special assignment was over, he told her all the nitty gritty details about the task force. Or at least the details he could share.

As she always did when she got to the gate, she pulled up and got out of her car to open it. Nox had given her the lock's combination so he wouldn't have to leave the gate wide open while waiting for her arrival.

He told her she could text him and he'd wait at the gate to open it for her, but she was quite capable of letting herself in and didn't feel the need to inconvenience him.

If they were still doing this routine come winter, she might take him up on his offer, but this evening was beautiful. The sky was clear and the temperature perfect enough for her to wear a pair of white shorts and a silky turquoise sleeveless tank, along with a pair of cute strappy sandals to show off her fresh pedicure.

As she walked to the side of the gate with the padlock, an unfamiliar male voice called out, "Hey!"

She abruptly stopped in her tracks since she'd never encountered anyone in the alley before. Was he calling out to *her*?

When she glanced over her shoulder, she saw a lanky man emerge from the shadows and head in her direction. With the limited light from the late setting sun, she noticed he had a straggly beard and the hood from his sweatshirt pulled over his head.

It was too damn warm outside for a sweatshirt. That wasn't suspicious at all.

Her spine began to tingle and tighten.

Should she engage or ignore?

"Ma'am!"

Shit. Her heart began to pound in her chest. Coming across a stranger in an alley in a town with a population of only one was a bit unnerving. "Yes?"

He jerked his chin toward the fence. "What's in that building?"

"I don't know," she lied since the Blue Avengers wanted the fact that The Plant was their clubhouse kept under wraps.

For good reason.

"You're headin' in there. Gotta have a reason for that."

When he stepped closer, she took a step back. "I sell real estate and the owners are thinking about selling. I'm here to meet them," she lied again.

It was best if he thought other people would be showing up soon.

Something about him was definitely "off." So, no matter what, she wouldn't open the gate while he stood there. She couldn't imagine anyone came to this town unless they were there to create trouble.

Or were lost.

This man did not appear to be lost. Though, he could be homeless.

The best thing to do would be to get back into her car, drive away and call Nox to let him know about this guy skulking around. She could return after the man moved on.

"Nice cage."

His use of a term only bikers living the MC lifestyle used made the alarm bells ring in her head and goosebumps to break out all over her body. She never heard weekend warriors or wannabes, as her father called them, use "cage" for a car.

Despite not wanting to take her eyes off him, with him standing between her and her Benz, her gaze automatically slid to her car when the thought popped into her head.

Maybe he only wanted her car.

The high-end Mercedes was sitting there running with the keyless fob in the cup holder. As well as her wallet on the passenger seat.

Good going, Liyah. Not smart. You should know better.

"What do you want?" she asked him.

"Wanna know what's behind the fence."

"Like I said, I'm only here to obtain a listing from the owner."

"Thinkin' you're bullshittin' me."

"I'd show you my business card but it's in the car."

His gaze once again landed on her AMG GT. A vehicle that cost her six figures.

"I can grab it for you." Her plan was, if it worked, she'd climb in her car while pretending to get a card and then get the hell out of there.

"Who're the owners of the buildin'?"

"Sorry, I can't remember their names off the top of my head. I'd have to check my paperwork."

"Which I bet is also in that sweet-ass cage."

Of course, the non-existent paperwork was in her car. "It is."

He licked his lips and glanced one more time at her Mercedes Benz. "Must be rich to be able to afford a ride like that."

"I got a great deal on it."

"I'm sure I can get a deal on it, too. It's called a five-fingered discount."

"Is that what you want? My car?"

"Ain't all I want."

That declaration raised the fine hairs on the back of her neck. Especially with him standing—on purpose—between her and her escape. "Just take it," she said.

"Plan on it. But ain't all I'm takin'."

"My money's in my wallet on the passenger seat," she volunteered.

Why wasn't he jumping in the car and leaving with it? Why was he getting closer and into her personal space?

"Look, the car's insured, the money's replaceable. Just take it and go before the owners show up."

"You don't get to tell me what to fuckin' do, bitch."

She raised her palms in surrender. Should she bother to tell him that she was a single mother raising two boys?

Fuck. He probably didn't have an empathetic bone in his body. She doubted he'd care. He was one of those selfish assholes who didn't care if he destroyed someone else's life to improve his own.

She knew plenty of men like him. Only, she never met any in an alley.

"You a part of the bullshit task force in that fuckin' buildin'?"

Oh shit. "I don't know anything about a task force."

"Thinkin' you're lyin' and you're one of 'em."

She had to play this right because if he was a biker, he probably hated law enforcement as much as her father. "One of who?"

"Them! The pigs! Gotta fuck up everything."

"Again, I don't know what you're talking about. I'm a real

estate broker. That's it. I'm not on any kind of task force. Why would you think one is here?"

"Don't worry 'bout how I fuckin' know. I just fuckin' know."

"Well then, if you know so damn much, you should know I have nothing to do with it." *Don't poke the bear, Liyah. Speak softly, but stand strong.* "If you're going to steal my car and cash, just do it and go."

"Like I said, ain't all I want."

Her heart leapt into her throat. "What else do you want?" she whispered, not liking the evil smile that crossed his face.

Why the hell did she leave her cell phone sitting on the seat next to her wallet and not keep it with her? She should know better.

She wasn't a small woman, the hell if she'd let him to anything to her without a fight. Even if she broke every one of her damn nails scratching his eyes out. Even if she broke every one of her teeth ripping out his throat.

She had Magnum's blood running through her veins. She was not a wilting flower, she was a queen.

She raised her chin and straightened her spine. Her eyes hardened as she stared this motherfucker down. "Take the fucking car or get the fuck out of here before you do something you'll regret for the rest of your life." Guaranteed that life would be shortened if he did something stupid.

And he was about to do something stupid.

She got ready for whatever it was by spreading her feet.

Just as she screamed out Nox's name, the man launched himself at her.

She jammed her forearm into his throat and scratched his face, causing him to back off slightly but only for a second.

Then he went after her again.

"Nox!" she screamed again, fighting off the guy as best as

she could as he tried to get a good hold of her. "I promise you, you're going to regret this."

"Shut the fuck up, bitch!" he shouted in her face.

She tried to skirt around him and thought she almost got away when he slammed his hand against her arm so hard, he almost knocked her off balance.

She managed to stay on her feet, but not for long.

As a euphoric feeling swept through her, making her head swim and her body feel sluggish. Preventing her from being able to move quickly. To escape. To fight him off.

When her knees began to buckle, she realized he didn't punch her.

No, the motherfucker stuck her with a damn needle.

"Nox," came out slurred as she slid to the concrete.

She was powerless to do anything when he grabbed her arms and dragged her across the concrete to her car.

Chapter Forty-One

Nox put down the crime thriller he was reading and picked up his phone to check the time. After getting the original text that she was on her way, he'd gotten no update from Liyah saying she was running behind schedule. Her running late happened often but she usually gave him a heads up.

It was one reason why she didn't want him waiting for her at the gate.

She could be five minutes or fifty-five minutes late. It all depended on how her day went.

But tonight? She was forty-five minutes past her arrival time.

He didn't like that.

He sent her a text. *You okay? Expected you here at six.*

He forced himself to wait five more minutes. Long enough to give her a chance to respond before he called her. After three rings, the call went to voicemail.

"Liyah, are you on your way? Call or text me as soon as you get this. I want to make sure you're okay."

With a frown, he hung up and stared at the phone in his hand.

He didn't like this. Not one bit. She'd never ignored his texts or calls. Not once. If she was busy with a client, fellow agents, or even her sons, she shot him a quick text to let him know she'd get ahold of him once she was free.

If she didn't own that fancy car, he would only think she didn't want to call or text while driving. However, her AMG had all the bells and whistles, including hands-free text and calls, so she had no valid excuse to not respond.

Unless something happened to her.

He shouldn't think like that but being a cop, it came with the territory.

He'd give her another twenty minutes before he went out searching for her.

Surging from the couch, he began to pace across the length of his apartment with his phone in his hand and his eyes watching the time tick by minute after minute.

With every minute that went by without a response, a new scenario would run through his head.

Her phone battery died.

One of her sons broke an arm and she was currently at the ER.

She was somewhere without any cell phone reception.

She lost her phone.

She'd been in a car crash.

Before he could stop it, his thoughts turned even darker.

She was injured and no one found her yet.

She was dead.

The last possibility made his mouth go dry, his stomach twist and his heart squeeze hard enough that pain shot through his chest.

"C'mon, Liyah," he whispered. "Don't leave me hanging like this."

He sent one more text. *If I don't hear from you in the next five minutes, I'm coming to look for you whether you want that or not.*

He shouldn't even wait another five minutes. Her situation—whatever it was—could change for the worst in five minutes.

Fuck it.

He ended up spending that next five minutes, in addition to another fifteen, on his bike as he raced over to her place, hoping at least one of the boys was home so he could find out where Liyah was.

Only no one answered the door.

He couldn't see into the garage, so he had no idea if her car was parked inside. He walked around the house, peering through any window he could.

The house appeared empty.

None of that made him feel any better. No, instead it sent him into a spin.

When he finished rounding the house and got back to her front porch, he called her office. The agent who picked up the phone said he hadn't seen her and they were about to close the office for the night.

He muttered, "Shit," more times than he could count as he strode back to his bike with his mind spinning on how to handle this. He could get his brothers involved but he wasn't sure that would help. He could call the police department that covered the area where she lived or...

Straddling his bike, he pulled out his phone and scrolled through his contacts to find the person possibly able to help him with his next option.

The second Axel Jamison answered, Nox asked, "Where does Malcolm Moore live?"

"Who?"

Shit. "Aaliyah's father."

"Why the fuck do you want to know where Magnum lives?"

"He doesn't live in the Dirty Angels' gated community with you?"

"No. He—"

"Just get me the address, brother. I tried googling it, but nothing came up."

"No surprise. Since ol' Magnum and I aren't best buds, I don't have his address but I can find out easily enough. You're not planning on actually going over there, are you?"

Yes, it was a risk showing up at the Knights' sergeant at arms' door uninvited. It wasn't like he had a choice. Liyah could be over there with her sons. "Just get me the address." He added, "Please."

"Why do you need his address? Is there a problem?"

"I don't know yet. I'm hoping not."

After a slight hesitation, Jamison finally said, "I'll find out where he lives and text it to you."

"Thanks, brother."

"Stay safe. And if you need anything..."

"Hopefully, this is simply some misunderstanding."

"Nox, what's going on?"

His grip tightened on his phone to the point of pain. "I haven't heard from Liyah, and I just want to check to see if she's over there. Just get me that address as soon as you can."

Relief rushed through him when Jamison responded with, "Will do."

THE TYPE of house Nox thought Magnum lived in was not what he found at the address texted to him by the BAMC president.

He hadn't expected it to look so... normal.

Like Magnum was some upper middle-class banker or something. It certainly didn't fit the image most people had of the Dark Knight member in the least.

When the door was flung open, he stared at the most probable reason why.

Caitlyn Moore, Liyah's stepmother.

"She here?"

Cait's eyebrows pinned together. "What?"

Nox forced his way into the house by pushing past the petite blonde. "Please tell me she's here." He glanced around, but he didn't see her. He didn't hear her. He didn't even see or hear Kee or Dev.

The alarm bells in his head began to ring at a deafening level.

"Liyah? No. What's going on?"

He had to fight the temptation to grab Cait and shake the answers from her he wanted to hear. "I was hoping she was over here."

"We haven't seen her. What's going on?" she asked again.

Her confusion was not helping his spiking blood pressure. "Liyah's gone."

She pulled her chin into her neck. "What do you mean, gone?"

He managed to swallow down his scream of, *"She's missing! She's nowhere to be found!"* But that wouldn't help anyone. He needed to keep his shit together. To keep his head on straight and refrain from taking out his frustration out on someone not deserving of it.

He pulled in a deep breath to keep himself from unraveling in the house of someone who considered him an enemy. "She was supposed to come over to my place but never showed up."

Cait's brow furrowed. "She's always running late."

And while that was true... "I'm used to her being a few minutes late but after texting me that she was on her way, she never showed up."

Cait started to pick up on his uneasiness. He could hear it in her voice when she suggested, "Maybe she's at home."

"That was the first place I checked."

Her blue eyes widened. "At the office?"

He shook his head. "Called there, too."

Her cheeks lost all of their color. "Meeting with a member of her grief group?"

While that technically could be a possibility, she would at least tell him she had to make a detour before heading to his apartment.

Not once had she left him in the dark like this.

Not fucking once.

This was not good.

The second he shook his head, she turned hers and yelled, "Magnum!"

Shit. Fuck. Shit.

Nox went over to their house for a reason, and he heard that reason's heavy footsteps lumbering in their direction.

This was either going to go well, or it would be a disaster.

He braced for the initial impact of Magnum's larger than life attitude. The man would not be happy that a cop was standing in his foyer.

Fuck him. He'd just have to deal with it. Nox was damn certain that Magnum would consider his daughter more important than his hatred toward anyone wearing a badge.

Or at least he hoped so.

"What the fuck you doin' in my house?"

Before he could answer, Cait did it for him. "Nox thinks Liyah's missing. He thought she might be here."

The big man went completely still. So still it was almost like he morphed into a statue.

Suddenly, that statue came back to life and all it took was him barking, "What?"

"I said—" Cait started.

"Heard what the fuck you said, woman. Need more than that." His dark eyes turned to Nox. "Better fuckin' explain and better fuckin' do it quickly."

With a single nod, Nox did just that.

Chapter Forty-Two

THE SECOND THE last word of his explanation slipped from Nox's lips, the man before him turned into an atom bomb and exploded.

Nox never heard so many curse words used in one sentence. So many that it might not have been a sentence at all.

"Magnum, calm down!" Cait grabbed her husband in attempt to do that, but he shook her free to face off with Nox. "You won't do anyone any good if you have a damn heart attack."

"Who the fuck took her?" he roared.

On a good day the man was larger than life, but pissed off...?

No matter what Liyah's father did or said, Nox would not back down. It was possible that Liyah's life was at stake. Until he knew for sure, he would assume the worst and hope for the best. "I don't even know if she was taken. But it's not like her to send a text to tell me she's on the way and then not show up. Or not respond to any of my calls or texts."

"Maybe you pissed her the fuck off and she's just done with your goddamn pig ass." He shook his head, his face still a mask of rage.

"Magnum!" Cait admonished him.

Nox needed to keep his cool and not match the man's energy. If he did, it would get them nowhere. "You're right. Maybe she got sick of my pig ass. But tell me, when have you known Liyah to not say what she meant? She has a lot of your blood running through her veins. If she didn't want to see me anymore, she'd tell me that to my face and not avoid the situation."

Magnum took a breath so deep that his chest expanded to an almost impossible breadth. When he released it, "One of your enemies, then. You pigs got a long fuckin' list of them," came with it.

"Possibly. I'm sure you have a few yourself."

Liyah's father shook his head. "Got no fuckin' enemies. Took care of that problem years ago."

"There's no point in debating this!" Cait exclaimed. "You two need to put your differences aside to find Liyah."

Nox agreed with that. "If she was physically taken, why her? Why not go after me? Or you?"

"Always go after a man's weakness, not after the man himself."

Damn, that made too much sense. "Sounds like you have experience in that."

As Magnum's upper lip began to curl, Cait stepped in front of her husband, making their size difference even more obvious than normal. She asked, "Where are the boys?"

Oh fuck. His pulse sped up another notch. "I figured they were here with you. I went to the house first and no one was there."

"They took the boys, too?" Magnum roared so loud, Nox

was surprised the windows didn't shake.

"I don't know," Nox answered. "Could they be at their grandmother's?"

"They better fuckin' be." Magnum jabbed a thick finger in his direction. "I bet you fuckin' caused this bullshit. Things were quiet for fuckin years, then you showed the fuck up..."

"Baby, we don't even know what happened yet. I can call her mother and go pick up the boys, if you'd feel better with them here." Liyah's stepmother added, "Just in case."

"Fuck that. If they're there, gonna send one of my brothers over there to get them. Don't want you leavin' this house. *No one* leaves this fuckin' house 'til we know what the fuck's goin' on." He twisted toward Nox. "'Cept you. If you got nothin' useful to give me to help find her, you need to get the fuck out."

Nox fully expected the next answer to enrage the big man again, but he needed to know. Because Magnum and his brothers might be able to handle the situation better than Nox and his. One MC's actions were restricted due to the law. The other didn't give a fuck about any laws. Just like the Demons didn't.

"It could be the Demons." Or one in particular. Possibly two, depending if Saint was also involved.

Nox wouldn't put it past the former prospect to try to snag Liyah. Especially when he had the balls to kidnap Sloane right from Decker's house.

He hoped to fuck he was wrong. But how would the asshole even tie Liyah to him? Or know that Nox was on the task force trying to put them all away?

Someone had tailed him back to The Plant the other day. Had it been that fucking dickhead?

Had T-Bone or Saint spotted Nox surveilling him at the motel?

Had they seen her coming and going from The Plant?

His runaway thoughts were interrupted by a bellow.

"The Deadly fuckin' Demons? Those dumb mother-fuckers?"

Nox pinned his lips together and nodded. At least he and Magnum agreed on one thing: that the Demons were mother-fuckers. The dumb part was debatable.

"Why the fuck would the Demons give a shit about you?"

Nox had no choice but to tell the man the truth and since the task force disbanded, its existence no longer needed to be kept a secret. "I was on a federal task force investigating them."

Magnum stared at him.

Nox waited.

Magnum stared at him some more.

Nox waited.

Finally, the man blinked.

Nox finally breathed.

"Did she know you were fuckin' with the Demons?"

"What would it matter if she did?"

His thick brow furrowed. "The word on the street is, the goddamn Sicilians took all those fuckers out. Wasn't no task force."

"Not all of them. But you're right, La Cosa Nostra got to them before we did. Even so, I have a feeling this was a former Demon."

"He got a bone to pick with you?"

"Funny you mention bone..." Though, no one was laughing.

"What the fuck does that mean?"

"T-Bone was one of their prospects. He got kicked out because he was skimming meth from their stash and using it to keep women on the hook."

"Explain," came the demand.

"He was getting them strung out and then pimping them out for cash."

"He the only one involved in this goddamn bullshit?"

"No, I recently witnessed a patched member involved."

"Name?"

"Saint," Nox answered.

"For fuck's sake. We got no more time to waste. We need to find Aaliyah and we need to find her now."

Magnum wasn't the only one with a clock ticking loudly in his head.

"When was the last time you heard from her?"

Nox quickly checked his texts for the time stamp. "Five-forty."

"What fuckin' time is it now?"

"A little after seven."

"For fuck's sake," Magnum once again grumbled. "Gotta get on this. Too much time's passed."

"Magnum, maybe we should let law enforcement handle it since a federal task force was involved."

Nox got what she was hinting at. Apparently, so did Magnum.

"Caitee, if you haven't fuckin' noticed, he's a goddamn pig. If he wanted them to handle it, he wouldn't be standin' in our fuckin' house."

Not one hundred percent true. "I came over here to see if she was here before I took any other steps."

"And you fuckin' stayed 'cause you want me to handle it."

That part was truer than Nox would like to admit. "I recognize the fact you might have more... *effective* means to find her if T-Bone did take her."

"What do you know about him?"

"Besides him being a piece of shit? He's done this before

451

with another member of our task force."

"What the fuck?" Magnum barked. "And he lived to do it again?"

"Unfortunately. We thought we had a way to handle him without getting our hands dirty, or exposing our task force, but apparently, it didn't work the way we hoped."

"Wanna hear that fucked up story, but we got more important shit to deal with right now. Like findin' my baby girl."

Nox couldn't agree more. Time was ticking, and, if T-Bone played a part in Liyah's disappearance...

Yeah, he didn't give a shit what happened to the former prospect if he touched even a single hair on Liyah's head.

"So, now what?" Nox asked.

"Now you get the fuck outta my house before I make it so you can no longer walk seein' it's probably your fault it happened in the first fuckin' place."

Nox pulled back his shoulders and looked Magnum straight in the eye. "I'm not leaving. We need to work together on this. Both of us want her found. Both of us want her safe. Both of us... care deeply for her."

Magnum cocked a dark eyebrow and warned, "You stick the fuck around, you might get some fuckin' dirt under those clean fingernails of yours."

"If I do, I'll deal with it."

A cell phone appeared in Magnum's massive hand and a second later so did a pair of reading glasses. He jammed them onto his face and scrolled for another second. Then he snatched his glasses off as he put the phone to his ear.

Nox had kind of hoped he'd put the caller on speakerphone so he could hear the whole conversation instead of only one side of it.

"Brother... Yeah... They got my girl... No, Aaliyah. Got

the pig who's doin' her standin' in front of me sayin' it could be members of the Deadly Demons... Yeah, those mother-fuckers... Thought so, too. Some musta been lucky, but not for long... Tell me what you need from me to find her. It's gotta be quick. The asshole might've drugged her and wants to..." Magnum sucked in an audible breath. "She could be drugged. Need to find her as quickly as fuckin' possible. Don't give a shit what it costs... Yeah. Got it. She was last heard from in a text over an hour ago."

When Liyah's father pulled the phone away from his ear, he must have turned on the speaker function because Nox heard a deep, grumbly voice asking, "You have no idea where she was taken from, right?"

Magnum's dark eyes met Nox's. He assumed the man wanted him to answer, so he did. "No."

"Didn't see her car anywhere?"

"No," Nox repeated.

"What did the text say?"

"She was headed to my place."

"Where at?"

"Rockvale."

"Rockvale? Nobody lives in Rockvale."

"I do."

There was a slight hesitation before he heard, "Was she coming there from her place or from work? Did she plan on doing any stops on the way?"

"Her place. And that's a negative on the stops."

A deep grunt came through the phone. "Name of the Demon you think is the culprit."

"Could be two working together. T-Bone is a former prospect who got booted from the MC for skimming meth. Saint's still a card-carrying member."

"T-Bone and Saint. Got it. Know what they drive?"

Nox gave whoever was on the other end of the line descriptions of the vehicles and Harleys he'd seen them both use.

"Descriptions of both bikers," was demanded next.

Nox gave the no-nonsense man that, too.

"Got their real names?"

He certainly did, so he shared that info before offering, "I can also get you their mugshots."

"I can do that myself."

"How?" Nox asked in surprise.

Of course, he didn't get an answer.

He was starting to get a good inkling on who Magnum called. A source Nox never would have approached on his own since they did sketchy shit to get the job done. But he knew the Shadows were good. So good, they managed to keep their own asses out of prison despite how much illegal shit they pulled. No matter how deep they got mired in shit, they always somehow emerged squeaky clean. It was a goddamn skill for sure.

"Shadows" was the perfect descriptor for the team of mercenary veterans.

Magnum told the man on the phone, "You find her, you find them, then you let me handle their fuckin' asses."

"You got it, brother. We'll take it from here, then I'll let you take it from there."

The call ended abruptly.

"Who was that?" Nox hoped to confirm his suspicion.

"Don't fuckin' worry 'bout it. Got this. That's all you gotta know. They can find a fuckin' goldfish flushed down a city sewer. Now... Guess I gotta finish the job the Sicilians started. Touchin' me or mine is a guaran-fuckin'-teed way to meet your goddamn maker. Whether it's the man above or the devil below."

Chapter Forty-Three

Nox was tempted to call his brothers to assist, especially Finn and Rez, but he really didn't want them getting caught up in anything illegal. And there was no doubt Aaliyah's father would leave no stone unturned to find her. No matter what the Knights' sergeant at arms had to do to flip over those damn stones.

For now, Nox would let Magnum do what he needed to do with the help of the Shadows and he'd keep his brothers out of it. However, he would take a ride over to the motel to see if T-Bone and Saint were stupid enough to take her there.

Truthfully, he hoped they were. It would make the search for Liyah easy and short.

"When you find him, I want to spend some time with him," Nox informed Magnum as he followed him out the front door.

Her father said nothing.

"He took what's mine."

That statement got the man's attention like he figured it would.

Magnum slammed to a stop and spun on him. A muscle jumped in his cheek as he growled, "She ain't fuckin' yours. She's mine." He slapped a hand against his massive chest. "My blood. My responsibility. You're only fuckin' temporary. A toy for her to play with. You and your pig bullshit put her and my grandsons at risk."

"Those are a lot of assumptions you're making."

"What part wasn't fuckin' true?"

"You want to blame me for this when we're not even sure what happened yet. But even if it has to do with me being a cop or on the task force, that means if I caused it, she's my responsibility. And as for temporary, you only hope that's true."

Magnum leaned in closer. "You're fuckin' temporary. I'll make sure of it."

Do your best was on the tip of his tongue but he swallowed it back down. They had no time to waste so he needed to let it go. For now.

"Where are you headed?" Nox asked.

"None of your goddamn business."

"Liyah is my business."

"Once again, you're fuckin' wrong," the big man declared as he strode down the sidewalk to the driveway. He glanced at Nox's Harley, snorted and shook his head. "Goddamn wannabe!"

"Why the fuck would I want to be like you?" Nox yelled out.

That had the massive man spinning on his boot heel and charging Nox. He tried to brace as a big fist headed in his direction. He tried to duck out of the way, but was a fraction of a second too slow to avoid the sledgehammer that slammed him right in the face.

———

Nox worked his jaw, wincing from the pain. It was already swollen despite waking in Malcolm Moore's driveway with his wife pressing ice to the point of impact.

"Are you okay?"

While he "rested" on the pavement, he had blinked up at her with his brain still rattled. "Is this Heaven?"

"No, it's our driveway."

"So, it's hell then," he had concluded, carefully sitting up and taking the Ziplock bag full of ice from her fingers.

"I'm so, so sorry he did that. He can be very passionate."

"You call that passionate? I call that assault." He had slowly climbed to his feet, testing his balance since his brain had been knocked loose.

Cait Moore had her bottom lip grasped between her teeth and a worried expression on her face.

"Your husband needs to learn how to control his impulses."

"He's better than he used to be."

"Well, that's a fucking relief," Nox said dryly, pressing fingers to his face and testing to see what hurt and what didn't.

Nothing like being cold-cocked by a man thirty or forty pounds heavier than him. Add in the element of surprise.

He shouldn't have let his guard down. A mistake he wouldn't make again around a man so "passionate."

He slowed his bike to take the turn into the motel where he last saw T-Bone and Saint. He wasn't sure if they'd be there since they hadn't been the morning after the "massacre" when he and his BAMC brothers went looking for them.

Of fucking course, finding them couldn't be that easy. Once again, no one was parked in front of the end room and T-Bone's, Saint's and Liyah's vehicles were nowhere to be seen. Nox took that as a sign that the duo had figured out he'd been stalking them and decided to move elsewhere.

If they discovered he'd been watching them, it made Nox more certain than ever that it was one of them who tailed him back to The Plant. Even though he lost whoever it was that night, all they had to do was come back to Rockvale, find a good hiding spot and wait for Nox to return to figure out where he lived.

If someone was determined to find out that info, it really wasn't that difficult since he had no choice but to come and go from The Plant. The only other option would've been to move and that wouldn't be practical.

So, *yeah*, his gut was telling him that T-Bone was the one who took Liyah. But why?

Revenge? Retaliation? Easy opportunity?

He hoped like fuck that the asshole hadn't had any of his sketchy clients lined up and ready to take advantage of Liyah in whatever state she was in.

If that motherfucker allowed...

Nox's nostrils flared and he squeezed the handlebar tighter, imagining it was T-Bone's neck.

Taking her had earned that lowlife a death sentence. No judge, no jury, no trial. And he was pretty damn sure Magnum would be the executioner.

Nox would do nothing—not a goddamn thing—to stop it. In fact, he would be silently cheering it on.

"Touchin' me or mine is a guaran-fuckin'-teed way to meet your goddamn maker. Whether it's the man above or the devil below."

That was one opinion Nox shared with the man who had cleaned his clock. While he could live with a physical bruise or two—as well as a bruised ego—he was thankful his clock didn't have a broken nose.

Before he left Magnum's house earlier, he gave Cait his cell phone number and asked if she could text him with any updates because he knew he wouldn't get any from the man himself. Thankfully, she agreed.

Now he had to hope Magnum would keep his wife in the loop.

Straddling his bike in the motel's parking lot, he wasn't sure what to do next. He wasn't sure where to go.

He thought about the Demon-owned businesses that still stood. Would they dare take Liyah to one of those?

He'd waste too much time checking them all out. *Hell,* they could've taken her into Ohio or West Virginia. If they did, they might still be traveling.

He pulled out his phone, hoping Liyah had texted or called him during the ride to the motel so he could laugh off this whole thing. What he saw—or more like what he didn't see—did not make him laugh.

Liyah had not reached out.

Dread quickly filled his chest all over again and he decided to text Cait. *Any word?*

Nothing yet, was the answer he got in return.

"Fuck," he muttered. *Boys there?* he asked next.

Yes, they just arrived was her response.

That should've helped him breathe easier, but it didn't. He hated being in the fucking dark, not knowing what the hell happened.

Feeling utterly helpless.

He couldn't just go back to The Plant and wait. He would lose his fucking mind if he did.

No, it was time to head to Shadow Valley and at least do something. He circled the motel's lot and headed out. On the way to his police department, he kept an eye out for her car. He also rolled slowly past the community center. Her car wasn't there, either.

Where the fuck else could she have gone?

As soon as he walked into Shadow Valley PD, he went directly to an unoccupied computer and looked up Liyah's registration plate. He then filled out an entry in the common-wealth's law enforcement network for a missing and endangered person, putting in her physical description, her car's info and the plate number.

It still wasn't enough, he needed to do more.

"Goddamn it," he growled, almost coming out of his skin.

He kept picturing Liyah in Sadie's place. On that bed. In that sleazy Ohio motel. Naked and abused.

He couldn't shake it.

"Holy shit," he heard.

Nox glanced up to see his supervisor staring at him wide-eyed.

"Let me guess. You showed up unannounced at Magnum's house. You should put some ice on that."

He wasn't worried about his face, he was worried about Liyah. "Thanks for the medical advice, Sarge."

Axel Jamison perched on the edge of the desk. "Did I ever tell you about the time Magnum's pale counterpart knocked me the fuck out when I was over at Bella's house?"

"No."

"Diesel might not be Bella's father, but he certainly made himself her protector. He, like Magnum, isn't a fan of cops. Let's just say he was not thrilled to catch me in Bella's bedroom."

"Damn, with your pants down?"

Jamison scratched his ear and shrugged. He then rapped his knuckles on the desk. "Okay, so what the hell's going on?

Why did you go over there? Why did Magnum introduce you to his fist? And why are you here on your day off? It can't be anything to do with the task force."

He wasn't sure how much he should tell Jamison. Especially since Magnum and the Shadows were involved. Normally he wouldn't care if any of them got popped for doing something illegal.

But this situation was different.

Nox didn't give a shit what had to happen to find Liyah. He only wanted her found.

More importantly, he wanted her found safe.

He *needed* her found safe.

Now that she was in his life, he couldn't bear losing her.

His heart squeezed painfully.

"Yeah, it's something for the task force and since the computers were removed, I had no way to look up the info."

"What is it? And why would Magnum be involved?"

"Magnum has nothing to do with the Demons, I... I can't talk about the investigation." He hated lying to his brother, but it was in Jamison's best interest.

"I thought the investigation was over. Especially after what the Russos pulled."

"It is for the most part. There's just a few loose ends that need to be dealt with for any remaining indictments and trials."

Jamison's steel blue eyes locked with his for a few seconds and Nox waited for his sergeant to call him out on his bullshit. Nox breathed easier when the BAMC president finally nodded, got to his feet and sighed. "All right. I'm headed home. Take care of that face. It's not a good look while on patrol."

Chapter Forty-Four

WHEN HIS PHONE rang while walking out of the station, he jerked it so quickly from his pocket, it almost tumbled to the ground. Once he had a better grip, he saw it was Aaliyah's stepmother. With his heart pounding, he put it to his ear. "Yeah."

"They tracked both her car and her cell phone."

She had to be talking about the Shadows. They probably knew how to hack into any program. Even the government's. A skill that Nox and his brothers did not have and one highly illegal. "And?"

"And the phone was dumped in Rockvale, but the car wasn't. One positive is that they did take her car, Nox, because the guys can track it. Hopefully, those assholes don't figure that out and abandon it somewhere along the way."

The guys. Like they were part of some "boys next door" club and not ruthless mercenaries. "It's still on the move?"

"Yes."

"What direction are they headed?"

"South."

Most likely to West Virginia. "But we don't know if she's in the car." It wasn't a question but a common sense assumption.

"No."

"Do they have eyes on it?"

"Not yet," she answered, "but they're catching up."

"Magnum told you all of this?"

An irritated sigh hit his ear. "Not willingly. However, I told him that if he didn't keep me updated that I wouldn't... Well..." Cait cleared her throat.

"Got it." He didn't want to make her admit out loud that she threatened to withhold sex from her husband if he didn't cooperate with her demands. The threat worked and that was all that mattered.

Thank fuck Cait was willing to go to that extreme to keep Nox updated.

"I appreciate the info, Cait, but I need to know where they're headed. I need more than the direction."

"Well... I shouldn't tell you this because if it gets back to Magnum, he won't be happy and then my threat won't matter because I'll be the one sleeping in the doghouse."

Nox waited for her confession.

"I'm able to track his phone, so I know exactly where he is."

Hot fucking damn. That was good news.

"Does he track your phone?" Nox asked out of curiosity.

"Since day one."

"Well then, turnabout is fair play. He shouldn't get pissed about it."

"*Mmm,*" she murmured. "We're talking about Magnum here. He thinks it's okay to track me because he has made himself my protector. He'll think I track him because I don't trust him."

"Do you?"

"Not since the day I met him have I not trusted him one hundred percent. And so you know, I met him when I was around fourteen. I'm now forty. Not once in all those years has he done anything to make that trust waiver."

Damn. The man might be an outlaw biker, but he was a loyal one. Nox had to respect that about him.

"Okay," he said, striding to his bike, "I'm going to start heading south. What do I have to do to get you to keep me updated on a regular basis?"

"Be good to Liyah and the boys."

That was too easy. "You got it."

"I just want her to be happy."

"You're not the only one."

"And safe."

"Ditto."

"Will your job be at risk by getting involved?" she asked.

"It's possible."

"But you're going to do it anyway."

He answered simply, "I want her back safe and sound."

"I like you, Nox."

That almost made him smile. "I like you, too, Cait. I appreciate you sticking out your neck."

"She might officially be my stepdaughter, but she's almost the same age, so she's more like a sister. I'd do anything for her."

Nox grunted. He would do anything for Liyah, too. "Please keep me updated."

"I'll text you with his last location once I get off the phone and can check it."

"Thanks, Cait."

The call ended.

He considered going back to Rockvale to grab his truck so it would be easier to check his messages as he drove, but that would waste time. Plus, he could travel faster on his Harley than in his old Chevy and he wanted to catch up before either T-Bone or Saint, or whoever snagged her, took their final breath.

He had questions.

He wanted answers.

If it was Saint and T-Bone, Nox wanted to know why they took Liyah and how they tied the two of them together. After that, he didn't give a shit what happened to either the former prospect or the strip club manager.

He'd even help throw gas on the fire as they burned in hell.

His phone dinged just as he threw a leg over his bike. He checked his texts to see a screenshot of a map that included Magnum's last location.

Thank fuck for Cait.

He started his Harley and raced in that direction.

———

Nox WAS thankful he had a full tank of gas because for the whole trip, he kept the throttle twisted hard as he chased the group chasing Liyah's car.

He hoped to fuck this wasn't a wild goose chase and someone else had her vehicle. One method to throw them off track.

Were T-Bone and Saint smart enough to think of that? He hoped to fuck not.

His thoughts as he rode never stopped spinning. Did those stupid fucks even know who they were fucking with? Who Liyah had ties to? He wasn't thinking about himself, but Magnum and the Dark Knights.

Two assholes versus an army of ruthless, pissed off bikers. Then add in the Shadows.

T-Bone and Saint would lose and lose big.

Magnum considered his daughter Dark Knights property. And no one got away with touching an MC's property. And lived to talk about it afterward.

Even Nox knew that.

So yeah, those dumbasses probably didn't have a clue who they were fucking with.

But they would.

Soon.

Nox already decided he wouldn't do shit to stop them. If anything, he'll be silently cheering them on.

Did that go against his morals? Normally, yes. But this situation was far from normal.

Would not stopping their demise make him a bad person? If it did, he didn't give a fuck.

Every twenty minutes, he'd pull over, quickly check his texts and get his bearings. Thank fuck Cait was on it with sending him regular updates.

He'd owe her at least two dozen roses.

Hell, a trip to Fiji.

Once he crossed the Mason-Dixon line, he pulled over once more, glanced at his phone and noticed that she sent a message telling him they stopped, and she even drew a big X on the map where they did so.

Nox didn't have far to catch up. He memorized the location, shoved his phone in his pocket and sped off.

Eighteen minutes later, he pulled up to a motel that made the one in Ohio, where they found Sadie, look like a five-star resort.

In fact, the motel had been abandoned and was beginning to collapse. Just the condition of it made his stomach turn.

Then he spotted a large vehicle that looked like it belonged in a dystopian movie.

Along with a half dozen Harleys.

In the large SUV, or whatever it was, was a couple of men.

He quickly parked his bike in line with rest but as he dismounted, a big man exited from the driver's seat of the vehicle. As soon as Nox saw the man's size and scarred face, he knew exactly who it was.

Ryan Mercer aka Mercy.

The man might be older, but he was still intimidating. Being in his crosshairs was enough for anyone to shit their pants.

Nox figured it was pretty damn obvious to Mercy and his crew that a white guy on a Harley wasn't a Dark Knight. That meant the Shadow was about to run interference for Magnum.

"You are?"

Nox faced him. "Here to get Aaliyah."

"That didn't answer my question."

"Liyah's mine."

Mercy's head tipped to the side and his steel gray eyes narrowed. "You're the cop."

"I am."

"You sure you want to be here?"

Nox raised his chin and answered, "If she's here, one hundred percent."

"She is."

"Then I don't have time for this chat."

Did the man's lips twitch? "You're aware those men in there don't like cops."

Nox pointed to his bruised and swollen face. "I'm aware."

He lifted the eyebrow with the scar running through it. "But you're here anyway."

"Damn right."

The second Mercy gave him a single nod and headed back to his monster vehicle, Nox headed in the opposite direction.

The motel room's broken door gaped open a bit. Whether it had been like that previously or someone recently kicked it in, Nox didn't know or care. He shoved it open the rest of the way, making quite a few heads turn toward him.

What Nox didn't expect was the electricity to be on in the rundown and abandoned business. It made him wonder if the Demons owned this trash dump and if so, for what reason since it wasn't bringing in any money in the condition it was in.

"Who the fuck's that?" he heard.

"That's the pig datin' Liyah, ain't it?" another Knight asked. "Remember him from the club run."

Magnum grunted and a whole lot of unhappy filled his face. "Didn't give my ol' lady enough info for you to find us, so guessin' I gotta have a fuckin' discussion with her."

"Don't blame her, I forced her to cooperate."

Magnum grunted again and didn't look like he believed him.

Nox's eyes scanned the small room. It appeared even smaller with the group of Knights filling it.

And...

Goddamn T-Bone and Saint.

Both sat on the floor. Both still breathed.

"Where the fuck is Liyah?"

"Think you can just fuckin' come in here and make demands?" one of the Knights sneered.

"I'm doing it, aren't I?" Nox slapped back. "Where is she?"

He was surprised when Magnum answered. "Bathroom. Romeo's in there with her."

Was that last part a warning? "Were you too late? Was she..."

"Don't think so," Magnum answered his unspoken question. "She's still too out of it to tell us much."

Nox pushed past the group and peered into the tiny bathroom to find Liyah propped up on a closed toilet seat with the Knights' president assisting her. He had a water bottle in one hand and a wet rag in another.

Nox nudged him out of the way and squatted in front of Liyah, brushing his knuckles down her cheek. When she slowly lifted her eyes, he saw her pupils were blown.

"You okay?" he asked softly.

Her answer came out slurred. "I don't feel right." When she began to lift her hand, it flopped back down into her lap like she didn't have any strength.

"That's to be expected. It'll wear off soon. I promise. Just hang on a few minutes, then I'm going to get you out of here." He got to his feet, his rage beginning to rise. It was about to boil over. "Watch her," he instructed Romeo. "Be back in a minute."

"Don't take orders from the likes of you, pig."

"Rome..." Liyah whispered.

"Yeah?"

"Don't."

Romeo's jaw turned to steel as he glanced from Liyah to Nox. "Got so many better fuckin' options than him, woman."

"You think right now's a good time to discuss her fucking love life?" he snapped at the MC president. "Save it for another goddamn day."

Nox didn't wait to see if he responded before striding out of the crowded bathroom and directly to the two mother-fuckers sitting on the floor. Not only were they gagged, but their hands were tied behind their backs and their ankles bound.

Perfect.

Ignoring the circle of Knights, Nox leaned over and went nose to nose with T-Bone, jamming a finger into his chest. "You. Fucked. Up." He then straightened and put every bit of strength he had behind the fist he pounded into the former prospect's nose, breaking it once again.

Nox felt the satisfying crunch before seeing the gush of blood. Then he shifted over to Saint, lifted his leg and slammed his boot right into the Demon's face, breaking a lot more than his nose.

He turned to Magnum. "They say why they took her?"

With his hands on his hips, the big man shook his head. "Not yet. With those bandanas in their mouths, they've been pretty fuckin' quiet."

"Find out before you finish them off. Need to know why they targeted her."

One side of Magnum's mouth pulled up. Did Nox see a sliver of respect in the man's eyes?

"Wanna know that, too. Plan on gettin' more info than that outta them. And if we can't convince them to talk, the men outside sure fuckin' can. And I can guaran-fuckin'-tee these two motherfuckers don't want that." He glanced over at

T-Bone and Saint and made his point by saying, "That's gonna be a horrible way to fuckin' die."

"Then I'm glad I'm not in their shoes."

"Not yet, anyway," Magnum muttered under his breath.

Nox ignored the threat. He had both the man's daughter and wife on his side. He doubted that Magnum would cross either of those women, no matter how big of a badass the Knight was.

"I also want to know how they tied her to me." Even though he could guess, he wanted to confirm his suspicions.

"Not sure why you think you can make fuckin' demands. Just be glad you're not sittin' on that floor next to them."

"And what do you think your daughter would say to that?"

Magnum's jaw shifted. "Get her the fuck outta here. We'll take care of the rest." He locked eyes with Nox. "But you saw nothin'. Got me?"

Nox nodded. "I'll take her to the ER."

"The fuck you will. You take her home and that's it. If she has any kinda issue, you take her then and not before. And if you do, you make up some fuckin' story that ain't gonna trigger an investigation. We don't want shit on record. You got that?"

"I do," Nox answered.

"Now get the fuck outta here before I decide I don't give a fuck what my wife or daughter think."

"Need the key fob for her car. I brought my bike, and I don't think she'll be able to hang on in the condition she's in." He'd worry about his Harley later. Liyah was more important to him than a fucking bike. It was replaceable. She wasn't.

Magnum stared at him for a heartbeat or two, then with a grunt, he dug deep into his front pocket, pulled out the Mercedes' key fob and tossed it at Nox. "Since you're all fuckin' cozy with my wife, let her know where you're takin' Aaliyah and the second you fuckin' get there. Don't make me fuckin' hunt you down."

"I'll take care of her while you take out the trash. Deal?"

When Magnum gave him a chin lift, Nox returned it and headed back into the bathroom to grab Liyah and get her the fuck out of there.

Chapter Forty-Five

"I GOT out to open the gate and..." Aaliyah's voice caught and cracked. "He ambushed me, Nox." Her tongue not only felt twice its size when she tried to speak, it was bone dry, too, no matter how much water she drank.

Hopefully the man driving her Mercedes understood what she said.

"I know. I should've been waiting for you at the fucking gate."

When she looked over at him, she noticed he was gripping the steering wheel so tight, his knuckles had turned white. His jaw was also sharp enough to cut glass. "It's not your fault."

"The fuck it isn't," he growled.

He was wrong, but she didn't have the energy to argue. "What did he inject me with? Why did I feel that way?"

"Since the Demons were selling meth, my guess is, he shot you up with that."

"That would make sense. At first, I experienced some sort of adrenaline rush. My heart raced so fast, I actually thought it would explode. After that, I hovered in this weird state of euphoria. It was both calming but frightening because I hate the feeling of helplessness. Worse, I was powerless to stop any of it."

She had to be crashing now since her head throbbed, she felt physically drained, and her limbs had grown heavy.

"Do you want to go to the hospital?"

"My father probably told you not to take me there." The tightening of his mouth was her answer. "I don't want this coming back on him. And you know if I go, there will be questions." She sighed softly. "I'll be fine. I was drugged, not injured or beaten." Or even raped, thankfully. "It'll wear off."

She wanted to say she was lucky, but it more had to do with timing than luck. She was sure she would've been sexually assaulted and worse if Nox hadn't notified the cavalry.

"Thank you for going to my father. And dealing with his stubborn ass. I know that couldn't have been easy."

"He has resources I don't, and I wanted you found as quickly as possible."

When she reached over to squeeze his thigh, he grabbed her hand, gave it an answering squeeze, then kept it enveloped in his.

"Did he do that to your face?" If so, she was going to have a serious sit down with her father. He needed to learn to accept Nox, especially since she planned on keeping him around for a long time.

And if it was up to her, forever.

Instead of answering her question, he deflected with, "Where do you want to go? My place? Yours?"

She tried to clear her dry throat. "Do you know where Devyn and Keenan are?" She needed to know her sons were okay and hadn't been targeted, too.

"Your father had one of the Knights pick them up from

your mother's and take them to his house. They're safe with Cait. Is that where you want to go?"

Her first instinct was to say yes because she wanted to see for herself that they were safe but earlier she had taken a peek in the small mirror built into the sun visor. She didn't recognize herself.

The way she looked right now might upset her boys.

"Not yet. I don't want them to see me like this. Can you take me home so I can shower, change and sober up some more before I go get them?"

"Whatever you want, baby. You also need to get more fluids in you. Food, too. And some sleep. If you want, I can get them after you clean up and while you take a nap."

"I don't want them to know what happened."

"I won't say shit but I'm sure they're wondering why a Knight picked them up early."

He was right, but she didn't want them to know she'd been abducted and drugged. She'd need to come up with an excuse. One that would pass muster with a fifteen-year-old. Devyn was too damn smart for his own good.

"It was crazy, Liyah," Nox murmured. "The Dark Knights rolled out to save you like they're white knights instead." He turned his head to glance at her. "I don't know what I would've done if they hadn't."

She interlaced her fingers with his, holding on tighter. "Yes, you would've. I have no doubt you would've done whatever you needed to do to find me."

His fingers twitched against hers. "I might never had found you without him and his contacts."

"That's what I'm saying. You did what needed to be done. You realized it was better to let him handle it and you didn't interfere, whether he would deal with it legally or not. You didn't let your ego, or your job, get in the way." Her eyes began to sting when she whispered, "I thank you for that."

His voice sounded huskier than normal when he said, "Anything for you, Liyah."

It had to be the drugs wearing off, because she was not expecting those four words to make those tears fall.

But despite everything that happened tonight, her heart was full.

———

It was late. The boys were in bed asleep. Nox had picked up a meal for her to eat on his way back to her house with the boys.

She had showered and then climbed into bed while waiting for him to return. During that time, she had fallen asleep and didn't wake up until he climbed in with her, offering her a bag emblazoned with "Bangin' Burgers."

Her boys' favorite.

She sat up and accepted it. "Are you staying here tonight?"

"Planned on it. You okay with that?"

"Yes." Before she could dig into the bag, Nox did it for her, pulling out a container overflowing with fries, as well as a wrapped burger. "Was my dad home when you got there?"

"No," he answered after popping one of the fries into his mouth. He offered the next one to her.

She took it from his fingers with her mouth, savoring the salty crunch. "What about your sled?"

"I'll worry about that tomorrow."

"Nox..."

"You're more important to me than any fucking bike, Liyah. Eat, then we can talk."

They remained quiet as she did so. She could only manage half of the burger, so he finished off the rest.

Once he did, he gathered up the trash, tossed it out, then got undressed and slipped back into bed with her, immediately pulling her into his arms.

She curled around him, placing her cheek on his bare chest. Listening to his strong, steady heartbeat. Basking in the warmth he emitted. Feeling secure and content enveloped in his arms.

"It could've turned out so much worse," she whispered.

"Yeah," came out on a breath.

"Someone was looking out for me."

"His name is Magnum." His fingers strummed soothingly along her arm. After a few more heartbeats, his low voice rumbled against her cheek. "I've decided to move out of The Plant and find somewhere safer to live."

He was going to do what? "You don't have to do that."

An idea popped into her head.

Should she mention it?

She didn't want to freak him out.

Screw it. "You could move in here."

His brow wrinkled and his fingers stilled as he echoed, "You don't have to do that."

"Of course I don't."

"Liyah..."

"I'm throwing it out there as an option, but don't feel pressured."

"Moving in with you is a huge step."

She couldn't get a good read on the idea in either his expression or his tone. "You're right, it is. And I'll understand if you're not ready." She wanted to give him an out without feeling guilty.

He tucked a finger under her chin and tipped her face up. "Are you?"

She shrugged one shoulder. "Tonight made me realize that life is too damn short to waste time. You need to make the most out of every day."

One eyebrow rose. "You only realized that tonight?"

"No, it whacked me right in the forehead when Mark died. As I'm sure it did for you when you lost Jackie, but tonight was a rude reminder."

"It was. For both of us."

"Think about it. No pressure. No rush. The offer will still be on the table tomorrow, a week from now, or even months from now."

"Months? Do you think we'll last that long?"

She lifted her head and watched him carefully. "Don't you?"

Instead of answering, he reached over to the nightstand and grabbed his cell phone. He activated the screen and a few seconds later, began typing.

He was texting someone *now*? In the middle of their conversation and—she glanced over at the clock—this late? "It must be important if you're sending a message at one in the morning."

She always caught him texting at the oddest times. And once he would send the text, she never heard a ding or vibration to indicate an incoming response. Nor did he ever read any reply.

He lifted his hazel eyes but didn't answer. Again, his expression was locked down tightly.

Since she was not one to beat around the bush... "How come whoever you text never texts you back?"

"Because she can't."

What the hell did that mean? Who was *she*?

Even though she wasn't jealous, she was now curious.

When she put out her hand, palm up, she expected him to balk. To make excuses.

To keep whoever he was texting a secret.

Jason had never let her see his phone. He had always kept it locked unless he was using it.

Liyah didn't want to be with someone she couldn't trust. Trust should be mutual.

Nox surprised the shit out of her when he placed his unlocked phone in her hand with the string of texts still pulled up on the screen.

Now she was unsure if she should even look. She might be violating his privacy.

Her stomach dropped when she quickly scanned the texts. All of them, every last one, written by Nox. None answered by whomever he was texting.

She glanced at the name at the top of the screen. The person he was texting so often.

Holy shit. He'd been texting his late wife.

She made sure to keep her expression as locked down as his and not make any sounds while she scrolled up and took a closer look at the messages.

She scrolled even farther trying to find where his one-sided conversation began or where Jackie's responses ended. But as she slid her finger up the screen over and over, she realized it was hundreds of unanswered texts, if not thousands. The string of messages seemed endless.

After a bit, she noticed about two years ago the texts were sent almost hourly throughout both the day and night.

As she read, she struggled to breathe.

Why?

I don't know how to go on without you.

I miss you.

I don't know what to do without you.

I miss you.

I'm lost without you.

I miss you more every day.

I love you.

I should've been there for you.

I'm sorry.

I'm sorry.

I'm sorry.

I miss you so fucking much.

I can't do this without you.

I don't want to live without you.

Eventually they slowed to several times a day. One particular text caught her eye, causing a lump to get caught in her throat and her vision to blur.

We'd be celebrating her first birthday about now.

Guilt washed through her for reading such personal thoughts. Was she invading his privacy, or had he wanted her to see them all?

She risked a glance at him.

He was staring straight ahead with his face still a blank mask.

Since he hadn't told her to stop or snatched his phone away, she continued scrolling to see a year later, the unanswered messages were reduced to a couple of times a week.

Then in the last few months, it returned to once a day. Sometimes more.

She wondered what triggered him texting his late wife that often again.

She paused when she read the reason.

We found Sadie.

Another dark moment in his life. A discovery that made his healing screech to a complete halt.

As Liyah continued on, she knew the exact point when he met her. Every text dripped with guilt and self-loathing.

He beat himself up over and over.

She stopped skimming the painful thread when the following caught her eye: *I made a mistake. I'm sorry.*

She looked at the date to find it was sent after the first time they had sex.

I don't know what to do.

I feel so damn lost.

Each text cracked her heart even further until it was thoroughly shattered. But it was the final text... the one he just sent...

That made her stop breathing and that broken heart seize.

I love her.

Her eyebrows knitted together. Was Liyah the "her" in his text?

Did he love her?

She glanced up, her heart suddenly whole again and thumping so hard it made it difficult for her to hear anything else. "Nox..."

"I used to share everything with her." He squeezed his eyes shut. "Everything. I missed that. I know it sounds really weird—maybe even creepy—but at her funeral I tucked her cell phone in her coffin." He shook his head and his voice caught as he continued. "It's messed up, I know, but I was desperate to keep that connection somehow. I knew eventually the battery would die and no one would ever read the messages anyway..." He finally opened his eyes and met hers. "I thought it would help me cope or..." He shook his head. "Something."

She attempted to clear the thick from her throat. "Doing that didn't hurt anyone, Nox. If it helped, then that's all that matters. It's obvious that when you give someone your heart, you do it completely."

His fingertips skimmed over her cheek. "And now it belongs to you."

Holy shit. "You felt the need to share that with her."

"Yes. But now, I want to share everything with you."

She considered that statement along with the three simple words in the last text he sent.

I love her.

Simple but also not. The concept of love might be considered simple, but real relationships were complex.

"Nox..."

He finally tipped his face down to her, his eyes soft. "*Hmm?*"

She slid the pad of her thumb over his bottom lip and the corners of her mouth curled slightly. "I love you, too."

Chapter Forty-Six

It was his fault. He was the reason his baby girl was buried without a name.

Nox remembered the conversation perfectly. In fact, he'd never forget it.

At the end of every day, he and Jackie would lie in bed together and when she'd press his hand to her extended belly, her expression would turn soft, and she'd smile at him.

"We made her."

"Yeah," he turned toward her, rubbing her very firm stomach, *"we did."*

"I love her, but I can't wait until she's no longer riding my bladder. Until she no longer kicks my ribs. And until you can help take some of the burden off me."

He pulled up her nightgown to bare her stomach and pressed his mouth to her tight skin. *"She'll be here soon. I can't wait to hold her."*

"We need to pick a name."

This was something they constantly disagreed over. Jackie wanted to choose one so they could call her that from the start, *while he wanted to wait.* "Not until we see her. I want her name to come from the heart."

"But I have a long list. Will you at least consider some of the names on it?"

"Jackie, we'll know who she is once she's in our arms. There's no rush. I wanted the baby's sex to be a surprise and you strong-armed me into finding that out early. Let me have this, at least."

Jackie's fingers dragged gently through his hair. "Fine. We'll compromise."

"Right, a compromise," he agreed.

Liyah originally didn't want to help him pick a name for his daughter. But in the end, she gave him some great suggestions, leaving it to him to decide on the final choice. On her list was one name that stood out above the rest.

Amara.

Latin for "everlasting." It was perfect because his unborn angel would last forever in his heart.

He had her name engraved on the headstone under Jackie's. And for some reason, being able to see it and trace the letters with his fingers made him feel more at peace.

With snow falling around him and Liyah, and with the boys waiting in the warm SUV, she gripped his hand tightly as they stood together in front of the grave after decorating the plot with a Christmas wreath.

Earlier, Devyn had joined them when they did the same at Mark's grave.

Hearing Liyah sniffle next to him made him wonder if she was emotional from visiting the cemeteries or if it was because of the frigid temps.

"You want to go?" he asked her.

"When you're ready."

He glanced at the strong, smart woman who single-handedly set his life back on the right path. "I'm ready. And I'm sure your family is wondering where we are."

Liyah snorted softly and jiggled their clasped hands.

"Okay," he admitted, "Cait might be wondering where we are. Your father won't give a shit if I show up. Come on, let's go before the boys complain."

"They probably don't even realize what time it is."

"I'm sure their stomachs are growling," he said. They were bottomless pits. If it was edible, it disappeared like magic.

"True. Food is the only thing that makes them pause their video games. I'm sure they're trying to conquer a few more levels in whatever their latest favorite is since I told them once we arrive at their grandparents' house, the phones will be put away for the rest of the day. Christmas is a day to spend with family."

"Thanks for the warning. I'm sure their eyes and fingers will be twitching," he teased.

"Actually, I expect them to sneak upstairs to play on Caleb's gaming console."

"Won't they want their presents first?" The back of his new Chevy Tahoe was jammed-packed with wrapped gifts.

He didn't want to know what Liyah spent on all of that.

"Oh yeah. They'll rip through their gifts, shovel dinner into their pie holes and then rush upstairs and not be seen again for the rest of the evening."

"Sounds peaceful," he teased.

"Right?" Liyah laughed. "Until they begin to fight over the controllers."

"We'll just turn up the Christmas music to drown them out."

"That's the spirit!" she exclaimed as they walked hand-in-hand back to his vehicle.

Despite Magnum "taking care" of both Saint and T-Bone—and Nox didn't know or want to know the details—things between him and Liyah's father still remained tense.

Magnum had subtle ways of showing his displeasure about Aaliyah letting Nox move in with her months ago. He was slick enough to make sure only Nox noticed in order to avoid both his wife and daughter giving him hell about it.

But the big man left no doubt he was not happy about the arrangement since he wanted his daughter to be with anyone but a "pig." He'd even prefer Liyah be with Romeo, known for using women and tossing them away when he was through. A true pig in Nox's eyes.

However, somehow, they managed to keep things civil. Magnum tolerated Nox, only for the fact he wanted to keep his oldest daughter in his life. As well as his grandsons.

If that was what it took, then that was what it took.

If it wasn't Christmas Day, Nox wouldn't be hanging out with the whole family, anyway. When her father was home, Liyah normally visited by herself to keep the peace.

Even though there hadn't been any more "fist meet face" episodes, Nox tended to keep his guard up around the Knights' enforcer.

Nox stood in the corner by the roaring fireplace, taking in the disaster left behind after everyone opened their gifts. Boxes, torn and balled up wrapping paper, forgotten gifts, empty glasses, coffee mugs and spilled bowls of nuts and pretzels littered the room.

Of course, he and the big man did not exchange anything but guarded looks.

Now Nox sipped at a beer with his gut jammed pack from a great early Christmas dinner and even better huge slice of sweet potato pie, drowning in real whipped cream. One of Liyah's specialties.

She had brought over four pies. All four had been decimated.

Like Liyah predicted, Caleb, Devyn and Keenan snuck off while the adults cleaned up the dining room and kitchen. Her sister Asia, at fifteen, was now curled up in a recliner talking a mile a minute on her cell phone. She was having an animated discussion about boys with whoever was on the other end.

Unless her father was in hearing distance, then the conversation quickly switched to makeup and clothes.

One side of Nox's mouth pulled up as he silently wished luck on all the boys wanting to date the stunningly beautiful girl in the future. That grin quickly dropped when Romeo crossed the large living room with his eyes laser-focused on Liyah.

As soon as she spotted him heading her way, she lifted her hand with her palm out, stopping him in his tracks.

Not a word needed to be said.

With a shake of his head, the Knights' president grumbled something, took a wide detour around her and headed out of the living room.

The man had some fucking balls trying to approach Nox's woman when they were in the same room. He didn't know when to quit, even though Liyah was always clear with how she felt about the horn dog. To his face.

Nox guessed he took her as a challenge.

A challenge he'd never win.

Because Nox won. Not Romeo.

The grin he had lost once again spread across his face.

"Hey," he heard softly next to him.

He tipped his face down to the woman he loved more and more every day. "Hey."

She held out a narrow box. "With all the craziness earlier, this got lost in the pile of gifts."

He stared at it. "It's for me?"

She bugged her eyes out at him and shoved it at him. "No, it's for Romeo. Of course it's for you."

He took it from her fingers. "From?"

Why was she fighting a grin? He narrowed his eyes on her.

She elbowed him. "Just open it and stop asking questions."

He studied the shape of the box. It had to be a new watch since his went missing the other week.

"Stop trying to figure out what it is and open it!"

Why was she so damn antsy?

"I already know it's a new watch."

She rolled her eyes. "Men! So damn confident when they're wrong."

"It's not a watch?"

"Nox!"

He chuckled and ripped off the festive wrapping paper to find a plain white box. When he lifted the lid, he blinked.

And blinked again.

He lifted his gaze to see a huge smile on her face and her eyes held a gleam. "Merry Christmas," she whispered.

He forced, "Liyah..." up his throat. "This isn't a joke, right?"

She shook her head. "I wouldn't joke about something like this."

He dropped his gaze back to the item in the box. Then it slipped from his fingers and fell to the ground as he grabbed her in a bear hug and swung her around.

Her laughter was thick with tears as he did so.

He couldn't speak for a few minutes because if he did, it might just come out in a blubber. And he knew better than to show any kind of weakness under Magnum's roof.

Instead, he blinked back the tears, swiping at the stray one threatening to spill over, and focused on the woman in front of him, even though she was a little blurry.

"I'll take it that you're happy about this?" Liyah asked.

"After finding out he was going to be a father, how long did it take Jason to pack his bags?"

Her mouth dropped open for a second, then she shoved him playfully. "That is so not funny!"

He took her into his arms again, put his mouth to her ear, and said, "I won't be running for the hills. In fact, good luck getting rid of me."

"Remember you said that when you're changing poopy diapers in the middle of the night. Or pacing for hours, trying to get the baby back to sleep."

"Can I borrow a suitcase?"

She tried to glare at him but failed and laughed, instead. "You got jokes."

He leaned over and scooped up the positive pregnancy test. When he did, his attention caught on his now bare left ring finger. That would have to change. And soon.

"Should we keep this and frame it?"

Liyah wrinkled her nose. "No. Ick."

"Nothing *ick* about it." He held up the white and pink stick. "This is our future."

"We'll have much better things to frame."

"Like our marriage certificate?"

She pulled away and stared wide-eyed at him. "Are you proposing?"

He shrugged. "I was planning on it, anyway. I guess there's no time like the present."

"Well, this is highly romantic," she said dryly.

"Do you need it to be romantic?"

She tipped her head as she considered him. "Truthfully, I only need you."

He pressed a kiss to her soft lips, murmuring, "You have me. For now and always. Ring or no ring on my finger. So, if you don't want to get marri—"

She took his mouth, smothering the rest of his teasing. When they finally broke the kiss, she locked eyes with him and said, "Yes."

He pressed a finger behind his ear to bend it forward. "I didn't quite catch that."

"Then it's your loss. Okay, I'm going to go share the good news!" She pressed another kiss to his lips before practically running out of the room.

He continued to stare at the doorway she disappeared through, wondering what the hell just happened. Wondering how he deserved any of this.

Thankful for it all.

Then it hit him that the room was too quiet.

When he turned, he saw Asia grinning at him. She gave him a thumbs up.

For a moment, he had forgotten she'd even been in the room.

His soon-to-be sister-in-law put her phone back to her ear and her mouth began to move again.

He sighed and decided to go find Liyah so he could be with her when she shared the good news.

Maybe not so good for a certain someone...

Only when he turned, he slammed into a wall.

A big, dark, bald wall.

That wall was not smiling.

No, Magnum looked furious.

Nox braced for the fist that was raised.

But instead of it striking him, the fingers uncurled.

Nox stared at Magnum's hand before lifting his eyes.

The man wanted to shake his hand?

Had he been drinking?

The shake was firm, but not bone shattering. "You ain't the person I'd pick for her to have another grandbaby. But from what I was told, I ain't got a fuckin' say. I don't fuckin' like it but apparently, no one gives a fuckin' shit."

"Is that your way of congratulating us?"

Magnum grunted and stepped back. "Had Aaliyah when I was only seventeen."

Where was this going? "That had to be difficult."

"We were too fuckin' young to be parents and made bad choices. Those choices affected my kids, and it fucked up my relationship with them. Lost them for years. Finally got them back fifteen years ago. That's why you're standin' in my house. Make no fuckin' mistake, it ain't 'cause I like you. It's 'cause I love my daughter and got a lotta makin' up to do."

Nox guessed that whacked congratulations was better than nothing.

Magnum dropped his voice lower until only Nox could hear him. "That fuckin' said, if you do to her what that last motherfucker did, gonna hunt you down and do the same to you as I did to him."

"Do I want to ask what that was?"

"Best you don't," his future father-in-law warned before heading over to his youngest daughter, yanking the cell phone out of her hand while she was in mid-sentence and hanging up on whoever she was talking to. "Go get your brother and nephews and tell them to get their asses down here. If they're up there playin' video games, I'm gonna smash Caleb's game console and he ain't gettin' another one 'til he can pay for it himself."

Asia unfolded herself from the recliner and didn't argue. She only went and did what she was told.

Interesting. What teenager didn't argue?

"Take fuckin' notes," Magnum said as he lumbered past Nox and back out of the room.

Then Liyah was peeking around the wall separating the living room and the hallway.

"Are you checking to make sure I'm not lying in a broken heap?"

She entered with a smile. "Don't let him fool you. He's excited."

Nox's answering grunt wasn't as deep as Magnum's.

When she pressed herself against him, his arms automatically pulled her closer. "How did your father know before me?"

"I figured it was best to prep him and not just spring the news on him. I didn't want him charging you like a raging bull in the middle of celebrating Christmas. Plus, I figured the fact having another grandbaby on the way would soften him up a little today."

"He shook my hand."

"At least he didn't break it. Soon you'll be best buds," she quipped.

"How did this happen?" he asked.

Her eyes widened. "I figured by this stage in life, you'd know all about the birds and the bees. Do you need a step-by-step explanation?"

"No, you can do a step-by-step demonstration later tonight after we get home." He cupped her cheek. "I thought you were still taking your birth control. I didn't know you wanted another baby."

"I figured if we were going to do this, it needed to be soon. I mean, I'm forty now. Having a baby at this age comes with some risks."

Fuck. His heart began to pound in his chest.

"Nothing is going to happen, Nox," she assured him softly.

"You don't know that."

"I can't make promises, but I can tell you that we'll stay on top of this pregnancy every step of the way."

"It wasn't the pregnancy that killed Jackie," he reminded her.

"I know. But the fall would've killed her whether she was pregnant or not. Life isn't without risks. You know that. You take a risk every day at your job. We take risks driving our vehicles. You can't not live life because you're worried something might happen."

He wondered how much she worried about him dying in the line of duty. Like her first husband. She never talked about it. She never insisted he get another job. She lived with that daily risk.

If she could deal with that, then he could live with the risk she was taking by giving them a child together.

A child together.

He was going to be a father.

Holy shit.

"Liyah..."

"*Hmm?*"

"Will Cait think it's rude if we leave now?"

Confusion filled her face. "You're ready to go?"

"I'm ready to get naked with you."

"Let's go say our goodbyes and inform them the boys will

be spending the night." She wiggled her eyebrows, grabbed his hand and pulled him toward the hallway.

"Hold on..." He dug in his heels, stopping her forward motion, then tugged hard enough that she crashed back into him. "I need to tell you something important first."

Her eyebrows rose as she waited.

"I love you."

Her face softened and her lips tipped upward. "Right back at you, baby. Now let's go home so you can tell me that again while we're naked."

"Sounds like a plan I can get on board with."

"Good to know we're on the same page."

"Baby, we're about to start a whole new chapter."

Epilogue

"We did all that damn work and got fucked out of the fun of rounding those motherfuckers up," Rez griped.

Nox had only told Finn, Decker and Rez what happened with T-Bone and Saint because he knew they wouldn't say shit to anyone. Like he expected, they were happy that karma was served to those two particular assholes.

No matter who served it.

"You heard Crew," Decker reminded Rez. "He said the trials will start in two months."

"Two more fucking months. This has been dragging on forever!" Rez bitched some more.

"What's with you? Why are you being so damn dramatic? And today of all days. You know the wheels of justice are rusty and slow," Nox told his BAMC brother.

In the end, only a handful of Demons needed to be rounded up. If more had escaped the massacre by the Russos, they most likely went underground.

It was a damn shame it wasn't six feet underground but

as long as they never popped their heads back up in Pennsylvania again, Nox could live with it.

But if any ever did...

They'd deal with it then.

Or he'd have someone else deal with it. Because that defunct MC was now a target for another one that was strong and growing.

If Magnum heard any whispers about the Demons rebuilding their club, Nox was damn sure he would squash them under his massive biker boot like the roaches they were.

Nox would conveniently look the other way.

See no evil, hear no evil, speak no evil was the best means to deal with the situation.

Liyah waddled over to them with her enormous stomach leading the way. "*Umm.* Did you boys know Finn had the DJ bring a karaoke machine?"

"What?" burst from Rez.

While Decker muttered, "For fuck's sake."

"Did he also have the wedding planner bring earplugs?" Nox asked her.

"Sorry, I didn't see a bowl of earplugs on the dessert table. And believe me, I've been gazing—I mean grazing—at that table for the past half hour."

Nox looked from Decker to Rez. "That karaoke machine needs to mysteriously disappear."

Rez shook his head. "Who the hell has a fucking karaoke machine at their wedding?"

"You're actually surprised by that?" Nox asked. "We're talking about Heat Miser here. He thinks he could be on stage next to Pavarotti."

"Maybe he needs to be debarked like a dog," Rez suggested

"That's cruel," Liyah said, rubbing her stomach and wincing.

Nox had no doubt by now her feet were swollen painfully.

"To a dog, yeah. To Finn, no. Him singing is cruelty to our ears," Rez explained.

Decker elbowed Rez, tipping his head toward the DJ's table. "Let's wait until Paul takes a piss break and steal it."

Paul worked for Mel's club, The Pink Pearl, and had volunteered his DJ services for Mel and Finn's wedding. The strip club was so damn successful now that Rez was even thinking about retiring early from the Southern Allegheny Regional PD so he could help her out full-time.

"Steal it? How about smash it? It's probably the same one he uses during karaoke night at the Pearl." Rez leaned into Nox. "You didn't hear shit."

Nox laughed. "What? I couldn't hear you say shit because the music's too loud."

With a nod and a grin, Rez and Decker went to go create havoc.

"Isn't she the cutest?" Liyah asked, watching Valee Girl dancing awkwardly with Keenan.

"I'm glad Kee didn't brush her off."

"Truthfully, I think he's looking forward to having his own sister."

Nox pulled Liyah into his arms with her back into his chest so they could both keep an eye on the dance floor. He rested his chin on her shoulder and planted both hands on her belly, the wedding band Liyah slipped onto his ring finger at their small ceremony catching the light.

Before Liyah, he never thought he'd take off his old one, but he was okay with being wrong.

With his hands pressed against her baby bump, he'd occasionally feel his daughter become restless, most likely as anxious to meet them as they were to meet her.

It would happen any day now.

If Finn and Mel's wedding hadn't been extremely important to him, he would have kept Liyah home and off her feet. She was so damn uncomfortable at this late stage in the pregnancy.

They both hated the term "geriatric pregnancy" but at forty, that was what the doctors considered it.

He'd been a bit worried about her the whole pregnancy because it wasn't the same as when she had Devyn in her twenties or Keenan in her early thirties. He went to every appointment with her. Every ultrasound. Even though it annoyed her to be fussed over, he waited on her hand and foot.

It was the least he could do since his daughter grew inside her.

This time he had a name picked out. Even before they sat down to discuss it.

Destiny.

He didn't think Liyah would like it. He was wrong. She loved it and agreed it was fitting for their circumstance. Though, she joked that the name could be her stage name, too, if she ever decided to dance at The Pink Pearl.

At that moment, he almost picked another name.

As they slightly swayed back and forth to the music, he scanned the wedding venue, finding each and every member of his family. The people he could count on.

Keenan and Devyn.

Valee Girl.

Crew and Cabrera.

Decker and Sloane.

Rez and Sapphire.

Beyond the Badge: Nox

Fletch and Wilder.
Jamison and Bella.
Cross and Nash.
Monty and Clark.
Miller with his wife.
Frasier with his plus one.
North and Naomi, now no longer his fiancée but his wife.
And lastly, the bride and groom: Finn and Mel.

He was a lucky man to have them all in his life. He was even luckier to have the woman currently in his arms.

"Nox..."

"Hmm?"

"I have something important to tell you."

"That you love me?"

"No."

He lifted his chin from her shoulder and turned his beautiful wife around to face him. "You don't?"

"I do. But that's not what I need to tell you."

"What is it?"

She pointed to the floor. "My water just broke."

———

DESTINY MARIAH LENNOX JOINED THEM, kicking and screaming, four hours and thirty-eight minutes later.

———

"Grief is like the wake behind a boat. It starts out as a huge wave that follows close behind you and is big enough to swamp and drown you if you suddenly stop moving forward. But if you do keep moving, the big wake will eventually dissipate. And after a long time, the waters of your life get

calm again, and that is when the memories of those who have left begin to shine as bright and as enduring as the stars above." ~ *Jimmy Buffett (1946-2023)*

———

Sign up for Jeanne's newsletter to learn about her upcoming releases, sales and more! http:// www.jeannestjames.com/newslettersignup

———

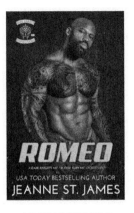

Romeo: A DKMC/BFMC Crossover

He's the president of the Dark Knights MC. She's the stepdaughter of a quiet, but deadly, member of the Blood Fury MC...

Romeo earned his road name honestly.

He loves the ladies.

Not one in particular. All of them.

But when he's finished with them, they don't love him back.

Simply put, he's a dog. Of the two-legged variety, not four.

He's charming when he wants to be.
He also has no problem dealing with threats.
Right now there's only one threat to his lifestyle.
Her.

Romeo: A DKMC/BFMC Crossover is an interracial romance that doesn't involve cheating and, as always, will give you a satisfying happily ever after.

Turn the page to read the prologue of Romeo: A Dark Knights MC/Blood Fury MC Crossover

Romeo: A Dark Knights MC/Blood Fury MC Crossover

UNEDITED Prologue

ROMEO TRACKED her as she walked across the Blood Fury's courtyard.

The young strawberry blonde with the big brown eyes.

The same as her mother.

The same as her younger sister.

She wore no one's colors despite being old enough to be an ol' lady. She appeared to only be a few years younger than him.

His best fucking guess? She had to be at least twenty-one now since she was drinking. Not that her doing so was a perfect indicator since Romeo doubted that the Fury gave a shit about underage drinking.

He could be wrong—that happened sometimes—since he heard Trip, the Fury president, was pretty damn strict. Totally fucking opposite of him, the president of the Dark Knights.

But then, he was younger than either president of the Fury or the Dirty Angels. Add in the fact he also liked to party fucking hard and often, he wasn't enough of a dick to police anyone in his club, or even connected to his club, unless he had no damn choice.

And anyway, he had his no-fucking-nonsense sergeant at arms to do that shit for him. No matter that Magnum no longer had youth on his side, he still fucking had it in him to pound someone into the ground or make someone shit their pants with one look.

He licked his lips as he thought about Magnum's hot-as-fuck, much younger wife.

That had him turning his wandering thoughts back to the woman heading toward the covered pavilion. Right now, the popular gathering spot was too crowded for him to approach. He didn't want anyone listening in on his "game." He'd find a better time when she wasn't surrounded by others who might interrupt.

When he could speak to her in private. Turn on his charm.

Test the waters.

Because he planned on having her before this wedding weekend was over.

The fuck if he was leaving Manning Grove without finding a willing woman to warm his bed every night.

It didn't have to be the same woman each night. He wasn't picky. His only requirement was soft thighs, big tits and an ass that wouldn't quit.

A mouth that wouldn't quit, either. And he didn't mean using that mouth in conversation.

He couldn't remember her name because, between the three clubs and all their sweet butts, hang-arounds and others that descended on the Blood Fury's farm for the wedding of Easy, a Fury member, to their president's sister, there were way too many goddamn people to remember.

If he had to be honest, he really didn't give a fuck what her name was. The second he kicked her out of his bed, he'd forget it anyway. What he wouldn't forget was if her pussy was tight, how wet she got, or how skilled she was with those soft, plump lips.

A grin crossed his face as he closed his eyes and imagined that one spread naked in the bed in his rented RV. The one parked in a field on the same farm where he stood.

Since the motels in town were booked solid due to the weekend-long wedding, he had no choice but to rent one. Unless he wanted to pitch a fucking tent.

And not one in his jeans.

Romeo did not sleep on the fucking ground. Ever.

Unless he was passed-out drunk.

And if he was, one of his brothers better move him to somewhere more comfortable. One of the many perks of being voted in as prez.

Not even an hour later, when his eyes scanned the crowd and the courtyard, he spotted her again. Mostly because she was so damn hard to miss.

The problem was, he wasn't the only one watching her.

He heard rumors about her stepfather—or whatever the fuck Shade was—watching over his ol' lady's hot daughters like a fucking hawk.

Magnum could be in-your-face deadly.

Shade went about it quietly.

He was the kind who'd slice your throat and disappear before you even knew what the fuck happened.

Breathing one second, bleeding out the next.

With one last glance at the strawberry blonde and the group she was in, he wandered away to find himself a cold beer.

And while he was sipping that beer, he'd work on his plan of attack.

Get the rest of the prologue and Romeo's story here: Romeo: A Dark Knights MC/Blood Fury MC Crossover

If You Enjoyed This Book

Thank you for reading Beyond the Badge: Nox. If you enjoyed Nox and Aaliyah's story, please consider leaving a review at your favorite retailer and/or Goodreads to let other readers know. Reviews are always appreciated and just a few words can help an independent author like me tremendously!

Want to read a sample of my work? Download a sampler book here: BookHip.com/MTQQKK

Also by Jeanne St. James

Find my complete reading order here:

https://www.jeannestjames.com/reading-order

Standalone Books:

Made Maleen: A Modern Twist on a Fairy Tale

Damaged

Rip Cord: The Complete Trilogy

Everything About You (A Second Chance Gay Romance)

Reigniting Chase (An M/M Standalone)

Brothers in Blue Series

A four-book series based around three brothers who are small-town cops and former Marines

The Dare Ménage Series

A six-book MMF, interracial ménage series

The Obsessed Novellas

A collection of five standalone BDSM novellas

Down & Dirty: Dirty Angels MC®

A ten-book motorcycle club series

Guts & Glory: In the Shadows Security

A six-book former special forces series

(A spin-off of the Dirty Angels MC)

Blood & Bones: Blood Fury MC®

A twelve-book motorcycle club series

Motorcycle Club Crossovers:

Crossing the Line: A DAMC/Blue Avengers MC Crossover

Magnum: A Dark Knights MC/Dirty Angels MC Crossover

Crash: A Dirty Angels MC/Blood Fury MC Crossover

Romeo: A Dark Knights MC/Blood Fury MC Crossover

Beyond the Badge: Blue Avengers MC™

A six-book law enforcement/motorcycle club series

COMING SOON!

Double D Ranch (An MMF Ménage Series)

Dirty Angels MC®: The Next Generation

WRITING AS J.J. MASTERS:

The Royal Alpha Series

A five-book gay mpreg shifter series

About the Author

JEANNE ST. JAMES is a USA Today, Amazon and international bestselling romance author who loves writing about strong women and alpha males. She was only thirteen when she first started writing. Her first published piece was an erotic short story in Playgirl magazine. She then went on to publish her first romance novel in 2009. She is now an author of over sixty contemporary romances. She writes M/F, M/M, and M/M/F ménages, including interracial romance. She also writes M/M paranormal romance under the name: J.J. Masters.

Want to read a sample of her work? Download a sampler book here: BookHip.com/MTQQKK

To keep up with her busy release schedule check her website at www.jeannestjames.com or sign up for her newsletter: http://www.jeannestjames.com/newslettersignup

www.jeannestjames.com
jeanne@jeannestjames.com

Newsletter: http://www.jeannestjames.com/newsletter signup
Jeanne's Down & Dirty Book Crew: https://www.facebook.com/groups/JeannesReviewCrew/

TikTok: https://www.tiktok.com/@jeannestjames

facebook.com/JeanneStJamesAuthor

instagram.com/JeanneStJames

bookbub.com/authors/jeanne-st-james

goodreads.com/JeanneStJames

pinterest.com/JeanneStJames

Get a FREE Sampler Book

This book contains the first chapter of a variety of my books. This will give you a taste of the type of books I write and if you enjoy the first chapter, I hope you'll be interested in reading the rest of the book.

Each book I list in the sampler will include the description of the book, the genre, and the first chapter, along with links to find out more. I hope you find a book you will enjoy curling up with!

Get it here: BookHip.com/MTQQKK

Printed in Great Britain
by Amazon

41118076R00293